T0209337

LIST OF OTHER BOOKS BY THE AUTHOR

Dryver's Fields

The Eighth Lion

ESCHATON
THE EIGHTH LION

BOOK 2

TONY THOMPSON

iUniverse

ESCHATON THE EIGHTH LION
BOOK 2

This is a work of fiction. All of the characters, names, incidents, organizations, and dialogue in this novel are either the products of the author's imagination or are used fictitiously.

iUniverse books may be ordered through booksellers or by contacting:

iUniverse
1663 Liberty Drive
Bloomington, IN 47403
www.iuniverse.com
844-349-9409

ISBN: 978-1-6632-2680-8 (sc)
ISBN: 978-1-6632-2681-5 (hc)
ISBN: 978-1-6632-2679-2 (e)

Library of Congress Control Number: 2021916987

Print information available on the last page.

iUniverse rev. date: 08/26/2021

I dedicate this book to those with Faith in their hearts, to anyone hoping the world could be a better place for our children, and to all who have kindness ingrained in their souls. Your conviction is inspiring.

~MAP~

THE KNOWN WORLD

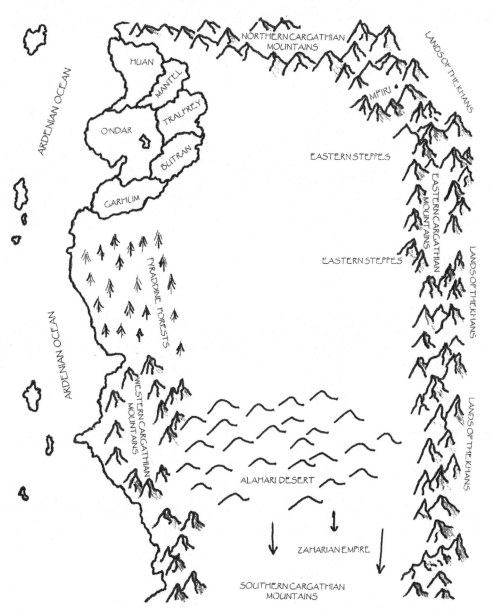

PROLOGUE

THE BROKEN WIZARD

"Where am I?" he asked aloud, the hoarseness in his voice adding to his bewilderment. His eyes had snapped open the moment the first snowflake settled gently on his warm cheek. It quickly melted and trickled down his face, leaving an icy cold trail in its wake. He lay unmoving, on his back, at the bottom of a narrow gorge, its rocky sides eroded long ago by a now non-existent stream.

His mangled body lay twisted in odd directions and he felt broken in too many places to count. Snow-covered mountain peaks lorded above, blanketed by a canopy of stars overhead, the unfamiliar constellations adding to his confusion. His body cried out silently against the pain radiating throughout his torso and out to his limbs. He refused to look down at his injuries, convinced that a thousand shards of broken glass had stabbed into him. Though his body shivered uncontrollably in the cold, he could not feel the light dusting of snow that shrouded him in flecks of white. The lacerations along his arms, legs, and chest stung harshly, and even though he refused to look, he knew he had many broken bones. Some parts of his body ached while others seared his mind with anguish. Looking upward, blinking against the droplets of tiny snowflakes as they landed on his face, he whispered, "Where am I?" and then he passed out.

Moments later, he awakened, remembered his injuries, and quickly decided to do something, or he would likely freeze to death, trapped between the large boulders on either side. The foreboding summits did not disorient him, this time, which he took as a small victory. He tried to roll over onto his side but stopped when he looked at his left leg. The severed bones of his mangled foot lay twisted at an odd angle. He took a few deep breaths, hoping to steady his mind against the pain. This time, he forced himself to remain calm, willing his mind to ignore the pain long enough to get his body moving before the elements took an even more tremendous toll.

Or before a Snow Leopard eats me! he thought. His mind raced with fear. He knew the types of predators hunting in these mountains. Many would enjoy scavenging on his body, even if he remained alive while they did so.

A gentle wind picked up, blowing wisps of snow in tiny circles around his body. The rising sun, still hours away before it would poke out between the peaks, could offer little warmth. His leg pain pulsated, the ache unbearable beyond anything he imagined possible. His right arm weighed heavily at his side, unmoving. Without looking, he could feel the trauma it had suffered. The fingers on his right hand extended outward, each pointing at odd angles in different directions. He tried to move them but did so in vain. Gathering enough courage to look at his right arm, he screamed in terror.

His right arm appeared charred to the bone, with the sleeve of his lavender robe torn away. Severely burned skin, pocketed with giant pustules of grey and black blisters, emanated pain from every pore, every skin cell. The agony was intense, magnified by the fear that started to creep into his mind each time his left eye looked at the blackened arm. He forced himself to look away, but like a magnet drawn to metal, his eyes continued to turn to the blackened arm.

His right eye had suffered damage, too, the contusion had swelled, and it closed completely. His vision in that eye, caked in a thick, syrupy layer of dried blood, would be of little use.

He could feel the broken bones in his cheek moving, grinding against each other. His jaw ached, and so did his forehead. His mangled face burned, adding to his suffering.

Sucking in the cold, refreshing wind, he gasped for air and then exhaled quickly. The agony came in like the waves of an ocean, each moment intense and cascading throughout his body. Slowly, the waves of pain receded, though the ebb and flow abated at a snail's pace. Each moment became more bearable, in time, buoyed by his commitment to focus on moving and surviving.

Lifting his head slightly, the purple hood of his robe falling to the ground behind him, he began assessing his surroundings. The narrow ravine, though rocky, was not very steep on either side.

His broken body, wedged between jagged rocks and giant boulders, had somehow maintained its grip on his oaken staff. He tightened the grip with his left hand. The wooden staff had snapped at the top end, most likely in the fall, but its presence offered him courage. Ornately carved with the images of hooded Cobras, it reminded him of who he was and how he had come to be here.

Mfiri, he thought.

He muttered, "I must get to Mfiri." His voice had gone, at least the power and strength it usually commanded. He made a few attempts to turn over, though the agony gripped him in blinding pain. Each time he tried, his body would involuntarily clench and then he would pass out. When he awakened, he remembered his purpose. He remembered the limitless power that was now at his disposal if he could make it back to his homeland. Finally, he lay on his stomach and felt elation surge inside his mind. Slowly, painfully, he lifted his left arm above his head, gripping the broken staff in his vice-like fingers. He pressed against the ground and started to drag his body forward, using his good leg for support. Slowly, looking like a giant, purple caterpillar, he began snaking ahead, inch by inch. Using all of his energy, he dragged his severely broken body out of the gorge.

New scratches, opened by rocks pocketing the ground, bled quickly, leaving a trail of blood in his wake. Inch by painstaking inch, he moved, passing out periodically when the pain became too intense or falling asleep, face down in the melted snow when overcome by exhaustion. His face snarled with rage, his body and soul burned with hatred. He swore revenge. It became his mantra, helping his mind force his body to continue, even when it begged to give up and rest.

Snow continued to fall across his mangled frame, though the cold revitalized him for a few moments. He was happy to feel it against his cheeks. His soft robe, with its deep-purple threading, offered little warmth. Somehow it had been torn into pieces, shredded into thin strips of cloth. The remnant, as he slithered against the tiny rocks and the edges of giant boulders, was nothing more than a delicate layering, offering no protection against the elements.

After three weeks, though his broken body was almost unrecognizable, he found the thick wall of fog that he had been seeking. He lifted his head to look at the whiteness as it disappeared into the horizon in both directions.

"Mfiri," he mumbled softly.

Elated, he dragged his body with fresh enthusiasm. Though it took almost seven more days, he smiled broadly the moment he spotted a large, wooden bridge, half of which poked out from the thick wall of mist. Circling to the entrance, he stopped a few feet away, face down, and waited for acknowledgement from the fiend before him. Though his body was in agony, and though his mind hovered on the edge of total exhaustion, he exhaled a sigh of relief. He looked up and stared into the eyes of the birdlike creature guarding the bridge.

He had climbed over the snow-covered terrain, had slithered between numerous crevices, and had pulled himself along countless cliffs. This time he faced the Guardian wounded and much weaker than before.

She looked at him passively, the big saucer eyes unsympathetic and uncaring. She stood to her full height, spread her wings and crooned, "I see that you have returned, Wizard, though this time you come before me hobbled and broken."

The soft, silky voice mesmerized him. He found the huskiness pleasing. It helped take his mind off the pain, which made the effort to speak difficult. Pain effused his entire body. He passed out, aware that he was utterly at her mercy.

He woke up disoriented, though it was short-lived. The womanly face, large and grotesque, topped the bird-like body, adding to the strangeness. Its human face looked beautiful in its countenance. He knew those dark eyes and voluptuous lips belied an evil spirit. The broken wizard lifted his left hand, and the staff's tip burst into bright, magenta flames. He wanted to show her, though weakened, some of his power remained at his command.

He said, "I have returned, Gamayun, as promised." His battered face offered a smile, met with a look of disdain by her features in response. It was clear that she regarded him with contempt.

"Do you have it?" she asked, leaning forward carefully. She knelt at the edge of the bridge opening, like an excited child, her eagerness apparent. "Do you?" The purple flames did not intimidate her. She lifted her wing, extended her long, grey fingers, and pointed at him.

The leathery skin repulsed him. His left eye squinting, he watched as she turned her hand over, palm up, and waited. *I would kill her if I had all of my power at my disposal.*

"I do," the broken wizard said. He lifted the staff above his head, swirled it in tiny circles, and smiled the moment three pulsating orbs appeared. Their soft, blue glow burst through the purple flames and helped calm his fears.

Gamayun tried to reach out, away from the bridge, but could not grasp the orbs. He smiled, the moment hidden by the painful grimace on his face. The wizard tapped the orb in the middle with the broken staff. Slowly, it floated away from the other two before landing in her outstretched fingers. Gleefully, the creature tucked the orb beneath one of her wings. She nodded to the wizard, stood up, and turned to leave.

"Wait," he called out, with very little energy left in his voice. "I must get back to the Lands of the Khans." He looked at Gamayun, waiting for her permission to cross the bridge into Mfiri. It did not come.

"Wizard, our deal allowed passage into the Known World through Mfiri. It did not offer passage back. Though not human, I allowed you to cross into one of the worlds of men," she sniped before continuing. "With our bargain fulfilled, Mfiri is closed to you."

He raised his hand to stop her from turning away. The gesture angered her, but he did not care.

"Unless you wish to offer me another of the Dragon orbs," she cooed greedily. Her smile angered him. They were both aware she held the upper hand in this negotiation.

"Unfortunately, I cannot. I require orbs to restore my strength, though even with their help, it will be hundreds of years before that happens. I need the power of the orbs if I am to find the one who will rid the Known World of men." Quietly, he berated himself for giving away some of his plans. She was not a creature to be trusted.

"Well then," Gamayun responded, "our business together is finished." She turned away and walked across the Bridge into the fog. The world went silent.

He waited patiently, his wounds aching, wondering if she had gone. "I offer you a Dragon!" he bellowed. Seconds later, the sinister-looking face peeked out from the thick fog, her eyes glimmering with elation. *She truly is a wicked creature.*

"A Dragon?" she asked, intrigued by his offer. Her saucer-like eyes sparkled with her disquieting intentions on full display.

"Yes, now let us begin our negotiations."

His words had aroused her curiosity. The broken wizard waited patiently, though the tortuous injuries made it very difficult.

"I have never had a Dragon in Mfiri," Gamayun said, elated at the prospect. She stepped out from the foggy curtain and moved back over to the bridge opening. "I admit, I did not think you would survive a battle with any of the original Titans, let alone all three at once. Yet, here you are. I did not think it would be possible." She looked down at the broken wizard, offered a smile, and waited for him to respond. His proposal had tamed her for the moment.

He ignored her taunting and responded, "I will make it possible for you to have a Dragon, Gamayun," he declared. "In return, I ask for safe passage through Mfiri and back into the Lands of the Khans."

Her words startled him, which he knew was her intention. "I am curious, how does a broken wizard come to know so much about

Dragons?" she asked curiously. "We both know they are extinct in both your world and the Lands of the Khans."

The Wizard looked up, chose his words carefully, and offered, "Wizards are not powerless. I discovered their existence and decided there must be a way to harness their power. A half a season before I crossed over, I disguised a warrior from our world and sent him through the mountains in search of proof."

He watched her features closely. The pouting lips, the porcelain skin, and the ruby-red lips all remained hypnotic. His tale had captivated her attention, though, and the glimmer of evil in her features returned.

"He was successful," she retorted sarcastically. "Otherwise, you would not have requested permission to cross over again." Gamayun crouched down, lowering her face closer to his working eye.

He nodded with affirmation, the effort painful. "Yes, though he almost failed. Through guile, he procured a copy of <u>A Brief History of Dragons</u>," he groaned, pausing at her raised eyebrows.

"The Historian!" Gamayun cackled in return. It was her turn to surprise him. "Many years ago, I ordered the master of the Stygian castle to send him to me before he crossed over. We talked for days before I would allow him to continue on his journey." She continued, "You would be surprised how much he left out of his book. I suppose, though, it was wise to do so. Otherwise, you would have easily defeated the three Titans, and we would not be in our current negotiation."

Did Pelinnedes hide information about Dragons? The Wizard's mind raced, tempted by the new information. He did not trust her words. *Does she speak the truth?* He decided against it and stated, "The warrior's bloodlust was too great to control. He gave away his appearance and began attacking men, spurred on by an ancient hunger. It took the combined force of a clan from the Steppes to drive him back into the Lands of the Khans." The anger on the Wizard's face grew, "Fearing my plans would be in vain; I closed the avenue into the Known World. I could not risk that others might attempt to follow his path, at least not yet."

He boasted, "The Dragons may try to follow me here, but I have used my powers to leave a false trail leading to that passageway. They will think

I have fled across and will immediately collapse the cliff walls further to prevent me from returning."

Gamayun smiled broadly and said, "That has been good for me; otherwise, you might have fled with that which I covet above all else. Though you are not human, I would have sent the Nameless Rider to retrieve you and the orb." He watched her fascinated. She repeatedly placed her left hand beneath her other wing so that she could caress the pulsating orb. She added, "I am happy that you fulfilled our bargain, though I must admit I find you repulsive."

He shrugged at her words. *She finds me repulsive?* he thought. Her words were incredulous, though not completely surprising. In their first meeting, she had jeered at his appearance. She had mocked the round eyes and the snake-like pupils. He had ignored her jabs, negotiating passage through Mfiri and into the Known World and the Lands of the Khans.

She waited a few seconds, gathered in her thoughts and giggled, "And now you offer me a Dragon."

Her raspy voice enthralled him for a few seconds. He nodded, acknowledging her words. He lifted his eyes to her face and nodded once more. Slowly, leaning on the remaining staff for support, the broken wizard lifted himself to a standing position. His left foot dragged limply on the ground. His right arm hung limply beside him, useless. He glowered at her but said with conviction, "Gamayun, offer me safe passage through Mfiri and back into the Lands of the Khans, and I offer you Norduir, the original Titan."

SIX HUNDRED
YEARS LATER

THE SLEEPING HILLS

ALONE IN THE DARKNESS, WITH THE DOOR SHUT QUIETLY BEHIND him, Landon did not fear what he could not see. When a child, the Prince had always enjoyed exploring hidden places in the darkness. He and Lyssa would play hide-and-seek throughout the unlighted recesses of his father's palace without a care in the world. Beyond that, he also had faith in the Eighth Lion. The ebony beast with the penetrating blue eyes had vowed to return him to the Dragon Arem's cave. Landon walked forward slowly, keeping the jar in his right hand close to his chest. If he lost his grip on the container and dropped it, he would never forgive himself.

He walked in silence for more than a minute, shrouded in darkness, before noticing the faint glow of a soft-blue light ahead. The tiny pearl beckoned to his soul, a beacon of hope from somewhere far off in the blackness.

The pathway must connect the den of the Eighth Lion to Arem's cave, he thought with nervous excitement.

Landon relaxed, doing his best to temper his elation. He stopped a few feet away from the edge of the darkness and looked around the cave. Even at this distance, he could make out the outlines of the glowing, oval-shaped eggs. Each appeared to be glowing more brightly, pulsating with a new intensity than they had before. Eerie shadows, cast by the wavering light, danced on the opposite walls. The shadows flickered mischievously, reminding Landon of the campfire in Mfiri.

The Dragon lay prostrate on the ground, his large head resting on the cave floor, with his eyes closed. He spotted Lyssa lying on her side with her right arm draped over the Dragon's neck. She was leaning against Arem, fast asleep. Landon was relieved to see his sister resting and safe.

Arem's yellow eyes opened slowly, but the Dragon did not move.

Can he see me? Landon thought with awe. Created by magic much older and more potent than anything thought possible, he wondered if the darkened passageway had masked him from Arem's sight. The Dragon's gaze fell on him and did not waver. Landon shrugged. Dragons were an ancient race with powers far beyond the ability and understanding of humans.

He looks different. Landon scanned the length of Arem's body, noticing the glowing scales flowing in pairs along the ridge of his back. Each usually black scale had turned lava red and pulsated slowly, the light rhythmical. Landon imagined it mimicking the beating of the Dragon's heart. Landon nodded to himself. The Dragon Arem was preparing to morph into one of the three Titan Dragon types. Once the Dragon morphed, no one could be sure whether the Captain would still be in control or whether the Dragon would absorb him into its awareness. If that happened, the true beast would return.

Am I too late? he wondered, frowning. Landon pushed the thought from his mind. It was time to take Lyssa back to O'ndar. This portion of his quest had ended. According to the Eighth Lion, the challenges that lay ahead held peril beyond anything he had ever faced. One misstep and the fate of the world would end with an Apocalypse. It was hard to imagine a world without humans, though that was a distinct possibility.

Silently, Landon stepped out of the pitch-black corridor and into the cave. He turned to look back, but the gateway had already disappeared, replaced by the rocky cave wall with its flickering shadows. He held the jar away from his body and high enough for the Dragon Arem to see it. The yellow eyes followed the container's movement closely, but the Dragon did not lift his head. Arem opened his mouth, exposing his forearm-length fangs, and smiled. The rumbling laughter, sounding like rolling thunder, began pouring out from the massive head. The boom echoed throughout the cave, startling Landon, though pleasantly. The laughter woke up Lyssa. Confused, she looked around to see what was happening.

"Landon!" Lyssa shrieked. She leapt to her feet, ran over to him, and threw her arms around his neck.

Landon winced in pain but returned the hug with affection. Breathing a heavy sigh of relief, Landon moved over to the large rock near the Dragon. He sat down gingerly, avoiding making eye contact. Finally, he looked up into his sister's eyes.

"Are you injured?" she asked. The worried look on her face was too much to bear.

Landon broke down, sobbing with large tears streaking down his face in large droplets. His shoulders sagged. He cried uncontrollably.

Lyssa sat down near him quietly and waited patiently for his emotions to run their course. She placed her hand on his shoulder but noticed the grimace on his face. Standing, Lyss pulled his shirt away and gasped at the deep, puncture wounds covered with a thick layer of dried blood on his neck and back.

The Dragon Arem watched in silence as Lyssa tended to her brother's injuries. She cleaned up all of the wounds. Lyssa tore strips of cloth from the bottom of her dress, dipped them in a water-filled basin and used them to clean away the blood. Finally, when Landon appeared to have gained his composure, the Dragon slowly lifted one of his clawed hands and waved the two of them over to him.

Landon frowned in sympathy. "What is wrong with him?" Landon asked Lyssa; he could see the worry lines on her face.

"He is about to change, brother. The scales on his back have been glowing and pulsating for at least a day. He can barely move. Doing so must be painful. I sat beside him, hoping to provide him comfort, but failed to do much else." Large tears ran down her cheeks, the droplets falling to the cave floor. "What else can I do?"

Landon reached up, hoping to comfort her but had no words to offer. The three of them knew this had been a possibility. It had been one of the reasons he had started the quest to Mfiri. He leaned down and spoke to Arem, softly but firmly. The Dragon's left eye looked at him passively.

"You were right, Captain Arem. I want you to know I understand why you brought my sister to the other side of the Known World. It would not have been wise to abduct me since I would not have believed you. You would have had to kill me in the process. Yet, by convincing my sister, I was encouraged to listen. I bear no ill will. Do you understand me?" The Dragon did not move. The yellow eyes sparkled with acknowledgement. That was enough for Landon.

Landon looked to Lyssa and then said, "The orb. Bring it to us." The command in his voice startled her, though she turned to comply.

Lyssa stood, hurriedly retrieved the glowing orb, and then handed it to Landon. Landon thanked her with a nod, moved the sphere over to the Dragon's hand and leaned it against one of the ebony talons. Landon looked to his sister, using a gesture with his head to bring her closer. After she kneeled beside him, they both placed their hands on the pulsating orb.

"Welcome back, Prince Landon," the Dragon offered. His hoarse voice sounded less commanding than it did when Landon began his journey. Landon frowned, aware of how difficult it must be for Arem to speak.

Lyssa smiled widely, happy to hear the Captain's voice. It pleased Landon to see the vitality in her eyes. She was the most positive person in his life, and her spirit and energy were infectious. That vitality had always been one of his greatest pleasures and had many times pulled him out of a depressed mood.

"Was the journey as dangerous as we thought it would be?" There was a pause. Landon could hear the difficulty it took for Arem to communicate. It was his turn to be sympathetic. Captain Arem had endured a lot with the hopes of saving Princess Lenali. Rather than give in to his circumstances, Captain Arem had persevered. The Captain had abducted Lyssa so that Landon would follow the two of them across the Known World and enter into Mfiri. The Captain had never given up, even though trapped inside the body of this massive, black-scaled Dragon. He worked tirelessly to save the Princess from her glass prison. He had realized that his transformation was imminent, bringing the two of them to this place so that they might save their birth mother from her imprisonment.

This man has a sense of duty ingrained into his soul, Landon thought. *It is an inherited trait, not something to be taught. It is just who he is as a person.*

"Yes. But, we were successful," boasted Landon, gesturing with his head over to the jar. He looked at the pride in Lyssa's face. It buoyed him immensely.

"You have been injured and need rest Prince," Arem's voice fretted. It pained Landon to hear Arem worry about him. Unfortunately, he had to push the concern he had for Arem out of his mind. His attention, his focus, would need to be on other things.

"I appreciate your concern, Captain Arem. However, we both know there is no time for rest. How long is it until you change? My guess is less than a day."

The Dragon acknowledged, "You are very perceptive. I have," he paused for a few seconds as a wave of pain flowed through his body, "less than a few hours until the change occurs. After that moment, I can no longer guarantee your safety." His eyes grew severe, almost callous.

Landon nodded. He turned to Lyssa and said, "It is time for us to go, Lyss."

"Go!" she cried, much too loudly. "We cannot leave. Arem needs our help." She said the words but knew there was nothing that she could do for Arem. She leaned in and kissed the Dragon on top of the head.

Lyssa asked, bewildered, "Where do we go?"

"We have to go back, across the Celestial Plane," Landon responded firmly, "Arem is a Dragon. He has the power to send us back to O'ndar."

"You have done this before, Prince, but please remember, you must not open your eyes until both of you have stopped moving across the Plane," the Dragon's voice instructed.

Landon wished he could offer some solace to Captain Arem. The effort required to communicate must be intense. Even using the orb, Arem's voice quivered.

"Neither of you has metal on you?" the Dragon asked. "The journey will take some time since I am not at my full strength. Keep a tight hold onto the glass container."

The Dragon paused for more than thirty seconds to gather his strength. He continued, "Princess, I am sorry for taking you away from your home. I wish there had been another way." The sincerity in his yellow eyes was moving.

Lyssa listened quietly, without responding. The tears continued to streak down her face.

Arem's deep voice said, "Lock your arms together and close your eyes."

Lyssa locked her left arm through Landon's right one. He pulled the container close to his chest.

"Frathma ark frathman, eriden a frathma. Frathma ark frathman er Ferlynne's cave. Frathma ark frathman er The Sleeping Hills."

Arem's powerful voice weakened and faded away; it reminded Landon, oddly, of an autumn day when the multi-coloured leaves fell from the trees and were then swiftly picked up by a gust of wind, blown away forever.

Landon felt the familiar tug on his waist. Without looking, he knew the two of them were once again travelling across the Celestial Plane. He imagined thousands of versions of them strung out from Arem's cave, across the mountains and lakes, and through the forests, all the way to O'ndar.

Before they started, he reminded Lyssa, "Do not open your eyes, sister. No matter what happens." The return journey took longer than his original. Finally, after a few hours, they came to a rest in a clearing in the middle of a forest.

"Be safe, my young Prince and Princess. It is with a heavy heart that I started you on this journey. It is with a happy one I send you back." The voice of the Dragon Arem trailed off at the end, but it was enough to end the spell.

Landon opened his eyes, lifted his head, and watched with fascination the moment their souls began to collapse into each other. Each version, hundreds of them, reconnected with the nearest one, snapping into each other with force and racing quickly to reconnect with his body. They pulled away from the Dragon Arem's cave until they reached the two siblings in O'ndar. The collision between souls and bodies flattened them back onto the ground.

"You may open your eyes, sister," offered Landon, though he warned, "I would recommend waiting a few minutes before you try to stand. You are going to experience a wave of nausea. It will pass." He listened to the silence around them, happy to hear the familiar sound of insects.

Lyssa opened her eyes and looked upward at the stars in the darkened sky. She could see the outline of trees surrounding them and asked quietly, "Where are we?"

"Do not fear. We are back in O'ndar," Landon responded. "More specifically, we are almost back to the spot where my journey began."

"We are not near the castle?" she asked, confused by their location.

"No. We are in the middle of the Sleeping Hills Forest. By the look of this clearing, I would say we are outside Ferlynne's cave." Landon turned his head a few inches, looking over to the cave. A large pile of boulders sealed the opening. He smiled to himself, knowingly.

"I am confused, brother. If your journey began inside the cave, why would Arem return us here but keep us outside the cave?" He could not see her eyes clearly but was impressed by her curiosity.

"There would be no way to escape if we became trapped inside the cave." Lyssa had not seen the boulders blocking the mouth of the cave. "Turn your head, look over there to your right."

"He did not want us locked inside by those boulders," she said, pleased by the Dragon's gesture. A few minutes later, she sat up. The world seemed to spin but stopped seconds later. She took a few deep breaths to steady herself. "You need to rest and need time to recover. What can I do to help?" Lyssa asked, concerned.

"We must do one more thing before I rest," he offered. Landon forced himself into a sitting position. Gently, he set the jar down on the grass, stood up, and walked over to the mouth of the cave. He looked the boulders over closely, wishing that they had the light from a torch to help.

We must start with all of the smaller ones. Once cleared, we will remove the medium-sized stones and then do our best to roll the larger ones at the top away from the others. We only need to make a space large enough for us to squeeze through.

Lyssa walked over to the cave and leaned on his left shoulder. She asked, "Why are we in front of the cave, brother? I think we need to get going to the castle?" She was worried about Landon, and the concern was evident.

"We will go to the castle, but not just yet. We need a safe place to rest so that I can recover. Also, we need to go into the cave to visit an old friend," he offered sarcastically.

Lyssa looked at him, puzzled by his words.

Landon offered, "We need help getting into the castle if we are to get close enough to Qui Oto without arousing her suspicion. I would like Ferlynne's help." He expected her puzzlement and smiled at her proclamation.

"But he is dead. You told me so yourself," Lyssa blurted.

"Maybe, but I suspect Captain Arem placed us here with a purpose. Why not place us inside the castle or back into our rooms?" Landon asked excitedly. "Why not place us beside the bed of the sleeping Queen? Why here?" He looked at Lyssa's face, watching her eyes widen. He appreciated her enlightenment as her head nodded in understanding.

"Do you think Ferlynne is alive?" she whispered.

"I do not know, for sure. But there is only one way to find out," he answered. Landon climbed up the pile of boulders and began slowly tossing smaller ones aside. He smiled when Lyssa joined him at the top.

They worked for more than an hour before stopping to take a break. The soldiers had done their task well, sealing up the cave tightly. It was challenging to work, especially with his injuries slowing him down. The two of them appeared to be no closer to getting into the cave than when they had started.

While they rested, Landon told Lyssa everything. He smiled when her eyes widened at his description of Gamayun and the Children of the Night. She remained silent, hoping he would continue unabated. Landon paused the moment his story brought him to the door of the den of the Seven Lions. He smiled at her disappointment when he said, "We should work some more; I will finish the story later." Slowly, he stood up and helped pull her to a standing position. They moved back over to the cave and climbed the pile of boulders once more.

The work, done with the light provided by the stars, was difficult. The heavier boulders were cumbersome to move. There were a few scary moments when it felt as if the boulders beneath had shifted and might collapse. Eventually, when they had safely rolled the smaller ones away, Landon sent Lyssa back to the bottom and directed her to move out from the opening. Slowly, though his neck ached and he was physically exhausted, Landon made some headway by rolling some of the medium-sized rocks away. An hour later, Landon climbed down and signalled that he needed to rest. The Sleeping Hills Forest was just beginning to see the light of the coming day. It was pleasing to Landon to be in a familiar place.

Landon did not rest long. He looked at Lyssa. She sat beside him, patiently waiting for him to continue his story. "Where was I?" he asked, smiling.

"I believe you were standing in front of the cave of the Seven Lions," she answered, shrugging. He appreciated her curiosity and admitted that it was cathartic to get to share everything that had happened.

Landon continued describing every minute detail that he could remember. This time, Lyssa gasped and stopped him to ask questions. It pleased him knowing that he had made her proud.

"Arem was right about you," Lyssa said firmly. She continued, confident in her words. "He told me I should have faith in you." Once again, her words and her support filled him with happiness.

He finished the tale by describing how he felt when he first saw that she was safe, sleeping across the Dragon's neck. He had left out the coming war with the warriors from the Lands of the Khans. Nor did he mention his intention to honor the treaty with the Sultan. Lyssa would need to go south very soon. His heart wore heavily with this knowledge.

I cannot tell her at this moment, he thought, his mind clouded with emotions. *There are too many things that must fall into place. Otherwise, it will not matter. If I fail, the Apocalypse and the end of the world will happen. The rest will not matter.*

Moments later, light from the sunrise flooded the Sleeping Hills Forest, piercing through the trees and across the landscape. Landon appreciated the coming dawn since he did not want to enter the cave in darkness. He pointed and said to his sister, "We have made enough of an opening to make it through."

Slowly, Landon climbed up to the small space, it was wide enough for the two to slide through together, but he insisted that he go in first. Landon retrieved the glass container and handed it to his sister.

"Hold onto this," he started, "Once I am inside, and my eyes have adjusted to the light, I will have you hand it down to me. Then, I will put it aside and help you through."

Lyssa held the container up to her face. *My mother is here. Is she aware of all we are doing? Is she listening?* She wondered in silence, watching Landon slither in through the opening at the top of the boulders. A few seconds later, he called to her softly.

"Hand me the jar. There is more than enough light inside the cave." He helped her through, insisting they wait a few minutes for her eyes to adjust. The coolness of the cave felt welcoming.

When they arrived at the living quarters, Landon smiled knowingly. There were two lit torches mounted on opposite sides of the cave walls. Someone had lit a small candle and placed it upon a wooden table. He walked with Lyssa over to the bed, watching her eyes widen as they looked down at a desiccated corpse covered haphazardly with a thick, cotton blanket. Two gold coins covered the eyes.

"I am sorry to say, dear brother, Ferlynne is dead," she whispered, hoping her voice would not be too loud.

Landon could see that the withered remains worried her. *Does she wonder if he will awaken from the dead?* He listened to her speaking quietly, knowing that she did not want to find out. When they were younger, one of her nannies had told them tales of corpses rising from the dead to devour little children who did not listen to their parents.

"Come, Lyss. Let's sit for a little while." Landon grabbed one of the chairs on the other side of the cave and pulled it closer to the one near the table. He sat down, patted the seat of the other chair, and placed his fingers to his lips, reminding her to sit quietly.

They sat in silence for a few minutes, listening to the trickling of water droplets echoing somewhere from the back of the cave. Lyss started to speak but stopped when Landon raised his hand once more.

"We do not mind waiting here all day," Landon declared, much too loudly. His voice bounded with force to the back of the cave, its strength shocking Lyssa. They listened to see if there would be a response. Landon heard Lyssa gasp.

"I am happy to hear your voice, Prince Landon." The man had spoken the words, yet he did not sound sincere.

Lyssa detected an edginess to his voice. *Anger?*

"Have no fear, Ferlynne. Or should I call you General Faron?" Landon asked sternly.

"Ferlynne will be fine, Prince. I lay no claim to the life I lived before becoming the feeble man you met a few nights ago. General Faron died many years ago." The voice resonated from somewhere deep within the cave.

"I see you have brought your sister back from the clutches of the Black Dragon. Welcome, Princess." With these final words, Ferlynne rounded the corner and stood before the two of them.

REBIRTH & RESURRECTION

LYSSA OPENED HER MOUTH TO SPEAK, LOOKED TO THE CORPSE LYING silently on the small cot, and decided to wait instead.

The elderly man standing before them chuckled with amusement and said, "My apologies, Princess. Had I known you were with your brother, I would have hidden the mummy before you arrived." His eyes fell to the corpse.

"Mummy?" Lyssa asked, fearful at his words. "What is a mummy?" Ferlynne's declaration piqued her curiosity.

Ferlynne smiled at her question before responding, "I come from a part of the world with scorching temperatures and a dry climate. Our Priests have developed certain techniques to preserve a body by removing all the moisture. Although I lacked some of the necessary equipment and the chemical resins needed to complete the task, I did mummify him, though not as properly as we would do in Istanabad. The actual process requires wrapping the body in a specially treated cloth to ensure that it remains preserved through eternity. For my purposes, I did not need to wrap his body. I only needed to convince the soldiers of my demise." The man grinned at Lyssa, the glee in his eyes very apparent.

"I purchased his body a little more than a year ago. I mummified him hoping to slow the rate of decomposition. I knew the wretched Queen would send someone to verify my death. I am sorry to refer to your mother in such a manner, but she is an evil woman." He pointed to the shriveled up body while finishing his statement. "He was an elderly gentleman, resembling me in many ways. I was hoping the deception would be enough to fool the Queen's lackey. I believe I have been successful since no one has returned."

"And the coins?" Landon asked. The presence of the coins intrigued him.

"Ah yes," Ferlynne answered with enthusiasm, "the soldier who entered the cave was supposed to place the coins over my eyes. Just before leaving, though, he retrieved them both. In my native country, to gain access to the Afterlife, a person's soul must be ferried across a great river. The coins are the price of passage. Once the soldier left, I placed two more coins over the eyes to help this poor man finish his journey."

Landon shook his head and laughed. He looked to his sister and asserted, "He wanted to fool anyone else who looked inside this cave. Everyone needed to believe Ferlynne had passed away. He gambled a second soldier would do the same as the first. Pocket the coins without looking closely at the body. He needed the Queen to believe that he had died. Both soldiers would have reported the same story to the Queen, that his eyes had been covered with the coins." He motioned with his head to the corpse.

"Precisely!" Ferlynne's green, bird-like eyes glowed with ferocity in the dim firelight.

"Landon!" Lyssa yelled. She leapt forward, catching her brother the moment he began to slump out of the chair. "Help him, please," Lyssa pleaded. She looked to Ferlynne with worry on her face. Landon's body weight was too heavy for her, and he started sliding to the floor. Ferlynne jumped over to them quickly, surprising Lyssa with his strength. He lifted Landon without much effort.

He paused for a few seconds before responding. "Let us put him on the cot." He smiled when she shook her head slightly, the fear of having to touch the corpse evident. Ferlynne walked to the cot and moved the body to the floor. Together, they lifted and dragged Landon over to the bed. They lay him on his back, covering him with a blanket. Landon, semi-conscious, mumbled quietly, but the words were gibberish.

Lyssa leaned over and felt his forehead. "He's burning up. Do you have any water? I told him he needed rest, but he insisted on continuing." She worried that Landon might push himself too far, and now, he had collapsed from the fatigue.

Ferlynne nodded in the affirmative and went to retrieve it. Lyssa soaked a rag in the cold water, wrung it out, and used the compress to wipe Landon's forehead. Ferlynne opened a small, black chest. He rummaged through the bottom, found an item and brought a glass jar containing a white powder to Lyssa.

"Salt?" Lyssa asked. Her eyes gave away her suspicion.

Ferlynne shook his head and said, "Not at all. It has medical properties that will be helpful." He brought a bowl and thistle over to his table, poured a small amount into the mixing bowl, and began grinding it. Satisfied, he added a small amount of water and stirred the mixture. When it was ready, he poured it into a glass.

"We need to sit him up and get him to drink this," he said matter-of-factly. Lyssa did not argue. The majority of the concoction ended up on Landon's chest, but Ferlynne seemed pleased. He helped ease the Prince back onto the cot.

It's the fever. Landon needs rest, and hopefully, he will recover, she thought. The uncertainty assailed her.

"Do not worry, Princess. I have given him a sedative. It will allow him to sleep peacefully. The powder has healing properties to take away a fever." Ferlynne looked at Lyssa, smiled, and nodded.

She thanked him profusely. "He needs a few days to rest and recover," she added. Lyssa stood and walked over to one of the chairs. She had been so worried about Landon that she had not paid heed to her exhaustion.

"It looks like you also need rest," Ferlynne asserted. He brought a cup of water to Lyssa, but she looked at it with misgivings. "Do not worry. I have not added anything to it." She took the water and gulped it down, the coolness refreshing.

"I will take my rest but was hoping you would sit with me for a while and we could talk," Lyssa proposed. She quietly hoped Ferlynne would agree to her request since she had many questions. She could see the misgivings on his face, but eventually, he agreed.

Ferlynne pulled up a chair and sat down opposite Lyssa. He wore a pea-green robe. His green eyes perched beneath a clean-shaven scalp sat above a hawk-like nose. His wrinkled face and thin frame made it difficult to discern his age. "What would you like to know?" the old man asked. Alyssa's request pleased him. She projected calmness and sincerity, qualities that he respected.

"I would like to know everything. I know you are General Faron, Captain Arem's father." Her final words struck home. Ferlynne frowned, and tears welled in his eyes. Lyssa thought he might leap from the chair and disappear into the back of the cave.

"The Sultan is Captain Arem's father," Ferlynne agonized. The aching in his voice cut through Lyssa. The man's shoulders sagged the moment he uttered the words.

I cannot truly appreciate all that he has been through, she thought.

Lyssa countered, "No. He was never Captain Arem's father. We both know the truth. I was able to watch them take Arem away from the two of you. You leaned in to hug him one last time before saying you will always be his one and only father."

"Stop!" Ferlynne demanded, the anguish in his voice apparent. He leaned forward with his eyes closed. Slowly, Lyssa reached out her right hand and placed it on top of his head. She caressed his head softly, cooing to him all the while.

"You are his only father. I believe Captain Arem would have wanted me to tell you this." The two of them cried together for a few minutes.

Ferlynne spoke smoothly, his voice no louder than a whisper. "Is he....dead?" he asked, afraid to hear the answer. His eyes pleaded for some good news.

"I do not know. Arem has begun his transformation, and only time will tell whether Captain Arem controls the Dragon or whether the Dragon controls Captain Arem. We may never know."

Ferlynne accepted the news as a General would welcome a military report. He nodded but never said a word.

Lyssa asked, "I am confused General, How did you come to be here? There are too many things yet unknown. Would you tell me everything?" Ferlynne stood up quickly and walked to the back of the cave, disappearing for a few minutes. For a few minutes, she thought the conversation about Arem had been too much, but then she could hear him rumbling through things. He returned, holding a brown-leather bound book close to his chest. Ferlynne sat down in his chair. He held the book out to Lyssa, watching her with pride.

"I decided, for posterity, to write down the story of my life. It gave me some comfort to express my failures as a father and my heartache at losing my son. Years ago, I provided a false narrative to your parents, hoping to keep the Queen from becoming suspicious. After I completed the imaginary story of Ferlynne, I felt inspired to write the correct version of my life." The old man placed the book onto Lyssa's lap, the title face down. He smiled, leaned in, and tapped the cover with his finger.

She turned the book over and read the title aloud. "Rebirth & Resurrection: From Faron to Ferlynne." Lyssa was fascinated. She enjoyed reading immensely and admittedly looked forward to figuring out how Ferlynne fit into this puzzle. Slowly, she opened the book and began to read.

Rebirth & Resurrection: From Faron to Ferlynne

My name is Jirani Na'im Faron, and I was born into a small, rural village in the western part of the Zaharian Empire during the early spring of what villagers liked to call the year of the Ram. Since my birth, the year of the Ram has come and gone more than four times, though my body, in all its frailty, would cause others to believe I am much older than I appear. My mind, though, is full of vitality and continues to house a keen intellect.

The village itself is unimportant, other than it was the spot where my birth father, a General in the Zaharian military, met my birth mother. The two of them fell in love at first sight. The result was a marriage and, of course, my birth. I do not remember the name of my birth father. I remember nothing of him other than he brought me into this world to fulfil his commitment to honour and serve Sultan Muraffe III. Nor do I remember the name of my birth mother. She died during childbirth, thus earning me the wrath and disdain of my father. I do not ask for sympathy from the reader. I offer these morsels only to create an understanding of who I was and how I came to be.

In the seventh year of my existence, Horsemen from the Eastern Steppes killed my birth father in a bloody skirmish. When told of his death, I did not react and returned quickly to my training. As the son of a General, my military training began when I could walk on my own two feet. I was a quick learner, much more advanced than most other children, even those four to five years older. I did not grieve since I had already forgotten much about my father. At a young age, taught to view the Sultan as our true father, I latched onto this motto feverishly. I often wished he would adopt me into his household to prove my value as a son. It was something that I yearned for from the bottom of my soul.

At some point, I remember learning I had brothers and sisters by birth, but they are of no import in the story of Faron.

One afternoon, when I was eight years old, three older boys set upon me. I made them angry because I had stolen their mid-morning meals. I was not aware the Sultan Muraffe watched these events unfold from on high. I have often wondered whether he set the events into motion to see how I would respond. He is devious beyond description, using others for his wicked amusement, regardless of the costs.

My initial reaction gained me the upper hand. I feigned submission, crouching in supplication. The boys believed my ruse and came closer to offer me a beating. I attacked them with ferocity. I provided them with viciousness in a battle that they were unprepared to answer. I have used a similar tactic throughout my military career. Often, I would have troops appear to retreat only to have an opposing army over-commit. Once they were overly confident and attacked, I would have my own troops counter-attack and use the element of surprise to defeat them. My outnumbered forces have won the field and the day in countless battles.

I attacked and, within minutes, slew the three boys with my short sword. They came to offer a beating and left without their lives. When the soldiers arrived, I calmly waited for the sentence and the punishment. I knew my death would be the result. I had killed without an order to kill.

Instead, the Sultan brought me into the castle and adopted me as his son. Pleased, I offered my life in his service. It was the one pledge that I had prayed to be able to make, and it came to fruition. Little did I realize that I did not have to make that oath; any Sultan's son must be prepared to die on his behalf even with only a moment's notice.

Thus, when I was eight years old, Jirani Na'im Faron, the son of a General, officially became the adopted son of Muraffe III. I immediately entered his household, placing me in a favourable position. I became a student of the best military minds in the land. In the year of my adoption, there were thirty-two other sons adopted into his household. One would think it an honour and a privilege to be the adopted son of the Sultan, the leader of the world's greatest Empire. It was neither. From the day of our adoption, thirty-three sons were encouraged to compete, to fight, to savage, to steal, to beat, to harass, and in time to kill each other in the name of the Sultan. In Muraffe's house, sons and daughters exist for one purpose only, which is to serve the whim of the Sultan. We live to carry out his orders, without hesitation, as if a god gave them. In some manner, I guess one did.

While I am intentionally vague on details of the remainder of my early years, suffice it to say I excelled in every category and every challenge thrown at me. Eventually, I rose to the rank of Captain. I led squads into battle, displaying the necessary courage and skill to earn a promotion to become a General. While pride is ultimately sinful, I take pride in being one of the most successful military tacticians in the Zaharian army.

As I age and mature, though, I have realized that my life did not truly begin until a little more than twenty-two years ago.

My life, my Rebirth, began on the day of the birth of my son Arem.

I met my desert flower Ocotillo, Arem's mother, while leading a group of Zaharian soldiers back home, following a successful military campaign. She was a tiny waif, one who had come to a nearby oasis to gather water for her family. I watched her from the other side of the water, enthralled. Her skin was the colour of the sand, and her brown eyes those of a doe. Though adorned in my military garb, she looked at me unafraid. The moment our eyes met, I knew she was the love of my life. As a General, I was within my rights to take her into my house, even without her permission. Instead, I approached her father and asked for his permission to take his daughter as my wife.

Requesting permission from Ocotillo's father would have caused a scandal had the Sultan known of my approach. Muraffe would have had the entire family slain because of my weakness. Love cannot influence Muraffe's generals.

Ocotillo's father was a timid man, especially standing in front of a General of the Zaharian military. The man threw himself down at my feet and held up his hands in supplication. He agreed to my request without argument or complaint. I chose not to accept this. I was in love and did not wish to coerce Ocotillo or her family in any manner.

I looked to the father but spoke to the daughter. I knew she listened from the next room. I professed my love for Ocotillo. I swore I would honour her wishes without hesitation. If she did not love me, I would ride away, never to return. Her family would be safe from any reprisals. If she assented, I would marry her the moment we returned to Istanabad and received the permission of the Sultan. Though her father had fallen prone onto the floor, Ocotillo stepped out from the other room. She looked me in the eyes and responded. She, too, had fallen in love with me. She felt the same connection I felt the moment we looked into each other's eyes. She raised her father and affirmed my previous words. He had nothing to fear. She kissed her mother and her father goodbye and rode away with me, back to Istanabad. On the remainder of the journey, I explained my plan regarding our approach with Muraffe. The Sultan would be ecstatic with my military victory and would be pleased that I had lusted after Ocotillo. I would not allow him to believe I was in love. We agreed to keep our love for each other secret. We would be the only two ever to know we were in love. The Sultan readily agreed to our marriage and personally performed the ceremonies.

My rebirth began the moment our son Arem was born into this world. His tiny fingers grabbed onto mine the first time I held him. Though I would have never done so in public, I shed tears of joy when he entered this world. I looked into my wife's eyes, thankful she had come into my life and grateful she was healthy. History had not repeated itself.

My life had been a constant struggle. My emotions, walled up since birth, burst forth without restraint. Joy leapt into my heart. Arem had sprung out of the love I held for my desert flower. Named for a common desert shrub with deceptively beautiful, red, cone-shaped flowers, Ocotillo brightened my life as much as the flowers brighten the desert. Ocotillo, who had invigorated my life, did so again by bearing me a son. I, the military tactician responsible for slaying hundreds of men with his bare hands, stood in awe while looking at my son. During my military career, I had ordered entire villages burned to the ground without thinking about my actions. The tiny hands of a babe conquered my hardened soul.

Outside our home, though, our love for Arem remained a closely kept secret. I had grown accustomed to life in the presence of madness. My wife and son had not. Though Ocotillo had grown up in poverty, she lived in a loving family. Neither of the two loves of my life would know how to deal with the jealousy of a Sultan. I swore to protect them from Muraffe's rage by feigning indifference.

I protected them as best I could by trying to keep them away from the view and the attention of the Sultan. Eventually, though, my military exploits could not deter the Sultan from his tradition of adopting his general's sons into his household. This strategy offers two advantages to Muraffe. First, with the proper training and guidance, these sons would grow up to replace the leaders of Muraffe's military. Thus, the military machine remained in capable hands. Secondly, it kept Generals in check. Each General would be wary of attempting a coup with the eldest of their sons required to live within Muraffe's house.

In time, the Sultan honoured me by adopting Arem as his son. I understand, to the reader, how my words can seem a contradiction. It is necessary to comprehend how tradition and training instill habits, which are difficult to break. Though the Sultan had stolen Arem away from me, I periodically think his methods to be honourable to his Generals. These emotions are a contradiction, as I have stated. It has been ingrained into my brain for so long that it is hard to break these misguided beliefs.

I knew the moment would come and dreaded it with trepidation. Ocotillo and I agreed to spend those precious years with our son Arem and not focus on what we hoped would be the distant future.

However, he was now the son of the Sultan. At night, his mother and I would hold each other and speak of him quite often. I did not disclose to her all I knew about life in the Sultan's house. Arem lived in the House of a lunatic. As the Sultan's son, he would have to be vicious, uncaring, and callous if he were to survive. I had needed to suppress any compassion I might have for others in the name of survival. The same would be expected of Arem.

Years later, when Arem rose to the rank of Captain, he was required to whip me in public for my insolence to the Sultan and Elzahari. Each moment the lash cut into my back, I never stopped loving Arem. If anything, I loved him even more and used this love to deal with the pain. Please understand I never stopped loving him.

Lyssa stopped reading, looked up from the book, and said, "Captain Arem was emphatic that I see this moment in his life because it brought him back from the precipice."

"What do you mean? Please explain," Ferlynne lamented, his voice full of fear and hope.

"I know the Sultan had Arem whip you to test his loyalty and resolve. Muraffe's plan backfired. Instead of binding him to Muraffe, it freed him. He had already shown me the day of his adoption. He remembered your words and wholeheartedly feels you are his only father." Lyssa felt obligated to let Ferlynne know she understood what the two of them had experienced. Without waiting for a response, she looked back to the book and continued to read.

Years later, the Sultan ordered Captain Arem to escort one of his daughters, Princess Lenali, north to O'ndar. Two days after the group left Istanabad, heading north across the Alahari Desert, my wife and I received an unannounced visit from the Sultan. We immediately fell to our knees, bowing in subservience. I had been unaware of the presence of Elzahari, the Chosen One. The Sultan did not say a word. He entered our home uninvited, which is his right. Muraffe walked around the two of us silently. Finally, he commanded me to stand. I did so, shocked to witness Elzahari's purple body wrapped around Ocotillo, its face hovering a few inches above her head.

The Sultan gave me a choice. Ocotillo had been hesitant in kneeling in the presence of the Sultan. Her offence required punishment. He commanded Ocotillo to look up. She did so, frozen in fear with the Cobra's face less than an inch from her own. Elzahari would bite Ocotillo, or I could take her immediately to the public square and give her twenty lashes.

The thought of the pain of the Cobra venom wracking her body was too much. I scolded her for her insolence. I dragged her, without

hesitation, angrily from my home and to the public square. The Sultan did not understand that I did all of this out of love. Ocotillo and I had prepared for this moment, realizing that someday, I might need to be harsh and uncompassionate in the eyes of Muraffe. We had agreed to this, hoping that ultimately it might save our lives.

The Sultan smiled wickedly. He followed us out of our home with his pet close behind. I immediately took my wife to the square, stripped off her shirt, tied her to the whipping pole, and began to whip her. While binding her hands, I leaned in quietly, offering my love. She returned my words with her own words of love and affection. I now know how difficult it must have been for Arem to whip his father. At least, I hoped he struggled with the act as much as I. When the first lash landed across her back, the spectacle began. I looked up at one point to see the Sultan standing at the edge of the square. I had hoped to brand her back lightly with the whip, yet he had come personally to ensure that I did not hold back. The look of glee on his face angered me, though I was careful not to let him see it.

When I finished administering the twenty lashes, the Sultan left the two of us alone. I removed the bindings and held my dying Ocotillo in my arms. I had been too diligent in metering out the punishment. Moments before she succumbed to the wounds, she asked me to make a promise to find Arem. Ocotillo, the love of my life, the one who helped me be reborn, made me promise to locate him and never return to Istanabad. It was a vow I was ready and willing to make. Seven nights after Arem's group left Istanabad, I stole out of the House of the Sultan Muraffe III, hoping to follow my son to O'ndar.

Years of training for warfare in the desert had not prepared me for the grief when I found Arem's remains partially buried beneath Princess Lenali's tent. The goat hair abode, only partially exposed by the time I arrived, confused me. I spent a day digging the sand away only to find Arem's body lying next to the body of a little child. Distraught, I spent an entire night in anguish. My mind screamed in agony. In my misery, I cursed the Sultan, swearing revenge for the death of my beloved Ocotillo and our son Arem. After giving him a proper burial, I swore an oath to find the soldiers accompanying Lenali and confront them for their dereliction of duty. We are all brothers, and as such, he deserved better than he received. It was all I could do to hold onto my sanity, which battled with my grief for control of my mind. They would, without a doubt, quiver in fear at the arrival of General Faron, the lion of the desert.

Fate has a way of dipping its hand into each of our lives in ways that we truly do not understand. It is difficult enough to unravel the mysteries of the universe. Yet, I believe it was my destiny to find Arem's body. Fate also placed me in the path of a Private of the Zaharian military. Within a day of exiting the vastness of the Alahari Desert, our paths crossed. The Private, immediately deferential, rambled incoherently for hours. Following Arem's death, Princess Lenali had ordered the Private and one of his Sergeants to complete a secretive mission. Privately, the two doubted the veracity of her claim that the Sultan had personally ordered the mission. Fearing any reprisal on that front, they completed the mission to deliver a glass container, filled with an unknown liquid, to a small village nestled high in the Cargathian Mountains in the northeastern part of the Known World. The Private was distraught over the loss of his Sergeant. The man died of an injury sustained when falling off his horse.

Although angered by the mistreatment of my son's body, the Private assured me the Princess had told them he succumbed to a highly contagious, desert-borne disease. Otherwise, they would have given Arem's body its appropriate care. After hearing the Private's description of the events, I decided to change course and ride to the northeast. As a military tactician, I am always prepared to change course on an as-needed basis to accomplish my objectives. I needed to find answers to some nagging questions.

What was the mission's objective? What was inside the glass container? How did it play a role, if any, in the death of my son?

Would Princess Lenali have known about the secret mission while Captain Arem did not?

The explanation she gave to the Sergeant, and the Private, seemed to be lacking in truthfulness.

I decided I could find and confront Princess Lenali at another time. She would be married to the King of O'ndar, and I could deal with her in the future. Therefore, I changed direction and headed to a village known as Mfiri.

Heading northeast with two glass containers, the Private told me the Sergeant panicked when a Dragon threatened to attack their horses. The Sergeant's horse took fright, bounding away with the Sergeant and leaving the Private to face certain death. Seconds before the Dragon attacked, the Private threw one of the containers at the Dragon. The powerful contents inside the shattered container knocked the Dragon unconscious. The Private tracked the cowardly Sergeant but forgave him immediately for his actions. The Sergeant lay dying, thrown from his horse. The Private planned to report the Sergeant's pusillanimity when the two returned to Istanabad, but decided to forgive and forget.

Once again, fate intervened mysteriously. The Private handed me a map showing the way to Mfiri. I thanked him and swore him to secrecy about our chance meeting. I also explained I was on a mission for the Sultan and would never return to our homeland. He agreed to my order of secrecy, offering the appropriate vows and left for Istanabad. I headed northeast.

Within days, I spotted the remote village from the top of a large hill nestled within the mountains. I planned to leave the following day but was weary from my travels and decided to get some rest.

I slept peacefully enough but was shocked the next day when I awoke. A giant, black dragon leaned over me. Startled, I reached for my scimitar to defend myself. Before I could grab it, though, the Dragon snatched me up in its claws and carried me up the side of the mountain. I was to become the Dragon's next meal. Inside its cave, the Dragon handled me gently and placed me on the floor. The Dragon signalled that I needed to put my hand upon one of its eggs, one that glowed eerily.

The moment my hands touched the glowing egg, words began flowing into my mind.

They were sporadic, often nonsensical. I remained calm, hoping at some point to plot my escape from the cave of the beast. Yet, the words continued repeatedly.

Arem. Alive. Father. Mfiri. Arem. Alive. Father. Mfiri.

It was then I realized the Dragon was attempting to speak to me. When he leaned closer, placing his face close enough to mine so that I could feel his breath on my cheeks, our eyes locked. It was then I knew. My body shook with confusion at this revelation. Somehow, this Dragon was my son. Arem's soul became trapped inside this beast. If this were true, it could only mean the contents of the shattered, glass container had housed a part of the soul of my son.

The other container must hold the rest of his soul. I did not know, but if even a chance existed for me to reverse the dark magic used to imprison Arem inside the body of the Dragon, I would need to go to this village to find it.

I felt that the village Mfiri held the answers I needed. I knew two things. Princess Lenali ordered my son's body abandoned after sending two soldiers on a secret mission. Now, his soul remained trapped inside the body of a Dragon. I was angry and wanted revenge, but misguided or misdirected anger never solved any problems. I calmed myself, knowing that I would need to go into Mfiri before avenging my son. I needed answers to many unspoken questions.

I spoke to the Dragon as if he were my son. I spent the next few hours telling him I loved him and thanked him for helping me to be reborn as a human. I spoke to him of his mother's death and the Sultan's part to play in it. There we were, father and son, a former General and a former Captain in the Zaharian military. I wept for the two of us when speaking of his mother and her dying wishes. Arem wrapped his massive claws around me, hugging me close. We held each other one last time in the darkness of the cave. A small part of me did not want to leave him alone. I had travelled across the Known World to fulfill an oath made to his dying mother and was leaving him alone.

Before we parted, I swore to him that I would find Mfiri and figure out a way to save him. He seemed troubled with my words but could not offer any communication to me about why my words caused him pain. I immediately left the cave and continued on my journey to Mfiri. My hatred for Princess Lenali grew with each step.

Finally, after walking for a little more than a day, I found the only entrance into the accursed village. A wall of fog, hundreds of meters high and bordered by a deep ravine led me to the bridge into Mfiri. The Private had not been entirely truthful in his description of the Guardian. It was not a woman. It was a creature with the face of a woman and the body of a bird. I have learned over the years to be a patient soldier before entering into a battle with a superior foe. I spent the better part of a day watching the creature closely. The monster coveted something hidden beneath one of its wings. She spent most of her time lifting the wing, peaking beneath, and smiling to herself. She would cover it lightly, speaking softly to the object, only to repeat the process every few minutes. After some planning, I decided the village held the answers I needed, and therefore I must cross the bridge.

Just before evening, the moment the creature had fallen asleep, my opportunity arose. All my years in the Sultan's house had given me the skills to lie, cheat, and steal. I used the latter skill to approach stealthily. Without arousing the creature, I snuck beneath her wing and snatched a large, shiny blue-black egg. It was unique in its size. It was unique in its texture. This egg, smooth as glass, emanated a pulsating light. I retreated a few feet off the bridge and turned to call out a challenge to the creature.

Startled out of her slumber, she awoke with an intensity of anger I had never before witnessed. I do not state this lightly, having grown and served in the house of a maniac. The creature was infuriated to find I had stolen the pulsating egg from beneath its feathered wing. It threatened to devour me unless I immediately returned its property. The wretched beast stood up to its full height, standing taller than four horses. I refused to heed its ultimatums but offered a trade.

Rather than listen to my offer, the creature moved to attack. It charged me but stopped at the edge of the bridge. I realized I was safe from it since the animal seemed restrained from coming any closer. An unseen barrier prevented it from attacking me. Smiling with this realization, I walked over to the edge of the ravine. I held the glowing sphere away from my body. The creature pleaded with me to be careful. I knew I would be able to ask for anything, and the beast would not be able to refuse. After some few minutes, of what could be described as haggling, though we both knew she had no room to negotiate, the creature agreed to let me pass safely and unmolested into Mfiri if I promised to return the egg. Moments later, I crossed over the bridge, keeping the fiend at a safe distance. I reminded the wretch that if attacked, I would toss the egg over the side. I crossed over, unmolested. Seconds before leaping off the bridge, I threw the egg back to the hideous beast.

Once I was across the wooden bridge, and the glowing egg was safely in its possession, the creature laughed insidiously, promising Mfiri had become my prison. The monster professed to know why I wanted to gain entrance into Mfiri. Inside one of the huts, I could find the answers I sought. I would only need to walk up and ask one of the residents for guidance. I did not heed her words.

I had entered the world a thief, having robbed my birth mother of her life. Thus, I entered Mfiri by stealing my way inside. Within the village, I found a black-on-black pathway. The surface was smooth as the creature's egg, constructed out of black, glasslike material. The path wound its way across the entire village, crisscrossing back and forth.

As a General in the world's most powerful military there are few things in the world capable of striking fear into my heart. Mfiri is one. Even today, I awaken from my dreams covered in sweat. I will see creatures in a darkened corner that turn out to be only a mirage. Mfiri is a desolate place, devoid of ordinary life. The horrible place houses many fiendish sorts of creatures.

I traversed the entire village many times before realising I had no idea where to find answers about my son. Finally, in the act of desperation, I decided to follow the bird-like creature's advice and seek the assistance of a hag with a face covered in giant warts. She had already come to the causeway numerous times to scold me for ignoring her reprehensible children. They had been harassing me relentlessly whenever I passed by their home. Finally, I stopped to ask her if she could provide me with the answers I needed. The evil woman smiled sadistically. She lied to me by saying she could offer the answers I sought in exchange for a small price. I only needed to step off the walkway and walk with her to her house. Desperate, I stepped off the blackened pavement. The heinous offspring attacked me, scooping me up into their arms. I initially thought there were only two or three, but I realized there were more than thirty when they lifted me above their heads. They carried me screaming into one of the darkened houses.

These evil children were abominations. There are no stronger terms to describe them; otherwise, I would do so in another manner. I soon realized the little monsters were cannibalistic, and I was to be their dinner. They began arguing profusely about which one would get to eat the tastiest parts of me. Held immobile by tiny hands, I refused to let fear overtake my senses. Though reaching the point of insanity, I mumbled Arem's name repeatedly to help maintain my balance.

The witch angrily stared them into silence and instead offered them another option, my blood. She told them that if they kept me alive, they could consume me for years to come. Thus, gagged and bound, the demonic children locked me inside a cage near a large fireplace, the logs of which burned with black fire. The darkened flames offered no warmth and little light, but I could see them flickering inside the hearth.

Each morning and each evening, the children arrived at the hut. They would drag me out of the cage. They held me firmly while a few guarded each doorway to prevent my escape. The witch would slowly drain me of half my blood. It was an existence that left me lethargic and miserable. This routine went on for an eternity. Slowly, during the moments not drained of my blood, I became acquainted with the witch. In the first five years she avoided having any conversation with me. It took years, but finally, she and I began to have small chats. Her trust in me grew, as did her obvious affection. I bided my time and gained her confidence slowly. In time, the witch began to teach me some of the rudiments of healing and spell making. I was careful in the way I phrased my questions but was able to gather some practical knowledge.

As a resident of Mfiri, she used her cauldron to watch events while they unfolded in the outside world. She verified for me that the Dragon was my son Arem. Her words only confused me.

Why had Arem insisted I come to Mfiri? He was safe, though, and it helped to know he was still alive, in some manner.

The witch also told me the Guardian, a creature named Gamayun, was a vile creature. The old crone arrived in Mfiri thousands of years before my arrival. Gamayun would place all manner of creatures inside Mfiri and then never allow them to leave. Gamayun had tricked the witch aeons ago, and she too was a prisoner to Mfiri. She seemed delighted, though, to play her given role. Her duty was to trap other beings the moment they stepped off the blackened causeway near her home.

I sighed heavily, realizing Gamayun had only agreed to my demand for entrance into Mfiri, knowing she would never allow me to leave. For almost an entire year, I became despondent and refused any more attempts at communication from the witch.

Yet, I persevered. My captors, draining me of blood twice a day, came to believe I would not try to escape. They became lax in their duties. They allowed me the freedom to move about the tiny hut though they warned me against attempting to step outside. Other creatures might come to know of my presence. The children and the witch advised caution. While they only intended to drain my blood, some of the other creatures would eat my flesh. It was best to remain inside to prevent them from snatching me away from my captors.

Over the next five years, the witch fed on my soul while she and the children nourished themselves daily on my blood. One evening, while they were away, I happened upon a book, hidden away in a mouldy chest, in the back of the fireplace. Expecting my hands to burn, I plucked it from the flames. The fire turned out to be cold to the touch.

Inside the book was the revelation I had been waiting to find. The book offered a spell to send the soul of a person across the Known World. The soul could travel to any desired spot, and once there would bring the body out to its location, for a soul, and a body must always remain connected to stay alive. Thus, escape from Mfiri was possible. I spent the next five years biding my time and memorizing the spell. I carefully placed the book back into the flames, removing it only when it was safe to do so. Finally, one afternoon I decided to try my escape. It is difficult to tell the difference between day and night in Mfiri. The witch and the children had gone from the house. I decided if I were ever to attempt my getaway, it had to be now. I paused for a few minutes, trying to choose my next destination. I could not go to Arem's cave since there was no saving him. I could seek revenge on the one person I deemed responsible. I decided to go to O'ndar

It is a unique experience, removing a soul from a body and putting the two of them back together. It is unnatural, and when they collapse together, they do so violently. While I did not honestly know if it would work, it did. I landed on the outskirts of O'ndar and lay on my back in a grassy field. I sobbed, I cursed, and I thanked the universe. I was free. I laughed hysterically at the thought of the wicked witch and the evil children crying in desperation after finding the house empty.

Shortly, I found a nearby lake and bathed in it with utter joy in my heart.

A few hours later, I spoke with a passerby. He was on his way to the castle to offer a gift to the Queen. She was with a child, her first, and the pregnancy was not going well. Hiding my glee, I was astounded to realize I had only been in Mfiri for a little more than a year.

I hobbled back to the lake in my weakened condition and looked down at the water to see my reflection. I stared in utter disbelief. The witch had fed on my soul, and the wicked children had drained me of my blood. I thought Mfiri had trapped me for more than fifteen years. The toll on my body from the experience was expensive. I appeared to have aged more than twenty years from my dealings with the witch and the children. I am confident my frailty included the price I paid to escape Mfiri without Gamayun's permission.

I settled near O'ndar and eventually in my cave with the intent of taking vengeance, someday, on Queen Lenali. A few years later, when the Royal Guards demanded I help the Queen I feigned being frightened, hoping it would mask my excitement. I accepted, happy to use the opportunity to take both her life and the life of her unborn son. That was my original intention. Yet, filled with madness, the moment I was allowed to be close to her, I decided to delay my vengeance until her son reached my son Arem's age. Then I would exact revenge on both of them, robbing them the way she had stolen Arem. On that day, far in the future, I would kill the Prince, the Princess, and, if possible, the Queen.

I had become a lunatic though I masked it very well.

Mfiri is a magical place, yet if not in its presence, the magic loses its lustre and eventually, Mfiri slips away from our minds. Finally, as time elapsed, the memories of Mfiri began to fade away, seemingly lost forever, but what I knew about Arem did not. His recent reappearance, abducting Princess Lyssa at Lake Windain, has brought it all back.

My vengeance has not come to fruition, but I think my son Arem has the same goal. He swooped in from the sky, plummeting to the earth like a meteor.

After weighing out all of the possibilities, it is clear that he has done so to seek his revenge. When news of the abduction reached my ears, I hurried to the King and Queen and offered my services. The fools accepted my proposal, and I just recently aided the Prince in his quest to save his sister. It pleased me to know my son Arem would kill both of the children of Queen Lenali.

I am alone, residing in a cave sealed up by soldiers of the Queen. My body is too old, and I am too feeble to attempt my escape. I will work to finish my memoirs, tweaking them for the sake of posterity. Thus, Ferlynne has failed his mission. A mission based on a promise to a woman loved beyond anyone in the world. Ocotillo, my wife and the mother of my only son, helped me find something taken from me many years ago, my lost humanity. The love of my Desert Flower helped Faron to be Reborn. It is with a heavy heart I go to my ultimate demise. I have sinned many times; thus, I deserve a fate reserved for those who have sinned. The story of General Faron ends, trapped inside a cave, lonely and heartbroken once again.

Lyssa had difficulty making eye contact with the tired-looking man sitting opposite her on a rickety chair. In his writings, he had just admitted to wanting the two of them killed. She sympathized with the despair he felt, though. She empathized with his hatred of her mother. It would be not easy to understand, yet she felt it imperative to explain to him everything Arem had shown her. Once again, she lifted her hand and placed it on top of Ferlynne's head.

"I am sorry for everything your family has been through," Lyssa said gently. She stroked his head soothingly, trusting that he understood her emotions were genuine. "General Faron?" Lyssa asked.

The old man looked up once more and started to remind her, "I told you. General Faron is…"

"Alive," Lyssa finished his sentence. "You are no more Ferlynne than I am Queen Lenali. You are General Faron, given an opportunity to live again. Arem provided the spark needed to bring you back to your humanity. Arem does not know Ferlynne. He only knows Faron." Lyssa spent the next few hours telling General Faron everything that had happened to the two of them. He asked questions, sought clarification, but listened attentively.

During the next two days, they waited less anxiously than before. Landon's fever had long since broken. He rested peacefully. The two of them talked incessantly, each enjoying the company of the other. She quit referring to the him as Ferlynne. He no longer asked her to call him by that name. He seemed content to be the General once more.

At one point in their conversation, General Faron startled Lyssa with his words. "I had forgotten him. I had forgotten Mfiri and the witch and the Children of the Night and had forgotten my son." He teared up again but held his emotions in check. "When I first arrived in O'ndar, I was full of vengeance and hatred. As time moved on, though, I began to forget. I am not sure, but I suspect Mfiri, or Gamayun, or the witch cast a spell of forgetfulness on me. When the Dragon abducted you, my memories returned. They flooded back into me like water flowing from a river into a lake. I decided to send the Prince on his way, anticipating that my son, the Dragon, would gain our revenge. I am glad I was wrong."

Her eyes widened with wonder, and she nodded in agreement. She watched as General Faron retrieved something tied around his neck. He untied the strip of leather and held the item out to her.

"Arem gave me this before I left his cave," he offered, leaning in close to her.

"Is that a tooth?" she asked.

"Yes, he told me it would protect me from some forms of magic. I am sure it helped me maintain my sanity when trapped by the witch and the wicked children.

Lyssa smiled before pulling something from beneath her shirt. It was another tooth, tied safely by a leather string. "He gave me this, also," she added.

They continued their conversation in the safety of the cave, waiting for Landon to recover.

Finally, on the third day, a few minutes after they had finished sharing a cold biscuit and a slice of cheese, Landon sat up gingerly. He looked over to his sister and asked, "How long have I slept?"

MURAFFE III

THE SULTAN MURAFFE III LOUNGED LAZILY IN THE DARKENED ROOM;
the silky, lavender drapes pulled tightly across the stained-glass windows.
Plush pillows, purple-stained bear-skinned rugs, and thickly made
cushions with gold threading woven into the pomegranate fibre cradled
him in comfort.

An enormous serpent, a purple Cobra, slithered towards him
stealthily, the scales of its underbelly caressing his skin like fine sandpaper.
Pausing on his legs to soak up the warmth of his body, it inched its way
slowly upward. Elzahari's entrancing eyes never left Muraffe's face as her
body snaked back and forth across his own. The yellow-slits, hypnotizing,
bore into the man's countenance with a fiery intensity.

"I am ready, Elzahari, enlighten me," Muraffe whispered, pleading
with the Cobra for it to begin. There was no fear in the man's voice. This
scene had played itself out hundreds of times before. It was always a
gamble, but one that he was willing to take, just as long as he had Elzahari
beside him, guiding him and helping him to rule his Empire.

Turning his head slightly to the left, Muraffe lovingly offered his
throat to the snake. He felt the caress of the tongue, felt it kiss his skin
ever so slightly seconds before the snake sank its ivory fangs into his
neck. The Sultan felt a slight stab of pain, no more than a bee sting, as

the Cobra's tube-like fangs pierced through the skin. A trickle of blood slithered down his neck, a tiny stream of red. He wrapped his arms around Elzahari, holding the Cobra tenderly, offering the warmth of his body. Muraffe cooed to it softly, "We are one, my Elzahari. We have always been and will always be."

He could feel the gentle burning when the venom, a tiny, almost microscopic drop, entered his bloodstream and infused his entire body. Once again, he could feel the gentle heat that came when the Cobra's toxin began to spread through his whole body. Each time, the Sultan imagined an ounce of pure gold in its reddish-yellow form melted into a molten liquid, coursing through his veins, furling outward throughout his now paralyzed limbs. Eventually, as the heat wound its way to his heart, his eyes would glaze over, and the room would disappear, fading slowly into a shadow of mist. He could feel it in his upper torso, winding its way through the web of veins in his body.

Muraffe's body turned rigid, stiffening in response to the venom. His green, bird-like eyes rolled upward into his head. He was no longer in his room, no longer in Istanabad. He had taken flight, his soul drawn away from the physical Muraffe by unseen hands. The first time this had happened, he had screamed for Elzahari, pleading with the snake to bring him back, though it was to no avail. That was many years ago.

He had grown accustomed to the sensation and looked forward each time to flying above the clouds. It was breathtaking. Looking down from the heavens, he imagined himself to be a predatory bird, the view inspiring him beyond anything imaginable. He coveted these moments, and his heart thumped loudly with excitement. Casting his eyes below him, scanning with them as far as he could see, Muraffe knew that he was floating slowly across an ocean of darkness. Each time he took this journey, his eyes became accustomed to the murkiness, and each time, he could make out more shapes, more of the detail.

I am above mountains, he thought, wondering if they were the Cargathian Mountain range that bordered his lands and the rest of the Known World.

It was the same dream, the same hallucination, though he had come to believe in its veracity many years ago. Though they performed this ritual only a few times a year, it was the prophecy that Muraffe sought. He yearned for reassurance, hoping to use it to guide his decisions. It was the reason that he would never allow Elzahari to leave his side.

A few hours later, though in reality it had only taken mere seconds, he landed softly on the marbled floor at the end of a magnificent hall. Lavender pillars, each ornately carved to resemble Elzahari, reached upward to a vaulted ceiling. Muraffe's eyes followed the carved row of marbled posts before settling on a hooded figure at the end of the hall. The being sat upon a throne carved from the rare, Amethyst gem. Looking at the magenta throne, with its multifaceted cuts reflecting the torchlight brightly, Muraffe understood how its presence intrigued him. Its unspoken message offered the two things he coveted the most in life. Hewn from a block of a precious gemstone, the throne, as well as the meticulously carved pillars, called out to his soul. The bright mosaic of purple, lavender, and magenta-colored tiles forced his eyes forward and upward to the shadow sitting on the distant throne.

Standing in his lavender robes, woven from the finest silk in the Known World, Muraffe lowered his head in embarrassment. Once again, the magnitude and the affluence of this place humbled him to his core. There were no guards along the walls. The master of this place ruled with confidence, feeling little need to protect himself from those beneath him.

Muraffe could see him at the end of the great hall, waiting patiently for his minion to trek the distance in solitude. The first time he had done so, Muraffe had been unnerved. It was a long walk, more than ten minutes in length. As before, Muraffe began and ended his walk in silence, using the moment to reflect. The hooded figure used the enormity of the hall, the distance it took to traverse its breadth to his advantage, of that Muraffe was certain.

Muraffe stopped in front of the throne and bowed. The hidden features, buried deep within its cowl, remained motionless. "My Lord, I arrive once again as a beggar on your doorstep." Muraffe was sure that the people he ruled over, the millions who were a part of the vast Zaharian Empire, would be shocked to hear him speak with subservience to anyone. Yet, he did so with complete sincerity.

"It is good to see you, Muraffe," the master of the palace intoned. He watched, amused as Muraffe's face studied the Amethyst throne. Muraffe had desired the meticulously carved rarity the first time he had laid eyes upon it. Nothing had changed since their last encounter.

Pale, slender arms, the only parts of the master's body that were discernable, rested comfortably upon the throne. A crooked finger, grey and thin, lifted towards Muraffe demanding acknowledgement.

"It is good to see you, Lord. Once again, I come before you a beggar seeking your guidance to ensure that Elzahari and I rule the Known World, appropriately." Muraffe dropped to his knees, lowered his eyes, and placed his head upon the marbled floor.

"Soon," the shrouded figure hummed, "we will invade the Known World and together, our forces will overrun all who offer opposition. With my support, and because of your obedience, I will help place you upon this Amethyst throne, lording above all and bowing to no one, including myself."

"Thank you, Lord," Muraffe responded before lifting his green, penetrating eyes. The hooded figure, the Amethyst throne, and the marbled hall had all evaporated into nothingness, leaving him in solitude. Muraffe sighed, wishing he had been able to stay a little longer. He had many questions, too many misgivings, but it was the same as it always had been.

Muraffe lay unmoving on his back, fully aware that he had returned to his castle. Nestled comfortably, between a few thickly cushioned pillows, he thought about the words offered by the shadow on the throne and smiled. *Soon,* he thought, *Very soon.*

Elzahari, her yellow eyes gleaming, hovered above his face, barely inches away.

"It goes as planned, old friend," Muraffe whispered, caressing her lovingly.

UQUAY

"THE PLAN IS SIMPLE ENOUGH," GENERAL FARON ANSWERED IN response to Landon's question. It pleased Landon to know that Lyssa's calming influence had brought Arem's father back from the brink of despair. A military tactician was helpful at this moment. Leading an army successfully was akin to playing chess, the only difference being the loser typically lost their life. Each move always led to many possible countermoves. The most successful Generals were those who planned for their opponents moves ahead of time. With each scenario accounted for, they would be able to prevent the success of each strategic change. According to Captain Arem, Faron had been the most successful General in world history.

From the moment he had awakened, Landon quickly noticed the difference in General Faron's spirits. Though his family had endured pain, he was much happier. The man, reenergized, moved with a sense of purpose. As Lyssa told it, the two of them had spent the last three days talking about their pasts. Their discussions were cathartic for both of them. Landon found the sparkle in Faron's eyes infectious.

He has a new intensity about him, Landon thought.

"Often, the less complicated a strategy, the greater the chance it will be successful. Many of my opponents overthought their plans; thus, when it came time to make decisions, they were paralyzed and afraid to make mistakes. This fear often led to many mistakes, some of which could not be corrected."

The three of them talked for two more days, hoping to give Landon enough time to recover his strength. During that time, they kept themselves busy, mapping out alternate plans should their original scheme fail.

They agreed that they needed to get close enough to Qui Oto without arousing her suspicion. At some point, they would have to contend with King Ghardenne since he was oblivious to everything. Confused by their actions, the King would attempt to protect his Queen.

At one point, Landon offered to arrange a secret meeting with his father, predicting that he could sway the King into trusting their intentions. They talked through this option but agreed there were too many ways for Qui Oto to find out.

"How will we get the Queen to come to Lake Windain?" Lyssa asked with worry. "Are we sure she will leave the safety of the castle?" She picked up the glass container once again and spoke softly to the contents. "We are going to save you, mother. I swear."

Landon watched General Faron's face closely. His leathered face carried doubts about the contents of the container. Faron did not believe it housed the essence of Princess Lenali. Landon was convinced the General thought part of Arem's soul might still be in the container. His confusion wore heavily on his face.

He's not the only one who has doubts? We all do, Landon reminded himself.

Landon tried to reassure her. "It is because of you that Qui Oto will come," he offered. He decided to refer to the Queen by her demon name. It made it easier to maintain his resolve. "If she has made plans to remove your essence and take over your body, she will want to keep you in her sights the moment you are back in O'ndar. She will insist that she be here to greet us. After all, she is our mother and would be worried about our safe return." Landon spoke the final words sarcastically.

The plan was sound. Landon agreed with General Faron. The false Queen would come to Lake Windain, yet doubts assailed him about the rest of their designs. Landon stood, stretched, and paced back and forth for a few minutes. His body no longer ached, and he felt strong enough for what must happen.

"How will you get the message to the King?" Landon asked. He looked to General Faron, watching as he pushed the sleeves of his soft robe up above his forearms. The Purple Cobra tattoo caught Landon's attention, but he said nothing.

I have to deal with one challenge at a time. First Qui Oto. Then, if successful, I will deal with Muraffe.

"As a healer, I have developed many connections and have many friends who would be willing to deliver the message. Write a letter announcing your return. Ask the King to meet us on the shores of Lake Windain at sunrise. With the sun at our backs, hopefully, the element of surprise will be enough." General Faron paused for a few seconds before continuing.

"You will arrive by boat with a friend, one who helped save your sister. Declare that Princess Lyssa requires immediate medical attention. Such a letter will ensure the Queen's presence. She will not want to leave your health to the skill of her doctors. At least that will be her excuse to be alone with you."

"My face will remain covered until the moment we step off the boat. Trust me; if the Queen believes the Princess's health is in jeopardy, she will come. The moment I remove my hood, there will be a few moments of confusion. In that brief space of time you will have the opportunity to subdue the demon and pour the contents of the container onto her face."

"I will run interference with father," Lyssa stated. The three of them were relying on a certain level of bewilderment, hoping it would be enough to slow the response from the Guards.

"If needed, I will hold the Queen down until you can pry open her mouth. We must not fail. If it is as you have said, once the essence is inside her body, your mother will battle Qui Oto for supremacy." He hesitated and then continued, "If needed, pour the contents into her nostrils. We just need to get it inside her body."

"Will it be enough?" Lyssa asked, afraid they might have missed something. "Is she strong enough to win control? Will she even remember who she is and where she has been? How will we ever know?"

Landon nodded in affirmation, though he shared Lyssa's apprehension. *How could they ever know? Qui Oto was clever and fooled us for almost eighteen years.*

"I do not know of any other options. If we go to the castle, Qui Oto has many avenues of escape. The only chance is to draw her out into the open where we can catch her off-guard. The demon must not escape us. If she does, we will never be able to convince our father of the truth," he responded, wishing that he could have his father's counsel to help guide them. Landon paused, his eyes caught up in the torch flames. They flickered hypnotically, casting dancing shadows on the cave wall.

There is more at stake than just our mother. We must prevent the destruction of the Known World! Landon did not want to focus on the 'what ifs but found it challenging. He shivered with trepidation.

The three of them sat silently for the next few minutes; each caught up in their thoughts. Lyssa held the glass container in her left hand, lifting it periodically to her face to study the liquid inside. Landon sat on Faron's cot with his back against the coolness of the cave wall, his eyes closed. General Faron studied the purple Cobra, painted vividly on his shield. Etched and painted with care, the Cobra's eyes were still hypnotic even after all these years.

Finally, the silence became too much to bear, and Lyssa asked, "Where do we begin?"

General Faron stood, walked over to his table, and picked up some stained parchment, its yellowish texture making it look old and worn. He walked over to Landon and said, "Write the letter. Be specific and leave no room for the creature to become suspicious should she have the chance to read your words." He sat next to Landon. For the next twenty minutes, they wrote and re-wrote the letter until satisfied with its contents. They had torn up three parchments before ultimately agreeing on the final draft.

Landon stood and handed the letter to Lyssa. She read over it carefully, nodding a few times while she read. "This is good." She handed it back to her brother and stood. "What is next?"

General Faron smiled and said, "Now we deliver the message." He walked to the back of the cave and disappeared from their view. A few minutes later, Faron returned with a small, brown bat. It rested quietly on the General's fingers, watching the three of them with curiosity.

"Is he big enough to carry the letter?" Landon asked with a grin. The tiny bat, smaller than Landon's fist, sat passively waiting. Landon doubted it could carry the weight of the parchment. He reached out, petting the bat's ears. The tiny creature rubbed against his fingers, relishing the attention.

"He is tiny," General Faron responded with pride. "Do not be fooled by his size, though. He is capable of carrying a rat twice his size back to this cave. I have seen him do it on several occasions. Hand me the letter." Faron spent a few minutes strapping the letter onto the back of the tiny bat. When finished, he whispered into the bat's ears. The pocket-sized animal lifted one of its wings and snuggled closer to Faron, enjoying his breath on its face. Gently scratching its neck and chin, the General returned the affections. Landon thought he saw the winged creature smiling at the man.

When finished, Faron lifted his hand above his head and said softly, "Fly away, little Uquay. You have been a good pet and a good companion. Thank you for listening to my ramblings without complaint. There is no need to return to our cave; you are free." General Faron frowned the moment Uquay flew out of sight. He turned to the two of them and said, "He will deliver his letter to a friend within an hour. We need to get some rest. In the morning, we will meet our destiny."

Landon lay down on the cot, covered himself, and quickly fell asleep.

Lyssa lay on her pallet in the cool darkness but could not sleep.

Silently, she watched Faron go to his table and begin writing by candlelight. He wrote for a little more than an hour, stopping periodically deep in thought, before finally closing his book with a heavy sigh. He looked sad, and for a few minutes, his mannerisms reminded her of Ferlynne, the quiet, lonely man living in solitude in this cave. The General grabbed his blanket before moving to the darker side of the cave.

Lyssa waited for more than an hour, and when convinced that he had finally fallen asleep, she went over to the table and sat down. She opened the leather-bound book once more and read his final words.

It is with a heavy amount of shame that I, the one who was born and reborn as Jirani Na'im Faron, must write into my memoirs the fallacy of my misguided hatred and my faulty casuistry. I require no recrimination. However, truthfully I would fully deserve it. As a General and a father, I have learned questions are better than answers, for they always lead to truth. Though it is in my nature to be investigatory, I allowed events and despair to fester into a rage against an innocent Princess, one plagued by a demon from the underworld. Whether a General, a Prince, a King, or a father, the measure of a man is whether or not he will rectify the errors he has made.

My anger led to delusion, and my hatred led to a fallacious understanding of events about the death of my son Arem. I know now I had never forgiven myself for not being able to protect my Desert Flower, my Ocotillo, nor my son Arem from the maniacal whims of a tyrant.

Ocotillo is lost to me forever. Arem, though he lives on in the body of a Dragon, is lost to me as well. This knowledge does not make life easier to bear, but it does provide me with a renewed sense of purpose. How do I atone for my sins?

The mistakes I have made are wholly my own. I will own them now and forever.

I came to O'ndar more than seventeen years ago with hopes that I would visit harsh retribution on the one guilty for inflicting an unbearable pain upon my son and my soul. The old man Ferlynne, the hermit and the healer, was to be the vessel of my revenge. Karma has once again placed someone in my path to alter what I thought to be my destiny. My son put the daughter of the one I believed to be my nemesis into my hands. I believe Arem sent her to my cave to help me heal myself.

In doing so, a resurrected General Faron can no longer be content to hide in the shadows of this cave, waiting for life to make decisions for me. Ferlynne will never return. He has disappeared into the sunset, though locked away inside the darkness of this cave is better stated. I did not know it, but he died the moment a soft-spoken Princess from the north placed her hand gently upon my scalp and shared the burden of my tears. She could have offered admonishment for my offences but instead showed me compassion. She could have offered me hostility but instead provided me only love.

I know not what the morrow holds and do not apologize for the wrongs I have loosened on this world. In the morning, I go quietly and with a conviction of righteousness. I must attend to a task, unfavourable, yet honourable. I go to my destiny with a swelling of pride in my heart.

Beware Qui Oto! The actions of the Princess, a flower of the north, are responsible for the resurrection of General Jirani Na'im Faron!

A QUEEN'S PREROGATIVE

THE BOAR, ONE OF THE HERITAGE BREEDS RAISED MILES AWAY ON AN open-pasture farm, had been slow roasted to perfection by the King's Master Chef. It was from a special breed of pig with ancestors raised for almost a millennial, living off the natural land without a fence to surround them. This particular swine, known for its rich, hearty taste, came from a farm located miles away, on the outer edge of O'ndar. It ended up on the table of the King, roasted and presented to him by order of Queen Lenali.

Because he had been cooking for the King for more than twenty years, the King's chef developed an almost uncanny ability to predict which meal would excellently match the King's current mood. An adequately roasted pig could always lift Ghardenne's spirits. From preparation to roasting, the entire process, including the serving of the pig, took a little more than four days.

Dug by hand, the large fire-pit located behind the kitchen and just outside the thick castle walls needed prepping by the kitchen staff before it would meet the standards the Chef required when roasting boar. The Chef spent a lot of time ensuring the bed of coals was just the right size. They needed to reach the ideal temperatures necessary for bringing the meat to exquisiteness. Three of his assistants dug a shallow ditch and used pea gravel to make sure the pit floor was flat and level. Afterwards, they confirmed the pit was large enough. They would need to rotate the boar throughout the process. After the Chef confirmed it met his expectations, the men meticulously worked as they carved the spit.

Though it happened only rarely, the Chef left the kitchen to supervise the pit's construction. He measured the spit. The Chef counted and measured the sticks. He watched closely the moment his assistants hammered them into the ground. They would need to be strong enough to support the weight of the massive boar. The Master Chef watched the wooden coals closely, ordering his assistants to do this or change that. Finally, when the coals were just a few hours away from reaching the proper temperature, he called for the boar.

He smiled, pleased that he had personally supervised the dressing of the pig. Days before, the Chef had carved away and removed the unsavory tissues and organs. An empty cavity always helped ensure the roasting process went smoothly.

His father had been Master Chef many years ago and had taught him well. He watched while his two assistants, one of whom was his son, cleaned the pig, wiping down every inch with salt, helping to kill unwanted bacteria. Then they rubbed in herbs and spices, a unique blend created by his father many years ago. When this step was complete, the Master Chef sent everyone out of the kitchen except his son. His other assistant guarded the door to prevent anyone from spying on the next step in the process. The Master Chef kept his son beside him so he might learn the secret family recipe. He wanted and needed his son to learn how to use the personal blend of brines and marinades that helped keep the pork moist and flavored throughout the roasting.

The two of them rubbed down the pig with a mixture of secret spices, including black pepper, seasoned salt, and paprika. The two slowly peeled a bushel of fully ripened apples, the ingredient needed to enhance the flavoring of the meat. The Chef complimented his son on his efforts, and then the Master Chef turned his attention to the remainder of the secret family recipe.

He helped his son place more than thirty apples, unsliced, inside the cavity of the hog. Each had been hand-rolled in a combination of sugar and cinnamon. Like his father before him, he explained each step to his son, encouraging the younger one to ask questions. He answered them patiently, pride beaming on his face.

When the two of them had finished placing the boar on the spit, they tied the midsection and the legs shut to ensure the apples remained inside. Though the preparation took three days, the actual roasting would only take twenty-four hours. Master Chef remained vigilant during the entire process, never once resting nor closing his eyes. During the roasting, he continued to marinate the hog, helping maintain the texture of the skin and the juiciness of the meat.

When it was ready, servants lifted the pig from the spot above the coals. Though exhausted, the Master Chef personally prepared the pig for presentation to the Monarchs. He ordered everyone from the kitchen, and once again, he and his son worked on the boar. They carefully removed the roasted apples and placed them into large mixing bowls. The young man added a slab of lard and some freshly churned butter with his father's directions. Another pinch of cinnamon and the smell of the apples, roasted to perfection, wafted throughout the entire castle. It was time to serve them to the King and Queen. Once again, the Master Chef refused to delegate this responsibility to others. He supervised the movement of the hog from the kitchen to the King and Queen's dinner table.

Ghardenne XVI used his plate and knife to carve large, succulent slices for the man and his family. The King was in high spirits, overjoyed at the Chef's efforts and immediately called the man back to the table. He thanked the Chef and bid him enjoy his meal with his wife and children, knowing he had excelled in his craft, once again.

The Queen requested the boar be ready for supper this evening, hoping it would lighten the mood and allow her to open up a reoccurring conversation she had been having with Ghardenne the previous nights. They had ended their chat last night frustrated with each other. Rather than leave well enough alone, Queen Lenali decided this would be her last chance. She must make one more attempt.

She watched the King enjoying his meal and thought, *If I cannot get him to agree to my plan, the meal may have to be his last.* Killing the King was not her priority, but she smiled inwardly at the prospect of ending his life. She had enjoyed her time in O'ndar, but she was ready to move on to new adventures.

He is a fool, she thought, the frustration with his ineptness almost maddening. She plucked an apple from her plate with her fork and bit into the fruit. It was delicious.

Maybe I will take the Master Chef with me? It could be a parting gift from the King to his daughter. The man would not be happy about leaving his home or his wife, but Queen Lenali was sure he would be agreeable if the order came from the King.

Watching the King enjoy his meal, she toyed with the possibility of gaining temporary control over Ghardenne's thoughts. It would require her to probe into his mind using the proboscis that she used to transfer her essence into the body of her victims. She had done this once or twice in her lifetime but did not relish it. Usually, the person died within a day or two. The long-term costs did not outweigh the short-term benefits. One of the instances almost ended with her death. It was a game of chance, and she did not wish to gamble her existence on its success.

Slowly, Queen Lenali pushed her chair away from the table, stood, and walked over to the fireplace. The spacious room offered comfort to the monarchs, always well-heated on cold days. She turned her back to the flames and watched the King eat. Ghardenne smiled at her a few times but remained silent during the meal. He enjoyed each bite of roasted pig, dipping the meat into the candied apples. When finished, he pushed himself away from the table but chose to remain in his seat.

"I surmise from your posture that you would like to revisit our conversation, My Lady." He had hoped to avoid the discussion for at least one night.

"Could we revisit the discussion one final time?" she asked politely. "I assure you, after tonight, I will no longer bother you with it." She watched the King sigh slightly, but he masked his annoyance quite well.

"Please review the options for me one final time, My Love," Ghardenne said as patiently as a father might to a child.

She reminded him, "In less than one month, if we are to honor the treaty signed between O'ndar and the Sultan, our daughter must begin her journey to Istanabad. She must be there before her eighteenth birthday; otherwise, the Sultan will consider it an insult."

Ghardenne looked into the flames, caught up in their movement while listening to the Queen's explanation. They had already reviewed the argument many times over, but he allowed her to continue.

"If Landon is not back shortly, I believe we must find a replacement and train her to act as if she is our daughter. Otherwise, O'ndar risks war with the Zaharian Empire."

"And you are of the mind the Sultan will not listen to truth and reason about the delay?" Ghardenne asked in disbelief. His response reminded her that he was unconvinced. He added, forcefully, "Muraffe seems a thoughtful ruler, he will be patient until we work things out with our beloved daughter's well-being." He stood and walked over to the fireplace, standing beside the Queen to enjoy the warmth of the fire.

"I am troubled about the prospect of war from our distant neighbor to the south, to be sure," Ghardenne began. "Yet, as a leader, I find it difficult to imagine the Zaharian Empire mustering their armies and travelling north over such a perceived slight. The cost would be tremendous." The Queen started to respond, but the King raised his fingers to his lips to silence her.

"I love you dearly and am happy always to seek your wise counsel. I must use honesty, not deception, in this situation. For the good of the country."

Queen Lenali did not try to hide her anger. It wore heavily on her face. She turned to face the King to argue her point one more time. A messenger arrived, interrupting their discussion.

The man entered quickly, bowed to the two of them and said, "Your Majesty. We have received a message from Prince Landon." He held out the rolled-up parchment paper, handed it to the King, bowed, and left quickly.

The King and Queen looked into each other's eyes before glancing down at the brown paper. His hands shaking, the King removed the thin string tied around the parchment. He spread the letter open and read aloud.

Your majesties! Father and Mother,

You may rejoice. Our Dear Lyss is safe!

I hope this letter finds you both well. My dear sister, your loving daughter, is safe from the clutches of the beast, which soared down upon us from the Wynde.

We will arrive on the shores of Lake Windain tomorrow morning at sunrise, crossing over by boat. Lyssa is sorely injured. She will need medical attention from our best physicians. She cannot walk and will need to Ryde in a carriage back to the castle.

We will see you on the morrow.

Your loving and dutiful son

Landon

Ghardenne clutched the letter close to his chest, allowing the tears of joy to streak down his face. The Queen smiled devilishly at him and nodded.

"Are we sure the letter came from our son?" she asked quickly. "Could it have been written by another's hands?" She looked deeply into Ghardenne's eyes, watching his every movement.

"Landon and I have a secret code, My Dear, developed to ensure that one of us had truly written to the other. Do you see the word Wynde and the word Ryde? Landon and I agreed to use these two words, though not in the same sentence, as proof," the King offered excitedly.

"A secret code?" Lenali asked, startled by the revelation. "Why was I kept unaware of this code?" Her anger flared.

"I am sorry, My Love, but a father and a son must have some secrets. Especially if one is King and one is a Prince. Do not be angry." He pleaded with her but was too excited about Landon's return to remain on the topic.

"I will send some guards to meet them at the shore in the morning. Escorted home, they will arrive within our castle walls by noon tomorrow," he jabbered, turning to yell for the Guards.

"We must meet them, My Lord," Queen Lenali said matter-of-factly. "If Lyssa is seriously injured, I would like to be with her when she is brought back by carriage. I need to be there to care for her."

"I am sorry, My Lady. I disagree. We will send the Physicians, along with thirty of the Royal Guard." He turned again to call for the Guards.

Lenali reached out her right hand and placed it on Ghardenne's left forearm. "My dear, before you call for the Guards, I need you to walk with me to our room, please. Landon left a letter for you to read should he return. You must read the letter before calling for the Guard."

She spoke softly, leaning on her husband's shoulders. Tears sprang to her eyes. She lamented, "It's disheartening to know it has come to this."

"A secret letter? Given to you by Landon. Secrets from the King?" Her words piqued Ghardenne's curiosity.

"Yes. A mother and her son must have some secrets too, My Lord. Landon sealed up the letter but told me of its contents should he find Lyssa. It implicates some of our Guards in a plot."

"Unbelievable!" the King responded, incredulously. His eyes widened a bit, and he gasped loudly. He turned to walk with Lenali to their bedroom. She leaned on him the entire way, patting his shoulder to comfort him.

When they arrived, the Queen held the door open for the King to enter. Once through, she turned to the two Guards and stated firmly, "No one is allowed to enter under any circumstances. Do you understand?" Both Guards nodded.

When the door shut behind them, Ghardenne asked quickly, "Where is the letter?" He looked to his wife, clearly in shock about her disclosure. The Queen moved around to her side of the bed before answering him.

"I will get it, my love. Please sit on the edge of the bed and give me a moment." Queen Lenali moved to her dresser and opened a drawer. She found a small bottle beneath some clothing, opened the lid and poured an ashy powder into one of her palms. She turned to keep the hand behind her back and walked around the bed. Without waiting, she bent down to look into Ghardenne's eyes.

The blown powder caught Ghardenne off-guard, halting his words in his throat. Before the King could respond, he fell backwards, landing softly on the bed, paralyzed. His eyes wide-open, the King's limbs weighed heavily next to his body as if bound by an invisible force. He listened with shock as the Queen threw the door open and yelled to the Guards.

"The King has been poisoned. You two help move him to the top of the bed." The two guards moved quickly to obey, gently placing the King's head on his pillow. One of them turned to leave the room.

"Where are you going?" Lenali yelled. She pointed to the guard and gestured him back to the room. He came timidly, confused.

"I am going to get the Royal Physician, My Lady," he stammered.

"The physician will be of no value here, fool. In Istanabad, our Sultan made sure all of his children became well versed in the art of dealing with poisons. I will administer an antidote, and the King will need rest, undisturbed. Send some guards immediately to the Master Chef and bring him to my anteroom. The two of you will guard this door and not allow anyone, including the Royal Physician, to pass. If anyone does, I will have your heads removed. Are we clear?" The guards had never seen the Queen this furious, and they both scrambled to obey her orders.

The door shut behind the two guards. Lenali smiled to herself, thinking, *They are cattle.*

She moved over to Ghardenne, placed her hands on both sides of his face, and turned his head so that she could look into his eyes. Tears welled up in their corners, streaking down his cheeks.

"Do not worry, my love," Queen Lenali whispered. She used the corner of his blanket to wipe his tears. "I will greet our son and daughter on the shores of Lake Windain and will make sure they arrive safely to our home." She leaned in close to kiss the King's lips but startled him when a hairy, tubular like proboscis slithered out of her mouth, slowly caressing his cheek.

Sitting up, the Queen retracted the proboscis back into her mouth and smiled. "Hopefully, I can be patient enough to wait until Lyssa and I are back in your chambers. You can witness what happens when Qui Oto removes the essence of the Princess and takes over her body. That is what I did many years ago to the previous inhabitant of this body." The Queen stood and left the room.

"Why are you shivering?" the Queen demanded angrily. "The fire provides more than enough warmth in this room. Are you trying to hide something?"

The Master Chef had been sitting at his supper table with his wife and three children when two of the Royal Guards burst into his home and demanded that he accompany them to the Queen. He did so but was unnerved when the two guards walked in complete silence, refusing to answer any of his questions. Now, facing the wrath of the Queen, he became afraid for the first time in his life. Even though he knew them quite well, the presence of the two armed Guards disquieted him. So did the absence of the King.

He stammered, "I am not cold, My Lady. I do not understand the reason for the armed escort."

"Are you claiming ignorance of the plot?" she ranted, raising her voice. The Queen leaned forward, menacingly.

"Plot? What plot, my Lady?" he asked. He glanced nervously at the Guards standing quietly behind him.

The Queen continued, "Quit looking at them and look at me, Chef!" Her piercing gaze was difficult to meet; the man lowered his eyes and waited.

"The plot to poison the King, of course," she jeered.

Looking up quickly, the man wore his shock well. He started to protest his innocence. "I have never known of and never would be involved in poisoning our beloved King," the Master Chef blurted. One of the Guards took a step closer, placing a hand to the hilt of his sword.

"I do not believe you. Moments after eating a meal, which you prepared, the King became deathly ill. Luckily, I alone know the antidote. And now, I must find out who else is involved in this plot, even if it means sending your family to the dungeons for interrogation."

Her probing gaze was too much for the Master Chef. The man lowered his eyes again. His lips quivered, and he began to cry. "Please have mercy, your Majesty. Please. My wife, my children are innocent. I am innocent." He fell to his knees, lifting his clasped hands in front of him. "Mercy."

The Queen waited for a few seconds before responding, "I will admit, Master Chef, you have been a faithful cook, and it would be a shame to have anyone tortured and hanged. I will therefore offer you a choice. You may go to the Dungeons, along with your family, or I will send you into exile. I only offer this because you have been Ghardenne's favorite and have served him faithfully all these years."

The Master Chef, caught off-guard by the offer, thanked the Queen profusely. "Exile?" he asked.

"Yes. Princess Lyssa is due to journey south to Istanabad. I would like you to travel with her and be her chef. Your wife will need to remain here in O'ndar, along with your oldest son. The one trained by you to take over as the King's Master Chef. You may take one of your children with us." The Queen paused a few seconds before continuing, "I mean, you can take one of your children with you to Istanabad. I believe you have a son who is four years of age. If you accompany my daughter, ensure Lyssa receives the finest meals while she lives among the heathens. Do you accept?"

It did not take the Master Chef long to accept the offer. He thanked the Queen once more and stood.

"Now go. You may speak to your wife and family, but do not speak to anyone else about my decision. I will follow up with you tomorrow, when I return. I will let my daughter know the moment I see her in the morning."

The Queen looked at one of the Guards when the Chef left and ordered, "Post a guard outside his home. Do not allow anyone to leave. Do we understand each other?" The Guard bowed and left.

The Queen sputtered to the other Guard, "Go quickly and find Captain Ryden. Let him know there will be hell to pay if he is not standing in front of me ten minutes from now." The Guard left in a rush. While she was waiting for the Captain to arrive, the Queen decided to stand once more in front of the ornately decorated, purple tapestry. She enjoyed looking up into the faces of Generals of the Zaharian Empire. She did not wait long for Captain Ryden. He arrived, panting and out of breath.

He entered and bowed humbly to her. The Queen began, "It has come to my attention, Captain, that the coins I provided to you for Ferlynne's eyes did not get placed on his corpse."

The Captain started to stammer but was stopped by the Queen, "Do not worry, Captain, I am willing to forgive your insolence, but will need you to do something to atone for your failure. I will need you to gather thirty armed guards to escort me to Lake Windain. We will need to be there in the morning, before sunrise."

"Thank you, My Lady; I will work hard to return to your good graces." He turned to leave, hoping to prevent her from changing her mind.

"Hold, Captain," she said, gesturing for him to sit. When he complied, she sat on a chair opposite him.

"Prince Landon has rescued the Princess. She is gravely injured, though, and will need to ride back to the castle, along with me, in an enclosed carriage."

"The Royal Physician will remain in the castle to await our return. Additionally, the King informed me this very evening that he suspects Landon may be under a spell by the Dragon. I cannot go into detail but will explain more once we return." She waited for the Captain to ask questions. He remained silent.

"The moment he steps off the boat, Prince Landon is to be placed under arrest and put in another carriage with four armed soldiers. Keep him safely away from the two of us. If he argues, he will need to be bound and gagged until we return." Queen Lenali dismissed the Captain with a wave of her hand.

The moment Captain Ryden shut the door behind him, the Queen returned to her bedroom. She sat down next to Ghardenne. His eyes remained open, and he was lucid, but he remained rigid.

Placing her hands upon his chest, the Queen whispered to him, "Are you not impressed? I used this woman's body for more than seventeen years, and no one was the wiser. How could you be?" She patted the King gently and continued.

"I have been a Queen nine times, thus far, and will admit that I did enjoy my time in O'ndar. Yet, I have tired of the north. I have tired of growing old, and I have tired of you." She stood and moved around to the end of the bed. Ghardenne's eyes followed her intently.

"I will also admit to some sadness on my part. However, it is not because of you. In my many lifetimes, I have been able to enjoy the moment a loved one watches, horrified when I change bodies. They are unable to do anything to save their daughter or wife, or mother. I am saddened because I have changed my mind, and I cannot wait any longer. I will not bring Lyssa back to the castle. When I am alone with her, I will rob her body of its essence and replace it with my own. Thus, Qui Oto will continue to live forever." She turned away, went over to her dresser, and reached into one of the drawers. She removed a small vial of liquid. The Queen returned to the foot of the bed and stared down at Ghardenne.

"Unfortunately, I cannot take a chance with Landon. He must die. At some point, he will come to Lyssa, ignorant that I reside within her, wishing to mourn your passing. Thus, before the night is over, the House of Ghardenne will come to an end."

"Are you not impressed?" she smiled at him lovingly, moved around to the side of the bed, and sat back down. Queen Lenali opened the bottle and pulled out the dropper. It was full of a bluish liquid. "Do not worry, Love. It is just a little arsenic to help you sleep." She put the tip of the dropper inside Ghardenne's mouth and squeezed.

The Queen replaced the lid and placed her hands on the side of Ghardenne's face. She caressed him softly, watching his chest rise and fall. Once, twice, and then no more.

The Queen leaned in close to his face, her dark eyes looking into his, and whispered, "Do not worry, My Love, this will all be over soon."

THE EMERALD DRAGON

A HEAVY FOG, A THICK, WHITE BLANKET OF MIST FLOATED IN ACROSS Lake Windain an hour before the coming sunrise. Landon, Lyssa, and General Faron climbed into what looked to be a rickety, old boat and reviewed their plans a few moments before Landon sat down and began operating the oars. The outer shell of the small craft was covered with a thin layer of green moss but seemed sturdy. The inside, made with very sturdy cedar planks, appeared well-kept and very clean.

Before agreeing to the purchase, Landon had searched bow to stern for knots in the wood but could not find any that caused him concern. The three of them had purchased the boat from an elderly angler, a man more than willing to accept the number of coins General Faron provided.

"We must get going," Landon demanded. The seriousness in his voice startled Lyssa. The sudden appearance of the fog made him nervous, but he hoped it would dissipate in the hours needed to row across the dark, blue waters of Lake Windain.

Before starting their journey, the three agreed General Faron would remain in the front of the boat but would keep his head covered with his hood. The General had changed his pea-green robe for one of a pomegranate color. Once they spotted others on the far bank, he would provide hand signals to guide Landon. They needed luck and the element of surprise to increase their chances of success. Lyss would remain in the back of the boat, acting as Landon's eyes by helping him make the adjustments signaled to her by the General. When close enough, she would feign being injured.

The moment the boat set out on the waters, the three of them lowered their voices, fearful that their words might carry across the open waters to wary ears.

Lyssa hoped to appear calm, but internally she worried about the strength of their plan. "Do you think she will come?" She had kept her nervousness well hidden, but wondered whether they could entice Qui Oto out of the palace. She had taken Landon's advice and no longer referred to the Queen as her mother or as Lenali.

"The Queen is hostage inside this glass prison," he had added while they walked to the Lake.

General Faron had wrinkled up his forehead, looking at the jar with puzzlement. He had seen enough in his lifetime to know there was true magic in the world, yet it was almost too much to accept. *Was it possible to imprison a person's soul, for eternity?*

Doubts continued to creep into Lyssa, but she bit her lip, hoping to hide her nervousness from her two companions.

"I believe she will come," Landon offered once again just minutes after he started rowing. The exertion made it challenging to speak, but in the small moments between, when he could gather his breath, he made sure to offer her a smile. *I do not want her courage to wane.* If they acted half-heartedly when the proper moment arrived, all would be lost. Uncertainty had a way of tempering one's actions.

Landon was thrilled to discover the boat double-oared, which allowed the trio to make good time on the calm waters. Frequently, he stopped rowing, allowing the boat to glide along its path. In those brief moments, he glanced over his shoulder at General Faron sitting stoically in the bow with his back toward the two of them.

"How are you feeling, General?" Landon pried. He knew the General disliked the boat and the water.

General Faron looked up, keeping his eyes forward, and frowned. "Man was not made to travel on water. If this were a chariot gliding atop a row of dunes, I would be much more comfortable." He realized he had not answered Landon's question, so he offered more.

"Our plan is sound. Travelling across the water is useful as it puts the rising sun at our back. It also provides an avenue of escape, if our plans have to change." He pointed behind Lyssa at the thick fog, "This, though, may dampen our chances of success. We still have another hour of rowing. Maybe by then, it will have burned off with the morning sun."

The three of them fell into a silence, each absorbed in their thoughts.

Queen Lenali sat in the carriage looking out the windows at Lake Windain, the dampness and the chilly air kept at bay by a velvety soft, emerald coverlet thrown over her legs. She had pressed the soldiers to hurry to the Lake, needing them to arrive at least an hour before the boat put to shore. The arrival of the morning fog forced her to second-guess her plan.

I do not like this fog. It prevents me from seeing everything around me. Should I return to the castle? Maybe it was a mistake to remove Ghardenne? Doubts plagued her. She listened attentively to the Guards since most had gathered into small groups around the carriages. There were no grumblings. She was confident Captain Ryden would obey her orders. By now, he would have already told his most trusted men of the plan.

She frowned again, looking at the fog with misgivings. *What do I do if Lyssa's wounds are too severe? If her body is not functional she will have to die, and so will Landon. Otherwise, I put myself at risk.*

Within an hour, the Queen looked out once more and smiled to herself. The soupy fog had begun to evaporate, though slowly. There were thin patches across the lake, but even these hovered more than ten feet above the water. She stepped down out of her carriage. Lenali pulled her fur-lined cloak, a mosaic of greens with a bright, yellow-eyed Dragon stitched onto the back, around her closely for warmth.

"There!" Captain Ryden offered excitedly. She spotted the boat, but at this distance, could not see the occupants.

The moment she arrives, I must get her into the carriage. It must happen on the way back to the castle. Then Lyss will explain the Queen Mother simply closed her eyes, exhausted, only to never re-open them. Once we return to the palace, the servants will make another discovery. The Guards will report Ghardenne has succumbed to his poison. When I meet with Landon to discuss the funeral arrangements, he too will die.

"Captain," Lenali challenged, "are the men prepared to carry out my orders?" The soldiers fanned out along the shore. A few had already drawn their swords.

Finally, Lenali thought, relishing the moment.

General Faron turned away from the other two occupants to peer up ahead through the impenetrable fog. It unnerved him, yet his years of training had prepared him to react accordingly to a change in circumstance. Actions required quick reactions, and he was ready to do anything to kill the Queen. He sat quietly, listening to the oars dip into the water each time Landon rowed. His mind flooded with misgivings.

The two of them are sincere. I must have faith that Arem sent them back to me with a reason. He admitted he had seriously considered killing them when they arrived, unannounced, in his cave. The spear was in hand the moment Landon had called out to him. Yet, something stayed his hand. *Why? Why did I not kill them? Then, I could have planned a way to kill the Queen.* He did not want to second-guess Arem's decision. Yet, until the Princess explained everything, he had reservations.

I must not falter if they fail. The Queen must die, regardless of the contents in the jar. He remembered how close he looked at the liquid when Lyssa had first shown it to him. During one of their long conversations, while Landon recovered, the Princess had become distraught. She feared the two of them might die before saving the Queen. If that happened, Queen Lenali would never be able to regain control of her body. Lyssa asked, then demanded, then pleaded for Faron to make vow to carry out their plan if he were the only one alive.

I lied to her. Faron did not feel guilt or even remorse about being dishonest. There had been too many moments of deception in his illustrious military career for him to feel emotions. This trait, hardened by years of violence, would have shocked the Princess to her core. *If the plan fails, the witch must die.* The Queen's harshness reminded Faron of the witch in Mfiri. The hag held him captive, in her darkened hut, without any reservations about what it was doing to his sanity. The Queen's exotic eyes and complexion did not fool him. The two beings were both uncaring, seemingly oblivious to the suffering around them. Queen Lenali was beautiful, yet in some ways, she was even more hideous than the hag. Their mannerisms, though, were the same.

She is a witch, and she must die.

What do I do if either of them tries to stop me? The possibility had crossed his mind, though he committed not to abandon their plan unless something went wrong. They had never received enough military training to account for this type of scenario. They did not know how to look for the nuances, watching for changes in order to make changes in a split second, if needed. If he decided to change their plans and they remained unaware. *Will I have to kill them?* He could kill Landon without remorse, but the General would struggle to harm the sister. *I have grown fond of her.*

Turning, Faron looked back to the two of them. Lyssa, caught deep in her thoughts, did not notice the look on his face. Landon continued to row in silence with his back to the General.

I will try to save her no matter what happens! he decided. He turned back to the water and looked through the fog once more. Faron's eyes widened when the mist started to dissipate. Minutes later, thin patches remained, hovering a few feet above the water.

Does the witch control the weather? General Faron leaned down to the right side of the boat and peered beneath the bottom layer of fog. He noticed the Royal Guards in their green chain mail and emerald cloaks arranged along the shore.

The first rays of sunlight, rising at their backs, started to push through the thinning fog, the cascade of light filtering through the openings and brightening up the morning horizon. General Faron had a sense of foreboding as he looked across the waters at the Guards.

They have unsheathed their swords, General Faron thought. His mind was in turmoil. Once again, he began to doubt their plan. He sighed quietly, looking for an opening to exploit.

Landon was happy to operate the oars and use the opportunity to work his muscles. His recent exertions had fatigued him, but rowing a boat was an activity that always pleased him. He bent forward, lifting the oars and dipping them softly back into the calm waters. Once they entered the water, he leaned backwards, dragging the oars smoothly and propelling them forward. The rowing gave him a chance to think about everything. There were many things that needed to fall into place, and he was not sure how to make all of them happen.

He looked to his sister, watching her sit in silence at the back of the rowboat. She had fallen into her thoughts and did not make eye contact.

I love her more than anything in the world. Yet, I know I will have to send her to the south to marry the Sultan's son. There is no other way. If Landon's plan with Qui Oto failed, it would not matter and humankind most likely faced extinction. *There is no other way.*

The night with the Four Horsemen had forced Landon to dread the possibilities that lay ahead. He trembled when thinking about that future. *I will be happy to discuss everything with my father. He will lead us through the coming Apocalypse.*

Landon longed to sit with his father and seek the King's advice. So far, he had been a pragmatic King, very practical. *He will know our best avenue.* Landon was sure his father would agree about Lyss and the necessity for her to travel to Istanabad.

Though the Sultan may come to regret our Treaty, Landon thought. He planned to force the Sultan to drop his goal of conquest. Trouble for the Known World lay ahead. They must prepare for a dire future. Those living on this side of the Cargathian Mountains had to unite and immediately. Muraffe might never agree. *We may have to force his acceptance.*

Landon focused on the Lands of the Khans and the legendary warriors residing on the other side of the Mountains. If thousands of those warriors crossed over the mountains, aided by a dark wizard with the power of Dragons at his disposal, a divided Known World would fall. *Even united, we may not stop Armageddon, but splintered, we are guaranteed to fail.*

I do not believe the warriors living in the Lands of the Khans are men? It has been hundreds of years since a warrior crossed into our world. Why is that? Landon thought. Man's indelible spirit would have looked at the mountains as obstacles needing to be explored, to be conquered. It was hard to imagine others had not tried to cross over.

The men on this side of the mountains feared the legendary warriors from the Lands of the Khans. That trepidation prevented men in the Known World from crossing over to the other side. Could the warriors in the Lands of the Khans be afraid to cross the mountains? Did the Dragons make them afraid? He doubted this to be the case.

Maybe they have been too busy fighting for their survival? he wondered.

It unnerved him to think the men residing in the Lands of the Khans might be trying to prevent their own Apocalypse and their own extinction. Yet, none had tried to cross over for hundreds of years. Something prevented them from doing so.

Landon continued rowing, enjoying the quietness of the lake. He paused for a few seconds before looking up at Lyss. She raised her eyes, looking across the lake. Turning his head, Landon was startled to see the fog had lifted. *When did that happen?*

He looked for a few seconds, spotting the Queen standing near the shore of the Lake. The Guards had fanned out in a line along the shoreline.

Unless I am mistaken, they have drawn their swords.

Will she even know who I am? Seventeen years, how could she know me?

How will I explain this to my father? How do I convince him that a demon has deceived him? Has deceived all of us?

Lyssa had been conflicted all morning about how to react once she stood in front of the Queen. This woman had raised her from birth. Yet, when she thought about the Queen, she could only imagine her as a stranger.

Were all those moments when she held me a lie? Lyssa had always favored her father, yet the Queen had been a dutiful mother. Lyssa had never known anything but love.

She did not treat me harshly, in the least. She held me. She cradled me when I was sad and scared. Was it all a lie?

The sound of the oars entering the water and the motion of gliding smoothly across Lake Windain was mesmerizing. Lyssa looked off to the side of the boat, caught up in her thoughts.

Brought out of her reverie, she looked ahead at a writhing ball of snakes floating in the water. The boat slipped by the snakes quietly. More than a hundred snakes slithered around each other. *Nature is such an oddity,* Lyssa thought, intrigued by their behavior.

She wondered what the snakes thought of them, the humans floating by in their wooden craft. *Do snakes think?* Lyssa noticed Landon smiling when they passed by the ball of water moccasins. She did not look up and acknowledge him. She had already recognized the poisonous snakes and pulled her hands out of the water.

Snakes are a part of nature. They may be poisonous and dangerous, but they are not like Qui Oto. She is a demon, more deadly than any snake. Other than Elzahari.

Lyssa was surprised to find herself thinking about the Purple Cobra of Istanabad at a time like this. *Was Elzahari a demon in the snake's skin? Was it like Qui Oto?* She noticed a similarity between the control Qui Oto and Elzahari extended over those in their orbit. She glanced sideways at Landon, watching him row in silence.

He has not told me everything about his plans. I know he is holding back about what we need to do if we survive Qui Oto. If we live, I will need to go south and marry the Sultan's son. The two nations must not go to war.

She suspected Landon had been holding back about his experiences in Mfiri. He answered all of her questions patiently, but some of his answers were vague, and he never quite answered them. *He has been through so much. I do not want him to feel I do not trust him.*

Finally, she looked up and smiled at him. He returned the smile and continued rowing with enthusiasm. *I love him more than anyone else in the world,* she thought. Up ahead, the fog lifted and hung listlessly above the waters, opening a clear path to the distant shore.

She did not focus on the guards spreading out along the banks of Lake Windain. She did not notice the glimmer of sunlight on their blades. Lyssa's eyes focused on the dark-haired, olive-skinned woman covered in a thick, emerald-green cloak. The woman stood along the shore, facing the waters with her arms crossed.

She has come. Lyssa's confidence drained away, her doubts resurfaced.

Landon realized there might not be enough time to put the boat ashore safely and react quickly to the guards fanned out along the shoreline, should things go awry. The unsheathed swords had caught him unprepared, but for Lyssa's sake, he chose to keep his nerves bottled up. He considered turning the boat and rowing away but did not do so since it would raise suspicion. Qui Oto might flee back to the castle, thus putting their plans in jeopardy.

Refusing to show any hesitation, Landon pulled on the oars with all of his energy. The boat picked up speed, closing the gap between the two groups. He listened to the chatter of the Guards, some of whom he and Lyss had known since birth. In response to his efforts, Landon heard General Faron grunt, "Good."

Landon imagined the excitement the General must feel each time he went into battle. *He is like a predator. His eyes gleam with zest moments before the oncoming clash.* Landon was thankful to have the warrior with them, hopeful that his eyes would notice subtle things that the two of them might miss.

When they were halfway across the lake, Landon remembered a tactical military lesson taught by one of his father's Generals, years ago. The man expounded on the importance of doing the unexpected.

"When in doubt, do something unexpected. Surprise may buy enough time to turn the odds in your favor," the General had told him. Landon was thankful for the lesson.

Landon's response to the Guards on the shoreline had pleasantly surprised General Faron. Landon refused to cower from a fight and his efforts had been noticed by the General. They were attacking rather than fleeing, which might provide them the shock they need to succeed. He had heard the approval in the General's voice, and it gave him courage. His actions would surprise Qui Oto, even if only for a few seconds.

When they were less than ten yards from the bank, Landon lifted the oars, stood up, and turned to face the waiting soldiers. He bellowed as loudly as he could, "In the name of my father, King Ghardenne, I command all of you to hold!"

The boat rammed into the shore with a jolt, the momentum carrying Landon forward. He took a few steps, leapt past the General, and landed solidly on the grassy bank. He yelled, once again, commanding the soldiers to hold fast. He did not notice General Faron step out of the boat behind him.

Landon turned to the Queen, his voice full of bitterness, "Hello, mother. Or should I call you Qui Oto?"

His words had the desired effect. Four of the closest Guards, including a Captain with whom Landon was on good terms, stopped walking briskly towards the three of them. Two of the guards held bindings, which they immediately lowered to their sides.

Landon's statement caught Qui Oto caught off guard, but the revelation lasted only a few seconds.

Queen Lenali ranted at the Guards, pointing at the Prince, "Seize him. I command you to seize him!" She turned and glared at Captain Ryden, who once again moved towards Landon. This time, though, he did so timidly.

"Captain Ryden, as the heir to the throne I command you to hold. Do not make the mistake of ignoring my commands." The Guards were deeply confused; heavy tension filled the air.

Without turning, Landon said quietly to General Faron, "General, we have the element of surprise; shall we give them one more." He smiled when the man lifted his hands to his hood and dropped it onto his shoulders.

"Alive! He's alive!" The Queen, her eyes glaring, turned and pointed to Captain Ryden, "I shall have your head for this Captain." She turned and yelled at the other Guards. "Seize them, all of them, including the Captain. They are traitors." None of the men moved to obey the Queen. Her cheeks reddened with anger.

Lyssa moved to the front of the boat slowly, struggling to keep her footing. Keeping her eyes fixated on the Queen, she made it to the bow. A shadow, cast by an object in the sky behind her, made her turn to look across the lake. A large animal flew towards them, hovering just above the rising sun.

"What's that?" she yelled loudly. All of the soldiers turned in unison, many lifting a hand to shield their eyes from the sun. A large, green bird dropped quickly down to the lake, flying a hundred feet above the water, aiming directly at those gathered along the shores.

"Dragon!" one of the soldiers screamed. He turned to flee in terror.

The Dragon flew swiftly, its massive wings beating the air. Within seconds, it pulled in its pinions and swooped down toward the blue water. Just before it crashed into Lake Windain, the Dragon opened its wings, gliding parallel to the open waters.

Captain Ryden met the fleeing soldier and slapped him harshly on the side of the face.

"You fool. We have to protect them!" Ryden pointed his sword to Landon and Lyssa. The man, embarrassed by his cowardice, turned to face the oncoming Dragon.

Lyssa jumped up and down in the boat excitedly. She yelled with exuberance, the happiness in her voice apparent.

"Landon! Look to the sky, brother! It is Arem! He is an Emerald Dragon!" She turned to look at Landon, wanting to share her excitement, lost her footing as the boat tilted and fell backwards, with a loud splash, into the Lake.

Landon looked at the growing form filling the sky. He saw it shoot toward the earth like a meteor and felt a sense of *Deja Vu* the moment the Dragon opened its mighty wings. This time though, the Dragon was much larger, more than twice the size of the one that had scooped Lyssa up in its talons. This Emerald Dragon, covered in thick, interlocking green feathers, glided toward them effortlessly on a cushion of air.

It took a few seconds to realize the Dragon was not alone. Its size masked the smaller Dragons, flying alongside. There were more than twenty black Dragons, each about the size of a horse. Initially, tucked in a row directly behind the Green-feathered Dragon, the undersized Dragons fanned out to the side, reminding Landon of a flock of geese as they flew south for the winter.

Landon appreciated his sister's enthusiasm as a shiver of excitement ran up his spine, though it was short-lived when he heard her splash. He looked to the empty boat, realizing that Lyssa had disappeared beneath the water.

The Guards, urged on by the Captain, moved to form a protective circle around the group on the shore. Each man had trained for this moment, pledging to give his life to protect the nobles. Though they were going to die, they chose to do so with bravery. Thirty soldiers stood at the ready, their swords unsheathed.

Seconds later, the Emerald Dragon was upon them, emitting an ear-piercing screech. The invisible flame, high-pitched and noise deafening, hit everyone like a shock wave. Most of them flew backwards and then crumpled to the ground, unconscious. The others, those who maintained their footing for a few seconds, tumbled and then lay immobile, paralyzed by the Dragon's scream. The Dragon soared past the group, circled back with its mighty wings spread wide, and dove once more like a meteor towards the bank.

On the grassy bank, three figures remained standing.

THE STRETCHING OF THE SOUL

Lyssa, General Faron, and Qui Oto remained standing, unaffected by the Emerald Dragon's ear-piercing flame. Qui Oto vaulted forward to grab a sword from the hands of one of the paralyzed soldiers. She tripped over the man's immobile body, stumbled a few steps before recovering her footing, and turned to Landon, his body lying frozen and rigid upon the ground. With her lips snarled in anger, she raised the sword above her head and charged.

"Traitor!" she shrieked; her voice hollow and shrill.

General Faron had been able to keep his focus on Qui Oto the moment the feathered Dragon's screech knocked everyone else to the ground. With his senses heightened, as they always were before a battle, Faron experienced the next few moments in slow motion, fully aware that Qui Oto was charging towards Landon, intending on taking the Prince's life.

She truly is a demon! he thought. General Faron's eyes widened, yet the years of military training, the thousands of battles, and the hundreds of skirmishes, guided his reaction. The moment the soldiers began to fall, he moved quickly to place himself between the Prince and the demon.

He watched the Queen rush at Landon and witnessed her shock to find him blocking her path, though the surprise lasted only briefly.

Qui Oto raised the sword and brought it crashing down harshly. Faron instinctively raised his hands to block the sword aside, though the sleeve covering his forearm offered no protection against the bite of the tempered steel. It was a feeble attempt at self-preservation. Wounded in battle many times, he had always emerged victorious. He steadied himself, bracing his mind to deal with the impending pain. The blade opened a gash along his forehead; the finely honed metal sliced deeply into his forearm. Blood cascaded down his face and into his eyes, blinding him for a few moments. Even though everything appeared to be moving in slow motion, General Faron did not see the Queen raise the sword with both hands and drive the blade down into his chest. He felt the bite when the tip pierced his skin, quite surprised that it did not hurt as much as he would have imagined. Faron wiped his eyes with his other sleeve, cleared the blood away, and looked with hatred into Qui Oto's eyes.

His adrenaline rush tempered the pain as the sharpened sword sliced into and through his chest cavity. The General looked down to watch the blade enter into his chest, somewhat relieved that his eyes, once more covered with oozing blood, could not see clearly. This time the General's luck had run out; the blade had done its damage, wounding him mortally.

I am dying.

He shuddered at the finality of the moment. *I have failed my son once more.*

General Faron shuddered. He felt the stabbing pain when the blade slid through his body, surprised that he felt the tip exit his back. The warrior within him refused to succumb. He locked his hands around Qui Oto and squeezed her close to his body, feverishly trying to protect Landon for as long as he could.

Lyssa heard the loud screech above her even as the water swallowed her whole; it was deafening, the water offering little insulation from the sound. She struggled to stand, found her footing in the muddy water, and stood up next to the boat, her left hand holding it for support.

Are they dead? she wondered. Pushing the thought aside, she trudged through the water as quickly as she could move. The water, soaking her clothing, dragged against her movements, making her efforts sluggish. She wanted to run to Landon to check on him but watched in horror as Qui Oto drove the sword into General Faron.

"No!" Lyssa screamed. Slogged down by the weight of the water on her clothing, she ran up the grassy bank, frightened to see the tip of the sword as it exited the General's back. Briefly, the old man locked his arms around Qui Oto, pulling the demon close against his chest. Within seconds he collapsed to his knees, his grip on Qui Oto loosened, and then he started to crumble. Lyssa caught him before he fell backwards. Looking into her eyes, Faron lifted his right hand and caressed her cheek. He gasped for breath, thick puddles of blood trickling between his lips and down his chin.

"My northern flower," he whispered, his breathing labored. The General looked upward into her eyes and warned, "Beware."

Snarling, the Queen kicked her left foot against Lyssa's shoulder, yanked backwards with all her might, and shrieked loudly when the sword exited General Faron's body. She raised it high above her head and turned back to Landon. Before she could take another step, the Emerald Dragon swooped down, knocked her backwards, and pinned her to the ground. Razor, sharp claws wrapped, vice-like, around Qui Oto's struggling form. The green-feathered Dragon turned and looked to Lyssa.

He sputtered, his voice deep and resonating. "The container, where is the container?"

Lyssa left General Faron lying on the ground, ran to the boat, and jumped inside. She walked to the back of the rocking skiff, carefully trying to maintain her footing. Grabbing the glass container tightly, the Princess jumped onto land. Holding it tightly against her chest, she ran back up to the Dragon Arem. In his new form, the mosaics of green were mesmerizing, the feathers rippling like the waves on an ocean. Arem had almost tripled in size and now towered over them. He held the demon firmly against the dew-covered grass. Qui Oto raged against the Dragon, cursing its very existence.

"Release me; you cursed beast. I am the Queen. Release me," she pleaded and then begged, but to no avail. Finally, when she realized the Dragon would not heed her pleas, Qui Oto paused, turning her dark eyes to Lyssa.

"Lyss. Daughter. You are safe. Thank the gods you are safe. Please help me! If you hold sway over this creature, order it to release me. Help your mother, please!" Her eyes bore into Lyssa, pleading for her help. Lyssa looked, emotionless, at the Queen, offering no sympathy to the struggling woman. Even when the tears came, Lyss's features remained stern and uncaring.

I can see the demon now that I know what I am looking at, Lyssa realized, looking at the demon's face with a newfound revelation. She shivered with the knowledge that they had lived, unaware, all these years with a monster in their house.

How will I explain this to our father?

"You are not my mother, Qui Oto. You never were," Lyssa proclaimed sternly. She lifted the glass container out in front of her and said, "Hopefully, I will meet my mother today, for the first time."

Qui Oto's eyes widened, and her nostrils flared. "You dare disobey the Queen! I will see you in hell, daughter. I promise you I will see you in hell!"

Lyssa started to move forward but stopped. Goosebumps appeared on her forearms. Three probing proboscises exited Qui Oto's nose and mouth. The tubes slithered back and forth against the Dragon's talons, touching the feathers, but they did not latch on.

The Dragon's large, green head turned to Lyssa. He spoke softly but with command. "Do not fear. You are safe. Bring me the container." Arem's yellow eyes bore into her with an intensity she had never experienced. Even though he had tried to lower his voice, it was still very intimidating.

Lyssa moved beside Arem and leaned over to look into Qui Oto's face. The demon continued to writhe, but the weight and the strength of Arem's clawed hands were much too powerful.

Arem's face leaned to within a few inches of Qui Oto's, a few of his emerald feathers brushing her cheek and forehead lightly. Yellow eyes, hypnotic and serious, fixated on the Queen's contorted face. A deathly silence settled in along the shore; even the insects had ceased their chirping. Without warning, the Dragon's green feathers ruffled vigorously, each standing on end. He shook them violently, the loud vibrations echoing across the silent waters. It reminded Lyssa of a rattlesnake that she and

Landon had seen when they were children. She stood entranced, for a few seconds, watching Arem's intensity with fascination. His mouth was open; his long, ivory fangs glistened in the morning light.

Qui Oto stopped squirming, frozen by the rattling sound. The two remained motionless for a few seconds, each sizing up the other. After another moment of silence, the Dragon Arem lifted one of his claws and touched the squirming Qui Oto on the forehead. The demon's eyes glazed over, hypnotized.

The tip of the ebony talon remained pressed against Qui Oto's forehead. The yellow eyes, snakelike, glared with fury.

Arem's voice boomed loudly, "Fretha N Onleqt, Menalin Su Tfrathk. Mafwfira un Qui Oto."

Qui Oto's body convulsed once, twice, and then she opened her mouth, expelling a green vapor into the air. The Dragon lifted his claw away from her forehead, placed it just outside the floating mist, and drew an invisible circle around it. He whispered, "Endinda." The cloud hovered a foot above the physical body of Queen Lenali. The gaseous substance gelled together and swirled slowly.

The moment Qui Oto blew the vapor into the air Lyssa removed the glass top of the container, leaned over, and poured the greenish liquid into the Queen's mouth. She fell backwards, expecting an explosion. There was none. The Queen's eyes remained open, but they were vacant and unaware.

Arem spoke softly to Lyssa, "The container, bring it closer, beneath the cloud."

Lyssa did so timidly, watching Arem lift his clawed hand once more. He circled the vapor once and pointed into the jar. The liquid formed into a stream and flowed quickly into the container. When all of the contents were inside, Lyssa replaced the cap. She held it up to the Dragon Arem's face and smiled. He nodded in return.

Lyssa held the glass container to her face and said smugly, "Hello, Qui Oto. Are you not impressed?"

"You aware of everything, even though you were locked inside this perfume jar?" Landon asked.

He had awakened from the paralysis to find the Dragon Arem cradling General Faron the way a mother cradles an infant. He watched, saddened, when the Dragon leaned its head up to the sky and screeched in pain, the sound rolling into the heavens like thunder. The younger, coal-black Dragons continued flying in wide circles overhead. They responded to Arem's screams by shrieking loudly in unison. They were aware he was mourning, though none understood why the Dragon would mourn for a human.

Arem held General Faron gently, rocking him back and forth. The General, moments away from death, lifted his right hand and caressed the side of Arem's face. Some stained crimson red, the green-feathers shuddered as large tears began streaming down the massive face.

"My son," Faron whispered lovingly. "I promised your mother I would find you." He coughed a few times, the blood splattering outward to land on his chest and shoulders. "I have fulfilled my pledge and die peacefully knowing I was able to see you one last time." The General's arms fell to his sides. His eyes closed, and he breathed no more.

Landon stood up slowly, made sure his legs would hold him, and walked over to Arem. He reached up and patted the Dragon. "Captain Arem, I am saddened for your loss. He was a good man. We had only recently been able to get to know him. He loved you deeply."

The massive, green-feathered shoulders bounced up and down, gripped with sadness. Arem closed his eyes as the teardrops streaked down the feathered face. The Dragon pulled the lifeless body of General Faron up to his face and hugged it closely. Everyone present was captivated, watching with amazement as the Dragon mourned the fallen General.

Once they recovered from their paralysis, the soldiers gathered into a group near the carriages, waiting for Landon's orders. They listened intently to the conversation between the Prince and the Emerald Dragon of the Forests. They all knew the legend. They had learned about Pelinnedes and the pact made with Meeha almost a thousand years ago.

Landon walked over to Lyssa and the Queen, both of whom sat on the ground talking. He wanted to give Arem a chance to grieve in private. Walking into the middle of their conversation, he had asked his question.

Queen Lenali looked upward at Landon and smiled timidly. She said, "Yes. I saw each of you the moment you were born. I cannot say I experienced the pain of childbirth, but I was able to see the two of you. My awareness, always veiled behind a thin mist, allowed me to see everything the demon could see. I wanted to run to you each time you fell, cried, or argued. Yet, I could not move. It was agony. Everything Qui Oto experienced…" she paused for a few seconds and then continued, "I was aware when it happened."

Landon felt a twinge of sadness knowing his mother, his real mother, never experienced how much he loved her. He promised himself he would get to know her, and he planned to spend the remainder of his life making her happy.

She has been through so much, he thought sympathetically.

Landon kneeled and hugged Queen Lenali. The three of them sat and talked for more than half an hour. Finally, when Landon felt the time was right, he stood and excused himself. He walked back over and looked sympathetically at the mighty Dragon. Arem, his head bent, sat motionless with his eyes closed.

Is he praying? Do Dragons pray? The question had been on Landon's lips, though he refrained from asking.

After a few minutes of silence, the Dragon Arem opened his eyes.

"I thank you, Prince. My father is gone, and I am saddened. Yet, with both of your help, I have fulfilled my duty." His voice was heavy and grave.

Landon nodded in acknowledgement. He looked back to Lyssa, sitting beside the Queen, the two of them whispering.

"I am sorry for the death of General Faron. Moments before we left his cave this morning, he stopped us at the entrance. He asked the two of us, should he fail to see you again, to tell you he loved you and your mother." Landon considered ending the conversation, but the loss of a father must be painful and needed more words. He had made a promise to the General and wanted to see it through. More than anything, he wanted nothing to go unsaid.

Landon tried to lighten the mood. He grinned at the Dragon and pointed to the flock of black Dragons flying in circles overhead. "It seems you are now a father," he said with a hearty laugh.

The Dragon looked upward and smiled. The long fangs glistened, once again in the sunlight, though this time with pleasure. "I do not mind being their mother. I guess I can be both. There is not a rule book for parenting."

Landon watched, fascinated when three of the black Dragons landed nearby. Arem spoke to them softly in the Dragon tongue; the words sounded raspy. The ebony Dragons shrieked in return, flapped their wings enthusiastically, and darted off briskly across the sunny sky, heading southward.

"I am sending them south along the Cargathian Mountains. I would like them to check on Muraffe's progress. They should return in a few hours."

Landon thanked Arem, "We will need to head to the castle quickly so I might explain everything to my father." Arem's expression puzzled him. Once again, sadness had appeared on the Dragon's face.

"I am disheartened to say this to you, King Landon, but your father has suffered the same fate as mine." The tips of his green feathers swayed gently in the wind. The Dragon Arem waited a few seconds for the shock of his words to sink in before standing.

"I will take my father into the forests to grieve and to offer the proper ceremonies. My daughters and I will return this evening. I am sorry you will not have much time to mourn, but there are tasks to complete," the Dragon Arem said, his voice booming.

Landon's mind barely registered Arem's words. He fell to his knees, placed his face into his hands, and sobbed.

FARON SENDS HIS REGARDS

BY THE TIME THEY REACHED THE CASTLE, WORD HAD ALREADY spread about the appearance of the Emerald feathered Dragon at Lake Windain. Tales of the exploits grew exponentially, and they all ended with Landon being the hero. He had saved the Princess from the clutches of an ebony Dragon and then, through heroism and bravery, had liberated the Queen from demonic possession.

A few soldiers had ridden ahead, sent by Landon to report and prepare the King for their arrival. When the news arrived at the door of his bed-chamber, the two guards nervously took it to the King. They entered quietly, preferring not to disturb his majesty should he be sleeping. Instead, they found his lifeless body. This discovery spread like wildfire, and by the time Landon and his escort arrived, everyone kneeled to the Prince, who by birthright would become the new King of O'ndar.

Lyssa bore no grudge about Landon's deeds, many already spreading into song throughout the Kingdom. She could have been dismayed that her efforts were excluded or were added in as an afterthought. She could have felt slighted but chose not to do so. She loved her brother dearly and knew he carried a heavy weight upon his newly crowned shoulders. Freeing her mother had been a heart-wrenching experience. As the new

King of O'ndar he would need to figure out how to prevent the coming invasion, and do it quickly.

She had seen Muraffe's plans, allowed to observe the War Council across the Celestial Plane and with the help of the magical power of a Dragon orb. She knew the planned invasion could be months, weeks, or even days away. Landon would not have time to mourn Ghardenne properly, and for this Lyssa was saddened. Her father had been a wonderful man and a great King. His steady leadership had allowed the country to prosper while enjoying a long peace with its neighbors. His steadfast qualities kept the tribesmen of the Eastern Steppes from invading and raiding the villages. Even beyond that, he was a marvelous father.

The moment she witnessed Landon falling to his knees, his face pressed firmly against his hands, Lyssa knew her father had perished. She watched, stunned as the Emerald Dragon gathered the body of General Faron, leapt cat-like high into the air, and flew with the other Dragons southward, out of sight. Lyssa wanted to run after Arem to beg him to return but did not do so. She stood, walked over to Landon, kneeled next to him, and wrapped her arms around him. They sobbed into each other's shoulders. Queen Lenali came over and did the same. The three of them grieved for the loss of the King.

After a few moments of silence, a change of mood came over Landon. He pulled away from his mother and sister, shrugging. His countenance hardened. He looked at the two most important women in his life, yet he was no longer a Prince. He was the King. He ordered the soldiers to help the Queen and Princess into the carriage and to escort them safely back to the castle. Mounting one of the horses, he galloped away escorted by five heavily armed soldiers.

By the time the carriage arrived at the castle, the entire nation seemed to be abuzz. Met at the castle gate, Landon listened intently while two generals explained the fate of King Ghardenne. He commanded the Generals to call for a War Council, ordering them to meet with him at evening-time in the open courtyard. Shrugging aside their many questions, Landon went to his father's room, kneeled, and paid his respects. The soldiers guarding the door closed it behind the new King, offering privacy so that he might spend time alone with his father. When finished, Landon ordered the men to bring in the Priests to prepare the body. He left the room, issuing orders to those he passed before moving to the courtyard to find his Generals. While waiting, Landon dispatched riders to all of the neighboring countries. He tasked them with presenting a letter, written by his own hands, that explained the demise of the King. He also issued a call to arms, declaring that the northern nations were at risk of an impending invasion by the Zaharian Empire.

Later that evening, just as the sun had begun to dip below the horizon, the Dragon Arem returned, landing lightly in the courtyard. The heavy flapping wings blew out three of the recently lit torches. Joined by twenty-four coal-black Dragons, the Dragon Arem kneeled to the ground and lay down on his belly. The other Dragons did the same. Determined to wait patiently for Landon to join them, the Dragon watched the gathering onlookers stoically.

Servants hastily carried wooden chairs, placing them in the courtyard in a semi-circle facing the Dragons. Landon led his Generals across the yard. Many sat down, afraid to move any closer to the Dragons. He commanded the Generals to sit and observe, ordering them not to interfere with the discussion. Awed by the mere presence of the Emerald Dragon, protector of the House of Ghardenne, none of them would have dared to do so.

Although Landon had chairs brought for all the Generals, he chose to stand. His coal-black hair, washed and combed, glistened in the torchlight. His green tunic, with its gold threading, matched the color of the Dragon's feathers perfectly. Landon was sure Arem would understand the significance. Pacing back and forth in front of Arem, he turned and smiled at the Dragon. "My apologies, Captain, but would it be inappropriate to ask that we forego conversations about our fathers? I have not had the appropriate time to mourn, and I cannot afford to let emotions cloud my thoughts." Landon was proud that he could be honest with Arem about his pain. Diplomacy and planning for the Zaharian threat would require that he keep his emotions in check.

The Generals gasped loudly when the green-feathered Dragon responded, "I appreciate your words. Yes, I agree. There are more pressing matters at hand."

A slight breeze kicked up in the courtyard, lifting the tips of Arem's feathers for a few seconds before they smoothed back into place. The Dragon sat up on his two hind legs and crossed his arms, the thickness of his robust frame intimidating. He stared down at Landon, waiting patiently for the new King to begin the conversation. Landon started to speak but stopped as the Dragon lifted two clawed fingers, gesturing for him to hold. Arem tilted his head to the sky, listening to something that Landon could not hear.

A minute later, Landon could hear the flapping of Dragon wings. Three black Dragons landed softly in the courtyard next to the Emerald Dragon. One of the Dragons hissed softly. It stood on all fours, reminding Landon of one of his hounds. Arem listened, all the while nodding at the smaller Dragon. Finally, when the ebony Dragon finished, Arem smiled and pointed to the other Dragons. The three black ones joined the others, bringing the count of the smaller Dragons to twenty-seven.

"We are not too late," the Dragon Arem offered. The corners of his mouth curled upward into a sinister grin. His voice echoed through the courtyard. A deep baritone, his voice resonated like thunder inside the hearts of those listening. "My daughters have flown into the Cargathian Mountains. The pass through the mountains is less than a month away from completion. They flew further south and found the supplies and weaponry heading northward at a slow and steady pace. It will take at least two weeks more for them to arrive in the north."

"Which means Muraffe's generals will begin moving their troops shortly after," he added, pleased that they were not too late. The tips of the green feathers lifted again, blown gently by another gust of wind.

Landon listened closely. When Arem finished speaking, he turned to the Generals and explained. "The Zaharian Empire has secretly built a passageway through the Cargathian Mountains. They are moving enough weaponry into place for two hundred thousand soldiers, maybe more. Unhindered by the heavy weaponry, the troops can move with speed to the north until they link up with their weapons. By the time they arrive, Zaharian slaves will have already punched a passageway through the mountains. The military, larger than armies of the northern countries combined, plans an invasion." He could feel the goosebumps gathering on his forearms.

The Generals were shocked. Startled looks soon turned to anger. Some mumbled quietly to each other. A few stood, placing their hands on the hilts of their swords.

"This is why the Emerald Dragon has come," one said. He looked admiringly at Arem and the other Dragons.

"Nearly a thousand years ago, the green-feathered Dragon swore an oath to help the House of Ghardenne," another whispered to the General sitting next to him. Many of them nodded in agreement.

They had all heard the Dragon speak and proclaim the northern nations were almost at war. Silently, each General stood and then kneeled before Landon. Cries began to grow on Landon's behalf. At first, the exclamations came from the kneeling Generals. They grew into a swell of exultations from the hundreds of onlookers gathered to witness the arrival of a daughter of Bosque.

Prince Landon had rescued his sister from the clutches of a Black Dragon. He recently had saved his mother from a demonic possession. Now, the Prince would command the largest, best-trained military of all of the northern nations. Bravely holding counsel with the Emerald Dragon, his mannerisms inspired the onlookers to sing his praises.

The crowd of onlookers pushed forward to be near Landon, excited about his recent exploits. The kneeling Generals gestured to the surrounding soldiers, ordering the Guards to move the crowd back while servants retrieved the crown. Each of them kneeled in supplication. When the servants returned, the crown passed from one General to the next so that each might kiss it and swear an oath of loyalty to Landon and O'ndar. Landon, surprised by the quick turn of events, did not know how to respond. His cheeks reddened.

Arem's voice boomed out over the courtyard. "Bring me the crown!" The final General holding the crown did not hesitate. Standing quickly, he walked it over to the Dragon. He bowed, held the crown up high, and waited for Arem to take it. When the Dragon held it aloft in the tips of his clawed hands, the General returned to his seat.

"Prince Landon, come closer and kneel." A hush went over the crowd, which by now had grown to at least a thousand people. Arem's voice boomed, carrying loudly throughout the courtyard. It seemed the entire world held its breath. Landon knelt in front of the Dragon Arem, looking upward into the intense, yellow eyes.

"I crown you King of O'ndar. Wear the crown as faithfully as your father and as honorably as his memory will allow. I crown you King and name you Ghardenne XVII." Arem bent forward, his feathers a mosaic of greens. Slowly, he placed the golden crown upon Landon's head. The emeralds, the bloodstones, and the jade stones sparkled in the torchlight. Landon stood with the jeweled crown perched atop his dark hair. He turned to the crowd. Cheers erupted and spread to a nearby village.

Ghardenne XVII? He always knew the day would come but hoped it would be years later. He wanted to spend more time with his father.

It is a tradition that not all Princes ever get to enjoy. His father had complained to Landon, once, when he was a little boy. "The hardest part about becoming King is getting used to having a new name." His father's words seemed sarcastic, but ended with his grin expanding into a broad smile.

He remembered the King saying, humorously, "I was Almaric for almost twenty-five years. Then, all of a sudden, I was Ghardenne. Can you imagine?" The King smiled, again, to soften the blow.

Landon came out of his reverie and looked up at the Dragon Arem. *I am now Ghardenne. It will take a while to adjust,* he lamented. Arem's yellow eyes twinkled with pride. The Dragon remained sitting on his hind legs, arms crossed. He waited for the newly named Ghardenne to speak.

"I thank you for the tribute done to me, Captain Arem," Landon shouted for all to hear. He leaned in and whispered, "It will take me a while to get used to this. I will always think of myself as Landon." He laughed, watching the Dragon Arem nod in agreement.

"I have asked emissaries from the northern countries to join us, requesting all of them to immediately send as many soldiers as they can spare. These troops will join us at the foothills of the Cargathian Mountains."

He spoke to Generals and Dragon alike, saying, "Generals, I need a plan ready by tomorrow morning, since by sunrise, hopefully, we will be on the move. Our military can get us started. Have any remaining soldiers, including those from the other countries, catch up to us as quickly as possible. Captain Arem, would you be kind enough to join us on our journey to your homeland?"

The Dragon smiled wickedly, causing the hairs on many of the General's necks to stand on end. Arem nodded in acknowledgement, and without saying another word, flapped his wings and flew swiftly out of the courtyard.

~Six Months in the South

Two days later, Landon rode in front of ten thousand soldiers, heading south towards the Cargathian Mountains. He commanded five thousand archers, three thousand foot soldiers, and a calvalry of two thousand. All of the northern countries had pledged more troops, but he decided they could not wait for them to arrive.

The O'ndarian military was in high spirits with an escort from the Emerald Dragon and her twenty-seven black Dragons soaring in circles overhead. Landon had spoken with the Dragon Arem, and they agreed the younger Dragons would remain close. They did not want the Zaharian slaves to learn of their approach. The element of surprise was essential.

When they arrived at the foothills, Landon ordered the horses tethered and guarded by two hundred soldiers. Before continuing, he ordered his men to rest.

When they were ready, he led them up through the foothills, winding their way upwards, between the massive, Red-Barked trees. Halfway up, he paused and turned back towards the north, looking across the sunlit sky.

Is this where it all began? Where Pelinnedes met Meeha for the first time? He relished the knowledge that he was, in some, small way, reliving history. When he finished his meditations, Landon sent a few soldiers back with fresh orders. The guards needed to be prepared to bring the horses up through the mountains at a moment's notice.

The rest of the O'ndarian army, led by Landon, wound their way up through the mountains on foot. They crept quietly, walking around jagged outcroppings and giant boulders. Scouts went ahead to locate the Zaharian engineers, ordered to do so stealthily. That evening, while the Zaharian slaves and their guards settled in for the evening, Landon arranged his archers into position, allowing the high ground to work for their advantage. While the Zaharians slept, the O'ndarian military surrounded the encampment.

At sunrise, moments after the Zaharian engineers had directed the soldiers to rouse the slaves from their slumber, the Dragon Arem and his daughters appeared. They flew in sweeping circles overhead, screeching loudly. The slaves fell to their knees in fear. The hundreds of soldiers guarding the slaves were startled to see the Dragons flying overhead. They were even more shocked to see the O'ndarian military arranged in the mountains around them. Five thousand archers stood at the ready, supported by heavily armed foot soldiers. The presence of the soldiers and the Dragons worked quickly to subdue any thoughts of fighting. The surrender was complete and unconditional.

All of the Zaharians expected a quick execution, as was customary in the south. Zaharians were not allowed to surrender.

Landon ordered their weapons brought forth and placed at the edge of the camp. He then ordered the Zaharian soldiers to return to their encampment. He spoke to his Generals, commanding them to ensure that all prisoners were treated with dignity.

"They obey Muraffe's orders. I am not Muraffe and will not treat them as such," he commanded.

Stepping away from the others, he moved to a hilltop to wait for Arem. The sound of wings flapping reached his ears, and he watched silently while the Dragon landed next to him.

Arem asked quickly, "Would you like me to collapse the passageway that they have carved through the mountains? We could knock these mountain peaks down from here all the way south. It would set their work back many, many years."

Landon listened to the offer and shook his head, "I have other plans for this cobblestone highway. It is time the south and the north became acquainted. I would ask if it would be possible to leave ten of your daughters to help guard the Zaharians. We could continue onward with our troops."

He smiled at the look of surprise on Arem's face.

Landon returned to his Generals and ordered them to bring three Zaharian soldiers and three Zaharian slaves to negotiate. They agreed to meet with the King, even though they were suspicious of his intentions. Many had seen their comrades executed by Muraffe on a whim.

Ordered to kneel more than thirty yards away, King Landon, with his archers at the ready, addressed the motley group. Looking gaunt, with their clothing in tatters and each covered with dirt and grime, the men looked at Landon with a boldness that surprised him. His gaze bore into each of them as he stared at them silently for a few minutes, the intensity forcing them to lower their eyes.

The six men were shocked to hear the King's voice.

"Look up at me." Each man raised his head and looked at the King. His olive skin, coal-black hair, and brown eyes were features of those who lived in the south. "I would like to make you an offer. I plan to have two fortresses constructed to guard this pass." He pointed to spots along the ridgeline. "There and there."

"If they are well-underway and serviceable when I return, I will spare your lives. I will also grant freedom to all the slaves who work on these fortresses. I will allow any soldier who wishes to enlist in our army to do so. Those who wish to return to Istanabad will be allowed to do so un-encumbered, yet free." The three men representing the slaves smiled broadly. The soldiers frowned, knowing the reception waiting for them when they returned.

"Do not worry. The Istanabad you knew will have changed by the time you arrive. I promise you," Landon offered with conviction. He recognized the fear in the soldiers' eyes. "All of you are expected to work, slave and soldier alike. There will be no more whippings." He pointed at the black Dragons flying overhead. "My soldiers and my friends will ensure that you are well treated. The Dragons will eat you if there are attempts to rebel." Landon waived them away, sending them back to the camp to discuss his offer.

The discussion did not last long, and the leaders returned. They accepted the deal, assuring him that they had surrendered all of their weapons. When Landon's army set out along the gravel highway, the Zaharians had already begun to work on the foundation of one of the fortresses.

Landon stopped less than a half-mile away and waited patiently for the horses to catch up to their position. Once they arrived, the O'ndarian military was once again on the move.

"Have you left enough men?" The question came from one of his Generals, the doubt in the man's face easy to read.

"I could leave one soldier, General. The presence of the ten Dragons is enough to keep the soldiers and the slaves from revolting. Plus, the promise of freedom is enough to ensure the slaves will keep the soldiers from trying anything irrational."

Three days later, Landon's scouts reported heavily loaded wagons lumbering through the mountains, and heading in their direction. His troops moved quickly and found the wagons camped in an open plateau the next night. Once again, he placed his archers and his soldiers on higher ground. He moved one thousand of his heavily armed cavalry in place to block the pass heading north. He doubted the lumbering wagons could escape quickly, whether they headed north or south, but did not want to leave anything to chance. Landon asked Captain Arem to have ten Dragons take up positions above and beside the cavalry. He also arranged for Arem and seven black Dragons to land behind the wagons to prevent escape.

When morning arrived, Landon ordered the O'ndarian trumpeters to announce his presence. Once again, the sight of the Emerald Dragon, along with the thousands of archers and troops were too much. Slaves operated all of these wagons since they required no soldiers to guard them. Each knew the Zaharian military would be less than a week or two behind, preventing any chance of escape to the south. There were also Zaharian soldiers up ahead, guarding the other slaves.

Landon accepted the surrender of more than one thousand slaves. Once again, he met with three leaders and made the same offer, which the slaves readily accepted. Before sending the empty wagons northward to work on the two fortresses, the King had the weapons removed from the wagons and moved into the mountains, out of sight.

When asked by his Generals if they should continue, Landon insisted they wait. "It is time we rest and let the very lightly armed Zaharian army come to us." He set up sentries, sent scouts to monitor the movement of the Zaharian military, and had the soldiers eat heartily and rest.

"I am very impressed, King Ghardenne," the Dragon Arem intoned. He smiled widely, his long ivory fangs glinting in the firelight.

"Please, Captain Arem," Landon responded, "please refer to me as Landon. I know, for ceremonial purposes, I am now Ghardenne, but I cannot help but think of myself as anyone else."

The yellow eyes offered sincerity and friendship, "You have not lost one soldier. Muraffe would have ordered thousands to impale themselves upon your arrows with the hopes that they might overwhelm you with numbers."

Landon listened, accepting the praise, but offered, "The true challenge will come next. Hundreds of thousands of soldiers, many battle-hardened veterans, even though lightly armed, will be dangerous. Many will carry scimitars at their sides. They will not be cowed into submission like the others."

Landon and the Dragon Arem spoke well into the night. A bright moon hung high in the star-filled sky before the two bade each other good night. Before entering his tent, Landon received word that the reinforcements from the border countries had arrived. Fifty-thousand heavily armed soldiers were less than a day behind, including an additional seven thousand archers. He took the news heartedly, entered his tent, and slept soundly until just before sunrise.

The following day, just at sunrise, a shocked Landon exited his tent to find ten men bound and kneeling before him. The Dragon Arem sat twenty yards away, watching with amusement.

He is like a cat with an unsuspecting mouse, Landon mused.

Landon called out to Arem, "Good morning, Captain Arem. I see you have been busy." He walked over to the Dragon and offered a warm smile.

"My daughters and I could not sleep. We decided to visit the Zaharians and invite some of the generals to negotiate." He pointed with his talons at the bound men before continuing, "I will not need to translate for you as I did before. Muraffe requires all of his highest ranking Generals to be fluent in many languages."

Landon laughed with joy, turned, and gestured for the Guards to bring the Generals closer. They did so, instructing the bound men to sit down.

"My name is Ghardenne XVII, and I am the newly anointed King of O'ndar. Your Sultan signed a treaty with my father many years ago. It has come to my attention the Sultan does not intend to live up to this treaty. I do not require you to acknowledge the truth of this. Your presence in these mountains is proof enough." Landon paced back and forth, choosing his words carefully.

"The Emerald Dragon," he pointed to the Dragon, the yellow eyes gleaming with intensity, "the one who has long been the protector of the House of Gheldari, has already verified it for me."

"I stand before each of you, offering a way out of war. I prefer to avoid wasting any lives, but I plan on moving south and intend on having words with Muraffe." Landon paused a few seconds and asked, "Who among you speaks for the soldiers?"

Nine of the Generals looked down at their feet, waiting in silence. The tenth one, a tiny man with a clean-shaven scalp and dark skin, looked up at Landon. He was a lean man, his intense blue eyes held Landon's gaze without fear. He was unflinching and projected authority.

The King looked to the Dragon Arem, who nodded. He ordered the man freed and asked him to come closer to Arem so the three of them might converse quietly.

"I will not surrender, your Majesty," the old General stated matter-of-factly. "I have more than two-hundred and thirty-seven thousand troops following close behind. Another one-hundred thousand will join us in less than a month. You may have the Dragons and the higher ground, but the Zaharians are used to turning the tide of battle when the odds are against us. And unlike the northerners, we do know how to kill dragons."

Landon flinched at the old General's words. *Is this boasting true?*

He did not have time to reflect on the sincerity of the tiny man's proclamation.

Arem's booming voice startled Landon and the General, "General Hurrte, you would be wise to negotiate with the King." Arem leaned in closely, his yellow eyes blazing. If he had thought to intimidate the General, it did not work. Life in the Zaharian military had exposed the General to a multitude of threats to his life. This tiny man had survived them all. The General turned and locked his eyes with the Dragon. Landon, fascinated by the exchange, decided to take another approach.

"We are not asking for your surrender, General. We are asking for an alliance." Landon hoped and was pleased when the General asked him to explain.

"I recently had the pleasure of meeting a former General from the Zaharian Empire. The man came to the north and eventually took up residence in O'ndar. I am sure you know him. Before I mention his name, though, be warned, this Dragon has a personal connection to the General and will not allow any admonitions regarding the General's character. Are we clear?"

An intrigued General Hurrte readily agreed. Landon continued, "I have brought a letter written by the General. He asked, should I make it this far, to give the letter to one of Muraffe's other Generals. I am assuming the two of you know each other." Landon pulled the letter out of his tunic and handed it to General Hurrte. The General opened the letter and read it silently to himself. He returned the letter to Landon and stood quietly for a few minutes, processing the contents. He turned to look at the others, bound with their hands behind their backs but did not offer any words of encouragement. His face remained passive, hiding his thoughts.

While the General weighed out his options, the Dragon Arem asked Landon about the letter's contents, "What did my father write?" The letter had been a surprise, even for the Dragon. The King handed the letter to the Dragon. The yellow, cat-like eyes quickly scanned the letter; a broad smile appearing on his green-feathered face. The large head nodded approvingly.

The two looked back to General Hurrte as they waited patiently for the military veteran to counter the offer. Hurrte turned to Landon, nodded at the Dragon, and then kneeled before the King. He offered pointedly, "We surrender. What is your plan?"

After speaking with Hurrte for another fifteen minutes, Landon sent him back to the others so he might explain, persuade, and, if necessary, order their compliance. When the old man walked away, the King turned to the Emerald Dragon and said, "It is difficult to comprehend, yet it took only three words from General Faron to cause the surrender of more than two hundred thousand soldiers."

The Dragon spoke with conviction and with pride, yet Landon heard the pain in his voice, "I told you, my King. General Faron is well-known, well-respected, and well-feared. He is a man few have been able to emulate." Arem leapt into the sky with those words, flapped his mighty wings, and flew higher into the mountain peaks to mourn his father.

Three weeks later, Landon arrived unannounced at the gates to Istanabad with more than fifty thousand soldiers. The Generals of the other northern country had come days after the surrender of the Zaharian army. Many of them, furious to find a graveled highway constructed for the sole purpose of invading the north, demanded the King execute their prisoners in retaliation. Landon promptly refused.

The northern Generals had already heard about the presence of the Dragons. By the time the coalition arrived at the gates to Istanabad they had grown used to their company. The march south was quick, and the morale of the soldiers was extremely high.

Commanded by General Hurrte, the remaining Zaharian Generals had surrendered on behalf of their soldiers. They met with the Zaharian military and ordered them to hand over their swords. Landon left three thousand of his troops to watch over them. The Dragon Arem was more nervous about the size of this army and left ten of his daughters to assist, ordering them to slaughter the Zaharians if they offered any treachery.

Landon insisted General Hurrte and five other Generals accompany the northern coalition as it made its journey south. The old General had taken a liking to Landon and the King returned the affection with sincerity. He liked General Hurrte. The two spent most of the march, riding side by side and talking. He continually asked about General Faron. Landon held nothing back, telling Hurrte everything, including the fate of Faron's wife and his son.

Finally, without incident, the army arrived under cover of night and camped a mile outside the western side of the famed, white-walled capital. They had skirted the Alahari, using Muraffe's plan to their advantage. Landon, pleased by the speed of their progress, posted sentries, and sat down with his Generals and his guests.

The King explained his plan, "Just before sunrise, one of Arem's daughters will carry General Hurrte over the walls and place him safely inside the courtyard. He will order the Guards at the gates to lay down their arms and will personally see to the opening of the city."

One of Landon's Generals protested, the worry in his voice apparent, "Your majesty, do we dare give up a Knight for a Pawn?" Hurrte listened passively, fascinated by the exchange between the Monarch and his general.

"The concern is fair, General. General Hurrte, though, is a man of courage and honor. He will abide by his words. I have made a promise that other than the Sultan, no harm shall befall any other citizen of Istanabad, as long as they offer no violence. My long-term goal is an alliance. I must use our treaty to unite our lands." He looked to Hurrte and nodded. The old General nodded in return.

When Landon finished speaking, the Dragon Arem asked if he could have words with the King. "Surely, you do not mean to go through with the treaty," he declared grimly. "Muraffe used it to it to mask his intentions to invade and conquer the north."

"It is what I intend to do, Captain Arem. These countries will be allies by treaty and by blood. In less than a week, Lyss will begin her journey southward, though it will be a much easier one than the one taken by my mother all those years ago." The Dragon flinched at the words.

"I do not mean to sound harsh. The highway between our two lands will make trade much safer. I will have my sister escorted by a thousand soldiers."

Arem started to respond but halted as his attention was drawn away by the screeching of three of the black Dragons. They seemed to be flying in random circles overhead. He watched them for a few seconds, and when they settled down, he turned back to Ghardenne. "I will send those three back to help escort your sister. They will leave in two days."

Landon recognized the concern on the Dragon's face and asked, "Was anything wrong?" gesturing with his left hand to the Dragons flying overhead.

The Dragon frowned, "I cannot explain it, My King, but all of us feel a tugging on our souls. It is as if a magnet is pulling at us daily, filling us with the urge to fly eastward, beyond the Cargathian Mountains. The sensation is minute, and I can resist the urge. Yet its power grows stronger daily, and my daughters are too young to ignore its call. I have been using my influence to help them, but these three cannot bear it any longer."

Landon, fascinated by the Dragon Arem's words, declared, "I did not realize Dragons have souls." He looked into the yellow eyes, trying desperately to find Captain Arem.

"This Dragon does, My King. And thus, by extension, my daughters do, too."

The following day, with the sun still dipped below the horizon, one of the ebony-scaled Dragons lifted General Hurrte quietly but swiftly over the white-walled city. Landon watched intently, waiting for a sign from the General. Suddenly, one of his Guards pointed at the gates.

The massive, wrought-iron gates of Istanabad, the largest and most prosperous city in the Zaharian Empire, swung inward seconds after the massive portcullis rose. Three Zaharian soldiers stood silently next to General Hurrte, waiting, their weapons placed on the ground.

Landon and the Dragon Arem had agreed that the Emerald Dragon and four of his daughters would fly closely overhead, monitoring the courtyard for signs of trouble the moment the King entered the city gates. If needed, the Dragons would swoop into the plaza and offer protection from an ambush.

King Landon entered Istanabad unopposed, accompanied by one thousand soldiers, including four hundred archers. Hurrte had explained that in the south, because of the intense heat, most residents of Istanabad did not rise from their beds until well after the noon hour. Other than the Guards at the gates and a few hundred soldiers on foot patrol, the city streets were desolate. Landon left five hundred soldiers and fifty archers guarding the opened gates. If needed, the rest of his troops could infest the city in less than ten minutes.

I am nervous, he admitted. *Muraffe, even caught unaware, is dangerous.* Landon could feel a bead of sweat trickling down his neck.

General Hurrte guided Landon and the remaining soldiers through the quiet city streets. Whenever he met an armed foot patrol, the General ordered them to lower their weapons and go to the gates to await his return. Eventually, the group arrived at the walls of the Sultan's citadel.

The Dragon Arem landed inside the courtyard of Muraffe's castle and opened the gates, Landon entered with one hundred soldiers and twenty archers.

Before entering the Sultan's castle, he turned to look at the Emerald Dragon with sincerity, "The last time I was here, you were showing me violence resulting from thousands of years of tyranny. Let us hope we can avoid the mistakes of the past." General Hurrte looked puzzled by Landon's statement, but he did not ask the King to elaborate.

Landon entered the familiar halls, with their marbled floors, and walked decisively. The Dragon Arem had given him a chance to visit Muraffe's castle, using the power of one of his orbs. Landon walked past the pomegranate tapestries, the ones that had drawn his attention when he visited Istanabad's past. He followed and then led General Hurrte to the throne room. The General ordered the soldiers guarding the doors to lay down their weapons, and they complied without hesitation. They left the castle to join their comrades, waiting with the O'ndarian soldiers posted in the courtyard. The guards looked fearfully at the Emerald Dragon towering over them and the black figures flying overhead in sweeping circles, their ebony bodies sleek, silent, and ominous.

Silently, Landon entered the empty chamber ahead of the others. This time there were no guards with purple shields arranged along the walls. The King positioned ten of his men along the walls, raising his hand to signal them to remain silent. He signaled the archers to stay at the ready.

Landon moved forward alone, stopping at the bottom of the marbled stairs. He looked up at the Diamond Throne, remembering the awe it instilled in him the first time he saw it. The lavender cushions were still on the throne, covered by a deep-purple bearskin throw. The massive gem sparkled in the light cascading through the windows.

It looks the same. Nothing is different. What will I say to the Sultan? Should I be angry? Should I try to appease him and offer an alliance? He knew a partnership with the Sultan was out of the question. One with Istanabad would be acceptable. The Sultan could no longer rule the Zaharian Empire, though.

Landon, startled by a slight movement on the throne, cursed himself for daydreaming. He knew the perils of this place, knowing that losing focus could mean the difference between life and death, especially if caught unaware. Landon had overlooked the camouflaged Cobra until it slithered off the throne and down the steps. It had been lounging on the thick cushions, blended in perfectly. Elzahari raised half of its body off the marble floor. Its yellow eyes fixated on Landon's face, hypnotic and unblinking.

The King heard the familiar sound as the archers notched their arrows, but he raised his right hand and bellowed, "Hold!"

The archers lowered their bows. Landon met the Cobra's gaze unflinchingly. Without taking his eyes away from Elzahari, Landon offered, "It is good that you could join us, Sultan."

At Landon's words, Sultan Muraffe III entered his throne room. He glided, as quietly as a snake, to the throne before stopping to place an arm on the backrest. He noticed the heavily armed, foreign soldiers, with their emerald chain mail, arranged along the walls. Yet, with Elzahari at his side, he felt invincible. The Purple Cobra had always protected him from his enemies since birth. He had faith it would save him again.

"I will have you drawn and quartered, General Hurrte," Muraffe ranted, froth spraying from his lips. He walked forward, glaring at the tiny General standing with the O'ndarian soldiers at the back of the room.

"Do you hear me? I will have you, NOOOOOoooo!" he screamed.

The moment the Sultan had threatened General Hurrte, Landon unsheathed his sword. He lifted it with one hand, swinging it quickly in a sweeping sideways arc. The slashing sword cut through Elzahari's neck, separating the Cobra's head from its body.

Muraffe collapsed to his knees and crawled over to the Cobra, crying out in anguish. He glared at Landon, the young King standing silently with his sword at his side. Elzahari's blood dripped from the blade and onto the marble floor.

His dark eyes blazing with the ferocity of an African Lion, Landon smiled. He waited a few seconds before adding.

"Sultan, General Faron sends his regards!"

Landon spent the next four months finalizing the Treaty with the Zaharian Empire. He ordered all of the Elzahari killed, their magenta-hooded heads separated from their bodies. The Sultan's generals feared the Cobras, but the O'ndarian archers did not. Each snake, hunted down and impaled by the arrows of his highly trained archers, were then cut in half by razor-sharp swords.

The second thing Landon did was ask the generals about Murad, the fourteenth and eldest living son of Muraffe III. The boy appeared to be of good character, even though he had grown up in the house of a maniac. The Generals affirmed his belief that Murad would rule Istanabad compassionately. When Lyssa arrived, Landon participated in the lavish ceremony that wed the two nations. The festivities were magnificent, offering breathtaking fireworks for seven nights. New energy flowed through the streets of Istanabad.

The King had been true to his word. No citizens of Istanabad lost their lives during the invasion.

The moment he had separated Elzahari's head from its body Landon turned to General Hurrte and offered, "General, his crimes against your people outweigh my emotions. I offer you the right to make the final decision. Shall I slay him or leave him for the Zaharian military."

General Hurrte stepped forward, eyes gleaming. He thanked Landon for the offered sword and immediately beheaded Muraffe. He explained after the act, "There are some, even our Generals, who fear him so much that his living presence might cow them. Better to leave the legacy of Muraffe on the floor next to his lifeless body."

Before the wedding, the Generals met with Murad and offered loyalty, but only at the price of change. There were to be no more adoptions of the Generals' sons into the House of the Sultan. The Generals agreed to maintain tradition but would no longer sit aside quietly and allow the Sultan to commit atrocities against the populace. A Monarchy, but one with limits, would rule the Zaharian Empire.

O'ndarian emissaries, escorted by Zaharian soldiers, visited all parts of the Empire on behalf of Sultan Murad I and King Ghardenne XVII of O'ndar. They offered freedom and relief from the taxing demands placed on them by Muraffe. Awed by the presence of the Dragons, they readily accepted the offer.

Six months after embarking on his mission to halt the northern invasion, Landon kissed his sister goodbye and left with his troops. They travelled northward at a leisurely pace, providing Landon with the time to explain the warning he had received from the Four Horsemen and the Eighth Lion.

Before exiting the graveled highway, just before it ended at the northern tip of the Cargathian Mountains, Landon inspected the three forts built to protect travel between north and south. The former Zaharian slaves had been ecstatic with the King's offer of freedom and worked day and night to finish the forts, adding a third one in their enthusiasm. Fort Almaric named for his father, Fort Faron named for General Faron, and Fort Arem named for the Captain who had become a Dragon; all stood sentry to travelers, offering safety and protection. Landon dedicated all three personally.

When they were less than an hour away from leaving the Cargathian Mountains the Emerald Dragon of the Forests asked the King to stop to have a discussion. Twenty-seven ebony Dragons flew high overhead, screeching loudly and enjoying the clouds and the sun.

"King Ghardenne, my apologies, King Landon, I have fulfilled my duties to your mother. Now, I must honor the duties I have to protect my daughters from danger. Dragon Song is calling all dragons to the East, over the mountains. It is becoming challenging to resist. I am sure a Dragon is not the source. I must take my daughters and fly west." The Dragon Arem's green feathers blew gently in the wind. His yellow eyes looked into Landon's, and he bowed deeply.

"I thank you, Landon, who was once a Prince and is now King Ghardenne XVII."

Landon felt a surge of love for the Dragon and the Captain trapped within. He offered, with genuine affection, "Go in peace, Captain Arem. Please know that the Emerald Dragon of the Forests will always have the gratitude of the House of Gheldari."

The Green Dragon spread his wings and leapt, once more, cat-like, into the air. He flapped his mighty wings, flew higher and higher into the western sky and disappeared into the clouds, heading west towards the Ardenian Ocean.

One of the Generals riding nearby asked Landon, "Why do they leave us, your Majesty?"

The King shrugged his shoulders and answered, "I am not quite sure. I think they fear something from the other side of the Cargathian Mountains, yet, they have nothing to fear. No one has crossed over in more than five hundred years. I am not sure anyone ever will."

CHARDON II

ON THE DAY OF HIS RETURN TO O'NDAR, THE OTHER MONARCHS FROM the northern countries, most of whom were his cousins, greeted Ghardenne XVII enthusiastically. Messengers rode ahead to prepare the populace for the return of the young King. He had successfully led a coalition of soldiers, comprised of men from the six northern countries, south to prevent an invasion by the Zaharian Empire.

Each of the other five monarchs left the safety of their castles to pay homage, in person, to the newly crowned King. The accompanying celebration was festive and lasted for more than two weeks. The ceremonies included re-enactments of the invasion of Istanabad and the beheading of Elzahari. During this time, loud cries for the *Ascension* turned into demands from the soldiers and the citizens. On the fourteenth day of celebration, the other monarchs unanimously voted to promote Ghardenne XVII to the status of Chardon II, supreme ruler of all the northern nations. For the second time in the history of the House of Gheldari a King's exploits had risen to greatness, requiring the ultimate acknowledgement.

Thus, in less than a year, Landon had given up his name to become Ghardenne XVII. Shortly afterwards, he traded the name Ghardenne XVII for the title Chardon II. There was a whirlwind of celebrations.

Landon had not forgotten his plan to unite the Known World, but the importance of why it needed done had faded away.

As was tradition, each of the other monarchs, which included *Huan, Butran, Tralfrey, Mantel, and Garhum,* offered their thrones to Chardon II. He accepted the honorary title and the oaths of loyalty. He spoke with each of the other Kings personally to explain that it was time to make the Known World one. Many of them had been life-long friends and enthusiastically agreed with his goal.

Thanking the other Kings for the respect shown to him, he insisted they retain their titles and rule their countries' on his behalf. Each monarch gratefully accepted his offer and swore an oath to serve and protect their domains in his name.

On the evening of the crowing, Landon, who was soon to become Chardon II, enjoyed a light supper with his mother, Queen Lenali, to discuss the upcoming events.

"Must I accompany you, my son?" she asked woefully. The recently freed Queen resisted making the required journey to visit the other five nations of the north. She did not argue with him much after he reminded her that as an unwed King, he would need her eyes to help pick a worthy bride. The opportunity to find a suitable partner for her son changed her mind, and Queen Lenali quickly dropped her opposition.

"Don't feel too bad, mother. I have had two name changes recently and must admit that I will always think of myself as Landon, regardless of the title."

Continuing a tradition that had happened only one time before and hundreds of years prior, Chardon II began touring the northern countries accepting the fealty of the populace. The tour allowed the citizens to celebrate him and enjoy the triumph of the armies of the north. Though accompanied by Queen Lenali, he granted his mother's request to remain away from the spotlight. She was not required to attend any of the ceremonies since her years in captivity wore heavily upon her. She preferred solitude whenever possible. Landon enjoyed spending time with her and worked diligently to build their blossoming affection for one another. The Queen wrote letters to Lyssa twice per week, including descriptions of the northern Castles, detailed illustrations of the lavish costumes required for the various ceremonies, and broad narrations about the pomp and circumstance. She included the recipes for the best of their extravagant meals.

Starting his tour in the south with Garhum, its populace widely celebrated Chardon II and his visit. After spending a month in Garhum his entourage moved due East and visited Butran. Landon remained conscious of the need to stay the same amount of time in each of the five nations. Once Butran offered its congratulations, he moved north to Tralfrey, followed by Mantel, and finally swung west, back toward the Ardenian Ocean and Huan.

A little more than six months later, after crossing the border back into his own country, the citizens of O'ndar welcomed him home with glee. Queen Lenali, thankful to be back home, swore an oath never to leave again. Worn out from the journey's demands, the exhausted Queen asked for and received the opportunity to return to the palace to spend time recuperating.

Once more, Landon gathered his Generals in the same courtyard where they had held counsel with the Dragon Arem. This time, he reiterated his plan to unite the Known World.

"We have the southern alliance in place, and it is holding strong," Landon started. "Trade between the two nations has been bustling for the last six months." Lyssa had already written him numerous times, the last letter announcing that she was with child and hoped for a healthy birth, though it was still three months away. Landon had been happy to read the letter from his sister. He immediately sent gifts to her and the new Sultan, begging for weekly news of her progress.

He continued speaking with the Generals, explaining, "The northern nations are one and are allied with the south. Thus, two parts of the Known World have united, and only one remains."

General Trijan, the highest-ranking General in the O'ndarian army, declared surprise, "The Eastern Steppes. That is a challenge, Sire. It may be impossible." The tribes of the Eastern Steppes, known for their ferocity, were wildly protective of the freedoms that came with living off the land. The grizzled General tugged on his handlebar moustache, the blackened whiskers having turned to grey long ago. He waited for a response from Landon but turned to listen to one of his comrades.

The other General offered, "The Tribes will never unite. They are fiercely territorial and are an uncivilized conglomeration of clans." He looked to the other officers for support, hoping he would not be the only one doubting Landon's assertions.

Landon allowed each of his officers to speak in the council. He asked questions, affirmed some of their fears, and then countered, "My Generals, uniting the wild clans is only possible if we try something never before attempted. I will travel to the Eastern Steppes so that I might challenge the Chieftain of each clan to armed, one-on-one combat."

Shocked by his words, many of his Generals jumped to their feet in protest. "You must not, Your Majesty," one of them yelled. General Trijan quieted them with a look, his grizzled features stern. He waited patiently for Landon to explain further.

"The Chieftains of the Eastern Steppes follow one code, the strongest warrior rules the tribe. If we wish to unite the North with the South and include the East, it is the only way. I will leave in the morning, just before sunrise. I would like three soldiers to accompany me to the Eastern Steppes. It is the only way. I will have witnesses to all that happens. If successful, the Eastern Steppes will unite with the rest of the lands, and the Known World will be one."

The King's plan excited the O'ndarian military. Doubt turned to hope when they helped to overthrow the Sultan without losing a single soldier. Hope, if cradled and nourished correctly, turns to Faith. Once Faith is established, anything is possible. Landon was proposing something many in the War Council knew to be an impossible task.

The Generals had always dreaded launching a full-scale invasion of the Eastern Steppes. The army would need to battle the semi-wild Frontier people first. If they made it through, they would then encounter the feral tribes of the Eastern Steppes. While the tribes were fiercely independent of one another, they had united before to repel invasions by armies of the north. They had even successfully repelled the invading armies of the Zaharian Empire.

Chardon II, the hero of the modern age, was proposing something never before attempted. Quietness overcame those attending the council. Many of them had personally trained Landon in the art of warfare, including how to handle a sword. Some of them acknowledged there was no more exemplary warrior with a sword in all of the northern nations.

After a few minutes, General Trijan stood, looked to his fellow officers, and kneeled. "My Lord," he began. He looked to the others and then back to Landon. "You are rightful Majesty to us all. I offer my eldest son to accompany you on your journey. He is a Captain in our Cavalry. He is young and full of vigor. Please allow him to be one of the three who will accompany you on your pilgrimage." When Trijan, a well-respected General, accepted Landon's proposal, two of the other Generals followed suit. They offered to send their sons with the King on his quest.

Thus, after spending a little more than three weeks in O'ndar, on an early summer morning Landon, accompanied by the sons of three of his Generals, mounted his horse and galloped briskly toward the Eastern Steppes. Earning the respect of his comrades in battle had enabled General Trijan's son, Balthason, to rise to the rank of Captain in the Cavalry. Broad-shouldered, with thick blonde hair flowing down to his shoulders, Balthason was excited about riding into the Eastern Steppes to challenge the Chieftains to combat. He proudly accepted his father's offer to accompany the King.

The second son, Melkior, slim of waist and lean, walked with cat-like grace. His always-pleasant demeanor boasted of confidence in his abilities. His father had told him of Landon's plan late last night. Excited to ride into the open Steppes on a quest, Melkior spent the night sleepless, imagining the exploits to come.

The third son, Gezpar was swarthy, his complexion much like Landon. Yet, his hair had flecks of red intermingled with the black. His mother had been the daughter of one of the semi-wild frontier families. His parents met, by happenstance, when the O'ndarian army had been returning from its effort to drive some raiding clans back into the grasslands.

Landon sized up his comrades the moment their fathers introduced them. The three young men, each older than him, had used their wisdom to lead O'ndarian soldiers successfully. He could not have asked for better companions.

It would be far easier for four soldiers, instead of an army on horseback, to circumvent the semi-wild peoples populating the Frontier. Landon, fascinated that they had moved through the wooded Frontier unchallenged, admitted amazement when the four exited the woodlands unscathed. The companions halted at the edge of the forests, scanning the horizon. Without a glance backwards, they entered a vast ocean of prairie grass that extended in front of them as far as the sky overhead.

Large herds of elk and deer routinely migrated around the Steppes, followed by the nomadic tribesmen and the smaller clans. It did not take long for one hundred warriors from one of the tribes to ride out and challenge the presence of the four soldiers.

Typically, warriors killed invaders quickly, without an afterthought. These warriors paused, impressed by the audacity of the four soldiers who did not attempt to hide their presence from the warriors, as most others would have done. Approached by the warriors of the Ngari clan, including the Chieftain, Landon lifted an amulet off his neck and held it out before him.

"Greetings, horsemen. I show you an amulet given to me personally by Adeban, Rider of the Red-Horse." Many of the warriors recognized the snarling wolves locked in combat. Their soft voices carried across the open grass. Some of these warriors had great grandfathers who witnessed first-hand the prowess of the red-skinned warrior. Though many assumed his exploits to be mere legend, his tales, sung around the campfires, frequently scared the younger ones into compliance. The internal debate among the warriors bought Landon enough time to state his purpose and issue his first challenge.

He looked directly at the Chieftain but spoke loudly for all to hear. "I have earned the allegiance of Adeban, the blood-stained warrior and rider of the Red Horse. Thus, I have earned the right to challenge you to armed combat to be the Chief of the Ngari tribe." He pointed directly at the chieftain, dismounted his horse, and quickly removed his green cape.

"It has been a century since the blood-red warrior feverishly ran across these fields, slaying those who stood before him. How is it that you, a King from the northern nations and an outsider, earned his allegiance?" the Chieftain demanded, glowering.

Landon expected this challenge. He answered quickly, with conviction. "Two nights ago, the rider of the Red-Horse visited me from across the wastelands as I sat around the campfire with my companions." He gestured to the others and continued, "Adeban looked out from the flames and demanded I go forth and offer my challenge. As proof, he handed me his amulet from within the fire. Though the flames burned with intensity, my skin was undamaged." Once again, Landon held up the amulet for them to see.

Landon's memory of Adeban had grown foggy, but he knew the tribesmen of the Eastern Steppes would accept an explanation if it included something of the supernatural. These tribes honored their gods and spirits. There was a deep fear of the unknown, even in the wildness of these great warriors.

The Chief was a large man, muscled, and powerful. He laughed at the challenge given by the young soldier standing before him. When his warriors nodded at Landon's explanation, he knew he would have to act to save face.

When they first rode out to challenge the four riders, he chose not to have his men slay the four. Silently, he cursed himself for the mistake but knew there was no turning back. Many of the accompanying warriors had already accepted the challenge on his behalf. To refuse would usurp tradition. It would damage his ability to lead the warriors. His ability to be Chief of the Ngari tribe swung in the balance.

Cursing the young man before him, he loudly accepted the challenge. He dismounted, lifted his sword, and charged without waiting. Landon met the on-rush of the man, and the two swords clashed loudly against each other. The clanging steel reverberated across the open plains. The Chieftain, almost twice the size of the young King, realized that he was outmatched. He had the size and the strength, but the King was young and full of endurance. The King, well versed in the art of the sword, had destiny on his side.

The battle was brief. Within a few minutes, Landon's swordplay bested the Chieftain, knocking the sword from the Chief's vice-like fists. Knowing he was doomed, the man squatted down to await his fate, kneeling before Landon to wait in silence for the death blow.

"Rise, Chief. I would have your name," Landon ordered.

The Chieftain looked confused but obeyed Landon's command. He responded, "I was named Cleopte, Chief of the Ngari tribe. I am now nameless and await the final judgement. My life is yours to take, as Chief."

Landon nodded approval and added, "Rise Cleopte, Chief of the Ngari tribe. I return your name to you, though it is mine to keep. I did not challenge you to take your life. When visited by Adeban, from the other side of the flames, I was tasked to unite the clans." Landon lowered his sword to his side.

"I am Chardon II, the King of the Northern nations. I have united all the nations, both in the north and south, under one banner. I offer an alliance with all the clans of the Steppes. In exchange for your allegiance, to my cause, I would require you to rule the Ngari in my name. Thus, as demanded by the Rider of the Red horse, uniting our world." Landon looked to the stunned warriors sitting on their horses and offered more.

"I will accept all challenges, but I will not spare any more lives. From this day forth, any warrior from the Ngari who challenges me and falls before my sword, his head shall be forfeit."

Cleopte, the Chieftain of the Ngari tribe, accepted the offer, knelt before Landon, and swore an oath of loyalty.

Over the next three years, Landon and his companions Balthason, Melkior, and Gezpar visited each of the major tribes of the Eastern Steppes. He challenged the leaders of the *Ngali, the Ngeti, the Ngepi, the Ngati, and the Ngema* tribes to armed combat. Each Chieftain fell, defeated by his sword. Landon continued his effort to unite the Known World under one banner. His body became battle-scarred and hardened from the years of living on the Steppes. His companions tended his numerous wounds, offering friendship and encouragement for his efforts. They accompanied him across the grasslands of the Eastern Steppes, never leaving his side. Letters, sent back to O'ndar detailing Landon's exploits, kept Queen Lenali and the populace informed about events as they unfolded.

Once he had conquered the Chieftains of the powerful tribes, Landon set his sights on the minor clans. In less than three years, the *Nfali, the Mgata, the Mgendi,* and many others swore their allegiance to Chardon II, the Greatest King in the history of O'ndar and now the Emperor of the Known World.

Three years after heading out to the Eastern Steppes with his three companions, Landon and his three wise men rode back into O'ndar received as heroes. News of his exploits had swept across the open frontier, spreading quickly through the villages in the northern nations. Cartographers, tasked with mapping the Known World, added the Eastern Steppes to the lands falling within the dominion of Chardon II, officially uniting The Known World.

On the day of his return, Landon accepted the offer of marriage to the Princess Cecilia of Garhum. His mother, Queen Lenali had arranged it dutifully, and he was excited to meet his soon to be wife. A year later, in a magnificent ceremony attended by the monarchs of the other five nations of the north, representatives of the Zaharian Empire, and Chieftains from ten clans of the Eastern Steppes, Chardon II wed Princess Cecilia. The two monarchs settled in to rule their empire.

ESCHATON

LANDON PLACED THE LETTER FROM HIS ELDEST DAUGHTER ON THE nightstand next to his bed. Night had come on quickly this evening. He and the Queen had spent a few hours lying in bed, discussing the happenings of the day. Tiring, she kissed him and bade him good night. Within a few minutes, with the Queen fast asleep beside him, he retrieved the letter from a pile on his desk. Silently, he finally read the letter delivered to him early this morning, beaming with pride and excitement. His daughter Marinda was twenty-nine years old and had recently given birth to her fourth daughter. For more than thirteen years, her marriage helped cement an alliance with Huan, one of the neighboring countries in the north.

Landon and his wife, Queen Cecilia, a Princess of Garhum, had given birth to three daughters. Each of them had married Kings of the other Northern countries.

Getting out of bed, Landon walked over to the large oak table holding a large map of the Known World. The evening chill was kept at bay by large draperies pulled across the windows. Flames roared in the large, stone fireplace. Landon listened to the quietness of the castle, turned to put his hands close to the fire, and smiled.

I am pleased, he thought.

The Known World remained united. The populace lived in peace for the last thirty-five years. Turning away from the fire, the King, with his long, grey hair held in place by an emerald-colored leather headband, placed both hands on the map and leaned in slightly. In the last thirty-five years, the Tribesmen of the Eastern Steppes had honored the alliance forged years ago by his blade. The southern nations, including the Zaharian Empire and beyond, continued to maintain the coalition. With peace holding, all of the countries on the Known World prospered with the booming trade.

He turned quietly to look at the portraits of his mother and sister mounted above the fireplace. *I do miss you both,* the King brooded, his heart constricting with grief. Queen Lenali had passed away in her sleep, peacefully, a little more than twenty-five years ago. Landon had grieved silently at her passing, wishing he could have spent more time getting to know her.

His sister Lyssa had died during childbirth eighteen years ago. She had become beloved by the Zaharian Empire, and one of her sons currently sat on the throne, married to a Princess from Mantel. Landon looked at the paintings of both women with pangs of sadness in his heart. The two women, who had meant the most to him in his youth, were gone. Without them, he would not have been able to gather the nations of the Known World beneath one banner.

He sighed. *I am tired and need to sleep,* the aging monarch thought. He returned to the bed, blew out the lamps, climbed in, and covered himself with thickly woven quilts. He listened for a few minutes to the Queen's soft breathing, and eventually fell asleep.

With the heat of the sun beating down on his face, Landon woke up alone, lying atop a wind-swept dune. He sat up confused, looking around at the nothingness before him. The sun bore down upon the desert with an intensity he had never before felt. The oppressive heat made it difficult to breathe. He looked at the miles of dunes disappearing into the horizon.

Is this the Alahari? The hot sand burning his hands forced him to stand. Landon could see waves of heat rising above the dunes. His lips felt parched. His throat ached with thirst.

Landon shielded his eyes from the sun, its brightness blinding him briefly. He lowered his eyes to the ground, shutting them tightly, and waited for his vision to return.

Where am I? The King looked down at his hands, shocked. They were not the wrinkled hands of an older man. He could not find any of the familiar liver spots. The grey hairs covering his forearm had changed back to the black hairs from many years ago. They were the hands and arms of a young man. He felt his face. It was clean-shaven. The beard he had sported for the last twenty years had disappeared.

A light breeze blew gently across the open desert, kicking up sand in its wake. The tiny, silica pebbles swirled around Landon's feet like a snake. The breeze did not dispel the heat. It only made it more difficult to breathe.

"Eschaton!" The word carried across the dunes in a whisper.

"Hello. Who is there?" Landon asked, confused by the words. His heart raced; fear of the unknown crept into his mind. The King turned, looking around in every direction, seeking the source of the phrase. He was alone.

Landon lifted his right hand and pointed. "North?" He asked aloud, though he was sure he knew directions even out on the open desert. "That makes you south, west and," He paused. The moment he turned to the east, a bolt of lightning crackled in the sunny sky, miles away. The flash of light streaked across the sky in a crisscross pattern, quickly followed by another. Landon looked at the dunes. They flowed outward, into the horizon like the waves on the ocean. He gasped to see a set of muddy footprints tracking ahead of him, across the dunes, heading in the direction of the lightning bolts.

Landon started walking, following the muddy prints, but stopped when a heavy drop of rain struck him harshly in the forehead. It stung. At first, he thought that a rock had struck him, thrown by some unseen hand. The second drop and then the third hit him squarely in his face. Both of them stung, harshly. He lowered his head, determined to continue walking in the same direction as the muddy footprints. The power of the stinging rain increased. A fierce wind picked up, blowing heavily against his body. He kept walking, even though it felt like nature was determined to prevent his progress. Landon lowered his head, trying to avoid the pelting raindrops on his face. He kept his eyes open slightly, vowing to follow the tracks to their destination.

Rain, in the desert! He had never known desert life, though he was sure there was very little rain year-round. The force of the wind increased, blowing against him and pushing him back three steps before he could right himself. He struggled to move forward but did so inch by inch. Slowly, he trudged along, leaning into the wind, using the strength of his legs to keep moving forward.

I must not allow it to blow me to the bottom of the dunes. Landon remembered Captain Arem's advice about desert travel, given to his mother many years ago. *The Singing Dunes.*

Shielding his eyes with his right hand, the King wiped the rain away from his brows. He was startled to find his fingers tinged with red; the water drops had turned to blood.

Landon turned, looking behind him with astonishment. The dunes had turned crimson, pelted by the deluge of red droplets. The power of the rain and the wind increased once again. Red beads hammered the desert, melting the tops of the dunes beneath the torrent. Soon, nothing remained but a bloody Plain. It flooded quickly, turning from a pond, to a lake, and then to a sea. Landon shuddered at the sight.

Turning back into the wind, Landon again saw the crackling of lightning in the eastern sky. Though harder to make out in the torrential rain, Landon could see the outline of the muddy footprints. Once again, he slowly walked forward, making sure to place his feet squarely in the muddy footprints.

"*Eschaton!*" The words, carried on the wind, were little more than a whisper. Landon cursed silently but continued on his path.

The King walked for more than an hour in the relentless storm. He barely noticed the dunes ahead of him, though each time he passed one, it quickly melted away, replaced by the scarlet sea. Slowly, the dunes ahead thinned, and the ground flattened. The power of the rain and the wind lightened considerably. Landon had come to the end of the desert.

Landon looked up at the last crimson-colored dune, its silhouette standing tall against the backdrop of an ocean of blood. It had not melted beneath the torrent. An older woman sat cross-legged at the apex. Ignoring Landon, her eyes remained fixated on the lightning bolts in the eastern sky. Her drenched clothing had turned as red as the surrounding dune and the scarlet sea.

Landon yelled with glee. It was his sister, Lyssa. Scrambling up the side of the dune, he knelt in front of her, happy that she was with him. He leaned in to hug her. Tears streamed down his cheeks. He no longer cared about the wind. He ignored the pounding rain. He had missed her, immensely. His heart surged, feeling as if it could burst with excitement while at the same time seeming to be drowning with pain.

The old woman smiled, the twinkling in her eyes reminding him of the good times when they were kids. Her skin had darkened with her life in the south. Her hair had greyed along with her age. Yet, it was Lyssa, to be sure. She said gently, never taking her eyes away from the east, "The End of Days is almost upon us. The fate of humankind hangs in the balance."

Grimly, Landon stood and turned his eyes away from her. This woman was not his sister. She looked like Lyssa, she sounded like Lyssa, but something was missing. *Maybe her soul?*

He looked into the lifeless eyes. They returned his hopeful regard with a vacant stare.

Even so, she is here to remind me of something I have forgotten. Something has escaped my attention, and now, humankind faces a calamity from which it may not survive, Landon thought. It bothered him that he could not remember something that he had sworn to do.

Landon walked in silence back to the bottom of the dune. Without looking back, he stepped onto the muddied footprints and continued on his journey.

The moment he stepped away from the last of the dunes, the land changed instantly to a snow-covered, pristine forest. Massive, Red-barked trees, the bark flecked with white, stood sentinel, majestic, and powerful.

Landon recognized the Sleeping Hills Forest, the trees growing for miles in every direction. He had been through the forest enough in his lifetime to be able to identify the trees and the footpaths running through them. This forest, though, were desolate and frozen. Icicles dangled from the trees. The frozen ground, covered with a blanket of snow, seemed lifeless. He could still see the footprints, though they had changed from mud and sand to snow and ice.

Flashes of lightning bolts brightened the cloudy sky, far ahead.

I have been walking for hours, Landon thought, weary from the journey.

He considered stopping to rest, but each time he did, the words, **"*Eschaton!*"** echoed gently through the air. The words frightened him, growing louder each time they were spoken. Landon looked around once more, looking to find the source but could see no one.

The cold did not bother Landon. He had grown up in the north, his body accustomed to the ground covered with snow and the trees covered with ice. Soon though, large snowflakes began to fall from the cloudy sky. Landon once again lowered his eyes, trying to shield them from the flakes as they struck him brutally on the face. As soon as the snow struck his face, it melted and slithered down into his eyes. He used his hands to wipe away the moisture, startled to find his fingers tinged with red. He turned away from the wind and looked into the forests behind him. The snow-covered ground had shifted from white to scarlet. Cherry-red icicles hung from the trees, dripping ruby droplets onto the land.

Landon worried about what lay ahead and his apprehension turned to fear. He slowed his pace, wanting to delay the inevitable. At the edge of the forest, Landon found an elderly man sitting alone, resting on a fallen tree trunk. It was his father.

Immediately, Landon stepped off the footpath. He ran to the King, kneeling in front of his father. His father shivered with cold as blood-red snowflakes landed on his shoulders. Removing his cape, Landon draped it across his father's wet shoulders. He leaned in and hugged the old man. Landon's tears streaked down his cheeks. He had never been able to say goodbye. The sadness in his heart reminded him how much he missed the man. His father was and always would be the greatest King.

His father returned the hug affably. He smiled and said gently, "Remember, do not fear the storm. Fear what comes after."

Landon smiled in return and stood. When he was a child and frightened of storms, his father would sit with him, tell him stories, and talk to him calmly. The King always said to Landon, "Do not fear the storm. Fear what comes after." He would fall asleep next to his father, feeling protected and safe.

"I thank you, father, for all your words. I also thank you for your love, given unconditionally and returned whole-heartedly." Landon turned away from his father, stepping back onto the snow-packed pathway. He turned and walked out of the Sleeping Hills Forest, the trees thinning until they disappeared. They were replaced by tall prairie grass. He had arrived at the Eastern Steppes.

"*Eschaton!*" The words floated once more across the air, whispered into the winds, but growing in strength as they echoed to Landon.

The sky had begun to darken. The bluish sun blazed less brightly overhead. Looking at the evening sky gave Landon a sense of *Deja Vu*.

"I have been in a village with a sky similar to this," he said aloud. *But where was it?* He could not remember.

A pathway of trampled grass ran for miles in the distance ahead, continuing into the mountains that loomed on the horizon. Encouraged by the words of his father, Landon picked up his pace. His father's words buoyed him. He was no longer afraid. Chosen for something years ago, he had forgotten an original purpose. The demands of ruling a united land had clouded his memory, but now he remembered. Instead of dreading the storm ahead, Landon hoped to prevent what came after.

I must have Faith!

Less than an hour into his walk, the tall, wind-swept grass to either side of him caught fire. The surrounding flames shot high into the sky. The intensity of the heat forced Landon to lower his eyes. Beads of sweat drenched his forehead. Landon shuddered as he used his hands to wipe away the vermillion tinged moisture. Landon turned back to look at the grasslands behind him. Entire fields of grass burned brightly, the red flames flickering wickedly, the towering flames licking the sky with wild abandon. Landon turned away and continued on his path.

The moment the burning grass faded away behind him, Landon spotted three men standing on the edge of the field less than a hundred yards ahead. He refused to look behind him at the ravaging flames.

A cheer of excitement burst from him the moment he recognized the three. Stepping forward, he offered, "You three are well-met." The King smiled widely, shaking each of their hands. Standing before him were his three companions, the ones who had spent three years with him on the Eastern Steppes.

"Majesty," Balthason offered while grinning with pride. The man knelt and kissed Landon's hand. Standing, the soldier unsheathed his sword and handed it hilt first to the King. "A blade for your protection." Smiling, Balthason turned and walked into the fire consumed by the burning grass.

Landon turned to look at the second man.

"Majesty," Melkior offered, a broad smile settling on his face. The man knelt and kissed Landon's hand. Standing, the soldier handed Landon his shield. "A shield for your defense." Adorned with the face of Meeha, the original defender of the House of Gheldari, it helped calm Landon. Smiling, Melkior turned and walked into the fire, consumed by the burning grass.

Landon turned to look at the third man.

"Majesty," Gezpar offered, his grinning teeth glistening like fangs in the flames. Landon stretched out his hand. The man knelt and kissed it. Standing, the soldier removed the emerald-colored chain mail covering his torso. "Armor to guard you." The ringlets sparkled in the waning light. Smiling, Gezpar waited until Landon looked once again into his eyes.

"The Apocalypse is coming, My Lord," Gezpar warned. His smile disappeared, his eyes hardened, and he turned and walked into the flames, quickly consumed by the burning grass.

Landon's next step took him away from the burning grasslands and upward into the foothills of the Cargathian Mountains. With each step, the snow-covered peaks loomed closer. His legs ached, the weight of the chain mail, the sword, and the shield slowing him down. He refused to put them down. He refused to rest.

The sun disappeared behind the peaks the moment the flames consuming the grasslands ceased to burn. The light dissipated quickly, replaced by eerie darkness. The setting sun, dipping behind the mountains, confused Landon. O'ndar was on the Western side of the Cargathian Mountains.

I am no longer on the Western side.

Landon swallowed convulsively as a shiver ran up his spine. *I am in the Lands of the Khans.*

The starless sky and a darkened moon, its outline barely noticeable above, worried Landon. He looked back over his shoulder but could see nothing behind except blackness. He was alone.

Turning back to the snow-covered peaks, the King noticed a glowing light up ahead. It pulsated brightly, blanketing the ground in an eerie glow of white and blue.

Landon followed the path and, within a few minutes, stepped out onto an open plateau. Thousands of Dragon orbs piled upon one another lay scattered on the edges of the clearing. The orblight ebbed and flowed like waves on open water.

A giant throne, made of human skulls, dominated the middle of the clearing. Stacked one on top of the other, the eyeless sockets infected Landon with shame. The two armrests were different, each adorned with the skull of a Dragon, the bones of one armrest scarlet in color and the bones of the other emerald.

Upon the throne sat a dark giant, his massive frame motionless. Though his features were manlike, he was not a man. His dark eyes, hidden beneath a thick, ebony pelt covering his head, bore into Landon with hatred. The head of a black-maned lion, its lifeless blue eyes rested atop the giant's head. The mighty fangs encircled the top of the black eyes and ended just below his muscular chin. These fangs, though once powerful, were devoid of life. They no longer posed a danger. The lion's massive jaws, forcefully pried open wide enough to accommodate the shadowy face of the sinister-looking giant, sent a shiver through Landon.

Landon surveyed the giant's face; his robust and wolf-like nose sat above grim, chiseled features. His face wore deep scars from an untold number of battles. The giant lifted his left hand and pointed in Landon's direction.

A wolfish grin spread across his features when the dark giant realized Landon had recognized the lion. The large warrior sat with pride upon the throne of skulls. A broadsword lay across his muscled legs, its blackened blade as long as Landon was tall.

He is at least seven feet tall, Landon thought, shuddering.

"I am here to trample on your Faith, and I will crush its bones beneath my feet. Your faith has led you blindly down the darkened alley without an end," a deep voice intoned.

Landon trembled at the words. He recognized the group of men standing motionless behind the giant and to his left. The Four Horsemen stood as still as statues, their eyes soulless.

Adeban, Abadi, Arksaerop, and the Nameless Rider. Landon looked into their faces, checking for recognition. Only the Nameless Rider offered a smile; his words etched into Landon's memory from their last encounter.

To the giant's right, hovering just behind the throne, stood another dark figure. Partially hidden in a cloud of mist and shrouded in a purple robe, the figure's eyes bore into Landon with hatred and contempt. Clawed hands leaned on an oaken staff, the being's long nails sharpened into talons. The slender fingers were pasty and pale. Yellow, snake-like eyes peered out from beneath the cowl, reminding Landon of the Cobra Elzahari.

Jochi, Landon thought. *Is it possible?* The conversation with the White Dragon, many years ago, flooded back into him.

The wizard whispered to the giant, who responded by smiling wickedly. He waved a hand, silencing the wizard. For a brief moment, Landon saw a flicker of rage across the features of the wizard.

Jochi hates his station, yet he bides his time, waiting for his moment. He is a danger to the warrior because, secretly, he does not wish to follow. He wishes to rule. Landon kept his thoughts to himself.

The giant lifted his massive hand. He extended his forefinger, the nail a sharpened claw, and pointed to Landon. He proclaimed loudly, his voice echoing through the mountains.

"The Amarok are finally united and no longer hunt alone. The age of humans is at an end. We will devour the human world, feeding our children for eternity. We will crush beneath our feet all who oppose us."

Lightning flashed across the sky. The orb light went dark. Another bolt of lightning flashed across the heavens. The skull throne and the giant had disappeared. Landon was alone, surrounded by complete darkness.

The lightning flashed once again, the sky above the mountain peaks illuminated with the face of an albino Dragon, its ice-blue eyes intense.

The mighty voice, one Landon had heard many years before, rang out into the surrounding mountains.

"Eschaton is upon us! It has begun."

THICK AS THIEVES

EARLY THE FOLLOWING MORNING, JUST BEFORE THE SUN BEGAN ITS ascent into the vast ocean of blue above, Landon sent messengers to find his three companions, Balthason, Melkior, and Gezpar. While he waited, the King broke his fast with a hearty plate of boiled eggs and pan-fried potatoes seasoned with pepper and lightly salted. He washed them down with a flask of the best wine in the castle. Waiting for his friends, he talked with his Queen about his intentions.

Sitting on his jade-colored throne, the King waited patiently for his three comrades though he was anxious to begin. When they arrived and had gone through the niceties required when greeting a King, he went straight to the point. "My friends, I require the three of you once more."

All three responded without hesitation, "We are yours to command, our King and dearest friend."

Landon spent the next few hours recounting his dream and the hidden memories it had awakened. "The end of the Known World may already be upon us. If it is not too late, I will have a hand to play in this saga."

Moments later, the Queen joined the three men bringing with her ten of his Generals. All listened intently. None doubted his words or their veracity since they had learned from experience to trust his instincts.

"I must admit I find it amazing that the Titan chose to awaken my memories by uttering the same three words written by General Faron to General Hurrte many years ago," Landon offered.

"It has begun," Gezpar whispered. His words, foreboding, hushed everyone in the room, all of them awed by the magnitude of the moment.

Later that evening, just before nightfall, a fifty-three-year-old Landon went into the royal vault alone. He passed by the crown, ignored the stacks of gold coins, and walked by the piles of rubies and sapphires without a second glance. The King looked over his shoulder a few times, ensuring that no one had followed him. Convinced he was alone, Landon removed a copper key from beneath his shirt. Tied with leather strings beside an amulet with two fighting wolves, it remained around his neck for more than thirty-five years, guarded. He used the key to open the iron lock that held thick, crisscrossed chains around a leather-covered chest. The King lifted the heavy lid and removed its contents, a glass jar containing a small amount of greenish liquid. He left the royal vault, locked it again, and went to see the Queen one last time.

Bidding Queen Cecilia goodbye, "Hopefully, not forever, My Love," he whispered. The King leaned down and kissed her passionately.

"Go, My Lord, knowing that you have the faith of a loving and dutiful wife," she responded. "The fate of the Known World rests upon your shoulders. It is a burden few others could stand to bear."

Landon met his friends in the courtyard, their horses already saddled.

"Does this make us the Four Horsemen?" Melkior asked cheerfully. They mounted and rode, at a gallop, out of the castle.

As nightfall settled in across O'ndar the four companions rode north by northeast towards the Cargathian Mountains. His three friends rode enthusiastically, the memories of their days living on the Eastern Steppes freshly awakened. They spoke joyfully about Landon's exploits. They talked gleefully of his challenges to all of the Chieftains on the Eastern Steppes.

He thanked them profusely, once again, for tending his wounds and for never abandoning him. They had stuck with him for the months it took to recover between each battle. Their support had never wavered, and because of their companionship, he had never gone to despair.

After two weeks of hard riding, with little rest on the open grasslands, they arrived at the foothills of the Cargathian Mountains. The King turned to his brothers-in-arms and halted them with an upraised hand.

He dismounted and spoke with emotion. "My friends, this is where we must part ways. I am required to make the remainder of the journey alone." He waited for the three to dismount before shaking their hands.

Balthason spoke; his voice layered with sadness, "Majesty," The man clasped Landon along the right forearm and placed his left hand gently upon the shoulder of the King. He knelt and kissed Landon's outstretched hand. Standing, the soldier unsheathed his sword and handed it, hilt first, to the King. "A blade for your protection," he offered with pride. Landon traded swords with the smiling Balthason. He embraced his comrade once more and thanked him for the offer of his sword. Balthason turned, jumped into the saddle of his horse, and waited in silence.

Landon turned to look at the second man.

"My Lord," Melkior offered the words with difficulty. The man knelt before Landon and kissed the King's hand. Standing, the soldier handed Landon the shield he had carried for almost a lifetime. "I offer a shield for your defense." Adorned with the face of Meeha, the original defender of the House of Gheldari, the shield reassured Landon of his purpose. A smiling Melkior received and returned the embrace. He turned, leapt into his saddle, and waited patiently.

Landon turned to look at the third man.

"My King," Gezpar beamed. The man knelt before Landon and kissed the King's hand. Standing, the soldier removed the emerald-colored chain mail covering his torso. He had spoken fondly of it for more than twenty years. Its interlocking rivulets had saved his life in battle more than a dozen times. "I offer you this to guard your body against the sharpest blade." The ringlets glistened in the waning light. Smiling, he held the shield while the King donned the chain mail. Then, he embraced Landon tightly. He waited until the King had looked once again into his eyes.

"I have thought deeply about your life, My Lord. Maybe you are the Apocalypse for what lies on the other side of the mountains," offered

Gezpar. His smile never left his face, even when he effortlessly leapt into the saddle.

Without another word, the three companions turned the four horses and rode away across the open fields of prairie grass. Landon watched, grateful to have had them for friends, until they disappeared from his sight.

And now it truly has begun.

This time, Mfiri was much easier to find. At the end of his second day, an hour before the sun dipped behind the looming mountains, Landon stood in front of the bridge. He looked once more at the Guardian and the wall of fog leading into the village. The waning light sent a shudder up his spine. Mfiri had left a stamp on his soul, and though he returned of his own accord, its painful memories flooded his nerves.

Overjoyed, Gamayun immediately stood up to her full height, towering over Landon. The King chose to remain on the ground, just outside the Bridge.

"My Lover," she exclaimed passionately. "You have returned to me at last. In all these years, I never lost hope. I always knew you would find your way back into my wings." The creature stretched out her wings in both directions, with the tips brushing against the sides of the Bridge. "Come onto the Bridge and embrace me. I have dreamt of our first kiss, always hoping it would not be our last. I am overjoyed."

"Lovers do not keep secrets from one another, Gamayun," Landon replied, the gravity in his voice stopping her from approaching. He watched her closely, remembering the long, razor-sharp talons hidden beneath her wings. "And you kept many from me."

"I kept no secrets, Prince Landon. Aha. You are no longer a Prince, are you," she began. "Yet, you come to me more than a King." Her eyes scanned him with ferocity. "Are you an Emperor? You have returned to me as the leader of the Known World. I knew you were a Chosen One."

He bristled at her words, angry once again to be standing in her presence. "You are correct; I am now an Emperor. Prince Landon will not beg for your permission to enter Mfiri. I stand in front of your bridge as Chardon II, the Emperor of the Known World. I order you to give me safe passage into Mfiri." He paused before adding, "It's the least you may do to earn my forgiveness for your deceit."

Gamayun smiled widely, her canines on full display. She jeered, "I only played a small part in your saga, though. Yet, your ancestors will remember it through the ages. I hope you remember I was guided only by a concern for your well-being and out of a deep love I hold for you."

The rosy cheekbones remained as soft as ever. Gamayun's womanly face exuded beauty. The eyes continued to be mesmerizing. Voluptuous lips pouted for a few seconds, and then Gamayun blew a soft kiss to Landon. When he was younger, the magic of the moment would have caused him to swoon. He would have been captivated with her beauty and her willowy voice, which even now was hard to resist. Now, though, he was an older and much wiser man. He had hardened during the years on the battlefield. Protected by the love he held for another, Landon ignored her wicked flirtations. He remained passive to her wiles, unmoved by her attempts.

Ignoring her words, Landon added, "I seek passage into Mfiri, Gamayun. I am here to keep a vow made almost a lifetime ago."

The bird-like body hopped loudly on one foot and then the other. The wicked dance would have been amusing if Landon did not know that it meant she was at her most dangerous. Her wings remained outstretched, blocking access to the Bridge, hatred and fury in her eyes. Landon could see the gentle, pulsating light tucked beneath a ball of feathers inside one of her wings.

Gamayun's eyes flared. Her lips parted to show her pointy fangs. "You dare! You know the rules. There is always a price to enter Mfiri, and there will always be a price to leave."

Landon waited patiently until the creature stopped her ranting. Amused, he laughed heartily and responded, "I well remember your rules, creature. Now though, it is time I told you my rules." He reached into his tunic, removed the glass container, and held it in front of him for her to see. The greenish liquid swirled inside, splashing up, and running down the sides. Laughing diabolically, he raised the container up above his head, bending his arm for the throw.

"What is that?" Gamayun screeched fearfully. She recoiled away from the bridge opening, taking a giant step backwards. She had immediately recognized the contents inside the glass container.

"I believe you know what is in this container, Gamayun. We will have to agree that now is not the time to play games. Do you know what is in this container?" Landon taunted. He did not wait for her to respond.

"I make you an offer, one which I do not believe you will be able to refuse," the King yelled loudly. His booming voice resonated across the Bridge. Gamayun's fear was evident. She refused to make eye contact with Landon, apprehension gripping her frame.

"The two of you have been as thick as thieves, Guardian," Landon accused, gesturing to the glass container with his eyes. "Therefore, I will give you two choices. The first is to have the contents of this container thrown onto you. I will then leave you and Qui Oto to battle for supremacy of your body." He smiled grimly, hoping her expression of horror was not an act.

"What is the second?" Gamayun demanded scornfully. Her nostrils flared. Landon could hear the forceful breaths taken as she spoke. For the moment, she held her fury in check. Her passiveness did not fool him. He remained aware that she could leap across the bridge in a split second, regardless of the distance.

"In exchange for sparing you from the first choice, I demand three things."

Once again, he did not wait for her response, adding without hesitation, "First, you will give me the orb hidden beneath your wing." He pointed to one of her wings. Gamayun protectively folded it against her body. "It was stolen by an evil wizard six-hundred years ago and given to you in exchange for trapping Norduir."

"Never!" Gamayun shrieked in exasperation. He could see the pulsating light, its beating rhythm increasing with each passing moment. The King wondered if Gamayun's emotions were the cause.

Raising the container as if to throw it, Landon looked into Gamayun's eyes and offered, "Fine, enjoy your life with Qui Oto."

"What is your second demand?"

Landon lowered his hand and looked gravely at the creature. He waited a few seconds before offering, "I will be allowed to enter and leave Mfiri of my own accord, without any strings attached."

Gamayun gasped at his words, looking at him with disbelief. Shock turned to anger and then to rage. Five talons extended from the tips of her wrinkled fingers. Landon knew she was sizing up the distance needed to get to him. He was safe, though, since she could not leave this side of the bridge. *I hope she cannot.* He had surmised that the same magic keeping others out of Mfiri trapped Gamayun within.

"And the third demand?" Gamayun asked in disbelief. Her voice had lost its energy, her fury dissipating along with her enthusiasm. Her raspy voice, previously enthralling, now sounded hollow and shrill. Landon felt a pang of guilt at having tamed her but continued.

"When I choose to leave Mfiri, I will be allowed to leave with Norduir, the original Titan. There can be no limitations and no restrictions."

"You dare!" Gamayun roared. Her blue-green eyes flitted back and forth, desperately seeking a way out of her predicament.

He wondered, *Have they always been that color?* It was troubling that he could not remember.

It was her turn to startle the King.

The smooth, silky voice returned, "I will make you a counteroffer," The bird-like creature moved forward a few feet before squatting once more. "In exchange for the bottle, I will order the Lord of the Dark Castle to release the souls of Queen Lenali and Queen Lyssa. They will walk once more amongst the living. You will no longer be alone, living without your mother and your sister. Both of whom you loved most in the world."

Landon gasped at the words. Years ago, he had fought desperately against the temptations placed before him by the Eighth Lion. It had nearly torn him apart, emotionally. Now, the two women who meant more to him than any others were gone, both dead for many years. The thought of reuniting with his mother and his sister tugged mightily at his heartstrings.

They could live once more, he fretted. *Is it possible?* He stared at Gamayun in disbelief. He had come to the Bridge seeking safe passage once more into Mfiri. He had assumed he held the ultimate coin and was sure Gamayun would yield to his demands. Instead, though, she had countered with a currency almost too powerful to resist. *Almost!*

The King noticed the creature inching closer, once again. He took two steps backwards, increasing the space between them. She recognized his response, her eyes flaring with frustration.

She knew the best way to distract me. She is a wicked creature.

Slowly, with their eyes locked onto one another's, Landon removed the cap of the container. He lifted his hand to throw the glass jar at her.

"Stop!" Gamayun bellowed, though the fight had gone out of her voice. "I yield to your demands and vow to honor them fully." Landon lowered the container but did not replace the lid. He looked at her full pouting lips, her rosy cheekbones, and her soft, porcelain-like face. In all his years, he had rarely seen such beauty. The creature started to sob. Large teardrops ran down her cheeks, landing with soft thuds onto the wooden planks.

"The orb, give it to me," he demanded. He held his breath until the creature removed the pulsating orb from beneath its wing and placed it gently on the ground just outside the bridge.

Landon ordered her to back away from the edge, watching her sulking eyes, full of despair, as she complied. He walked over and picked up the orb. Tucking it into the crook of his left arm, the King raised the container as if to throw it. He stepped onto the bridge and ordered the creature to move backwards. Though she had made a vow, he was determined not to let his guard down.

It was an awkward journey across the Bridge, his shield held in his left hand with the orb tucked behind it in the crook of his elbow. He kept the jar at the ready.

The moment they reached the end of the Bridge, Landon ordered Gamayun to step backwards off the bridge.

He moved past her, watching as Gamayun hopped twice and landed lightly back onto the wooden Bridge. She turned back to Landon and lamented, "I am no longer in love with you." She looked down at the orb on his arm and sighed heavily, her nostrils flaring once again. Angrily, she turned and walked back into the fog, disappearing from his sight.

Landon found the obsidian pathway and began retracing his steps from years before. This time, it was much easier to ignore the pleas of the Children of the Night and the evil witch when they came to the pathway to scold him. They noticed the sword at his side and kept a safe distance. He would have enjoyed running his sword through every one of them or slicing off their heads. The King taunted them as he passed, reminding them of General Faron's escape. He lied by adding that the man was living blissfully, enjoying the comforts of a large family and many friends. The witch shrieked curses as the children groaned. They covered their ears and ran back into their houses, wailing.

For Faron, he thought, remembering the General fondly.

Turning a corner, he stopped and quickly kneeled.

Norduir, the ice-Dragon, stood before him, straddling the pathway once more.

"My Lady, I have returned to fulfill my vow." He placed his shield on the ground, stood, and lifted the orb above his head. "I would like to offer my sincere apologies for the length of time it has taken, though." His guilt spread across his face as quickly as the grassfire in his dream.

"Do not worry, mighty Chardon. Do not feel guilty. When compared to the lifespan of a Dragon, thirty-five years is no more than the blink of an eye." The Dragon took the orb, placed it inside her mouth, and swallowed it whole. The wild, ice blue eyes looked at the King with a ferocity seldom witnessed by man.

"Eschaton has begun. Climb onto my back, your Majesty. Thanks to you, the magic holding me prisoner all these years is gone." Landon climbed up and settled in behind Norduir's head. He gripped a thick, white scale in each hand. The other scales clapped loudly, locking his weapons and shield into place beside him. The mighty Dragon hopped into the air flapping her wings gracefully. They bolted upward into the sky, a white meteor streaking into the heavens.

The moment they were free of the bonds of Mfiri, the Dragon doubled, tripled, and then quadrupled in size. They soared through the cloudless sky, the white wings stretching widely. Landon looked down and swooned. The mountain peaks rose ahead, but the village below looked like a speck.

"Where do we go, My Queen?" he shouted, his mind racing with the knowledge that he was one of only a few humans who would ever know the sensation of flying with a Dragon.

Norduir screeched loudly and breathed a blue flame hundreds of feet ahead of them. The flame hardened instantly as the frozen particles solidified into a wall of ice. Norduir circled back around and flew directly into the frozen flame, shattering it into thousands of icy shards. The collision sounded like a thunderbolt, echoing away and back to Landon's ears.

"We go into battle, My King!" the Titan yelled exuberantly. "We go into battle, and we must hurry."

Landon leaned down and asked, "What about Pahaida? What about Bosque? Should we call for their assistance?" He was shocked and saddened by Norduir's response.

"Pahaida and Bosque are dead. The Dark Wizard Jochi has slain my sisters. Their heads have become armrests, mounted on a throne of human skulls."

Landon shuddered at the words but listened intently. The Titan's anger and fury were on full display.

"They dare use a Dragon's head to rest their pitiful arms!" bellowed Norduir, her thunderous voice terrifying.

She shrieked savagely, "It is time we fly into battle. It is time the beast-like warriors in the Lands of the Khans and the Dark Wizard learn firsthand the power and the fury of the original daughter of Ea. It is time they tremble at the might and courage of the Emperor Chardon II."

The sun lifted entirely above the distant mountain peaks, casting brightly onto everything in the world.

After a few moments of silence, Norduir spoke once more, though more gravely, "We cannot arrive a moment too late. A champion has challenged Natus Khan to armed combat. The battle is just beginning."

"A champion?" Landon asked with his voice full of wonder. He was surprised anyone would be brave enough to challenge the massive warrior. The creature who sat upon the throne of human skulls, his face ringed in by the head of the Eighth Lion, was dark and foreboding.

"An Amorak?" Landon asked, remembering the dark giant's words. He imagined all the Amarok from the Lands of the Khans to be as forbidding as Natus Khan.

"No, My King. A human. A boy from another world has challenged Natus Khan in armed combat. Bravely, he has shouldered the fate of the Known World, though youth and inexperience may impede his efforts. If we do not arrive in time to lend our support, the Khan will slay him. Even now, the Khan's armies have encircled the two to witness the battle. If successful, the Khan will lead a ravenous, invading horde across the Cargathian Mountains. Khan has welded the untamable into a fighting force of unimaginable power. Dragons and humans alike will perish, engulfed in an eternal flame if he is not defeated. Righteousness must always fight evil. The true King of O'ndar must defeat Natus Khan, or the world and others will suffer the consequences."

Once again, Landon shuddered at her words. His physical prowess had waned as his age had grown in years. A challenge, one he hoped he could accept and overcome, had arisen in the East, and the fate of the Known World was at stake

Eschaton had begun

He leaned in closely to Norduir's neck, gripping her scales tightly and weighing her words with the seriousness they deserved.

With her final words, Norduir, the original Titan and one of the Three Daughters of Ea and Chardon II, the greatest King in the history of the Known World, turned and flew into the direction of the rising sun.

ANOTHER
WORLD

CHOSEN

IT WAS ON AN EARLY CHRISTMAS-EVE MORNING, AN HOUR BEFORE THE sun would brighten the wintery landscape, when the woman sat down quietly at her desk, praying to God that she had the emotional strength to make it through the day. She opened the office for the Belleville Memorial Hospital Physical Therapy Department, as she always did, arriving well before sunrise and before most of the therapists and other secretaries in her department. Flecks of snow swirled around the parking lot, the dimming lights enveloped by the surrounding darkness in the pre-dawn hours. Hypnotic, in a peaceful way, the heavy flakes reminded her once again that Christmas had almost arrived. Her heart filled with sadness at a time of year when joy and hope usually reigned supreme.

She and her husband Reggie had spent the previous three-hundred sixty-four days coping as best they could, leaning on each other and silently dreading the arrival of the holiday season. They had done their best to insulate themselves, even ignoring the calendars on their phones as December quietly approached. Once today and tomorrow passed, they would be able to lead ordinary lives at least for another three-hundred sixty-four days.

She loved her husband dearly; the two had been high school sweethearts, both graduating from Belleville West High school more than twenty years ago. He had been an athlete, running track for his favorite, Coach Segraves, all four years. Reggie had always strived to emulate the man.

"He is a family man first, a father, and then a coach," he told her one time when speaking about Coach Segraves. "He ran, and I mean he ran fast, for the University of Kentucky, excelling as both an athlete and a top student." He beamed everytime Coach Segraves' name was mentioned, even all these years later.

She, on the other hand, had been a bookworm and other than joining the Art Club her sophomore year, she kept her nose in her books for the other three. They had met at a track tournament hosted by Belleville West, on a sunny Saturday morning, when he was a junior and she a sophomore. He had flirted with her while waiting for an event, causing her to smile and swoon with excitement. The two became an item and never looked back.

Denise Rogers sat silently at her desk, scanning over the numerous charts, reviewing all of the appointments she had scheduled for today. Since it was Christmas Eve, Physical Therapy would be available only until noon and then she could drive home to Millstadt, a small farming community less than ten miles away. With Reggie gone until evening, the hours spent alone in their house would be the worst, but she would find ways to keep busy.

I have to keep busy, she thought, wishing that it was as easy to do as it was to say.

For the last seventeen years, it had been her job to pull the charts for all therapists before they arrived. Today would be a whirlwind of patients. Today, even though it was considered by many to be a holiday, there would be too many walk-ins, all of them arriving unannounced. They always demanded that she squeeze them into an already packed schedule. Silently, she hoped the gathering snow might discourage enough of them to stay home. *I doubt it will,* she thought.

Even with the shortened Christmas Eve hours, she had scheduled seven patients recovering from back surgeries, two who recently had suffered shoulder injuries on the job, and a mixed bag of other impairments sprinkled in for good measure. Everyone would have a busy morning.

The therapists always asked that Denise be the one to pull their charts. They wanted her covering the main desk, especially around the holidays. She had become very efficient at getting things ready before the first patient arrived. *Besides, I don't have any responsibilities at home that need my attention,* she reasoned, a single tear trailing down her right cheek. She pushed her sandy-blonde hair away from her eyebrows and looked at the first chart.

Many of the patients were in their sixties and older; she quickly reminded herself that she would join that age group in less than twenty years.

She scanned the list of names but knew her attention lay elsewhere. Sighing heavily, she turned on the computer. Her mind was full of worries, built up like the water near a dam after a heavy rain, ready to break over the top if pushed too its limit. In her case, that extra push could be an innocent look, a familiar name, or a simple remembrance. Her spirit, including her ability to cope with today, weighed heavily in the balance.

Waiting for the computer, she thought about her husband, Reggie. She wondered how he was doing. He often pushed his own emotions aside, focusing instead on helping her manage the day. They had sat together at the kitchen table less than an hour ago, eating a quick bite of breakfast. He ate his eggs and bacon in silence, mopping up the yolk with a lightly toasted and lavishly buttered slice of bread. He had worried about her this morning, as he always did. It was one of the reasons she loved him so much even after all of their years together.

She remembered looking at his mouth, the worry wrinkles standing out when he frowned, as he offered quietly, "You're going to be okay." He tried to state it matter-of-factly, but instead, it came out worried. She had fought back the tears, trying to smile for his benefit.

He was a muscular man, just forty-two years old, but his sleek black hair, which had not gone to grey, made him look much younger. Reggie had remained the man she had fallen in love with all those years ago. It was love at first sight.

She smiled with deep affection before responding, "I will." She reached out and patted his forearm lovingly. He returned her gesture by placing his other hand over the top of hers and giving it a gentle squeeze.

Reggie stood, kissed her on top of the head and said, "Call me if you need me. Otherwise, I will be at the job site until 6." She leaned her head into his arm, enjoying the touch. She stood up and walked with him to the door, waiting for his truck to pull away before she went to get ready for work.

The computer beeped, bringing her out of her reverie. It took a few minutes, but finally, the username and password screen popped up. Without thinking, she typed in the name Zachary. Denise stopped, her fingertips resting lightly on the keyboard. Slowly, she lifted her right pinky finger and hit the backspace key until Zachary's name disappeared. Another tear ran down her face.

Please, not today, she worried.

Today marked the fifth anniversary of her son Zachary's death. The previous four Christmas's had been stressful, emotionally draining, and heart-wrenching. Last year, Denise had not been able to make it through the entire morning without breaking down into tears, sobbing uncontrollably. Her co-workers had done their best to console her, but she ended up leaving early, needing to go home to deal with the heartache. She had been an emotional wreck, reminded later by her counselor that anniversaries, especially those involving the death of loved ones, constantly added to the anguish and increased the burden of guilt.

"Do I feel guilty that I am alive?" she whispered with despair, talking as much to the computer screen as herself. She and Reggie agreed that they had done all they could, but she always worried that she should have done more as a mother.

They had been excited beyond imagination after finding out that she was pregnant, especially after having tried to conceive for more than ten years. Just when they had given up all hope, the good news they had prayed for arrived. Nine months later, Zachary was born. They enjoyed the bliss of parenting, her son a precocious, funny, beautiful little boy whose arrival filled an emptiness in her life that needed filling. When he was just four years old, Zach had developed an unexplained fever and chills. They had been nervous but had faith the doctors would be able to cure him. They brought him home, but the fever and chills led to fatigue, and finally, they took him to a specialist in St. Louis. The doctor diagnosed him with Leukemia. It had been a big kick in the gut, and the two of them prayed that God would intervene and save their son. Each night they held each other for comfort, and once Reggie fell asleep, she would tip-toe to Zach's room and lay beside him, her tears staining the pillows.

The moments that she held him, especially when he came out of chemotherapy were traumatic. Despite some of the finest doctors in the United States, his little body could not fight off cancer. Denise remembered his final moments as if they happened yesterday; the five years since had not clouded the clarity of that time. His soft, blue eyes had looked into her face with one fleeting moment of recognition.

Tired, his tiny hand had caressed her cheek, and he whispered, "It's going to be okay, Mama."

His hand had slipped off her cheek, dropping slowly onto her right arm. She looked down at his hand, wishing he could caress her cheek just once more.

Sitting in front of her computer, she could not help but think of Zach and that final moment. It had been Christmas Eve. The tiny flecks of snow had pelted the hospital window, just as they were now. That morning, they had brought him a stuffed Winnie the Pooh, hoping to cheer him a little. She sniffled, remembering Zachary's reaction, thinking about the precious smile when they placed the tiny bear beside him. "Pinnie the Pooh," he whispered voicelessly. His smile had warmed her heart.

They had been to many specialists, but the disease ravaged his little body, and he had died much too early. *As if there is an age that isn't much too early,* she thought, morbidly.

Denise was a petite woman, barely five feet three inches tall. Her sandy-blonde hair and light blue eyes went well with her pale complexion. She pulled her sweater around her closely, waiting for the computer. The moments of silence, when there was nothing to do but wait, were the most difficult.

Responsible for scheduling the treatments for the Physical Therapy Department, Denise knew the coming day would be a whirlwind of activity. Yet, there would be tiny moments when there was nothing to do; those times felt like an eternity of solitude. She inhaled deeply, steadied her conviction to make it through the day, and prayed lunchtime would come quickly.

She started to pick up the phone but paused, listening to the growing sound of the helicopter overhead. The blades echoed rhythmically, the gentle *thwop, thwop,* keeping the beat with her heart.

"It's too early for sadness," she mumbled. The helicopter would land shortly on the helipad, across the grounds near Medical Building One. Its arrival meant that someone had been in a severe accident. She lowered her head and prayed.

The woman's soft voice offered, "Hey Denise." She recognized the number as an internal call but was still surprised to hear Lisa's voice.

"Hey Lisa," she answered warily. A lump built up in her throat, its tightness making it difficult to speak. Lisa had been the maternity nurse on duty for Zach's birth, had followed his progress and regression after his diagnosis, and became a close family friend, a shoulder to cry on many times.

Denise sighed, wanting the call to be about something other than Zach. She appreciated Lisa's concern, but it was eleven-thirty, and she wanted to finish the day without any more tears.

I have almost made it. She praised herself silently.

Lisa asked, "Did you hear the helicopter come in this morning?" She paused, waiting for Denise to respond. Lisa continued, "It was a twenty-two-year-old woman hitchhiking on Interstate 70 North of Lebanon. Can you imagine someone hitchhiking in this snow?"

"That poor thing," Denise offered sincerely. "Did she make it?" She had prayed for the unknown woman and hoped God had answered her prayers, even if it was for a stranger.

"Sadly, no," Lisa said. "But, her son did."

Denise leaned into her computer and asked, intrigued, "Her son?"

Lisa continued, "Yes, the poor woman was nine months pregnant. They airlifted her to us as quickly as they could. A semi-truck ran her over. The Emergency Room doctors did not think either one would make it."

With conviction in her voice, Denise said, "Thank God he's alive." Lisa's call confused her. Other than mere gossip, she had no reason to know about this woman's plight, though it did tug on her heart to hear about a baby.

"Okay. Well, thanks for letting me know. We were all curious when the helicopter came in so early," Denise said, pausing to give Lisa time to answer, "It was good to hear your voice. I hope to hear from you again, soon." Hearing Lisa's voice, especially during the holidays, brought up memories of Zach.

"Denise, the baby does not have any family."

"What do you mean he doesn't have any family?" Denise asked in surprise. Her heart ached to think that a child would have to grow up without his mother.

"We've checked all the records, made numerous phone calls. There is nothing, no one. The baby is all alone in this world," Lisa added sorrowfully.

"Lisa, why did you call to tell me this? You, of all people, know how hard today can be for us."

Lisa responded soothingly, "I know, that is the reason I called. We have talked it over with Children and Family Services, with our Human Resource reps, with the Doctors, and the team of nurses caring for him."

"Yes?" Denise asked, annoyed. Her emotions clouded Lisa's words.

"We would like you to be his mother."

Denise Rogers sat at her kitchen table, waiting for her husband to arrive with a nervousness that she had not felt in many years. It was thirty minutes past six in the evening, and he was due to be home any moment. She fidgeted, though it was with excitement mixed with a slight pang of guilt and topped with a large amount of anxiousness.

She heard Reggie's truck pull up and waited for him to come into the house, even though she wanted to run out to greet him.

"Hey, babe," he said, smiling. "You do okay today?" He leaned down and kissed her on top of the head. She patted his hand and waited for him to sit at the kitchen table.

"What's up?" he asked, curious. Denise had called him on his cell at six o'clock, excited. She refused to say why, offering that the two had something they needed to discuss when he made it home. She knew he could hear the enthusiasm in her voice, a giddiness he had not heard in years, but she refused to explain any further. Denise could tell that he had been worried about her call, worried that she had broken down again, and afraid that she had spent the day crying, alone.

"It was a pretty eventful day, today for sure," she started. Denise explained the arrival of the helicopter and Lisa's subsequent phone call.

Reggie listened intently, keenly aware of the direction the conversation was heading. Patiently, lovingly, he wanted her to express her feelings without any interruption.

She continued, "I went over to the Maternity Ward Reg, just to see him. When I clocked out, I admit I thought about getting into my car and driving home." She looked into his eyes, wanting him to see the seriousness in her expression.

"Why didn't you?" he asked, his eyebrows showing his confusion.

"I couldn't do it. I went over to the window and looked at him. And then," Denise paused, her eyes glazing over as if she were staring at the baby through the window, "I saw the most amazing thing I have ever seen."

Filled with curiosity, Reggie asked, "What? What did you see?" He forgot, for a brief moment, that he had already decided to oppose her proposal.

She could sense his curiosity and said, "A few moments before I arrived, the hospital had a power outage. It took almost thirty minutes for the emergency generators kick in. You can imagine the chaos, with the nurses worried about keeping the babies warm. They quickly put two babies in each bin. They did amazing work. I watched Lisa, and another nurse swaddle each baby in thick blankets. The soft glow of the emergency lights helped, but without the generators," she paused, looked down at the table to gather her thoughts and then continued, "I thought that they handled themselves very well." She lifted her eyes to his and smiled deeply

"Well, you can imagine how loudly they cried the moment the lights went off. I was standing outside the glass, watching and listening. It's not the part of parenting I miss," Denise sighed. She went to the sink and filled a cup with water. She brought it to her husband before continuing.

Reggie looked up from his plate and frowned, "Honey, why would you go there, especially today?" His worried look almost brought her to tears, but she decided to focus on the story.

"I know, but I was there for a reason," she offered, raising a hand for him to wait. "For a few minutes, there wasn't any power. The nurses placed him into a bin, next to the window, with another baby. In the soft glow of their cell phone lights," she stopped as Reggie asked.

"Cell phone lights?"

"Yes. The nurses turned on their cell phone lights. They must have gone to other departments because the whole place seemed lit up with candles." Denise had a bright smile on her face. "I was looking at him, Reg. He did not cry at all, and for a second, he looked up at me, through the window. I knew he was looking at me." She nodded as if the baby were there with them in the kitchen. "The poor baby next to him was crying so loud. He was terrified, and soon all the babies were crying. The nurses walked around, cooing to them, holding some, rocking them gently. Nothing helped. But then, all of a sudden, they all stopped crying."

"What do you mean they all stopped?" Reggie asked breathlessly with a look of astonishment on his face. Her words had captivated his thoughts. He needed to know what happened.

"It was like a light switch somewhere had been turned off. The moment it happened, all of the babies in that room stopped crying at the same time."

Reggie's curiosity got the better of him. He blurted out, "What happened? What made them all stop crying? Did the lights come back on?"

Denise shook her head.

"They all stopped crying the moment our baby reached out and touched the other one."

Reggie ignored a part of her statement and asked, "They all stopped crying when one baby touched another one?"

"All of them. It was like turning off a faucet. Instantly, all of the babies stopped crying. All of them, at the same time. It was quiet. Everyone looked around, awed by the moment. Lisa looked at me and shrugged. And then, he started cooing to them."

"He started cooing to them. Who started cooing to them?" Reggie asked, amazed.

"He did. Our baby. He cooed softly, chortling, for lack of a better word. All of a sudden, all of the babies started laughing and cooing to each other. It was the most magical moment I have ever seen in my life."

Denise looked up, smiling at Reggie. She leaned in, looked deeply into his eyes, and added, "I have never seen anything like it in my life."

She shrugged, adding with sadness in her voice, "Reg, he looked at me through the window, just before he reached out with his tiny fingers and touched the other baby. His mama has died. He has no relatives, no family. He is all alone in this world."

"Lisa," Reggie said, frustrated, "she knows better than to call you on a day like today?"

"Don't be mad at her, Reg. I was, too, at first. However, this baby's mother has died. I am a mother who has lost a son. Do you see? If someone doesn't take him into their home, he's going to go through this world all alone." Denise fell silent because she had rambled on far too long, but she also felt compelled to continue. She knew Reggie understood that she was pleading for his acceptance. She needed him to agree with how she felt.

It was Reggie's turn to be saddened, "This baby won't replace Zach." He wiped the tears from the corners of his eyes and swallowed, choking them back. His voice cracked, and he stopped speaking for a few seconds. He asked hoarsely, "Can we go through this again? Losing him was so painful."

She folded herself into his arms, holding onto the man she loved more than anyone in the world. Hugging him closely, she whispered, "Sometimes I feel like I don't know anything anymore, Reg. I do know that we are both people of faith. It's a word we use with conviction, even after losing Zach." She cried into his shoulder for a full minute before continuing. "How is it that we lost our little boy, and we still have faith? I ask myself this often, not to second-guess our faith, though, just to understand why. It's just that sometimes Reg, I feel like the two of us have been chosen for something."

"Chosen?" Reggie asked, surprised. He had not been expecting the conversation to turn to their faith. It had taken every ounce of conviction for him to maintain his faith for the last five years. They had done it together, leaning on each other for emotional support. He repeated the question, "Chosen?"

"Yes, chosen," she answered. "I don't know for sure if this baby has been chosen for us. I don't know if we were chosen for him. However, after what I saw this morning, I believe he has destiny on his side. God has placed us in each other's path for a reason. It is up to us, the both of us as parents, to help him find his purpose. To help him make sense of his life and everything that has happened." She hugged her husband, grateful to have his arms around her once more. She leaned into his shoulder and cried softly.

REGINALD 'RUSTY' ROGERS III

AS SHE SAT DOWN ON HER FRONT PORCH LOOKING ACROSS THE GREEN rows of ripening soybeans, Denise could just barely make out the top of the yellow bus when it pulled away from the school a little more than a mile away. It looked tiny, the gently sloping field making it difficult to see as it drove away from Millstadt Elementary school. It was three-twenty three in the afternoon, and the bus would take at least thirty minutes to get to their house, since it made frequent stops to let other children off at their homes. Watching the bus, she imagined it to be a yellow and black caterpillar inching its way back and forth through the streets in the newly built subdivisions.

Their subdivision and house, recently built in the tiny village of Millstadt, was going to be one of the last stops for the driver. In the last few years, the town's population multiplied and it was no longer the best-kept secret in southern Illinois. Millstadt was growing prosperous. It had an academically challenging school, a community of citizens who believed in strong family values, and many people of faith. Millstadt was the perfect place for a family to settle and a great place to raise children.

Eventually, after stopping a few times along North Polk Street before it became Saeger Road, the bus passed Kalbfleish Drive and slowly made a right turn into their subdivision on Adam Wendt Parkway. Denise sat impassively on her porch, waiting for the bus to crisscross its way through the subdivision, eventually turning right on Terrace View Court before stopping to let off four small children. The bus waited for the children to get into their houses before turning around in a driveway and heading back to Adam Wendt Parkway.

God bless that driver, Denise thought, touched by the care he had taken to ensure that all the children made it into their houses. She liked Millstadt. It had its faults. Every community did, but other than the few rotten apples, it was a great place to raise children.

It's our hometown, she hummed to herself, remembering an old hit from Bruce Springsteen. She sighed softly and starting singing the lyrics.

"My hometown," she crooned, the words trailing off at the end. Though raised in Belleville, most of her high school friends had been from Millstadt. They had always told her about their experiences in elementary school and Jr. High. The stories and their praise for the Millstadt teachers had touched her enough that she talked Reggie into buying a house. He admitted, often, that she had been right. They had settled in, made many new friends, and were raising their son to be a good kid.

He is a good kid, she thought, reminding herself to focus on the positive. The bus disappeared for a few minutes before reappearing a few blocks away.

She finished humming, turned her head slightly, and continued to watch the moving bus. With a heavy sigh and a worried frown, her face grew serious.

It's the most challenging part of parenting, she thought uneasily. *No one likes to discipline their kids, especially when they are only six years old.*

She turned her head to watch the bus and sighed loudly. Little Reggie, her six-year-old son, was sitting directly behind the bus driver, placed there by Principal Merleins. Usually, he did not sit directly behind the driver, and on a typical day, she did not wait for him on the front porch.

"I'm in Kindergarten now," he had told her on the first day of school. "I don't want my friends seeing my Mama waiting for me when I come home." He had been serious when he said it, his lower lip thrust out, almost daring her to argue.

Though it made her sad, she chuckled and made him a promise not to meet him outside. She always waited, peering out the curtains, until he walked into the front door. She had made that promise, but this time she needed to make a statement, especially after the call this afternoon from Mr. Merleins. Reggie must understand the seriousness of his behavior. If that lesson included his Mama waiting for him on the front porch, so be it.

A little embarrassment might teach him a lesson, she thought with disappointment. It was not something she liked to do, but after Mr. Merleins' phone call, Mama Bear needed a response that would get his attention.

Once again, the bus was on the move, turning right at Diamond View Court. It stopped at the last house at a dead-end, frequently disappearing behind some brick houses. Denise could hear the laughter of some of the children. She caught flashes of the bus as it turned around and headed back, eventually turning right and then right once more at Mill Park Court. They had the last house on the end of the street, which meant that Reggie would be one of the last ones off the bus.

Reggie and Suzie, she mused. They would exit the bus together in the same way they did every single day. Suzie was also in Kindergarten, lived next door, and the two had become inseparable. Finally, the bus stopped in front of their house, turned around, and let four children off at their driveway. Two of the children were Junior High students, both almost thirteen years old. Usually, they came off the bus laughing and joking with each other. Today was different as they both exited quietly, looking at her waiting on the porch.

"Hey, Mrs. Rogers," one of the boys yelled. He tried to smile, but his facial expression was somber, making her feel like he had expected to find her waiting.

I wonder if Reggie told him what happened? she thought, hoping that he was old enough to understand why she was meeting her son in the driveway. Not that it mattered, but she did not want the neighborhood kids to think she was an ogre.

The boy waved, patted Reggie on the back the way an older brother might do when offering words of encouragement. He gave a quick look of sympathy and said, "Good luck." He leaned in and gave Reggie a one-arm hug before turning away.

Turning back to her, he frowned and offered, "See you, Mrs. Rogers." He looked down once more and then walked to his house across the road. He waved to the other Jr. High student who lived three houses away.

"Hey Sam," she called back. She watched, looking at Reggie slow his pace as he strolled up the concrete driveway, eyes downcast. She smiled inwardly, imagining how much sympathy he had gained from the other neighborhood kids on the short ride home. *What did he tell them?* Denise was sure he had not told them the whole story. It was probably just enough to have the entire bus rooting for him.

She grimaced, thinking, *I am not the bad guy.*

Suzie had an arm wrapped around his shoulder; her blond curls pushed back with a hairpin. She began whispering into his ear.

It tugged at Denise's heart to see how hard the little girl was trying to keep him from breaking down into tears.

Denise watched Suzie's eyes flit quickly to the belt, and she offered a frown. Denise was sure the little girl had shaken her head with disappointment. *She's six and doesn't understand how serious this can be.*

Denise heard her say softly, "Don't worry, Rusty. It's going to be okay." The little girl gave him a quick hug, leaned her head against his, looked up and smiled, before adding, "See you, Reggie." She peeled off, walking to her house without looking back.

Reggie slowed, even more, his expression somber, looked up and added quietly, "Hey, Mama." He looked at the belt in her hand but did not look away.

Denise steadied herself. It was a lesson that she thought might come someday. She just did not believe it would be in his first year of school. *Boys fight.* She had convinced herself, after Mr. Merleins phone call, that this was a normal part of growing up. She reminded herself that she had to support the things he did well and needed to discourage the things that might get him into trouble. She loved her son dearly. She would not tolerate any fighting at school, though.

"Sounds like we need to talk," she said matter-of-factly. She hoped her face remained impassive, but her stomach churned with nervousness.

"Yes, Mama, I suppose we do," he responded softly with both his thumbs tucked into the backpack straps. He looked into her eyes; his lips curled downward.

Denise stood up, holding the belt in both hands. She waited a few seconds, sighed loudly with disappointment, and walked into the house.

"Now listen to me carefully. I need you to pay close attention. I want nothing but the truth out of you Reginald Rogers," she said. It was odd that she always referred to him by his first and last name when he was in trouble. Otherwise, she always called him Little Reg. She sat down on the living room couch, pulling him over to her. He remained standing with his thumbs still in the straps.

He answered, his voice sounding wounded, "I would never lie to you, Mama. You know that."

His words stung. Denise almost started crying but took a deep breath, wishing they would hug and make things better. She wanted to pull him close so that she could tell him it was all okay. She stopped herself, remembering that he had gotten into a fight at school today. It had been a shock to hear the Principal's voice, but her worry quickly dissipated the moment he described Reggie's fight. Her son had punched another Kindergartner. She offered to come to get him immediately, but Mr. Merleins had discouraged it. "We can put him on the bus, Mrs. Rogers," he said. "There are only thirty minutes left before we release the students."

"I can be there in less than five minutes," she had countered. She wavered and finally relented, agreeing to let Little Reggie ride home on the bus. She insisted, though, that he sit behind the bus driver.

Mr. Merleins offered, patiently, "I don't want to embarrass him." At those words, she wanted to argue her point again but stopped. She agreed to wait until Reggie made it home on the bus. She wanted to ask more questions. She accepted that the Principal had dealt with the issue. Reggie had served afternoon detention outside Mr. Merleins office. Instead of arguing, Denise thanked him and assured him that this was not acceptable and she would ensure that it never happened again.

Now here they were in the living room, mother and son, staring at each other, both waiting for the other to break the silence. Little Reg waited patiently, looking somberly into her face.

"So," she started, "you decided to hit Tommy Krueger in the face at recess." Her eyes were stern. The Krueger's were a friendly enough family. Descendants of one of the first German immigrant families to settle in Millstadt back in 1834, Tommy's parents owned the local hardware store. They were a large family, and Tommy was the sixth of seven kids.

Six boys and one girl, Denise reminded herself. She often sympathized with Mrs. Krueger, wondering how she had dealt with six rambunctious boys all these years.

Rusty nodded but did not answer. His brown eyes never left hers. He waited in silence.

"Do you remember what your dad and I told you?" she asked, frustrated with his silence. "The one thing we will not tolerate is fighting, especially in school." She had placed the belt next to her on the couch cushion, but picked it up and patted the leather strap into the palm of her left hand.

"Well, what do you have to say for yourself?" Denise demanded. She had to admit Little Reggie had a great poker face. His eyes, his mouth, and his forehead betrayed no emotion. She could hear the frustration in her voice but knew it grew out of the silence. *He's going to make this difficult for me,* she thought with despair. She would have preferred that he yell about how unfair she was acting. He did not. She would have preferred that he cry and plead for her not to whip him. He did not. Instead, he waited in silence, patiently.

After a few minutes, he broke his silence, saying softly, "I don't have anything to say, Mama. I punched Tommy Krueger in the face. I won't lie. I punched him." Reggie put his book bag down and took a step closer to her. He looked up and said, "I know I shouldn't have done it, Mama. I deserve the belt. I accept my punishment." He turned around and waited for the belt to land.

Denise was shocked. *Is he trying to use reverse psychology on me?* Six-year-olds could be manipulative though Little Reggie rarely offered her anything but honesty. Once, when he and Suzie had taken extra cookies,

Suzie told her mom they did not do it. Reggie, though, had stepped forward, looked Denise in the eye, and said, "Yes, Mama. We took the cookies."

He had even accepted the weeklong grounding from his PlayStation 3 without any argument or complaint. His only response was, "We did it. We should accept the consequence."

Reggie's reaction caught her off-guard for a few seconds, but Denise recomposed herself before placing her left hand on his shoulder. She stood up beside him, lifted the belt above her shoulder, and swatted him on the backside four times. The leather made a *thwack, thwack* sound each time it landed on his jeans. She could hear his tears.

Denise kneeled in front of Reggie and leaned in to hug him. "You know how much I love you," she said tearfully. It had been the first spanking she had given him, and she hoped it would be the last.

He hugged her back before answering, "I know, Mama. I know. I love you, too." His eyes filled with tears making her heartache.

"No more fights at school. Do you hear me?" she reminded Reggie. Denise leaned backwards, trying to read his expression and his thoughts.

"Okay. No more fights at school," Little Reggie answered with tears rolling down his cheek and dropping onto his shoulder.

She felt a pang of guilt for being happy to see the tears. Denise had been afraid of her response if he had not shown any emotion. She originally had toyed with grounding him rather than whipping him with a belt. Denise had always been hypersensitive about using physical punishment, but she also wanted him to know how serious it was to fight in school.

"Good," she responded, changing the subject, "now go get cleaned up and come help me make supper for dad."

Her heart thumped loudly in her chest when he said, worriedly. "He's gonna be mad, isn't he?" Little Reggie asked, ashamed. The little boy had already picked up his backpack and was sauntering to his room, eyes downcast once again.

"Probably, but you know the rules in this house. Your dad knows them, too. The biggest one is to take responsibility for your actions and take your consequence without complaint. If you earned it, accept it. After that, we let bygones be bygones." Denise hoped her words of encouragement would make facing his father a little easier. *Big Reg will be mad*, she thought, praying that he would accept that she had already handed out the punishment. Little Reggie's words made her worry.

"I hope so," he added warily. "I've never been in a fight at school, though." He plodded off slowly, keeping his head down with regret.

"So," his dad asked with a smile, "did you win?" They had finished supper in silence, enjoying a helping of smoked pork chops, sweet corn smothered in melted butter, and mashed potatoes.

Denise had decided to make a splendid meal, one of Big Reggie's favorites, guessing it would put him into and keep him in a good mood. She decided to help Little Reggie through this even if she had to do it by going through Big Reggie's stomach, instead of his heart.

Denise had wondered when Big Reg would broach the subject, but to her amazement, he had not mentioned anything about the fight during the entire meal. They talked, instead, about the upcoming football games this season with the Rams. Big Reg and Little Reg loved to watch the St. Louis Rams every Sunday.

Then, once they finished eating, his mouth widened into a smile as the three of them sat around the supper table. He asked again, "Did you win?"

"Reg!" Denise blurted out. "You know better than to make it seem okay." Her anger flared, only a little since she had to admit that she was curious, too, but could not bring herself to ask the question aloud.

"It wasn't a fight, dad," Little Reggie began with a scowl. He scraped his fork through the remaining mashed potatoes, fascinated for a few seconds by the tiny rows created by the tines. He looked at his mom and added without blinking, "I punched Tommy on the playground. He didn't even know it was coming." His brown eyes looked directly at his father with intensity.

"You punched him?" his dad asked, startled by Little Reggie's bluntness. He had been angling for a father/son moment but was at a loss about how best to respond. "You just walked up to him and punched him for no reason." He had pushed himself away from the table to listen to his son talk but scooted the chair closer, curious.

Denise could tell he regretted opening the discussion so flippantly.

"I had a reason," the little boy answered, glowering. His eyes hardened as he sat thinking about the moment that he punched Tommy in the mouth. They could see that he was playing the moment over again in his head.

Stunned by his words, Denise felt a twinge of guilt as it balled up tightly in her stomach, forming a knot. It had never occurred to her to ask Little Reggie why he punched Tommy in the mouth. She had taken the Principal's report as gospel, and that Reggie had started a fight and therefore deserved a consequence.

"What was the reason?" Big Reg asked, leaning on the table with his elbows. He looked to Denise and shook his head the moment she started to say something. Reggie wanted to hear his son's explanation.

"He was making fun of Clifton Fields," Little Reggie blurted out, overwhelmed with despair. He had kept it bottled up, and now, it ran out of his mouth like water when it spills over a dam. "I was playing on the swings and heard Tommy, and a few other kids laughing and pointing at Clifton. They were making fun of him." Reggie talked excitedly, looking at his plate and the potatoes a few times. He gathered his thoughts and turned to speak.

Denise cut him off. "What were they saying?" she asked. Somehow she knew that her son's answer was going to make her mad. She knew that it might even make her mad enough to want Tommy punched.

Little Reggie looked up and said with desperation in his voice, "You won't like it, Mama. I didn't like it the moment I heard it." He waited and added, "They were yelling at Clifton, and I am ashamed even to repeat what they were saying. But, Tommy and his friends kept calling him Clefty Fields."

Denise's fork dropped to her plate with a loud clank. She covered her mouth with her left hand, shocked. "Isn't Clifton the little boy with the Cleft Palate?" The blood drained from her face, showing her embarrassment.

"That's him. He cried, Mama. He cried hard. There weren't any big people around, so we called him over to our group and tried to cheer him up."

Denise smiled inwardly at his description, though her heart burned with anger. Little Reggie often referred to the adults as big people. She looked at him again, noticing he had paused to watch their reaction. She nodded for him to continue.

"Suzie was there, and so was Preston. We did our best. We told him to ignore the others, but he was sad, Mama. It did not help. Suzie even tried to make him laugh. She tripped and fell down a couple of times. We saw it on television,once. It did not work. He still cried."

Denise's face offered her disapproval with Tommy's behavior before she asked, "Speaking of Suzie, what did she call you when you got off the bus?" She remembered the words of encouragement Suzie had tried to offer when they were walking up the driveway. Denise was shocked for the second time when she remembered Suzie's words. *Good luck, Rusty.* She looked at her husband, shaking her head. "Did she call you Rusty?" she asked in frustration. Her anger had gone from one to ten in an instant. Big Reggie always told her that she was too protective of Little Reg. She did not care. When it came to her son, she would go from one to one hundred in an instant, if needed.

Her mom will be furious, she thought, her emotions boiling with outrage. The little girl, the one who had been in their home hundreds of times, the one who had stolen cookies and watched fireworks with their family, the one who had chased after and ran from their son called him *Rusty* as they walked up the driveway. Denise's heart lurched. His little friend Suzie had called her African-American son *Rusty.* The anger got the better of her, and she jumped up, stomped over to the phone, and picked up the receiver. Her shoes sounded like a horse, the noisy clomp, clomp echoing across the room. She was surprised that Big Reggie had not reacted as angrily as she had but turned to look at the two of them still sitting at the kitchen table. She started to dial, knowing deep down that she should take a few deep breaths before making the call.

Little Reggie jumped out of his chair and rushed over to her. "Wait, Mama. You cannot call her. It's not her fault." He tried to grab the receiver from her hands.

"What do you mean it's not her fault? She is calling you Rusty because of the color of your skin. Her mom will be livid, and I am beyond angry. I am seething. We adore her, but I am not happy with her at all. Where did she even get the idea that something like that is okay?" Denise asked, incredulous.

There was a short pause that seemed like an eternity. Little Reggie looked up at her and responded, "From me, Mama. She got it from me." He walked back over to the kitchen table and sat down. He placed his head onto the table and buried his face in his arms.

Denise watched Big Reggie look at their son with both admiration and astonishment, as if both were physically possible. She watched her husband reached out and pat Little Reggie on the shoulder.

He reached down, slowly, and took one of Little Reggie's hands into his own. "I am proud of you, son," Big Reggie offered. Big Reg understood something that Denise did not. He was doing what a father should do. He was supportive.

I should be supportive, too, she worried. She did not understand what had transpired at school and looked into her husband's face to see if she could figure it out.

Big Reggie had always been fond of saying, "It's the shoes. You can look at a masterpiece, a painting of near perfection and will only focus on the shoes." He liked to tease her that the slight imperfection with the shoes would take her attention away from the bigger picture.

She looked to Reggie and lifted her eyebrows, puzzled. *Where is this masterpiece? Right now, it seems like a crumby old pair of shoes,* she thought, perplexed by the turn of events.

Big Reg pointed to a chair lovingly and said, "Come sit down. Let's have him start at the beginning." The two, father and son, continued to hold hands. Little Reggie kept his head buried in his arms. He sobbed once, then twice, and began to cry.

She could feel her heartstrings strumming, mightily. She put the phone back down and returned to the kitchen table, waiting in silence for him to begin. Softly, she laid a hand on the back of his head and caressed his hair.

Little Reggie lifted his head, his tears dropping onto the table. He began, "Well. Tommy and his group of friends were making fun of Clifton Fields. It started at morning recess. They kept saying things like, "Why don't you go play left field Clefty Fields".

Denise blurted out angrily, "Why would they do that?" When the two of them looked at her, she raised her hands and said, "Okay. I remember. Focus on the big picture."

"We played kickball during morning recess. Tommy kicked a ball that went about a hundred feet into the air. Everyone thought it would be a home run, but Clifton stumbled over, nearly falling, and caught it. He ran almost a mile to get to it. We thought there was no way Clifton could do it, but he did. He caught the ball, fell, and rolled over. When he stood up, holding the ball up high above his head, the whole class went crazy. We were all high fiving him, and he was on top of the world." He looked up at Big Reg and added, "You should have seen it, Dad." Big Reggie smiled at him but remained silent.

The little boy continued, "Tommy was mad. He stared at Clifton but did not say anything. Ms. Thorne was watching. Clifton told me later that Tommy walked by and mumbled something about the catch. Tommy said, "Nice catch Clefty Fields." Clifton almost started crying then but was too embarrassed. I guess Tommy was still mad this afternoon when we went out to second recess."

"When his gang started making fun of Clifton, we brought him into our group. We could not get him to stop crying, though. It made us mad that someone was making fun of Clifton for doing something good. He caught the ball that no one thought he could catch," Little Reggie said, the excitement apparent in his face. He looked at both of them and continued, "We told him not to let the name-calling get to him. That did not help. He cried and told us that it was easy for us to say. None of us had a cleft palate."

Denise pulled her hands to her face, covering her mouth. She pressed her fingertips against her lips, forcing herself to allow him to continue, uninterrupted.

"We all looked at him, and finally, I said we all have stuff that other people will use to make fun of us." He looked at his dad for support. Big Reggie nodded in understanding.

Denise said, "Not the color of your skin, though. Some people will always try to do stuff like that, Reg. You know how your father and I feel about that topic."

"I do, Mama," Little Reggie beamed with pride. "You and dad have always told me the world is full of mean people. I am never to be ashamed. I cannot allow them to treat me with disrespect. None of us should sit around and watch others be treated with disrespect, though. Not black people, not white people, not kids with cleft palates, not bald people, and not fat people. No one in this world should make others feel bad for who they are. It's just what I believe."

Denise looked at Big Reggie, trying to gauge his thoughts. They had always tried to prepare Little Reg for the real world. As the first African-American student in Millstadt elementary and currently the only African-American living in the village, they had always feared potential bullying. For the most part, though, they had been pleasantly surprised at the reception and acceptance he had received.

Little Reggie continued, "That's when we had a great idea. We thought that each of us should come up with a nickname and show Clifton that names can only hurt you if you let them. We agreed that our nicknames needed to be something that would make each of us mad enough to want to punch someone for saying it." His voice became louder, his enthusiasm showing.

"What did you come up with?" Big Reggie asked, beaming with pride. Denise had the sneaking suspicion that he already knew the answer.

Reggie frowned and said, "Now, don't be mad, Mama, please promise." He raised his brown eyes to hers and waited for Denise to nod before he continued.

"Hold on," he added, "I need you to know that we all agreed that we are the only ones allowed to use the nicknames. Does that make sense?" he asked, looking to either one of them for acknowledgement.

"It makes perfect sense," Big Reg answered. His eyes gleamed with admiration.

"Well, Clifton is now Clefty Fields. He even laughed when we said it. Clifton did not flinch; he did not cry. I guess the nickname did not bother him when we said it because he knows we like him. We all agreed to keep his nickname until he has his operation. He laughed a couple of times, but I think it was because of Whitey B's antics. She can be so silly."

"Whitey B?" Denise asked, smiling when her husband raised an eyebrow.

"Preston is now Pooch Belly," Rusty added, ignoring her question. "I am Rusty, though I am okay with Rusty Rogers, or Little Rusty." He looked up and smiled at his dad. "Can I call you Big Rusty, dad?"

Big Reggie leaned back and laughed aloud, offering with sincerity, "Of course, my little man, of course." Denise noticed they were still holding hands.

"So, there's Clefty Fields, Pooch Belly, Rusty Rogers," he stopped for a few seconds and finished, "and Whitey B." Little Reggie shrugged before adding, "We chose our nicknames. We agreed that only the four of us could use them. Well, it worked. Clefty, I mean Clifton, laughed at each of our nicknames. We also made a promise that he could be in our group from now on."

Denise sat statue still, amazed by the number of emotions she had experienced in the last fifteen minutes. She had been angry enough to swat her six-year-old with a belt the moment he had come home from school. He had accepted the responsibility and the consequence, far better than she would have done at that age, especially for doing what she thought was the right thing. She had been angry to find out that he had gotten into a fight. She had been embarrassed when the Principal called her this afternoon.

Little Reggie's bravery, for lack of a better word, had quieted her anger. She began to feel guilty that she had not given him a chance to tell his side of the story.

I will never make that mistake again, she thought with apprehension, knowing full well that parenting was not easy and that she would make the same mistake a hundred times in the years to come.

It surprised her that a group of six-year-olds had attempted to help each other deal with a terrible situation by offering a truly unique solution.

Now that her son had finished his story, she still felt guilty but was proud of him.

"If Clefty," she corrected herself, "If Clifton was happy, then why did you punch Tommy?" Denise asked.

"You and dad have always told me that I should not be afraid to stand up to bullies. You have told me never to let anyone make me feel bad or sad because of my skin color. I think that also means that I should not let anyone make my friends feel bad just because they have a Cleft Palate." His lower lip stuck out again, daring her to argue against his logic.

Denise's lips thinned before she added, "You cannot save the world, Reggie Rogers. Unfortunately, there will always be bullies. But if you try to protect everyone, you will be very frustrated." Her words stung, feeling ominous.

"I know. I know," the little boy answered. "That's probably true, but I decided that I can protect Clifton. We were all happy when we made him happy. But Tommy needed the beat down, either way. Sorry, Mama," he added, watching her face. "He needed a lesson in manners. I walked over and taught him that lesson. I can tell you this Mama, I know that I promised that I would not fight at school, but if I catch Tommy making fun of Clifton again, I am going over to his house after school and punch him in the mouth again. Or, I will find him at the park and punch him again. Bullies need the beat down, every once in a while, just to remind them that they are not in charge."

Little Reggie leaned back, releasing his dad's hand, crossed his arms and said, "We should not let bullies rule the world, Mama. We just can't. Otherwise, why are we even here?"

Denise sat stunned. Big Reggie was speechless. They looked at each other, wanting the other one to say something to Little Reggie.

Something still nagged at her though she knew better than to ask. Ignoring the little voice in her head advising her not to do it, Denise frowned again and said, "Okay. I understand the Clefty Fields nickname, though I think it is despicable. I understand Rusty Rogers, though the logic of it bothers me. I'm assuming Pooch Belly is Anderson Compton though he comes from one of the nicest families in Millstadt, and I would be livid to find anyone making fun of his weight."

She looked at Big Reg, watching his big grin return.

She asked, confused, "But Whitey B? Why is she called Whitey B?"

Rusty looked up at his mom and said matter-of-factly, "Because she's white Mama and her last name is Branigan."

MAMA BEAR

"HAVE A GOOD DAY, RUSTY," THE TINY WOMAN OFFERED WITH A SMILE when she passed by him in the hallway.

He had gone back to his locker to find his math book. Stuffing it into his backpack, he responded, "You, too Mrs. Eckert," returning her smile with genuine affection. She taught seventh grade Science and was currently one of his favorite teachers. All of his teachers were awesome, but she took his favorite subject, Science, to an entirely new level.

Just this afternoon, she had wowed all of them with what she called the *Eggsperiment*. Rusty had watched, almost mesmerized, as she swatted a pie plate from beneath an egg. The egg had been placed on the standing end of an empty toilet paper roll. The students "oohed and awwed" in response when the egg, instead of flying away, dropped straight down into the glass positioned below the plate. It cracked, and yolk filled the glass. Mrs. Eckert explained that inertia kept the egg from flying across the room. She had called it "proof of the first law of motion."

"And what is the first law of motion?"

The whole class responded in unison, "Inertia."

The entire class spent the rest of the period using hard-boiled eggs to replicate her experiment. Many of them had difficulty knocking the pie plate away evenly. Rusty had done it quickly, three times, before Suzie asked him to show her what she was doing wrong. The class laughed, asked questions related to gravity and inertia, and had left more curious than when they had entered. *That's why she's such a great teacher,* he thought, reaching the front doors. He walked out, looked around, and spotted Suzie.

Rusty laughed to himself and thought with affection, *Whitey B.* Once they entered Middle School, Suzie decided that the nickname 'Whitey B' had to go. On the first day of school, the four friends gathered during PE to talk over her concerns. They listened patiently as each person in the group made their case. Clifton and Preston, who chose to go by his middle name, decided they were ready to drop their nicknames now that high school was just around the corner.

"Who wants to enter high school known as Pooch Belly?" Preston asked, looking to the others for support.

"I am good with that," he responded when Suzie suggested they drop the names for good. "I don't like Pooch Belly anymore either," he said, acknowledging her feelings about Whitey B. Preston had hit a growth spurt a little more than a year ago and was now the second tallest in the class. Both he and Rusty were a bit shy of six feet in height. Preston had also slimmed down considerably. Rusty suspected making the basketball team was the reason. The coach had the players running all the time, though this year, it did not include Rusty. Rusty had decided to take a year off from basketball even though his coach pleaded for him to change his mind. He had decided it was time to hit the weights and beef up for high school. In two more years, Rusty planned on playing football for the Belleville West Mighty Maroons.

Either way, they all agreed. "The nicknames have run their course," Clifton added. Rusty smiled inwardly, remembering how it all started years ago. Thanks to his mom and her efforts at Memorial Hospital, the whole town had gotten behind a fundraiser to help Clifton have his surgery for his Cleft Palate. It had taken two years to gather the funds, but back in the third grade, Clifton had his surgery, and only a tiny scar remained. The group of friends had continued to use the nicknames, more so out of tradition than anything else. The handles became terms of endearment, especially among the four of them.

"So it's agreed. We'll always be friends, but it's time to put the nicknames behind us," Suzie queried. She looked to Preston, who nodded with agreement. Clifton did the same. She looked to Rusty, who shook his head.

Standing outside the school, searching for his best friend, Rusty remembered the look of confusion on Suzie's face when he had shaken his head in disagreement. Before she could ask, he had added, "I'd like to keep Rusty if that's okay. I like it. I promise to stop using your nicknames, though." The other three had smiled, since they had expected him to say it. By the time they entered the second grade, he had insisted that his teachers and the other students refer to him as Rusty. He wore the name like a Badge of Honor.

Finding Suzie standing with a group of friends, Rusty walked out of the Middle School with a big smile on his face.

"Rusty, over here," she yelled. She waved him over excitedly and said to three other girls, "Okay. See you tonight." The girls boarded the school bus while Suzie waited for him to catch up to her.

"Where to first?" she asked. Their parents had permitted them to hang in town as long as they walked home together. Her mom had only agreed since Rusty would be there with her. They promised to cut across the recently harvested field instead of walking the roads home. Their mothers had hounded them, last night, insisting they stick together.

"Let's head to Leider," Rusty responded. Liederkranz Park was a favorite hangout for many of the Millstadt kids. Every Friday, many middle school students hung there playing basketball, throwing Frisbees, or sitting around the picnic tables. The kids used it as a refuge, the last chance to hang with friends. They walked towards the park located less than a fourth of a mile from the school.

"Let's get a soda before the walk home," Suzie pleaded. They had been laughing so hard at the park, enjoying hanging with their friends that she needed something to drink. Rusty nodded in agreement, and they started walking back to Main Street.

The two of them talked incessantly about their plans for the weekend. Suzie had a sleepover, and Rusty planned to play online on his PlayStation 3. "Who are you gaming with?" she asked.

Rusty laughed, knowing that she already knew the answer. "Tommy," Rusty responded. It had amazed his friends, but after he punched Tommy Krueger in the face in Kindergarten, Rusty worked hard to cultivate his friendship.

Back in first grade, when they had challenged him on it, Rusty explained that everyone made mistakes. "If we aren't willing to forgive and forget, no one will ever get along." It had taken them a few years longer than Rusty, but eventually, the other three agreed that Tommy was okay. Even Clifton had long since forgiven Tommy for his harsh words.

The two friends made it to the Four-Way stop at Jefferson Street and 158. With all its nearby businesses, the intersection was considered the heart of Millstadt.

Suzie started to cross the street, but Rusty held out his hand and stopped her. She looked puzzled.

"Why don't we go in here?" he asked, pointing to their right at Johnson's Convenience Mart.

Suzie frowned, shaking her head in disagreement. "I don't think that's a great idea," she answered. "Mom always told me there is a rougher group of people who shop at Johnson's." She grabbed Rusty by the elbow and tugged, hoping he would keep walking. "Let's keep going. The IGA is only a few blocks away."

Rusty resisted her tug, looking back at the grocery store. Mr. Johnson's store had been there ever since he could remember, but he could not think of a time that either of his parents had ever taken him there for anything. He turned and started walking, dragging Suzie along with him. "Come on, Suz. Let's save ourselves the steps, get a soda, and get home more quickly."

Suzie released his elbow before saying, "I don't think it's a good idea." She could not explain why not when he asked her for a specific reason. Giving up, she caught up to him just before he opened the door and walked in.

It was a well-lit store, clean, with items stocked neatly on rows and rows of shelves. They both heard the familiar eighties music from one of the classic St. Louis radio stations playing softly in the background.

Rusty could feel Mr. Johnson's eyes boring into him with suspicion when they entered the store. The older man stood behind the counter with his arms crossed. His face held a wrinkled frown. He huffed a little when Rusty, followed by Suzie, walked past and headed to the soda fridge.

An older woman, grey-haired and with glasses, walked by the two of them and cleared her throat rudely. Rusty's eyes followed her movements. She deliberately put her few groceries back onto the shelf, walked to the counter, and whispered something to Mr. Johnson. The man shook his head, apologizing to the woman. Rusty could not quite make out his words. The woman huffed loudly and left the store. The man's frown deepened into a scowl.

Suzie hurriedly grabbed a Mountain Dew, and a Pepsi and the two of them walked over to the counter. She placed both sodas before Mr. Johnson and began reaching into her pocket for the money.

Suzie halted when Mr. Johnson challenged them. "Did you steal anything back there?" the old man demanded sternly. He looked at Rusty without flinching.

"No sir, we don't steal," Rusty responded calmly. He maintained eye contact, watching as Mr. Johnson's face turned a darker shade of red at his words.

"All of your kind steals, kid. It is why I was watching you so closely. You are also scaring off my customers. There are people in this town who do not want you here. We do not want you in my store, we do not want you in our school, and we do not want you in Millstadt. You're spooky to us, kid. That's why we all refer to you as the Spook when we talk about you." The man finished, satisfied with his words. He crossed his arms, passively waiting for Rusty to say something.

Suzie laid two dollars on the counter, grabbed the sodas, and said, "Come on, Rusty. Mr. Johnson, we don't need any change, and you don't have to worry we won't be back." Her face, red with embarrassment, could barely contain the anger that she was feeling.

The man laughed aloud, his words following them out of the store, "Rusty! Rusty! Oh, that is priceless. Your nickname is Rusty." He cackled, his harsh words stinging into Rusty's soul.

The two of them exited the store without looking back. When they made it to the corner, Suzie burst into tears, crying, "I'm sorry. I hate that man." She handed Rusty his soda, confused by his facial expression. He opened his soda and calmly took a sip. He did not look angry. He did not look as though what had happened bothered him in the least.

"Aren't you mad?" she asked angrily, "I know why my mom told me to avoid that place. That man is wicked. So are most of his customers."

"He's not wicked, Suz," Rusty said gloomily. "That man is just a lonely man. I can see it in his eyes. I feel sorry for him. Honestly, I did not hear the conviction in his voice when he spoke. He does not believe in what he said. In a few hours, he will even feel bad about treating us like that." Rusty stated it so matter-of-factly that Suzie had difficulty arguing.

She thought for a few seconds, taking a deep breath to calm her nerves. "Not us, Rusty. You. You are sugar coating what just happened. That man is a racist, pure and simple. I hate him. I hate everything about him. I am sorry we went in there, and I will never go back," she bristled a little when he shook his head in disagreement. It was the one area that she thought the two of them would be in total agreement.

Rusty countered, "I think he said it because of the elderly woman. I do not hate him, Suz. I just feel sorry for him, that's all." He took another sip of soda and turned to walk home.

They walked in complete silence past the school, across the recently harvested bean field, and separated without a word at his driveway.

"Thank you, Maria. I do appreciate it," Denise said gravely. She had answered the phone as she and Reggie sat around the kitchen table playing a hand of Rummy. Rusty had already gone to his room without a word to play games on his PlayStation. It had felt odd, but they chalked it up to his interest in gaming.

The moment she hung up the receiver, Reggie could tell that she was mad. "What was that about?" he asked, the muscles in his shoulders beginning to tighten. Only a few things could bring out the Mama Bear. Somehow, he knew it involved Rusty.

"Maria said Suzie has been crying for about an hour. They went to get a soda at Johnson's store," she started, her voice heavy with frustration. She watched Reggie's face closely, happy to see the muscles in his jawline contract tightly.

"Well. Mr. Johnson let his racism get the better of him. He called Rusty a Spook and told him that most of the town didn't want him here," she finished, seething with anger. "This is the dark side of Millstadt though I am sure every town has its problems." Denise stood up, walked over to the sink, and filled a glass with cool tap water. Her hands were shaking.

She lowered her head in prayer and demanded, "Let's go." Reggie stood up, looking into her eyes. He recognized that look and headed to their bedroom.

"Where are you going?" she asked, puzzled.

Calmly, he turned to her and answered, "If you do what I think you are going to do, we better bring some backup." He disappeared for a few minutes into their bedroom. He had a jacket on when he returned, but she could see the bulge beneath, along his left side.

"Do you think you will need that?" she asked, the reality of the moment starting to sink in.

He answered gravely, "I do unless you have changed your mind about going." He knew that she had not considered changing her mind. Mama Bear was about to be on full display.

She grabbed the keys, went to the garage and picked up Rusty's Aluminum baseball bat. Big Reg did not flinch in surprise. Getting into their car quietly, they drove to town without saying another word.

"Store's closing, folks," Mr. Johnson said to the woman and the man as they entered. He looked up from his receipts, curious. "I must have forgotten to lock the door. Please come back tomorrow." He looked nervously at the baseball bat in the woman's right hand. They had entered so quietly that the bells hung above the door barely made a sound.

Denise Rogers entered the store quietly, ignoring the older man sitting at the counter. She did not make eye contact with him as she walked over to the soda aisle. Standing before the shelves of Pepsi, Coke, and Mountain Dew, Mama Bear turned and looked into Mr. Johnson's eyes. His eyes widened as he realized what she was getting ready to do. Mr. Johnson glanced at the man standing with his back to the door, his right hand hovering near the left side of his jacket.

Denise lifted the baseball bat above her right shoulder, brought it down in a wide arc, and smashed it into one of the refrigerator's doors. The glass shattered into a million pieces, with glass shrapnel flying across the rows of groceries in every direction.

"What the hell are you doing, lady?" Mr. Johnson yelled, reaching beneath his counter. He froze when Reggie reached into his jacket and pulled out a pistol. "I wouldn't do that if I were you," Reggie said, his voice flat and unemotional.

Mr. Johnson stood back up, looking afraid, and asked, "Why?" He turned to the woman waiting for her explanation.

Denise answered, looking at him with fury, her voice full of scorn, "I think you had the opportunity to meet my son this afternoon, didn't you?" She lifted the bat, stepped to the next glass doorway, and smashed it in.

Mr. Johnson jumped, startled once again by the sound of the broken glass. He stammered, "Ma'am, I don't know what your son told you, but it's not worth going to jail over." He lifted his chin, proud that he had kept his voice calm when threatening her with the police.

"I look forward to the police getting involved, Mr. Johnson. The moment I get out of jail, I will be coming back here to burn this place to the ground." Her nostrils flared wildly as she approached the counter with the bat in hand.

Mr. Johnson backed up away from her, the fear evident on his face. He raised his hands in surrender and said, "Okay. I will not call the police. Please stop, and we will just call it even." He looked to Reggie for support, shrugging.

Reggie shrugged back and said, "It's all up to Mama Bear." He looked back at Denise and waited patiently for her next move.

Denise leaned into Mr. Johnson and whispered, "If I ever find out that you mistreat my son again, we will be back, and as God is my witness, there will be hell to pay." She slammed the bat onto the counter, watching packs of gum fly into the air. Mr. Johnson jumped backwards, nodding that he understood.

Denise and Reggie drove quietly back to their home, allowing themselves the opportunity to calm down before going back into the house. They agreed not to take the anger with them. When they arrived, as Big Reg went to put his gun back into the gun safe, Denise went into Rusty's bedroom. It was empty.

"Reg, Rusty's not here," she said, worried. "His game is on pause, but he is not in the house."

"He is probably over at Suzie's," Reggie responded, hopeful that Little Reggie had gone to visit his friend. "She has some girls over, and it's his chance to flirt with a couple of them." He tried to chuckle but could tell by the look on her face that she did not find it funny. "Let's go over and see if he's there."

⚜

"Are you kidding me?" Mr. Johnson cried out, bewildered, the moment the door to his store opened, and he looked up to see Rusty standing before him. "Look, kid. You already got me into hot water with your parents. Why are you here? Did they send you back in for an apology? I am sorry. Okay, I am sorry."

Rusty looked at the glass shards covering the floor and said apologetically, "I am sorry Mr. Johnson. Sometimes my mom can be a little overprotective." He pointed to the glass strewn across the floor.

"Are you okay?" His genuine look of concern was too much for Mr. Johnson. The man shuddered and sighed heavily. He took a few deep breaths before looking up at Rusty, "Why are you here, kid?"

"I am here to ask you for a job?" Rusty answered with sincerity. "Before you answer, I need you to know that my parents did not send me here. If anything, they will be pissed that I came back into your store for any reason."

Mr. Johnson interrupted, "You want a job?" He looked incredulously at Rusty. "Are you serious? You want a job?" The tired-looking old man seemed confused by Rusty's presence.

Rusty nodded and answered with conviction, "Mr. Johnson, I told my friend Suzie that I don't think you are a mean man. While you said some hateful things, I want you to know that I am here to prove that you are wrong. I want to prove to you that how you feel about me and blacks, in general, is misguided. I am not a thief, and I never will be."

Mr. Johnson sat down on the stool behind his counter, thinking about Rusty's statement. He smiled slightly and said, "You have balls, kid." He paused for a few seconds and offered, "Yes, you can have a job, though I will admit to you but not your parents, especially that Mama of yours, that I like the idea that it might piss them off. I need someone to stock my shelves from five o'clock every evening until about seven o'clock. Agreed?"

Rusty smiled broadly and said, "Yes. Thank you, sir. I promise you that you will not be disappointed." He reached out his right hand and waited for Mr. Johnson's to offer his own.

Mr. Johnson shook it before saying, "See you Monday, kid."

Instead of turning to leave, Rusty went to the door leading to the back of the store.

"Where are you going?" Mr. Johnson asked in surprise. "You don't need to start until Monday."

Rusty answered, "I'm getting a broom. We need to get this mess cleaned up since you will have customers tomorrow." He spent the next thirty minutes sweeping up the glass and putting everything back into place.

"A job!" Denise said, her voice rising to an octave that Rusty had not heard in a long time.

The three of them sat around the kitchen table, reviewing the events that had unfolded this evening.

Rusty had arrived back home, aware that his parents could see his journey across the field from their vantage point on the porch.

He explained that he had overheard their conversation and knew they would give Mr. Johnson what he liked to call the beat down. It reminded him of his response to Tommy all those years ago.

"Yes. That is right, Mama. I am going to work ten hours a week stocking shelves for Mr. Johnson," he answered proudly. His lip thrust forward as it always did when he meant to stand his ground.

"But Rusty, that man mistreated you. You cannot change the evil that is inside a person's heart," she stammered, looking pleadingly at her husband for support. Big Reg was deep in thought, though, clearly fighting his feelings about what Rusty had just told them. "That man is a racist."

"He is no more a racist than I am, Mama," Rusty started. He paused when she blurted a response.

"You cannot be a racist. I have read you the definition and have told you that many times," she said, frustrated.

"Mama, first of all, I know the true definition of racism. I do not need the definition changed just to make me feel better about myself. Racism is racism. Whether it's white on black, black on yellow, or yellow on red, it does not matter." His words shocked her. Denise had raised him to be confident and to be an independent thinker. She did not understand how or why he had fallen into his beliefs.

"Sometimes, Mama, it is true that people are beyond saving. Sometimes it is true, but when I looked into Mr. Johnson's eyes, I did not see the evil that spilt out of his mouth. I saw a lonely man. I can feel it in my heart. It is not too late to save him."

Rusty watched Denise's eyebrows lift in surprise. She answered him, half-heartedly, "How can you know what is in a person's heart?" She could not argue with his reasoning. Wanting to save others, even if it meant saving them from themselves, was admirable. It spoke to their Faith and the core principles that she held close to her heart.

"I can, Mama," he responded, his face growing more serious. He threw both of them off-guard by changing the topic. "Do you remember when the lights went out when I was a baby?" Rusty looked up at the kitchen lights after he asked her the question, wanting the gesture to help prod her memories.

"How do you know about that?" Denise asked fearfully. She had never spoken to anyone other than Big Reggie about that moment. The effects of that day still gave her goosebumps these many years later.

Rusty ignored her question and said, "Mama. I remember looking up at you when all the other babies started crying."

"How can you remember that? You were just a baby?" she asked.

Rusty added, "The light from all the cell phones lit up the room. I looked up through the window and looked into your eyes. Do you remember?" He waited for her to nod before continuing. "I looked into your eyes. They held a deep sadness, and I knew it was not too late to save you," the boy offered. Rusty stood up, walked over to her, and leaned in to give her a big hug. "I knew you were lonely and still grieving. I could see it in your eyes. When people are lonely, Mama, it comes out in different ways." He hoped she could understand why he argued on Mr. Johnson's behalf.

"Sometimes it comes out in anger as it did with Mr. Johnson today. Even the older woman, the one who put her groceries back onto the shelf, is not too far gone. She can be saved."

Silence hung in the kitchen as the two adults listened intently to their son's words. "Sometimes it comes out in other ways, too. You were sad, Mama. Even as a baby, I knew I needed to save you from what you were about to do."

"Don't," was all that she could whisper in response. Denise shook her head from side to side, the tears leaking from her closed eyes. She put her face into her hands and started to sob.

Big Reggie leaned in close and asked, "Rusty, what do you mean? What was she was going to do?" The hairs on his neck stood on end at his son's words.

Rusty looked at his father and offered, morbidly, "I arrived just in time, dad. She was going to kill herself."

THE LAST HUMAN

THE MIDDLE-AGED WOMAN, SOMEONE WHOM HE HAD NEVER MET before, leaned over and whispered into Rusty's ear, "Young man, you have my deepest sympathy, and I want you to know your Mama is in our prayers." She reached out a white, gloved hand and shook his hand firmly, though she appeared more fragile than anyone Rusty had ever met. He returned the handshake, afraid that he might inadvertently crush her tiny hand.

Minutes earlier, she had quietly knocked at the door. Rusty, who had been sitting alone in the living room, greeted her and asked her to come inside. She refused the request, not wanting to impose as she had called it, before handing him a large bowl of spaghetti and meatballs. "I have known your Mama for more than thirty-five years," she started, a tear streaking down her left cheek. "We went to Belleville West High School together before my family and I moved away my senior year. Once a Maroon, always a Maroon, we used to say in high school. I also knew your daddy, though not as well as your Mama. God rest his soul." She shook Rusty's hand once more before turning away to walk back to her car. Her husband, a large man with a big moustache, sat stoically behind the steering wheel of the large, tan-colored vehicle. He waved at Rusty before backing the car out of the driveway.

Rusty shut the door, taking the food bowl to the kitchen to find a place for it in the refrigerator. *What am I going to do with all this food?* he wondered.

His mother had been placed on Hospice Care four days ago. A full-time caregiver had come to the house to provide her with the support needed to help make her passing as peaceful as possible. Rusty spent the last three days in shock, wandering from the kitchen, back to her bedroom to check on her, and then back to the living room. The days had been a monotonous whirlwind of well-wishers, people from the community who wanted Rusty to know that they were thinking about him and his mother. Cancer had come on quickly, and Denise, who Rusty considered the strongest woman he had ever known, seemed to have given up. Her body withered away quickly.

During these last few days, as she grew weaker, she asked for Rusty often. The nurse would bring him to her and then allow the two of them time alone. He sat beside her bed, holding her hand and whispering to her, "I love you, Mama." Most of the time, she would nod that she understood, and a few times, she became lucid enough for them to have a conversation.

"I miss your Dad, Rusty," she had said earlier this morning. Rusty leaned his head onto her blanket and sobbed in agreement. Almost a year ago, his father died of a heart attack while working on a job site. "He was a good man, and you are a good man," she continued, reaching down with her left hand and caressing the top of his head. Her voice sounded raspy and hoarse. "Don't be afraid, Rusty. The world is a big place, but your daddy, your brother Zach, and I will be watching over you. We will always help keep you safe." She smiled, even though the effort appeared more painful than it had been worth.

"I'm not afraid, Mama," he responded quietly. He looked up into her eyes and then lowered his head back onto the bed. Rusty offered a quick prayer, thankful for both of his parents. He could not imagine how life would have been any better if they had not chosen him. They were a family.

She continued, as if she had not heard his response, "I am glad you saved me, son. Without you, I would have left your daddy here all alone in this world." Denise patted his head and offered, "I want you to have Faith. Do you hear me?" The words came out with conviction and full of energy.

"You know I do," he answered breathlessly.

Rusty lifted his head off the blanket and looked into her eyes. "What did you say, Mama?"

Denise had mumbled something quietly, under her breath, that caught his attention. "They need you," she said, the words barely a murmur. She patted his head again and rubbed her fingers along his right cheek.

"Who? Who needs me?" he asked, confused. He grabbed her hand and pressed the back of it against his cheek, her hands cool and soft.

Her hand slipped off the side of his face, landing softly on the bed beside him. Rusty thought she had fallen asleep, or worse, but was pleasantly surprised to see her looking into his eyes, awake and her eyes gleaming.

"You saved me. Your task here is complete. By choosing me all those years ago," she started.

"We chose each other, Mama," he answered in response.

Denise smiled, her eyes tired, "You saved me. You made it possible for me to join your father. I thank you. Our world no longer needs you, son. His does, though, and desperately." She remained focused, staring at his face and waiting for him to answer.

Confused by her words, Rusty thought pain, her medications, or a combination of both might be causing her to hallucinate. "It is okay, Mama," he said, picking up her hand again and squeezing it gently. He tried to soothe her worries, speaking softly and nodding that he understood.

"Rusty," Denise began with her voice clear and stern. "My soul has been saved thanks to you, but the Devil incarnate is gaining an army. He wants to bring death and destruction to the world. Do you hear me? He brings death and destruction, violence and decay. I pity the innocent, Rusty, for there are far too many who simply do not know the evil that is about to be set loose upon the Known World." It was a moment of pure clarity, one that he had not seen from her in weeks.

"The Known World? Do you mean here, in Millstadt?" he asked, confused. He was grateful to have the opportunity to speak with her, though her words puzzled him.

His mom sighed but smiled lovingly. She ignored his question and added, "I don't know if you can save them as you saved me. Nevertheless, son, you have to try. You may die trying, but at least you died on the side of righteousness. That is not a bad place to be when you die. Do you understand?" she added, her words desperate.

He did not.

Denise paused, waiting as the hospice nurse came in to check on her. "Are you okay, honey?" she asked, concerned.

Rusty leaned around to look at his mother; she seemed to be fast asleep. The hospice nurse turned and whispered, "She's just resting. Maybe you should get some rest, too. I don't think you have slept in three days." Her worried look was almost too much for Rusty. He stood up to leave but noticed his mom's Bible on the nightstand beside the bed.

"When did she get that out?" he asked, curious. He had read the Bible with her many times but thought she always kept it in her closet.

"I don't know how that got there," the woman answered, "I have been with her the entire day, and I did not notice it."

Rusty shivered.

"We spent most of the day talking about you, those times when she could talk," the woman began. "She told me that you might go to Belleville West high school in the fall. She mentioned, more than once, how she thought you would be a big football star." The woman smiled, looking to offer some words of comfort to Rusty.

"It is strange, though," the woman added.

Rusty asked, "What's strange?"

"Each time she talked about you and football, she always added that you were going on a trip first. She said football would have to wait. I asked where you were going, and she always gave me the same answer. He is going to battle Lucifer."

She looked at Rusty bewildered before adding, "Are you sure you didn't get that Bible out while I was in the other room? It's okay if you did?" She raised her eyebrows, waiting for Rusty's admission. When he remained silent, the nurse shook her head disapprovingly.

Rusty picked up the Bible, perplexed. *Where did she think I was going?* he thought. With thick, gilded lettering, the red-leather bound Bible had always been one of his Mama's favorite possessions. He found her bookmark, opened it and read the title, silently, *The Book of Revelations.*

He tried to smile at the woman but was sure she could see his sadness and said, "I think I will go for a walk." The woman nodded as he stood up to leave. She went to sit in the chair next to his mother.

"I'm sorry to hear about you, mother," Mr. Johnson said to Rusty, deep concern in his voice. "I want you to know that you are always welcome to stay with me. Your mother and I started on the wrong foot. I am sure to blame. She was a strong woman, and I respect her very much. How many years have you been working for me?" he asked.

"Almost two," Rusty responded. Mr. Johnson and his mother had come to terms though it had taken almost six months before Rusty could talk her into returning to the store. By the end of the conversation, Denise had shaken hands with Mr. Johnson and thanked him profusely for allowing Rusty to work in his store. They had mended their broken fences.

"It's gone by that quickly?" Mr. Johnson asked, amazed. "I am sorry, Rusty. It is not fair to lose your dad last year and now with your Mama being in a bad way. Do not worry, though; you will always have a place in my home. We can help get you through high school and college. It's the least we can do for you." Mr. Johnson was fond of referring to 'we,' when he meant him, since he had never married.

"Mr. Johnson, you don't owe me anything. If anything, I owe you. You had faith in me even though you had no reason to believe in me. That takes guts, and it takes courage," Rusty added firmly, meaning every word. It filled him with pride to know that he had been correct about Mr. Johnson. *If we had not offered forgiveness and mended our fences, where would he be?*

"No," Mr. Johnson said quickly, "what I did that first day was cowardly. I knew it the moment you left the store. I regretted those words deeply. You saved me, son; you saved me." His final three words trailed off into a whisper. Mr. Johnson broke eye contact, looking downward at the counter, sheepishly.

Rusty smiled at his friend and offered a hand to shake. "Mr. Johnson, I am going for a walk. I will see you soon." Mr. Johnson looked at the Bible in his left hand and smiled.

He waved at Mr. Johnson and left the store.

Rusty turned south, walking along Jefferson Street, letting his mind wander while his feet went on autopilot. He kept thinking about his mother's words, about how a brain worked in strange ways, especially when a person was on death's door. *She thought I was going on a trip? And, who needs me?*

Three blocks later, Rusty looked up, startled to find he was walking parallel to Schmittling's Junkyard. The eight-foot-high, chain-linked fence ran the entire length of three city blocks before heading back west. Rusty looked at the piles of rusted cars, the rows of metal piled eight to ten feet high and stopped to stare in wonderment. There were numerous towers of car tires stacked neatly into piles of many sizes throughout the junkyard. His family had driven past here often, and each time he looked at the junkyard with awe.

Each of those cars has a story, Rusty thought. He had always wanted to explore the junkyard, but there never seemed to be enough time for him to do so. Rusty looked behind him and then to the left and the right. He was alone. "What the hell," Rusty said aloud. He needed a distraction, something to keep his mind off his mom since the morbid thoughts were difficult to keep at bay. Even though he appreciated others for the offer to live with them, Rusty's mother and father had been his world. He was going to be devastated without her. He was going to be all alone.

He leapt onto the fence. Rusty's fingers gripped the spaces as he poked the tip of his shoes through the holes below. He began to climb. He cleared the top before landing lightly on the ground on the opposite side, his hands in the dirt. Rusty stood up, brushed his hands off on his jeans, and whistled. "Look at all of these cars." He looked around once more to make sure that he was alone and started walking between the rows of cars, stopping periodically to look inside the windows. Halfway down the first row, his eyes stopped on a rusted out, red Acura NSX, and he stopped to gaze at it. The body and the design of the car made him wish he could drive one. *In two more years, I will have my license,* he thought. Rusty promised himself that he would look into buying an Acura when he had saved enough money.

Rusty walked for almost ten minutes, astonished that the rows and rows of cars seemed to extend forever into the horizon. He squinted, covering his eyes from the sun hanging barely above the trees in the distance.

With his attention focused on the rows of cars stacked one on top of the other, Rusty was oblivious to a small hole, a tiny puncture created in the fabric of air behind him. Hovering a few feet off the ground, the little circle, no larger than a dime, snowballed. The diameter of the dark, swirling mass of nothingness expanded, its edges tugged open further by two wrinkled fingers that worked quietly on the edges. The fingers enlarged the hole and soon, a pair of hands, pale and grey, joined in on the effort.

Spinning slowly, the empty mass of grey-black grew to more than three feet in diameter. Rusty held his mom's Bible close to his chest and bent down to pick up a rust-covered hubcap at his feet. Ignorant to the pair of hands reaching out from within the blackness, Rusty did not notice them encircling his waist until a split second too late. He looked downward in time to see the fingers of the right-hand lock onto the left wrist. He started to yell out in surprise but did not do so. The two hands yanked backwards, forcefully tugging him through the collapsing hole.

Dragged back into the swirling cloud of nothingness, Rusty tried to yell out in surprise, "What the hell?" His words were absorbed like a sponge and sounded no louder than a whisper. Seconds later, he landed harshly onto his back, looking up into a star-filled sky. The brightness of the sun had disappeared, replaced by gloomy darkness. The moon was out, full and bright, but it gave Rusty little comfort. He jumped to his feet with his arms flailing around in desperation. An older man stood a few feet away, his eyes sparkling with joy in the moonlight.

"Wait," the old man whispered. He raised the fingers on his right hand to his lips, trying to quiet Rusty.

"Wait!" Rusty yelled, his voice echoing through a row of trees.

Wincing at the words, the man looked around, worried. His eyes darted into the trees and then back to Rusty.

Miles away, a howling pack of wolves responded to his yell. Their calls, Rusty hoped they were a long distance away, came springing back quickly through the darkened woods.

"Quiet, you damned fool," the old man demanded, his voice barely more than a whisper. He turned around in desperation, his eyes searching the shadows in the trees. Rusty could see the worry lines on his forehead, even in the darkness.

The man turned and began trotting away, the quickness of his pace surprising Rusty.

He waved for Rusty to follow but did not look back. Tempted to refuse, Rusty changed his mind when another cacophony of howling, much closer than it had been before, prodded him to catch up to the man. They reached a shallow creek, but instead of crossing it, the old man turned and jogged in it, keeping his feet in the water. He gestured for Rusty to do the same. The icy water soaked through his tennis shoes and his socks, the cold heightening his senses. They ran in silence for more than an hour before finally coming to a halt at the base of a small waterfall. He gestured for Rusty to hurry before disappearing through the cascading water.

Rusty stepped through the water quickly, wiped the water from his face, and let out a surprise. Less than a foot away, a rock wall opened when the man pushed heavily against it. The space, just large enough for the two of them to slide into, remained opened behind them once they were through.

"Quickly, you fool," the old man hissed, gesturing for Rusty to help push the heavy boulder back into place. Once it sealed tightly, the man leaned down and locked it with a lever. He did the same midway up and then once again at the top.

Rusty's mind was in turmoil. Confused about what just happened, he needed time to process everything. The sound of the waterfall and the howling wolves had disappeared, replaced by darkness. He did not know which of the two he found more disquieting.

They were standing in silence for a few seconds. It unnerved Rusty. The old man snapped his fingers, and a torch, mounted onto the opposite cave wall, burst into flames. The light infused the narrow passageway, causing Rusty to blink against its brightness. Without a word, the older man turned and walked away. Rusty followed.

"Let me get this straight," Rusty cried out, bewildered about what the old man had already told him. The two sat around a small campfire, a pile of burning logs encircled by small, grey stones. They had talked for more than two hours, with the old man answering some of his questions but being evasive when asked to answer others. Rusty's mind was still racing, and his heart was pounding.

"I am no longer on Earth," he said incredulously. He had to be dreaming.

"I do not know of the place you call Earth," the old man answered. He smiled with pride, though his eyes held a level of weariness that Rusty had never seen before. "Is that where you are from?"

"I am from Millstadt. Yes. It's a tiny town in Illinois, which is in the United States, which is on Earth," Rusty exclaimed, trying not to lose his patience.

"Where am I, again?" Rusty asked, confused. He did not think he would get a different answer to the same question but decided to try anyway.

"You are in the Lands of the Khans," the old man said. "Please sit down, young man. I will try to do a better job of explaining." He waited for Rusty to comply before beginning.

The older man, his grey eyes matching his grey eyebrows, had a full head of hair. Streaks of long, grey hair fell to his thin shoulders. He sighed heavily. "I have lived in the Lands of the Khans," he said, holding his arms out widely, "for more than one hundred and twenty years. My family and I were farmers. It was a harsh life, working from sunup until sundown. We worked with the hopes of growing enough food to feed our family. Being a farmer and a gatherer is not easy. But, it was a life that we chose, and we were happy to be together. At some point, when I was little, the humans began banding together for protection against the predators of the forests."

"The humans?" Rusty interrupted. "Why do you say it like that?" The words made him uneasy even though he had heard the tale already.

"Because there are more than humans living in the Lands of the Khans," he added before continuing. "In those days, when I was just a child, rumors had come from the south. They described packs of vicious beasts hunting humans in the dead of night. Soon after, four of our bravest warriors did not return from an evening hunt. The elders ordered the villagers to cut down the tallest trees. We walled in our village, fearful of the creatures that lurked in the night. Other villages were encouraged to do the same. Soon, we all feared the darkness and hunting by moonlight became taboo."

"At night, the gates were bolted shut. Families stayed hidden behind the doors of our huts, hunkered down inside our villages until the daylight hours. One day, when I was just thirteen years old, my father took me to hunt the nearby forest. It had always been safe to hunt in the daytime, but it was more difficult to stalk our prey. We quickly felled a deer, and we were carrying it back to the village when a beast attacked."

"A beast attacked you?" Rusty blurted out, caught up in the story.

The old man nodded before responding, "Yes, it was a large wolf, at least seven feet in height. It walked on hind legs like a man, but its long snout and sharpened canines made it look ferocious."

"A Werewolf?" Rusty asked, ,shocked by the older man's description.

"I do not know of this, Werewolf, but here the creatures are called Amorak or Amoraki," the old man responded. "How do you know of such a thing?"

Rusty paused and then said, "In my world, we have our myths. One of them includes a wolf that walks on hind legs. The Werewolf craves human flesh, even though it used to be a man. In our world, though, they could only come out at night and only during the full moon."

Rusty looked into the old man's wide eyes, the eyebrows raised in astonishment. He waited for the rest of the story.

The old man continued, "We dropped the deer and turned to run away, hoping it was after our kill. Instead, the beast pounced onto my back. It was within seconds of clamping its fangs onto my neck when my father pulled his knife and leapt to my defense." His eyes teared up.

Rusty could tell that he was reliving the moment, remembering when his father had sacrificed himself so that his son might live. "I squirmed away delirious with fear. It was daytime, yet a beast was attacking us and ignoring the deer. It was after us. We were its prey."

"Before running away in terror, I watched the beast sink its fangs into the side of my father's face. The last sound I heard was the crunching of my father's bones as the creature began to feed on him."

Touched by the old man's story, Rusty asked, "He sacrificed himself for you?"

"Anyone can make the sacrifice; it just takes courage," the old man said gravely. "Do not be shocked at the callousness of my words. I honor my father, and I honor his efforts. His courage and his sacrifice made it possible for his son to live."

His face frozen in a grimace, he added, "As I was running, I heard the beast howl. I felt the blood in my veins freeze when more than a hundred howls answered in response."

Rusty remembered the howls that emanated from deep within the forest after he had yelled. He shivered.

"Stop," Rusty demanded. "If this is true, if all of this is true, why have you brought me here?" Anger bubbled inside him. "I need to get back home. Do you hear me? My mother is dying." He stood, paced back and forth, and glared at the sitting man.

The man frowned softly, his eyes sad, "I am saddened to say this to you, young man. Your mother has passed." He waited for Rusty to respond, his grey eyes impassive.

"How do you know this?" Rusty asked. His mind was in turmoil. He knew that his mother would pass but had prayed that he would be there when she did.

"I just know," the old man countered. He waited for Rusty to ask other questions.

When Rusty did not, he continued, "There is so much to tell. However, there is not that much time. A month, three months, I do not know. The creatures overran the Lands of the Khans and have grown into an army of unspeakable horror. He knows that we are in these woods, which is why he has some of them scouring the forests."

"Who knows? Who is he? Is that why we ran through the water so they could not track our scent?" Rusty asked, bewildered. His mind was racing. There were so many questions that needed so many answers.

Ignoring Rusty's questions, the old man continued, "They have been hunting me for years, and each time I venture out, which I have to do for food and firewood, they get closer and closer to finding me. What you said about water and our scent, both are true, yes. But, the Amoraki, or as you call them, the Werewolves, fear what might be in the water."

Rusty's eyes darted to the darkened recesses of the surrounding cave. "What do they fear that is in the water?" he asked, still confused. He paused before adding, "Who are you?"

Rusty's words brought the man out of his reverie. His nervousness disappeared, though his eyes continued to look fatigued. "My apologies," the old man said before standing up slowly. Rusty could hear crackling in his kneecaps, but his grey eyes were alert and twinkling. He walked over to Rusty, held out his right hand, and said, "I am Joshua, the last human in the world."

On his fourth day in the cave, when he finished answering Rusty's questions, Joshua directed Rusty to follow him. They walked along a winding crevice, deeper into the bowels of the cave, for what seemed like miles. Joshua began climbing upward along a narrow fissure. There were no stairs, so they had to find toe holds as they ascended. Rusty admitted to an admiration for the old man, watching him climb effortlessly upward, through the cave roof and out onto the top of a high ridgeline. Rusty asked, worriedly, about the howling animals below, afraid that they might be able to see them.

"Do not worry," Joshua offered with assurance, "the sides are very steep and unclimbable. Also, since we are on a flattened top, they cannot see us or smell us from down below." He had turned around in a complete circle looking at the world around. "It's the one place left on this side of the mountains that a human can feel safe.

Rusty lifted the wooden sword nervously in front of him, holding the hilt tightly with both hands. Joshua had tossed it to him on his first day in the cave only to follow it up with a challenge to a swordfight. Its weight surprised him, as did the older man who charged at him without warning. Rusty backpedaled timidly, swinging the rigid blade half-heartedly, hoping to avoid striking and accidentally hurting the old man. It had been hard to do, striking at each other in the dimly lit cave. Finally, when he was satisfied with Rusty's progress, Joshua insisted they move to a better location. Here they were, on top of the world, play fighting with wooden swords.

He's over a hundred years old, thought Rusty, remembering Joshua's original challenge. *A swordfight with wooden swords?* Embarrassed, he accepted, convinced it was the only way to avoid any more harsh words between them. They had already argued, back and forth, about Joshua's reason for dragging Rusty through the Void between their worlds. Rusty did not know what else to call what happened, but there had to be a connection between the Lands of the Khans and Schmittling's Junkyard back in Millstadt. He thought about it so much the first few days, deep inside Joshua's cave, that he finally admitted it had become an obsession. *Could it be related to gravity and inertia? What about Newton and his Laws of Motion?* he puzzled.

His thoughts were in turmoil as he watched Joshua counter each of his moves. He lifted the wooden sword, blocked one of Joshua's blows, and continued to think about everything that had happened so far.

It occurred to him that he might be like the egg in the Science class experiment. Somehow, Joshua had used the laws of gravity and inertia to knock Millstadt out from beneath his feet. The resulting jolt, and Joshua's hands locked around his waist, had pulled him away from Millstadt and into these lands. Joshua refused to answer the how but was quick to offer the why.

Rusty's focus waned as he became lost in his thoughts. Joshua surprised him by ducking slightly, leaping sideways, and swatting Rusty harshly on the back. The blow landed heavily, knocking him onto the ground. He landed with a hard thud, releasing the wooden sword from his grip. Slowly, he rolled over and sat up, his lip busted open. Blood oozed down the front of his chin, a crimson rivulet snaking its way down his face.

He glared at the man, standing above him passively. Joshua, a gentle smirk on his face, looked at him, waiting patiently for some type of reaction.

"Why did you do that?" the boy asked, his anger boiling up and spilling out in his voice. He had tried to be friendly, and this was his thanks.

"Why did you hold back?" Joshua responded, chuckling. His beard's long, grey streaks looked odd, the red beard from his younger days long since hidden. Rusty could almost see the youthful Joshua with his red whiskers. A gentle breeze kicked up, blew softly into their faces, and lifted the end of Joshua's beard, briefly hiding his eyes. When it died down, the newly exposed eyes hardened. He said sternly, "This is not a game we play. It is life or death. Trust me. I need you to control your agility and balance it with the strength that I know you have within you."

Rusty swallowed convulsively. "I do have strength," he bragged. "I can bench press two-hundred twenty-five pounds seven times." He cursed himself, realizing how childish he sounded. He stewed in silence, not wholly believing Joshua's tale about why he was here. *What did he call this place?* Rusty thought, desperately trying to remember Joshua's first words.

It took a few seconds, and then he remembered, *The Lands of the Khans.*

He stood, brushed away the grass and the dirt, and looked up timidly. Holding up his hands, with his palms out, Rusty offered his surrender, "I need a break."

Joshua looked at Rusty with disappointment in his grey eyes but nodded. They walked in silence to sit beside each other on a large log. From this vantage point, they could see the entire valley below. The thickly wooded forests, a canopy of greens, extended for miles in every direction. Rusty could make out the outlines of a few gently flowing rivers as the water meandered its way, snakelike, back and forth into the distance.

"War is coming. A false King has risen to power," he professed gravely. Joshua explained that the Lands of the Khans, once home to hundreds of thousands of people, was now desolate of human life, save for himself.

Rusty rolled the man's story over in his mind. According to Joshua, a dark wizard had worked a sinister magic by helping a giant Werewolf named Natus Khan unite almost all of the Werewolves into a bloodthirsty army. There were tens of thousands of these Werewolves, each as savage as the next. Trained by the wizard and their leader in the art of war, each Werewolf had become proficient with spear, sword, and bow. These Amoraki, as he called them, had the strength of twenty men. They had been unleashed, like an unholy nightmare upon the humans of this world. Before the rise of their leader and the arrival of the wizard, the Werewolves had been solitary creatures, existing only in scary stories told around campfires at night. Or, the wizard had gathered all of them from a multitude of worlds, bringing them here to rid the Lands of the Khans of humans. Whichever it was, the nightmare had come to life.

The wizard, a faceless demon shrouded behind the hood of a dark cloak, had searched for the giant for years. Together, the two of them had slaughtered and conquered the once independent clans of Werewolves. They have run amok, a berserker hoard of screaming Werewolves, bursting forth from the darkness and now the daylight to kill all in their path. Only a few northern clans of Amoraki remain unconquered. After adding them to his army, Natus Khan, the leader, would turn his sight and army onto the remaining humans in this world, and possibly others, with the wizard's help.

Joshua, initially, was not very forthcoming. Rusty continued to ask questions, teasing out Joshua's hidden purpose for bringing him here. Everyone in this world, all of the humans, had been slaughtered and devoured. Joshua was looking for a champion. He needed someone who could stand up for the humans of this world by challenging and defeating the Khan in armed combat. Rusty immediately argued with Joshua on this assertion.

"If there are no more humans, why do you need a savior?" he asked.

In response, Joshua pointed to the mountains on the other side of the valley. He told Rusty that hundreds of thousands of humans, if not millions, lived on the other side of the snow-capped peaks. If left unchecked, the invading hoard would slaughter every man, woman, and child that remained.

Rusty had been angry, at first, about being dragged without his consent into a world where humans were hunted and eaten by ungodly creatures. Rusty's mother had known about Joshua's purpose and his plan, somehow. She had known this world needed him. That knowledge helped soothe his frustration, but only a bit. *She gave me her blessing, wanting me to help these people.*

But how did she know? The thought plagued him until Joshua explained that he had been communicating with Rusty's mother in her dreams.

Just a few days ago, moments after one of their early morning discussions, Rusty turned his mother's Bible back to The Book of Revelations and spent the remainder of the day, when they were not practicing with the sword, reading. He spent all night deep in thought. *He is the Devil,* he thought, the hairs on his neck standing on end. *Is it the wizard, though, or the massive brute? Can there be two Lords of the Flies?*

Joshua had made that promise more than a month ago, and now, here they were, back on top of the world, practicing sword fighting. Rusty's lip started to swell, though the blood no longer trickled down his chin.

Sitting against a log, resting in the afternoon sun with a gentle breeze in their faces, Joshua looked at Rusty and asked, "What is the name of your home, again?" He smiled curiously.

"Millstadt. Millstadt, Illinois," Rusty repeated. He had spent the last few weeks mourning the loss of his mother, saddened that he had not been with her at the end. *I owed that to her,* Rusty thought. He resented Joshua for taking that chance away from him.

Joshua guessed where his thoughts were taking him and offered, "Do not be sad for too long. Know that she is with you in your heart and that I brought you here with her blessing."

"How is that even possible?" Rusty asked, intrigued. Rusty started to repeat his question but stopped at Joshua's upturned hand.

"I cannot explain it all. Some of it, even in my old age, I do not understand." Joshua answered. He gestured to the Bible on the ground next to Rusty. "You told me that this book, the one brought with you when you came to visit me, is a book of Faith, true?"

"You mean when you yanked me into your world," Rusty countered sarcastically. He looked down at the Bible, the leather binding pristine. He thought about his mother once again.

Joshua frowned and added, "I have told you, there are moments in all of our lives that we must accept on pure Faith. This moment is one of them. I was encouraged, for lack of a better word, to seek you out and bring you here."

Rusty blurted out, "You have told me that part already. Encouraged by who?" He could hear the frustration in his voice, elevated by Joshua's evasiveness.

Joshua's eyes brightened for a brief moment as he whispered, "The Eighth Lion. He warned me years ago, in a dream, that humans are destined for pain and misery unless..." his voice trailed off as his mind drifted.

"Unless, unless?" Rusty added. He watched Joshua's face, the intensity in the grey eyes magnetic.

Joshua shook his head feverishly from side to side, "You are here now. That is all that matters. My dreams showed me the way to bring you here. And now, unless you can somehow master the use of a sword, it was all for nought."

"It is not an easy thing, to operate your life strictly on faith. Do you understand me? Your mother did it, did she not?" Joshua asked, oblivious to the pain his words caused.

Joshua's words stung. Rusty looked at him angrily but answered with pride, "Yes, she did. His mother's words had always comforted him. Her faith had carried her throughout her life, in the good times and the bad. Each morning, before I went to school, she always said I should go in peace, knowing that He watches over you."

Looking at the wooden sword at his feet, Rusty said, "It looked a lot easier in the movies." "Never mind," he added when Joshua's eyebrows lifted in puzzlement.

I am ready to go home, he thought. Rusty looked away from him, turning his attention to the ocean of trees spread out before them.

On the other side of the vast valley, the snow-capped mountain peaks loomed in the distance. Rusty could see large objects flying in wide circles above the highest peak. "What kind of birds are those?" Rusty asked. "I am amazed that I can see them at this great distance." He pointed at the mountaintops, some of them disappearing into the clouds.

Joshua squinted, his eyes looking to where Rusty had pointed.

"Those are not birds, my young friend," the old man answered with amusement.

The twinkle in his eye brought a smile to Rusty's face, though it quickly disappeared when he added, "Those are Dragons."

THE RIVER DRAGON

AFTER HIS FIRST MONTH OF TRAINING, OFTEN DOING MORE TO AVOID accidentally hurting Joshua than learning how to use a sword, Rusty decided it best to train independently. Initially, the sword felt heavy, and his movements were slow and cumbersome. He waited patiently for his companion to fall asleep. Then he would grab the heavy, wooden sword, move to a quieter location further back in the dark cave, and repeat the training on his own.

When he had lifted the sword for the first time, he asked Joshua, "How heavy?" He assured Rusty that it was no more than five pounds, though he felt it might as well be a hundred. In his first few weeks, he had to use a two-handed grip to control the weight, making his attacks look like he was moving slowly. He would swing the sword in broad, heavy arcs. Afraid that his movements were too cumbersome, he dreaded the seconds it took for the blade to reach its intended target. *In that length of time, he will disembowel me three times over.*

In one brief moment, after he had frustrated himself for the hundredth time, Rusty leaned the sword against a large rock near one of the torches mounted along the wall, stepped back, and tried to study it with a fresh approach. According to Joshua, the sword's weight was equal to one with a metal blade; one that a human might wield in combat.

Rusty had not appreciated the description, "One that a human might wield." He said as much to the old man, who responded with sincerity, "The blades used by the Amoraki are much longer, and the swords are five to ten pounds heavier. Yet, when in a fury, they move through the air as if they are lighter than silk."

Remembering their conversation, Rusty sat down, enjoying the soothing coolness. His eyes traveled the length of the blade, stopping to study the design of the handle. He was sure he had seen a sword of a similar design somewhere else. He had even used it. He whistled softly the moment the epiphany hit him. When he was eleven years old, his dad bought him, without his mother's knowledge, a new PlayStation 3 game. Until *Dark Souls,* Rusty played *Call of Duty* games and *Madden* football exclusively. The new game mesmerized him with its groundbreaking graphics and the ancient swordplay. He spent hours mastering each of the moves before advancing to a higher level.

Sitting on the rock, he could barely make out Joshua's deep breathing as it mixed with the sound of trickling water from somewhere further back in the cave. The campfire still burned brightly. He could see the flames as they swayed slowly, casting long shadows on the opposite walls. He smiled, hit by the realization that he had been fighting against his training. *I am fighting against myself.* He stood up, mimicked the movements of some of the characters from *Dark Souls* and said, "It's in the footwork."

He picked up the sword, but this time held the handle against his body with the blade pointing upward, close to his face. Rather than swinging it, he practiced keeping it balanced in his hands as he shuffled, twirled, sidestepped, and charged. Rusty maintained his two-handed grip but forced himself to relax it ever so slightly. Once comfortable, he lowered the tip, pointing it at the cave floor and then repeated his movements.

Proudly, he murmured, "Now we are getting somewhere." He repeated the steps and then added in a couple of random movements. He pulled the blade upward, the wooden blade inches from his face, before shuffling forward, backward, and side to side. *I will control the sword. I must use it defensively and only strike when I have an opening.*

Slowly, after a few nights working to enhance his footwork, his reflexes quickened. *I have become stronger and faster,* he thought. Rusty did not disillusion himself about his sword-fighting abilities but felt his skills had been showing improvement.

When he tired, Rusty would sit in the darkness, thinking about the fighting styles of different characters from other games. Each time he would leap up and practice the steps, trying to recreate them from memory. Rusty practiced parrying an opponent's sword to one side, followed by a quick thrust with his blade. Spinning, he whirled the blade around his body, connecting it with its desired target within seconds, often lunging ahead to stab the tip of his sword into his invisible target.

This fight, at least my part of it, will come down to footwork. Rusty knew Natus Khan would be a powerful opponent. If Joshua's description of the Werewolves was accurate and Natus Khan had conquered each of their clans, then he would have to be the largest, the strongest, and likely the most cunning. Rusty was determined to keep the swordplay to a minimum. If he could frustrate the Werewolf, maybe Khan would make a mistake by overextending one of his attacks. If this happened, and it was a big if, Rusty could counter cut or stab quickly.

"I must not let him overpower me. I must wear him down, slowly," he mumbled.

Since Rusty's only experience with actual combat came from online gaming, his best offense would be to develop a strong defense. *I cannot let him pen me in,* he thought. *The blade is my only defense. He could rip me apart with his bare hands.*

During his training, Rusty thought about his father a lot. When he was seven years old, Rusty's father had told him the story of Muhammad Ali, the greatest boxer in the history of the world. Big Rusty's enthusiasm and admiration transferred to his son, and Little Rusty went to the library to find some books written about the Greatest of All-Time. He read them feverishly. *It's the rope a dope or the rumble in the jungle,* he thought, smiling at the memory of his father.

"Except," he said morbidly, "if I lose, I am dead." He peeked around the corner to the sleeping man. Joshua had not stirred.

Shuffling again, he practiced knocking an invisible sword away from his body, leaping backwards to avoid the imaginary sweep of a sharpened blade, and stabbing quickly before lurching to one side and bounding away as quickly as possible.

As he gained more experience training nightly for hours, Rusty felt a sense of gratitude for all of his coaches, even those who would have coached him from Belleville West High School. Months ago, before his journey into the Lands of the Khans, the Belleville West coaching staff found out that Rusty had been considering not playing football his freshman year. They sent an unlikely duo of coaches, as far as Rusty could tell, to offer some encouragement for him to play. The name Rusty had already heard from friends, Coach Flake, was as energetic in person as they described him to be in the classroom. His high school friends told him that he had to take a class with the Coach, just for the experience. The man was witty, funny, and serious about helping kids.

Joined by Coach Boyd, a young African-American teacher ecstatic to come back to his old high school to coach and teach, Rusty found the meeting inspirational.

They were genuinely excited at his potential but did not make him any outlandish promises. He appreciated their honesty. He liked their enthusiasm for the game; it felt good to see how much they cared about students in general. They sat down with Rusty, helping him devise a workout routine to improve his speed, strength, and agility.

He remembered Coach Flake's words clearly, "At the high school level, we win the game in the weight room. We just celebrate the victory on the field." Rusty genuinely liked him. If he represented the best of Belleville West, then Rusty was going to the right high school. His mother and father had spoken highly of the school, and he planned to continue that tradition.

Coach Boyd had been a football standout at West a few years before. His attitude and love for Belleville West made an immediate connection with Rusty. His words resonated; his voice was deep and powerful. "It is about setting yourself up for a scholarship. You have the athletic talent and the potential to earn one at any school of your choice. Then, let's turn that into an opportunity to continue your education and find work in a career you love."

Rusty immediately hit the weight room. His mother's battle with cancer occupied his mind day and night. If it had not been for the advice of Coach Boyd and Coach Flake, he did not know if he would have been able to handle her decline and maintain his sanity.

Lacking weights deep inside the cave, Rusty modified some of his workouts, focusing instead on callisthenics. As his confidence grew, Rusty's frustration with Joshua began to wane. *Anger was holding me back,* he thought. He remembered his mother's words, hearing her voice clearly, "Identify your mistakes. Own up to them. Then let us forgive and forget. That is all a person can do."

Mr. Johnson had been proof of that, he thought, remembering the man fondly.

Joshua had owned up to his purpose, he admitted. Whether or not Rusty liked the idea, he had to move on and plan for what looked like an inevitable confrontation with Natus Khan.

Besides wishing for a training partner who could push him to his limits, he liked the old man and enjoyed his company. Joshua had an indelible quality about him. Even though Rusty could see the fatigue in his eyes, it had not beaten Joshua down. Rusty had seen that look, once before, when watching the news one night. The segment focused on some villagers who had escaped from North Korea. Their vacant stares had burned into his memory forever. Emaciated, with dark circles beneath their weary eyes, each villager looked into the camera with a lack of the spirit that humans naturally carried with them. They had been malnourished for years, living under extreme conditions, hopelessly lost. Their eyes communicated exhaustion that spoke of crushed souls.

Joshua, though worn and tired, had a curiosity that Rusty appreciated. His grey eyes would twinkle when Rusty spoke about Millstadt and life on earth. He asked as many questions as he could, eager to listen intently to anything Rusty was willing to share. They had become friends, something that Rusty did not realize until recently.

Joshua was a desperate man, facing a sense of urgency that Rusty had just recently begun to appreciate. *He has been through far worse than*

I, Rusty thought, ashamedly. *The people on the other side have no idea the savagery they face. They don't know about his struggles to save them from a creature bent on their destruction.*

Rusty's frustration with Joshua had grown into admiration. He prayed, nightly, that he was capable of living up to the expectations that this grey-eyed, grey-haired, wrinkled hermit had for him. He doubted that he would be able to do so.

Rusty could not drive away his fears, most of them centered around macabre thoughts about dying. Like it or not, he realised that Joshua's expectations had brought him here, and there was no way back home without his help. Unless he fought and defeated Natus Khan, that help would not be forthcoming.

No one wants to die? he thought. "I don't know if I would want to live forever, though," he muttered quietly.

He decided to forgive Joshua. His fears and all that had happened to him would not be the old man's cross to bear. *They are my own, so I must own them.*

It was at the end of his second month of training, in a moment that Rusty felt the wooden sword was as light as a feather and that his footwork had reached a mastery level, when Joshua sat up and called out, "I do believe you are ready."

Retrieving the torch, Rusty picked up the sword and returned to the campfire. "I am sorry if I woke you," Rusty apologized. He sat down on the opposite side of the campfire, feeling pleased that Joshua had acknowledged his growth.

"No need," Joshua responded gleefully. "I have been listening to you these last two months and have to admit that I am glad you took up training yourself. I was holding you back. Your skill development is amazing." The sincerity in his words filled Rusty with hope.

"What is next?" Rusty asked, curious. "I am not saying I am a master with the sword, but I can hold my own if needed. But, we both know a wooden sword will not win this fight." The hairs on Rusty's neck stood on end as he realized he had finally accepted his fate. He would meet Natus Khan on the field and challenge him to armed combat. Only one of them would leave the field alive. *I am no longer afraid to die.* He was amazed by the shift in his demeanor.

"Do you remember when you asked about the Dragons flying around the mountain peaks?" Joshua asked. He waited for Rusty to acknowledge the question with a nod before adding, "There is a cave halfway up that mountain. Inside that cave is a sword that in the right hands holds enough power to defeat any Werewolf, including Natus Khan."

Tiny goosebumps sprang up on Rusty's forearms. He shivered and asked, "If you have seen this sword, why did you not bring it here with you?"

"I have not seen it in person," Joshua answered, shrugging. He raised his hands to keep Rusty from crying out in protest. "It was shown to me, in a dream years ago, by The Eighth Lion."

Rusty sighed heavily. He had listened to Joshua's talk about The Eighth Lion, intrigued at first. "Let's assume that there is a sword inside a cave. It is on the other side of the Lands of the Khans. Look to the sky. You said those are Dragons guarding it. If the Werewolves are scouring this land looking for you, how are we going to get there without being captured, killed, or even worse, eaten alive?" He inhaled quickly and then exhaled deeply to calm his nerves.

A twinkle re-appeared in Joshua's eyes before he responded, "First. The Dragons have gone with the Khan and the wizard to the north. They wish to consolidate their power over the Amoraki and will be gone for at least a month."

"Second, I have Faith. I recommend the same to you. The Eighth Lion has our best interests at heart. Speaking to me through my dreams, He," Rusty noticed the accentuation of the word, "assures us that the sword is in that cave. We must accept it as gospel." Joshua ignored Rusty's eye roll but smiled. "I understand that you do not believe, but that is not my fault. I cannot force someone to have faith. It must be something they have on their own, without any misgivings or any doubts. Faith is faith."

He watched Rusty's face before continuing, "As far as getting from here to there, I have a plan. I have planned for your arrival for many years, long before I found the spell needed to bring you here."

Rusty leaned in more closely at Joshua's words. It was the first time he had mentioned that it took a magical spell to pull him away from Millstadt.

"It will be tedious and taxing, physically, but we can do it." Joshua stood before adding. "I estimate it will take us at least seven days to get to the mountains."

"Seven days!" Rusty exclaimed. "I know it's a long-distance away, but we should be able to get there in no more than three." He pleaded with his hands for Joshua to explain.

"In normal circumstances, yes, I agree," Joshua's patient voice answered. "But, the Werewolves are watching these woods. We cannot just stroll through them, hoping to avoid detection."

"Well. Do these caves run the entire length of these lands? Are we going to follow them to the mountains?" Rusty asked, bewildered. His confusion added to his frustration.

"Unfortunately, no," Joshua smiled. "I wish we could remain underground. It would be a lot safer, but these caves stretch for no more than another half-mile. After that, we must ascend." He lifted his fingers, following them with his eyes.

"Then how are we going to get there undetected?" Rusty asked. Joshua's confidence did not alleviate his confusion.

The old man turned back to Rusty and answered, "We will have to go underwater." He stood up, motioned for Rusty to follow, and walked toward the darkness of the cave.

"You have to be kidding me," Rusty blurted out. His eyes widened the moment Joshua stopped in front of a sizeable vat of grease. A least three feet deep, a foul smell emanated from the thick, jelly-like substance. Rusty pinched his nose shut and looked at Joshua incredulously. The stench had been overpowering, and for a few minutes, Rusty gagged and felt that he might vomit.

They continued walking, guided by the torchlight, for at least fifteen minutes. Away from the campfire, without the flames to provide a sense of security, Rusty shivered as the temperature dropped by more than ten degrees.

"What is that stuff?" he asked, thumbing backwards over his shoulder.

Joshua said, turning to Rusty. "The creeks and rivers start at the mountaintops and crisscross our lands before heading off to the east for hundreds of miles. They are very cold this close to the mountains. For the most part, the river currents are slow-moving. The nearest creek connects to a larger, slow-moving river less than a mile from our location. The creek is about ten feet deep and the river, in spots, is no more than twenty. If we stay beneath the surface, the Werewolves will not be able to find us."

Rusty was full of questions, "Even with a slow-moving current, we cannot swim upriver." He waited for Joshua to counter his doubts.

"We will not swim. We will walk," he answered, looking at Rusty's raised eyebrows with a smirk.

Rusty's mind was full of questions, "They cannot smell our tracks through water, then?" Rusty asked. He remembered running alongside Joshua, staying inside the creek as they fled the Amoraki on his first night.

"That is correct. Remember, though, that the Werewolves avoid the creeks and rivers for other reasons, too."

"They are afraid of water!" Rusty exclaimed. He thought this knowledge might be helpful and was excited to hear Joshua elaborate.

"Though timid around water, it's not the water that makes them afraid. It's what might be in the water."

"What do you mean?" Rusty asked, worried. He could feel the worry lines on his forehead but did not know if Joshua could see them in the dim light.

"Just around the next turn, I will show you. Do not be afraid. You are in no danger, for it has long since died."

Rusty swallowed convulsively, held his torch ahead of him, and walked with Joshua, but his pace slowed considerably. The moment they turned the next corner, he leapt backwards, dropping his torch. Rusty retrieved it quickly, held the torch out ahead of him, and asked, "What the hell is that?" His heart beat rapidly, and it seemed fear emanated from his every pore; he was ready to run for his life.

"It is," Joshua offered, "a river serpent. At least it was until it died almost a year ago."

Rusty looked downward, his eyes staring at the large head. They trailed its length, stopping along the thick, muscled body before ending at the tail. "Is that an anaconda?" He asked, captivated. He had seen documentaries about the giant snakes from South America but had never seen one in person.

"Yes," Joshua answered, understanding Rusty's question. "Is that what you call them on your world?"

Rusty stepped closer, whistling loudly. He leaned in to look at the head. It was as big as one of his neighbor's bulldogs. He scanned the scales, a mixture of dark and light green with brown splotches. The dead snake's thick muscles rippled in the torchlight. *It could crush me in an instant.*

He stepped out the length of the snake. "It has to be at least sixteen feet long," Rusty exclaimed. He looked around, peering into the darkness to see if there were others.

"Do not be afraid, Rusty," Joshua assured. "This snake fell through one of the many crevices that pocket this cavern. The coldness of the cave was too much, and it died here. I must admit that I was happy it had died before I found it. Otherwise, I don't know how I would have responded. It had to be a gift, and now we will use it to our advantage."

"What do we plan to do with that?" Rusty asked. "We cannot carry it with us. It has to weigh at least three hundred pounds." Frustrated, he looked from the snake and back to Joshua.

"Let us return to the campfire, and I will explain my plan," Joshua said, encouraging Rusty to leave the snake. Rusty did not like to see the amusement on his face but followed him. Passing the grease pit, he pinched his nose once more. Finally, the two of them settled next to the warmth of the fire.

"Years ago, I began planning for your arrival. I have been collecting the grease, leftover from all of my meals, purposefully. When the snake died here, inside this cave, I kept it too, preserved for this moment."

Rusty cringed at Joshua's words. This man had scavenged to stay alive, yet a snake that size could have provided meat for at least a year. Instead, Joshua had chosen to give up many meals so that the anaconda would be available for the two of them for this moment. It spoke to his perseverance, his tenacity, and his faith in the Eighth Lion.

Excited, Joshua hopped to his feet and went to retrieve four sturdy, wooden poles. "We will use them to maintain our footing as we lean against the current." He smiled with pride. Rusty felt his enthusiasm and tried to put on a broad smile in return.

He nodded that he understood, though he remained skeptical. Doubts assailed him, but he pushed them aside. This man spent years planning for this moment. "I admit I want to argue with you, but instead, I will just have faith." He was happy to see Joshua's smile return.

Gesturing towards two nearby boards, Joshua retrieved them. Each plank, six feet long and two feet wide, had a quarter size hole drilled at each end. Joshua had strung thickly knotted rope through the holes and looped them together for footholds. "We will place our feet inside the rope to keep them fastened to the boards. You and I will use these boards to walk, moving together against the current. We must tether ourselves, using this rope. We will practice lifting a foot and a board before taking a step forward. The boards will keep us from getting mired in the muck." Joshua pointed to the end of each board. Molded with care, they curved up at the ends. "This is to ensure we do not get snagged on any logs or anything else."

"It is like long-distance skiing," Rusty responded with amazement. He looked at Joshua's puzzled face and added, "It's a sport in my world. Those who move across heavy snow use something similar. Though skeptical, I admit it makes sense."

"Thank you for being willing to try," Joshua answered gleefully, his grey eyes twinkling with happiness.

"Well," Rusty started, "you seem to have thought of almost everything. I have only one concern left." He knew he had many concerns about Joshua's plan, but arguing them at this point would not solve anything. He looked into Joshua's face and asked, "How do we breathe?"

Laughing, Joshua retrieved two leather bladders from the darkness of the cave, each the size of a small backpack. He handed one to Rusty. It weighed heavily in his hands.

Rusty estimated it to be about twenty pounds, with the end of some hollow vine-like tubing inserted into them. The free end of the tubing widened to about four inches and was stretched meticulously over a fist-sized piece of hollowed-out wood. Joshuah explained it would allow air to flow freely. The device looked simplistic, but it would function like scuba diving equipment.

"I have tested these, improved them as many times as I can, and believe we can use them to breath safely beneath the water for up to thirty minutes at a time. Any longer and I became quite winded and felt I might pass out. We will have to surface, often, to refill them with air."

"What are they filled with?" Rusty asked. Joshua's enthusiasm added to his curiosity. "They are heavy. I would expect that if filled with air, they would be much lighter." He picked one up and shook it lightly.

Joshua raised his hand quickly and said, "Gently. Gently. They hold tiny grub worms. Each bag holds hundreds of them." He watched Rusty's eyes as they filled with curiosity.

"When I was a little kid, our mother would send us into the forests to collect Chafers. They live in abundance in the trees, along the forests floor, and under rocks. Once, when my mother was not looking, I snatched three or four of them to keep as pets. I placed them in a leather pouch and closed them up, hoping to keep them safe. To my amazement, an hour later, the bag had swollen with air. I tried it again with the same results. Eventually, through trial and error, I realized that these Chafers give off air as they breathe." He looked up, excited to be telling Rusty about his discovery. "When I began planning our trip, I experimented with these worms. I found that I can put a hundred of them in these bags, and we can get about thirty minutes of air. I have also found that most of them die after a day or so in the bag."

Joshua continued, "I have added rocks to keep the bags from floating to the surface. We will just have to exit the water every thirty minutes and find more worms. It will be the most dangerous part of our journey."

Rusty offered, "Interesting. You became light-headed because we exhale a gas called Carbon Dioxide. I guess that these tiny worms breathe in Carbon Dioxide, especially if they give off oxygen. Eventually, the Carbon Dioxide builds up, replacing the oxygen. You are definitely on the right track. We just need to figure out a way to slow down the buildup of Carbon Dioxide and a way to keep them alive, longer."

Joshua felt Rusty's excitement before adding, "Is there a way to counterbalance this?" He waited patiently for Rusty to work it out in his head.

"We need to open one of these up so that I can inspect it." He watched while Joshua methodically unlaced the leather pouch. Joshua carefully tilted it until the contents spilt out onto the floor of the cave. A pile of yellow grub worms with orange heads, each less than a half-inch long, squirmed in the firelight. Joshua dumped the rocks from the bottom of the leather bladder onto the floor next to the grub worms."

"Could we lengthen this container?" Rusty asked, holding up one of the bladders.

"Definitely," Joshua answered. "How much longer do we need to make it?"

Curious, Rusty picked up one of the worms and held it to his face. He could feel the oxygen on his face, a tiny gust of air as it expelled from the worm's mouth. He watched the confusion on Joshua's face before he added, "Humans need oxygen. It is what we breathe in every day to help us live. You figured out the importance, which is why you are using these grub worms to help us breathe. The lungs in our body exhale Carbon Dioxide, which I suspect, but cannot prove; these grub worms use in their breathing. When you were exhaling through that tube, you put the Carbon Dioxide from your body back into the bag. The grub worms cannot keep up with the excess Carbon Dioxide. Too much of it must incapacitate them. We must slow down the amount of Carbon Dioxide that they have to contend with when breathing." He pointed to the rocks on the ground and added, "It was a great idea to add the rocks to counteract the buoyancy. We just have to figure out a way to keep these tiny worms alive for a little longer."

He thought for a few minutes. "We need deciduous trees," he exclaimed, his eyes brightening with the idea. "Trees with broad leaves or trees with flowers or spike-covered fruits. Any of these types of trees, we call them oak or walnut in my land, would be perfect." It was the most excited Rusty had been since arriving in Joshua's world. "Do you think we could gather some leaves? A lot of them. If we cut them fresh, they will act Carbon Dioxide absorbers just as they do in nature."

Joshua nodded and answered, "Yes. We can gather the leaves we need and as many Chafers as you think we need. We need to stay close and be very aware. It is fascinating to think that trees might play a role in helping humans to breathe." Joshua turned the bladder over in his hand and looked back up at Rusty.

Switching gears, Rusty asked, "Why the grease pit?" He had to admit that Joshua had planned meticulously, and his plan held merit, though the purpose of the grease escaped him.

"We will cover our bodies with a thick layer of grease. It will help keep us warm in the frigid waters."

Rusty laughed, clapped his hands and said, "I love science and need you to know that my teachers at Millstadt, and Coach Flake at Belleville West, would be proud of everything that you have discovered."

Joshua smiled before adding, "We should practice for a few days." He pointed to the items on the floor.

"I agree," Rusty said with invigoration. He was ready to be done with this cave. He did not think they were going to survive the journey. They would either drown, be attacked and eaten by another anaconda, or be found and slain by the Amoraki.

"And why the snake?" he asked, afraid to bring it up.

"We will attach the head, and the tail to each of us, fastened to our shoulders. Other predators, the snakes and crocodiles sometimes found in these rivers, will avoid us out of fear." He smiled once again when Rusty rolled his eyes. "This serpent is the largest I have ever seen. She is the apex predator. When we surface, we will start by poking her head out of the water. If any Amoraki is nearby, trust me, it will flee."

Rusty clapped his hands again, impressed. He leapt up and shook the old man's hand.

Joshua thanked him and added, "Let's get some sleep. Tomorrow, we begin our training. And then, when we are ready to begin our journey, we will have one magnificent meal to celebrate." Rusty could see the gleam return to Joshua's eyes.

"I have been waiting a long time to eat that damned snake."

By the third day, Rusty and Joshua agreed that they were as prepared as they could ever be. Joshua placed his hand upon Rusty's shoulder, offering his assurance that the plan was sound and that they would, with divine intervention, make it safely to the mountains.

"Let's go up one more time," Joshua added, pointing above them. "I would like to see the sunrise one final time before we begin our nocturnal journey." They had agreed to travel beneath the water during daylight hours, rising from the murky depths only at night and only when necessary.

Rusty nodded, though this time, instead of waiting for Joshua, he scrambled up the crevasse, bursting out from the ground into the fresh air above. The two of them sat down facing the east, waiting for the sun to shower the landscape with its golden rays.

Joshua thumbed over his left shoulder, saying, "Do you notice the Dragons are no longer circling the mountaintops. As I told you before, they have gone north with Natus Khan and will be there for at least a month."

Fascinated, Rusty asked, "Just how big are these Lands?" He swept his eyes over the landscape below, mesmerized by its beauty. He whistled, enjoying Joshua's smile and shrug.

"When I was a little boy," Joshua began, "I would often dream of crossing the Mountains to find out what was on the other side. Yet, now that I am the last human in this world," he paused before adding, "I mean as one of the last two humans in this world I fear the other side of the mountains. Natus Khan knows there are others like me. I do not want them slaughtered. I do not want their children to live in fear of the dreadful creatures that will burst forth from the night."

It was the first time since arriving in the Lands of the Khans that Joshua had shown this much emotion. It caught Rusty off-guard, and he did not know how to respond. "Why has no one ever cross over?" Rusty asked, curious. "In my world, there are vast mountain peaks and deep oceans that have been explored just to see what they hold. Has no one been curious?"

"The mountains are treacherous. Crossing over is a dangerous task. Fear of the unknown has always kept my people from exploring. I think many of us were afraid. If we crossed over, whomever or whatever lives on the other side might follow us back. It was a chance none were ever willing to take." Joshua inhaled deeply, closed his eyes, and seemed to absorb the golden rays shining brightly on his face. "Fear does many things," he added with his eyes still closed. "Yet, I have learned, after living with it for many years, that it can also push a person to do anything possible to survive. Fear can hold a person down so that they cannot live life to the fullest extent possible. If harnessed, though, it can be a driving force. It can spur on changes. It can help to ensure that a person stays alive." He stood, slowly stretched his arms over his head and said, "Let us leave this place, and hopefully, we will meet our destiny, whatever it may be, with courage and grace."

BENEATH THE WATER

It took three days of grueling practice before the two of them were able to walk in lockstep. At first, it had been challenging to get the boards moving in the right direction, without one of them falling flat on their face. Their misgivings, of which they had many, could not be used as an excuse. Finally, they felt proficient enough to put their plan into action.

They each took a deep breath, trying to soothe their nerves before slowly sinking into the shadowy depths of the nearby creek.

Joshua had assured him that the tube-like vines, freshly cut and molded, would withstand the rigors of the water and the current. He was confident that they would remain airtight throughout the journey. The green, fibrous vines connected the air-filled bladder to their mouthpiece. Strapping the packs onto their backs, they agreed it was time to begin.

Convinced that he looked nothing short of ridiculous, Rusty gave up on worrying about appearances. He did worry about whether or not Joshua's inventions would work.

They had settled on using about five hundred live grub worms, gently mixed in with as many freshly cut leaves as possible. Through trial and error, they found they could breathe safely for almost two hours at a time. Even better, since the worms had a food source inside the bag, they stayed alive, which meant that Rusty and Joshua would not have to stray away from the safety of the water.

Joshua insisted that he take the lead as he tied the much heavier anaconda head around his torso and onto his left shoulder. The large head hung limply, but Joshua guaranteed Rusty that it would float out ahead of him when they submerged themselves. "I know these lands far better than you and need to be the guide. Besides, if attacked, you are far more valuable than I," he said, matter-of-factly. Though he did not like to admit it, Rusty agreed with the older man's logic.

Rusty tied the anaconda's severed tail to his shoulder with leather strips threaded through its skin. Joshua insisted they both have a part of the river serpent with them.

"All other predators fear these Dragons of the river. Even the sight of its tail will frighten away animals approaching us from behind," he added, nodding at Rusty.

They spent most of a day carrying the materials to the narrow creek bank, moving slowly to avoid the unwanted attention of any patrolling Werewolves. The green, brackish waters looked foreboding, but Joshua assured Rusty, "There are no large serpents in this creek. When we get to the river, yes, but even then, they are a rarity."

If that is the case, how did one end up in our cave? Rusty thought, doubting Joshua's assurances. He could not bring himself to accept that divine intervention had brought them the dead anaconda.

A moment before they entered the water, Joshua stopped Rusty to offer an apology. "I wish there had been another way, trust me. I did not wish to take you away from your dying mother."

The sincerity in his voice made Rusty tear up. His throat choked with emotion, and he could not respond.

A few minutes later, Joshua placed his hands on Rusty's shoulders and said solemnly, "Let us begin."

Tethered together, the two settled on a rhythm. When walking along the bottom of the murky water, they would step, count one, step, count two, step, count one, step count two.

Joshua suggested that Rusty focus his thoughts on counting their steps and not the anacondas and crocodiles. Rusty promised he would try but knew that it would be impossible.

As Joshua had predicted, the slow current offered only slight resistance, no more than a gentle breeze if they had been walking on land. They used the poles to push themselves forward along the muddy bottom. Other than leaning forward, ever so slightly, they moved along with relative ease.

The first day of traveling went well, though the darkness ten feet below the surface unnerved Rusty. Locked beneath the water, away from the sunlight, he forced his eyes downward, fearing that if he looked up, the sun would beckon to him like a magnet. It would tear at his soul, calling him upward into the light. He longed to see the golden rays showering the landscape once more.

By the end of the first day, just as the light above began to wane, Rusty felt physically exhausted. The moment Joshua pointed upward, they turned the boards to the right and climbed the gentle slope toward the bank. Rusty sighed with relief. He had pushed his body and his mind to their limits.

Earlier, Rusty had meant to ask Joshua how he had acquired the glass to construct their rudimentary goggles. Unfortunately, the opportunity to ask never presented itself. The glass, thick and wavy, was not as clear and transparent as he would have liked. They could see many shapes with them at the bottom of the creek. Rusty spied numerous large catfish skimming along beside their feet, drawn to them by their movement. Each time Joshua turned to face them, the large anaconda head acted as a repellent, and the big fish sped away into the darkness. There had been quite a few orange and black banded snakes slithering through the water, searching for a meal.

Watching the snakes and the fish swim away, Rusty admitted to an appreciation of everything Joshua had done to prepare for this day. He also admitted, ashamedly, that his assumptions about Joshua's upbringing had led to some unfair bias on his behalf. He initially saw him as backwards and unintelligent. *I will never underestimate anyone again based on how they live and how they look.* Joshua's mind and his creative intellect had been on full display. It was clear to Rusty that Joshua was a genius.

Each time they ascended for air, it was not to gather more Chafers. Instead, they simply removed the snorkel from their mouths and waited for the bladder to expand. They never fully exited the creek, and both remained vigilant. Once the Chafers filled the balloon with fresh oxygen, they would slide down to the bottom of the stream and continue their journey.

It had been a long day, but Joshua pointed once more, upward, indicating that they needed to surface. As he had done before, he poked the nostrils of the anaconda slightly above the surface. Though darkness approached quickly, Rusty could make out some of the trees, but he could not see into the dense shadows of the forest.

The two travelers, weary from the exertion, collapsed into a pile on the edge of the creek. They kept their feet strapped to the boards, and their poles gripped tightly in their hands. The night air had turned chilly, with Rusty's breath visible each time he exhaled. The thick grease, smeared over his body, insulated him from the cold. Once again, he silently praised Joshua for his ingenuity.

We are a sight for sore eyes, Rusty thought, chuckling. *What would Suz say if she could see me now?* Pangs of sadness rushed over him, but he pushed her from his mind and waited for Joshua.

"We will sleep in shifts," Joshua whispered. His grey eyes were difficult to see in the approaching darkness, but Rusty knew they held an intense gaze. "If we hear a noise tap the other, and we will slide noiselessly back into the creek until we know it is safe." He gestured for Rusty to sleep, indicating his intentions to pull the first shift. Rusty did not argue, the fatigue weighing heavily on him. He fell asleep.

Rusty knew he was dreaming, but he did not care. His mom and dad were sitting at the kitchen table, laughing and enjoying each other's company. He smiled warmly, praying the feeling would never end.

"Hurry up, Zach," his mother shouted, putting her hand on his father's forearm. "Or else we are going to eat without you." She rolled her eyes at Rusty, the twinkle in them magical. A minute later, his older brother Zach bounded into the room, smiling from ear to ear. He scooted along the tiled floor, sliding effortlessly on his grey tube socks before he plopped heavily into the chair next to Rusty.

"You okay, little bro?" Zach asked with an infectious smile. His blond hair, paired with piercing ice-blue eyes, fascinated Rusty. Zach was the epitome of athleticism, intellect, and humor. He was the starting quarterback for the football team at Belleville West High School. Rusty's brother was an Honor student, liked by everyone in Millstadt. He was also a fantastic big brother. Every night, after they ate, he and Rusty would go outside and play catch, shoot hoops, or just hang out. Rusty was elated to be with his family. He hoped this moment would never end.

I will be just like him when I grow up, Rusty imagined, watching his older brother with deep admiration.

Other kids Zach's age did not hang with their brothers or sisters, especially those five years younger. Zach, though, laughed at his friends when they teased him about it. "He's cool," Zach would say, and Rusty could tell that he meant it.

Rusty felt Zach tap him lightly on the shoulder before he said, "Dude, it's time to wake up."

"What?" Rusty asked, confused. He looked at Zach and asked again, "What did you say?"

Rusty turned to his mom and dad, but they had gone. Zach had disappeared, too. He sat alone at the kitchen table.

He felt the gentle tapping on his shoulder and heard Joshua's voice, "It's time to wake up." Rusty opened his eyes, expecting it still to be dark. The sun had not risen, but the light from the pre-dawn hours had already arrived. Joshua had allowed him to sleep all night.

Before he could protest, Joshua raised his hands and they replaced their goggles. He gestured to the water and they slid back into the murkiness.

By the end of the second day, when they had pushed themselves almost to exhaustion, Joshua pointed once more to Rusty and turned the boards to walk up the gently sloping bank. This time, though, Rusty refused to sleep. Feeling worn down to a nub, he refused Joshua's offer to take the first shift.

"I cannot allow you to bear this cross all by yourself," Rusty added, smiling inwardly at his allusion.

Joshua relented, leaned his head down onto his forearm, and fell fast asleep. Joshua refused to admit to being mentally drained.

Rusty knew they had pushed themselves to their limits, but he was determined to remain awake, no matter how tired he felt, for the entire night.

Unfortunately, just a little past the midnight hour, when the full moon was directly overhead, he heard a rustling of leaves less than thirty yards downriver on the opposite side of the bank. He reached to tap Joshua on the shoulder but froze. Three enormous Werewolves exited the woods, slowly heading to the creek for water. The blades of their swords glistened in the moonlight. The first one leaned in to get a drink timidly, its red eyes searching the darkness for any sign of movement in the water.

Rusty had never seen any creatures as foreboding as the three Amoraki, even compared to the scariest Werewolves he had seen in movies. The beasts were tall. He estimated each of them to be at least seven feet. Their arms were thick and muscular, their shoulders broad. Covered with thick hair, Rusty could see the long, ivory claws on their hands and feet. It was difficult to see their facial features, though he could make out the outline of snouts, each with long, sharpened canines. They were Werewolves in every sense of the word.

The hair on the back of his neck stood on end. He shivered with fear but dared not move to tap Joshua. They would notice the slightest movement. Even if they did not, Joshua might awaken, be startled and give away their position. He chose to wait. If patient, the creatures would move on at some point. Rusty sensed their agitation at being so close to the water, especially at nightfall.

They took turns lapping at the water, their long tongues dripping with either water or drool; he could not be sure. Once finished, the three turned to move downriver but stopped when the closest one lifted a clawed hand. The third one, standing nearer the trees, grunted in frustration. Growling softly, it warned the others to move back into the forest, quickly. The one near the river lifted its head and sniffed the air. The others repeated the gesture.

Can they smell us? Rusty wondered fearfully. The thick, heavy grease was pungent.

Seconds later, a voice, thick and hoarse, shocked Rusty when it barked, "Smell human." The three Werewolves looked around, trying desperately to identify the source of the odor, but they could not see Joshua and Rusty lying motionless along the riverbank.

At this distance, they may think we are logs, Rusty thought. The hairs on his neck stood on end the moment he heard it speak. It was a startling revelation and spoke to the level of intelligence that they were facing.

They can speak?

The other two grunted in acknowledgement. The Werewolf nearest the trees leaned his head back, tilted his long snout to the sky, and howled loudly into the night.

The howling echoed outward, through the trees, before it disappeared into the darkness. Within seconds the howling of hundreds of other Werewolves answered the call. Rusty could hear the sounds of crashing bushes and running feet. Startled awake, Joshua moved without making a sound. Quickly and quietly, they replaced their goggles and slid back into the dark waters. Rusty cursed himself silently. He had allowed the three Amoraki to call for others, frozen in fear and unsure about what to do.

Worse than that, he panicked when they slid back into the water, losing his grip on one of the poles. It slipped out of his hand and floated upward, drifting along slowly with the current.

Before they sank beneath the water, Rusty was sure that he saw one of the Amoraki follow the floating stick as it bobbed up and down.

Walking became much more difficult from that moment on, but Rusty decided he would persevere without complaint. He refused Joshua's offer to give up one of his poles. The two continued making good headway, but the presence of Amoraki close to the river had unnerved them.

They had a substantial supply of air that would last for hours. Joshua mentioned the river was less than an hour away, and by then, the Amoraki could have dispersed. If anything, they might follow the floating pole downriver, expecting that to be where they were heading. The creatures would never suspect that they were beneath the water, walking against the current.

A little more than two hours later, moments before their airbags ran out of oxygen, Joshua guided Rusty up the sloping bank to refill their air. They were on edge, wary that the Amoraki might have figured out their plan. Once again, they felt drained.

"The river is around the next bend," Joshua whispered, his eyes furtively darting to the woods and all around them. "Unfortunately, the creek is too shallow in this location for us to remain underwater. We must carry our equipment, as silently as we can, for about ten minutes." He looked at Rusty to see if he understood. Joshua continued, "Once we are in the river, it will be much deeper than before, but the current is slow. The wideness of the river will make it easier to traverse. Its depth will completely hide the light from above." He gestured upward as if they were already below the surface of the river. "I believe that if we can make it safely to the river, then we will make excellent time for the remainder of the journey."

Stepping over scattered rocks, Joshua led the way, with Rusty following silently. They carried their equipment, having tied it together tightly. Rusty walked with embarrassment, unable to forgive himself for the earlier blunder. They moved quickly and quietly, staying as close to the bank as possible.

They reached the river without incident, though they cringed at every sound emanating from the nearby trees. They had agreed to make a break for it and run with all speed to the river if need be. Luckily, no Werewolves burst forth from the forest and its shadows.

Once they settled into the river and lowered themselves to the bottom, Rusty shivered, slightly. The grease had begun to wear off. It would only be a matter of time before the exposure to the cold caused hypothermia.

We better pick up our pace, he thought, worried about how they would handle the cold once the grease thoroughly washed away. They walked for almost three hours along the river bottom before moving up to the broad river banks. With dawn coming, Rusty could see three or four small crocodiles lounging along the banks, waiting for the warmth of the sun.

"They are only three footers," Joshua offered, watching the direction of his gaze. "When I mentioned they were a rarity, I meant the large ones. We have nothing to fear as long as they aren't longer than we are tall." His words offered no comfort.

On the sixth day of their journey, Rusty's mind began to ease. He tensed up, once, when a crocodile as long as the two of them together rubbed against his calf. Its scales, thick and rough, startled him. He looked to his left, spied the torpedo-like shape gliding parallel to them, less than two feet away. It had not made any move to attack them, though it remained by their sides for at least fifteen minutes. Suddenly, it turned and sped towards them. Rusty put out his pole, pointing the tip at it to discourage the huge croc. Joshua turned his body slightly, moving the anaconda head so that it looked in the crocodile's direction. The ploy worked, and the crocodile sped away. It did not return, though Rusty feared it hovered behind him, looking for an opening to attack.

Though they were making good time, they had to surface more frequently. The grease had worn away, and both needed to leave the water to warm up in the sun. Rusty's teeth chattered loudly. Joshua amazed him, once again, since it seemed the cold water did not bother him.

Finally, just before the end of the seventh day, Joshua whispered to Rusty as they waited for their airbags to fill, "We are less than two hours away from our destination. The next time we ascend, we will move away from the river, and with luck, we will be able to climb up to His cave." He accentuated the word purposefully.

Elated, Rusty forced the icy river and his chattering teeth out of his mind. The journey had been arduous, but they had persevered. Now, if their luck held, they would arrive at the cave and find the promised sword. Grudgingly, Rusty admitted that Joshua's faith in The Eighth Lion seemed to be justified. He wanted all of it to be true but still had his doubts.

Moments later, they slipped into the icy, cold river for one last walk along its bottom. Rusty shivered in the darkness below but did not mind. They were almost there. An hour later, Joshua turned to his right, slightly, and they began walking upward for the last time before exiting the water quietly. Joshua unpacked a leather pouch and handed Rusty some dry clothing.

Rusty dressed quickly, scanning the trees and listening closely for any signs of trouble. He could hear the birds chirping and the sounds of insects nearby. It sounded blissful to his ears.

Joshua hid everything in some thick bushes and waved for Rusty to follow him. The mountains loomed ahead. Rusty's looked up, awed as the tallest ones disappeared into the clouds.

They walked for more than thirty minutes; each caught in their thoughts when Rusty tapped Joshua on the shoulder. The old man stopped, puzzled.

"Something is wrong," Rusty said quietly. "Listen."

Joshua lifted his eyebrows before he answered, "I do not hear anything."

"Exactly," Rusty said. "The forest has gone silent. Something is wrong." He looked around, his eyes darting back and forth, but could not see anything.

"Do not worry, my friend, we are almost there. Just a little further," he offered. Joshua turned and led Rusty out of the forest onto a grassy plain. They froze.

They were surrounded by a thousand Werewolves, their large bodies jumping up and down as they howled with excitement. Rusty's body became rigid with fear, and it felt as if the blood in his veins had frozen solid.

NATUS KHAN

THE NEXT FEW MINUTES WERE AS CHAOTIC AS ANYTHING RUSTY HAD ever witnessed. He imagined a powerful tornado ripping trees out of the ground by the roots to be less intimidating than the mass of howling Werewolves. Powerful hands knocked them harshly to the ground. Rusty watched as the Werewolves seized Joshua, binding his hands before him with thick rope. They did the same to Rusty, and then his captors lifted the two of them roughly only to shove them forward. The Werewolves, each a massive beast, covered in coarse hair, no longer remained just creatures of the night. They were real. They were an intimidating mass of muscled bodies, sporting red, lustful eyes and sharp, razor-like fangs. They shoved each other back and forth, snarling and snapping loudly with wild abandon. A few heavy blows from a large paw buffeted Rusty's ears. He winced in pain, his ears ringing loudly.

"Human, smell human," one of them screamed excitedly, pointing at them with his broad sword. The gruff voice sounded odd, almost incomprehensible. Stunned, Rusty watched the Werewolf rush towards them before pummeled backwards by a larger, grey-haired Amoraki. Infuriated, it leapt to its feet, ready to attack but stopped as two of its companions fought to restrain it. Grunting loudly, snorting with fury, it repeated the word "Humans," numerous times. The fight to get at them seemed to have left it, though.

The older Amoraki, a Werewolf with battle scars crisscrossing its torso, pointed defiantly towards the younger creature. Rusty was at a loss to figure out what was happening. His head ached from exhaustion, the lack of sleep slowing his ability to process everything. His brain felt as if it could explode at any moment from the noise. He felt the trickle of blood oozing down the side of his from his left ear. The ringing in his ears began to subside, but most of their words sounded sporadic and nonsensical.

Surrounded by more than a thousand bloodthirsty Amoraki, Rusty became demoralized. His heart sank, and the fight rushed out of him like the air squeezed from a balloon. Exhausted, he wanted to drop to the ground but could not do so as they shoved him forward once again. In their zeal to bind the two of them, the Werewolves tossed them about like ragdolls. Half of the beasts were hell-bent on eating them. They howled with delight, jostling closer to get in on the feast.

Rusty did not know why the grey-haired Werewolf had spared them, though he was sure it was not on their behalf. Rusty could make out various pockets of Werewolves as the beasts separated. What started as a pack of mad, howling Amoraki melted quickly into a melee! Groups of Werewolves viciously attacked each other. The nearest ones had forgotten Joshua and Rusty, caught up in assaulting their comrades. Some battled with swords, swinging them wildly. Others, the ones who seemed to have lost all sense of sanity, dropped their blades so that they could claw and bite each other with a ferocity that sent shivers through his bones.

Is this blood lust? he wondered desperately. The pile of Amoraki or the Werewolves, as far as he was concerned, looked horrific. They were every Werewolf horror movie come to life, each wild and untamed, ferocious and savage. *How does he hope to control them?* During his training, Rusty had held out a small kernel of hope that he would defeat Natus Khan. The brute strength of these creatures, and the sheer ferocity with which they scratched, clawed and bit each other brought a harsh reality crashing down on him.

"All is lost," he mumbled, looking towards Joshua. The older man had sat down, waiting passively with his eyes closed. Rusty thought he might be praying but could not be sure. *How can he remain calm? I am terrified!*

Joshua seemed to be waiting patiently for the surrounding madness to abate, but Rusty knew that deep in his soul, he had to realize that all was lost.

"Humans cannot stand against this madness," Rusty yelled, bewildered. Joshua did not respond.

As soon as he had uttered the words, a gentle breeze picked up, blowing gently across Rusty's face. It was refreshing, but it did not push the fear from his mind. He looked up at the tops of the trees, watching the branches and the green leaves sway back and forth. Rusty was sure the forests remained silent, fearful from the presence of so many snarling Amoraki.

The grey-haired wolf seemed to be the leader of this pack. *Is he Natus Khan?* Rusty wondered.

The wolf growled an order to four of his companions, nodding approvingly as they quickly surrounded Joshua and Rusty, their swords at the ready. They looked menacing, clearly sending the message that they meant to prevent the other Werewolves from attacking the prisoners. The older Werewolf leaned his head back and howled loudly, the sound echoing through the forests. The cacophony of responding howls sent shivers through Rusty. Soon, the others nearby joined, and a symphony of howls reverberated. In response, the remaining groups of Amoraki ceased their fighting. They joined the chorus.

When the concert of howls died away, the grey-haired Amoraki raised his sword triumphantly above his head. "We go to Khan," it barked loudly. The creature lowered his sword, the tip of the blade pointing at the others, daring any of them to disagree. He snapped an order, chomping his jaws together savagely, and turned to walk through the throng. He waved the others forward, ordering them to follow him with the prisoners.

Rusty exhaled slightly, glad to have a moment's reprieve from the madness. His mind seemed addled, weighed down with the worries and the impossibilities of their situation. "I shall not fear," he whispered. He looked to Joshua who remained silent; his hands bound tightly before him, his eyes downcast.

Suddenly, when they were less than ten yards from the forest, a larger, darkly maned Werewolf jumped in front of them, blocking their path.

At least eight feet tall, the beast's shoulders were much broader than the other Amoraki. The creature's black hair glistened in the sunlight. The grey-haired Werewolf snarled with fury at the challenge to his command. The four Amoraki surrounding Joshua and Rusty paused in confusion, their eyes darting back and forth at the other two Werewolves. Rusty could hear a soft whining as many of the Werewolves shrunk away, opening a space between this Amoraki and the five surrounding them.

"One human," the black-haired Werewolf growled, his white fangs gnashing loudly. "We want one of the humans." His guttural voice was thick and heavy. The savagery in his eyes chilled Rusty to the bone. At first, the leader seemed unimpressed and continued marching them forward. Rusty prayed that the older Amoraki would stand his ground. He did not.

Just as it was in nature, size and strength ruled the day. Though the grey-haired Werewolf commanded this pack of ferocious creatures, it did not have the physical power to prevent the challenger from taking one of them to eat. The grey-haired Werewolf had intended on taking the prisoners to Natus Khan, but even with the support of the four behind him, he did not have the strength to enforce his command.

The dark eyes locked onto Rusty and then onto Joshua. Rusty could see his thoughts spinning around, weighing out which of them to give to the Werewolves. Slowly, the Amoraki lifted his sword, grunted softly, and pointed to Joshua.

The closest Amoraki caterwauled with anticipation. Their blood lust returned, and a desire for human flesh quickly built into a craze. Many of them hopped around, waving their swords over their heads, gesticulating with wild abandon. Tongues flashed, and Rusty could see large globs of saliva dripping onto the ground.

The black-maned Werewolf seized Joshua by the ropes, hauled him to his feet, and dragged him into a nearby circle of Amoraki. Massive claws ripped the rope-like thread, freeing his hands. They shoved him to the ground, and twenty of the nearest ones screamed with ecstasy.

Tossing their swords to the ground, strong hands, some white-haired, some grey-haired, and some black-haired, leaned down. They grabbed Joshua and shoved him harshly above their heads for the other Amoraki to see. Howls of delight mixed loudly with barks of pleasure. Rusty knew the end had come for Joshua. The old man had survived in these woods for more than a hundred years, avoiding capture. He had lived alone, in the darkness of a cave, plotting a way to bring Rusty into the Lands of the Khans. He brought Rusty to this world, hoping that the two of them would be the savior's of the human race. He had failed.

Seconds before they ripped Joshua limb from limb, hundreds of Amoraki, those on the edges of the group, exploded with sounds of adoration. "Khan! Khan! Khan!" Thousands began chanting the name with delight. Like a collapsing wave on the ocean when it crashes into land, the Werewolves knelt in supplication, lowering their heads in subservience. The Amoraki holding Joshua dropped him to the ground and released him. They kneeled quickly. The black-haired Werewolf remained standing, his eyes imploring his comrades for support. He released his grip on Joshua's wrist, shoved him harshly, and smiled when Joshua landed with a thud. The old man lay on his back, unmoving. Rusty could see his chest rise and fall and was thankful to see him breathing.

To his amazement, the sea of Amoraki parted slowly, making a wide path for the approaching Khan, a husky figure towering above all of them. A darkly cloaked figure, half the size of the Khan, hobbled alongside, leaning heavily against a wooden staff. The creature's snakelike features, partially hidden beneath the cowls of the purple fabric, reminded Rusty of a King Cobra.

Exasperated, Rusty cried out, "Khan is a human?" The surrounding Amoraki ignored him, their eyes focused on the approaching Khan. Rusty's head ached, the jolt of Khan's appearance striking him harshly like a bolt of lightning. He swooned and passed out.

His eyes came into focus quickly, though his heart sank again in confusion. Natus Khan, the leader of the Amoraki was a mountain of a man. At least, Rusty had thought him to be a man. He realized his error, looking more closely at the beast's features. Natus Khan was not fully human, nor was he entirely Amoraki. He was broad-shouldered with long arms, and the claws of a wolf. His eyes were dark and sinister. His jawline was humanoid, but ivory fangs protruded from the bottom and top lips. Khan had patches of black, wolf-like hair across his arms. His legs, though covered with tan pants, had tufts of hair protruding out at the bottom. He did not have the long, wolf-like snout, but Khan was part Werewolf, Rusty was sure.

His head, encased in the jaws of a large, black lion, sat upon a thick, muscular neck. The lion's fangs had been pried open, providing the illusion that it had tried to eat Natus Khan and had failed. The message, Rusty knew, was that even this beast had failed in its efforts to defeat the Khan.

Rusty looked at Joshua, wondering if the man doubted The Eighth Lion and his visions. Joshua had described the lion as a blue-eyed, black-maned protector. Surely he could see that Khan had chosen to adorn himself with the skin of a black lion with blue eyes.

The Khan's dark eyes were ferocious in their countenance as they locked onto the black-maned Werewolf with an intensity that Rusty had never seen before.

Natus Khan, his torso hairless and human-like, walked with a grace and a power that exceeded anything Rusty had seen from the surrounding Werewolves. He had slung a heavy battle-axe across his massive back. It dripped with fresh blood. Sheathed at his side, the jewel-encrusted hilt of his broadsword glimmered in the sunlight. Ignoring the kneeling Amoraki, the Khan entered the grassy plain, his long legs taking decisive steps. His eyes remained fixated on the Amoraki that had chosen to challenge his authority.

His dark eyes spoke of power and command. It was clear that when compared to Khan, the other Amoraki were mere pups.

Rusty would have liked more time to study Khan and his snake-faced companion, but the snarling Amoraki, his black-mane standing on end, lifted his sword in defiance. He barked a warning to the approaching Khan.

Rusty watched, shocked. If directed at him, he would run away in terror, cowed by the black Werewolf's dominating presence. The Khan, his face impassive, seemed unimpressed by the challenge. Rather than waiting, the younger Werewolf let out a scream of fury, raised his sword, and charged.

In the blink of an eye, with his movement almost too quick for Rusty to process, the Khan sidestepped the charging Werewolf. He drew his sword with his right hand before flicking it outward in a sweeping, sideways arc. The black-maned Amoraki, carried forward by momentum, took four steps past Khan. He did not turn back, though. His head, separated from the body, fell to the ground with a loud thump. The snapping head, its jaws snarling with fury, lay at Khan's feet. The body had taken one, two, three more steps with its sword raised for battle. Slowly, as the blade dropped to its side, the ebony body collapsed into a heap.

A thousand Amoraki howled with delight, acknowledging the Khan's victory with wild abandon. The Khan turned and locked his stare onto Rusty. He looked to Joshua lying prone on the ground and gestured with his sword to the grey-haired Werewolf. Silently, the Khan turned and walked away, escorted once more by the hooded figure with the snakelike eyes.

Rusty looked at Joshua to see how he was faring. His hands bound once more with the heavy rope, Joshua's eyes remained downcast. The nearby Amoraki seized them roughly, leading them away without any further protests.

They walked for about fifteen minutes, moving closer to the mountains when they reached another clearing. A few hundred yards away from the base of one of the peaks, the encampment held tens of thousands of Werewolves. Rusty's heart sank. What he thought had been a thousand Amoraki had been the tip of the iceberg.

How many are there? he worried. There was no way the humans on the other side of these mountains could stand against this hoard. *I don't think earth could stand up to them.* Shoved harshly to the ground and forced to kneel in supplication, Rusty looked up into the eyes of Natus Khan, King of the Amoraki, and ruler of the Lands of the Khans.

Rusty looked into the eyes of the beast, afraid. This creature was responsible for slaying every human in these lands. Its face offered indifference to human suffering. Human emotion would not sway this creature from its chosen purpose.

Natus Khan sat stoically on a large, ivory throne crafted from human skulls. Two Dragon skulls, molded into armrests, held Khan's powerful arms. It took Rusty a few minutes to realize the eyeless sockets staring back at him had once been human.

Rusty wondered, looking in awe at the size of the two skulls. *How could he kill a dragon?* He would have thought it impossible.

The Khan's eyes scanned Joshua and then Rusty. He raised a finger on his right hand, pointing at the two of them. "Jochi," he demanded with a deep and booming voice.

Rusty watched the features of the approaching creature closely. The face remained hidden beneath the cloak. *Is he angry? Is he afraid"* Whichever it was, the purple hooded figure hobbled closer to the two of them. He leaned in, sniffed loudly, and turned to speak to the Khan.

"This one is not of this world," he offered, pointing towards Rusty. "He does not smell like the other humans. His stench is foul, to be sure, but it is not the same." He waited for the Khan to speak.

"You," the Khan commanded, "Why have you entered our world without my permission?" His chiseled features and vice-like eyes gripped Rusty's heart.

Rusty was at a loss for words. He did not know how to answer the Khan's question. He did not want to give away Joshua's plan. Part of him still held out hope for a miracle.

The hooded figure, its purple robes rustling, turned and offered, "Should I strike him, my Khan?" He turned to hit Rusty with his staff but stopped when Khan raised his large hand.

"That is not necessary, Wizard," Natus Khan answered, pausing to look upward as three large shadows blotted out the sun for a few seconds. "Your Dragons have returned," he added smiling.

Rusty turned and looked upward. Three Dragons flew in wide circles, their screeches filling the air. When he first spied them, flying above the snow-capped mountains from the other side of the valley, the Dragons seemed no larger than bats. Now, though, Rusty could almost count the scales on their bodies. The Dragons were massive, majestic, and intimidating. The smaller one, a mosaic of charcoal grey and black sparkling in the sunlight, maintained a safe distance from the larger ones. The two others, colossal when compared to the black Dragon, were lava red with thick, interlocking scales covering their bodies. He was mesmerized and breathless to be so close to them. Their wings beat loudly, and many of the Amoraki whined in fear. Rusty looked up into the Khan's eyes, shuddering to think this creature could control Dragons. The dark eyes bore into him, and for the first time in his life, Rusty knew what it meant to be afraid to die.

Khan gestured to the wizard, a subtle movement, no more than a flick of the wrist, and immediately he removed the hood, exposing the snake-like countenance. He ordered the grey-haired Amoraki to clear the area of the other Werewolves. Barks of command filled the air. The sitting Amoraki leapt to their feet, scrambling to obey the Khan's commands.

A few minutes later, they were alone with the Khan, the Wizard, and twenty Amoraki. Rusty guessed that they must be the Khan's generals. Natus Khan barked an order, and the captives were scooped up, dragged over to him, and shoved back to the ground. Flanked by three heavily armed Amoraki, each holding battleaxes, Natus Khan looked at the two of them suspiciously. The dark wizard had moved to a spot behind the throne, his presence masked by the Dragon skulls. The Khan noticed and offered a broad smile, his razor-sharp fangs glistening with delight at Rusty's discomfort.

"They are trophies. If I so desire, you may earn the right to be added to my throne," the giant bragged, his voice deep and full of command. "I have questions. Beware, the Amoraki are all very loyal. If any of them detect hesitation from you or feel that you are not answering with the truth, they will kill you. Are we at an understanding?"

Rusty did not wait and blurted out, "We are, My Lord." He added the title, expecting it to appease Khan. The smug look of satisfaction told him that he was correct.

The Khan leaned his head back and tilted his ear to the wizard. His firm eyes fixated on Rusty's. They whispered back and forth for a few minutes. Nodding, the Khan leaned forward and asked, "If you are not of this world, what world are you from?"

"I am from Millstadt, Illinois," Rusty began, "It is a town in the United States of America on the planet earth." He saw no reason to hold back the truth. They were already doomed, and only the Khan's good graces would get them out of their current predicament.

"Why are you here, human?" the Khan nodded, accepting Rusty's answer. His voice dripped with distaste and hatred, causing the hairs on the back of Rusty's neck to stand on end.

"Aren't you a human, too?" Rusty asked. The nearest Werewolf stepped forward and struck him harshly across the face. His head snapped backwards, his blood splattering the ground behind him. He sat back up slowly and said, "I am supposed to kill you."

The Amoraki growled a warning. One-stepped forward, the battle-axe held high to strike a death blow. "Hold," the Khan ordered. He smiled, intrigued by Rusty's bluntness.

"It looks as though you will fail in your quest," he answered smugly. Once again, the Wizard leaned forward to whisper into his ear. Annoyed by the interruption, the Khan waved him back and looked down at Joshua.

"Old man, Jochi wants to know if this human knows about the sacrifice it took to bring him here." His words confused Rusty. He looked at Joshua, but the grey eyes refused to look up. "Does he know that the only way into our world is through the sacrifice of a loved one?"

The words stung Rusty to his core. Was it true? Did his mom have to die for Joshua to bring him here against his will? He could not read Joshua's facial expression. The Khan smiled, happy that his words had stung Rusty.

"We do not like humans, whether they are from our world or another. You are a despicable race, nothing more than food and sport. Once I have finished conquering the Known World, we may turn our attention to your world. Jochi is confident that he will be able to find a way into your world since you were able to cross over into ours." Satisfied, the Khan smiled, drumming the fingers on his right hand onto the Dragon skull. The sound echoed into the silence. He seemed to be contemplating something but did not indicate his plans.

Rusty could hear the sounds of chopping, the sound of nearby trees falling to the ground. He shuddered and began to wonder if they were going to burn him at the stake. A sense of foreboding fell over him. Rusty pushed the sound out of his mind, choosing to focus on the memories of his mother and father and his brother. A calm serenity passed over his face, and he looked up to smile at Natus Khan.

The Khan's jawline hardened. Fury flooded into his eyes. The smile had offended the Khan and that made Rusty happy. If he were going to die, it would not be in fear. *It's what the Amoraki part of this creature does not understand about humans.*

The Khan issued a command to the nearby Werewolves, his voice low but full of scorn. He focused on Rusty with a smile before saying, "Crucify him."

Howling with delight, five of the Werewolves hauled Rusty to his feet. A few others ran past him holding three trees, the trunks stripped of all their branches. The Amoraki spun him around and dragged him forcefully behind the others. Rusty looked back over his shoulder at the Khan; the brute had come down from his throne to follow them. They dragged him to a spot at the base of the mountains, beneath the circling Dragons. Their wings flapped loudly, drowning out most of the angry snarls.

Dropping him to the ground, one of the Werewolves pinned him down, the creature's weight making it difficult to breathe. Rough hands, the fingers clawed and hairy, forced his face upward. They held Rusty's head up to compel him to watch while the other Amoraki dug the hole. The Amoraki dropped one end of a tree into the hole and stood it up. They filled in the gap with dirt and turned back to Rusty. Rusty looked at the trunk; its branches stripped away and broken off remained knotted with sharpened edges from top to bottom. The two other logs were lashed together haphazardly, looking to Rusty like the wings of a dragonfly. He knew what was coming, but he did not fret. His mind filled with a sense of tranquility. His thoughts had emptied of all worries.

The mantra *I shall not fear* filled his heart and his mind. He had said these words so many times with his mother that they flooded quickly into his thoughts. He refused to let fear into his heart.

They stripped Rusty of his shirt, shoving him harshly against the two poles. The broken branches pierced deeply into his back, but he did not cry out. Clawed hands lashed his wrists to the poles with thorny vines. Inch long thorns punctured his wrists, and the blood flowed out of him like a river. Though the pain was excruciating, he refused to cry out. Four Amoraki lifted him off the ground and carried him howling with delight to the upright pole. They wrapped his torso tightly, once, twice, three times around the trunk. He could hear their celebration as more thorns cut into his waist. With his arms suspended at such an odd angle, Rusty tried to look down. One of the Amoraki jumped onto the shoulders of another, and soon they brought more vine and wrapped it around his forehead and face, binding his head against the pole. One of the thorns gouged into his cheek, puncturing clear through. He could feel the tip of the thorn on the inside of his mouth. Heavy blood flowed down his throat, gagging him. Rusty mustered all his will, refusing to cry out. The pain was intense. His body felt as if it was burning in a hundred places. His legs ached as they dangled freely, the weight of his body forcing the thorns more deeply into his skin. Patting each other roughly on their backs, the Amoraki turned to Khan and bowed, proud of their work.

With his eyes covered in blood, Rusty could not see Natus Khan's face clearly. He knew, though, that Khan was angry. He had expected Rusty to cry out in pain, to ask for forgiveness, and to beg the Khan for mercy. Rusty had cheated him of this satisfaction.

Standing before Rusty, his dark eyes peering upward, the Khan ordered, "Bring the old man." The Amoraki dropped Joshua below Rusty's feet.

Rusty's heart sank with sadness. Rusty could not see his face, but he knew the old man's heart had filled with despair. Joshua's shoulders sagged heavily. He could just make out Joshua's words, whispered for the Khan's ears, "He is innocent." He repeated the words a few times, lowered his head and once again, Rusty wondered if he was praying.

Rusty watched in horror as Natus Khan turned toward the others before saying, "Eat him." The Werewolves were delirious. Those with battle-axes unslung them, quickly tossing them to the ground. The grey-haired wolf, the one that had prevented the others from eating them earlier, threw his sword to the ground and crouched low, preparing to leap onto Joshua.

Joshua turned his back to all of them and said softly, "Remember always; you must have Faith."

Rusty could not see him clearly, but he tried to nod in response. "I will," he mouthed, the thorns making it difficult to speak.

In the few seconds before the twenty Amoraki pounced on him, Joshua stood up, raised his bound hands above his head and said to Rusty, "Anyone can make the sacrifice. You just need the courage and the faith."

Rusty hung on the poles in agony but was grateful to have the blood blocking out his vision. He wished, silently, that it could flow into his ears to block out all sound. Rusty did not cry out in anguish the moment the Werewolves ripped into Joshua's flesh. He refused to respond to the sound of crushing bones, though it was almost too much to bear. Rusty flooded his mind with images of his mother, his father, and his brother Zach. He thought about the four of them, sitting around the kitchen table as a family. They had never been able to do so in real life, but Rusty was grateful to have done so even if in his dream. He swallowed the impulse to cry out, feeling it would dishonor the courage Joshua had shown in the face of his impending death. It was over in minutes. Rusty's sadness drained away, replaced with a fury that he had never felt in his entire life.

Natus Khan stepped forward and looked up at Rusty's blood-covered body. "He is not of our world and does not deserve to be eaten by the Amoraki." He turned and spat on the ground. "We will leave him for the Dragons to devour at their leisure." Rusty expected the Khan to walk away but heard the soft footsteps of the approaching wizard.

"My Lord," the creature offered, "May I make a request." He handed Rusty's Bible to the Khan, pointed upward, and waited for the Khan to acknowledge him.

"Of course, Jochi, as a favored servant, I would be honored to hear your request." Rusty could hear the heavy sarcasm. The Khan had assumed his orders finished it and did not appreciate Jochi's interruption.

Their garbled words, spoken in whispers, confused Rusty.

"Yes," the Khan responded, "You have my permission." He turned to the nearby Amoraki and ordered, "Let it be known to all the others that his flesh is tainted. He is to be left, crucified on these poles, and untouched. In the morning, at sunrise, Jochi will sacrifice him. Then, when the remaining Amoraki arrive we shall cross over the mountains and invade the Known World. Soon, each Amoraki will have their fill of human flesh." The howls of delight returned.

The Khan turned to leave but halted. Turning back to Rusty, the Khan looked up at him and shook his head with disgust. He returned to stand before Rusty, kicked at the upright pole with all his might, and grunted with delight when the base of it snapped like a twig. Rusty teetered for a second and crashed backwards, with a loud thud, onto the ground. The blow knocked the wind out of him, the force jarring his body, the broken branches impaling him more deeply. The Khan dropped the leather-bound Bible onto Rusty's chest and turned to leave. The Amoraki howled with delight, and once again, Rusty passed out.

A CAULDRON OF UQUAYS

HE DID NOT KNOW HOW LONG HE LAY UNCONSCIOUS, BUT RUSTY WOKE
up looking into the vastness of the star-filled sky above. His whole body
ached. The muscles on his arms screamed in agony. He could feel the
puncture wounds along his body, each a slow-burning sensation from
the thorns piercing into his skin. The blood was no longer oozing, which
meant he had stopped bleeding. It did not matter, though, since all was
lost. Joshua was dead, and the wizard with the snake-like face would
sacrifice him tomorrow. Rusty shuddered. He could see the three Dragons
flying in wide circles around the mountain peak above. Their wings
beat silently in the night as they glided in silence, their dark silhouettes
blocking out hundreds of stars.

A movement from halfway up the mountain caught Rusty's attention
as something appeared over a rock ledge. Glimmering, a small apparition
began gliding down the summit slowly, its body shimmering with a faint
luminescence. Rusty inhaled slowly, wondering if the entity intended
to devour him. He thought he might be hallucinating, but the specter
continued its slow descent, unabated. Dried blood caked his eyes, making
it difficult to see clearly, but the approaching apparition took his focus
away from the pain.

Moments later, in the silence of the night, he looked up into the eyes of a floating spirit; a four-year-old boy with blond hair and shimmering, blue eyes. Rusty was sure that he was hallucinating, but he smiled with joy. He had hoped to be able to see this face one last time, before he died.

"You okay, little bro?" the phantom of his older brother asked. The voice echoed in his head, filling his heart with warmth. All of his pain melted away. Rusty had never met Zach, but he had known his brother's face. He had looked at it hundreds of times with his mother, wishing each time that he had been able to enjoy time with his brother. His mind flooded with happiness. He did not care if this was a hallucination.

"I miss you," Rusty said, his voice weak. "I miss everyone." He wished that he could wrap his arms around his brother and hug him tightly. *I would never let him go,* he thought, the heartache almost too much to handle. "I miss mom and dad. I am all alone," Rusty cried softly. He could not take his eyes off Zach's face.

"We know," the little boy replied. "We miss you too. Mom and dad wanted to come to see you, but only one of us could cross over. They wanted it to be me. So here I am."

"Are you going to take me with you," Rusty pleaded. He remembered the pain, afraid that if Zach left, the intense agony would return. It had grown to an unbearable level. He winced a few times, fighting back the tears but kept his eyes on his brother's ghost.

"Sorry, dude. It is not your time," Zach smiled warmly. The apparition reached out his left hand and caressed Rusty's face. "When it is, just know that we will all be together once more. We will always be a family. We can sit around the kitchen table, talking with mom and dad. I will even play catch with you if you like."

Frustrated, Rusty responded, "What can I do? I am trapped." Zach might be a fabrication of his imagination, but Rusty could not be angry. Zach's appearance had filled him with happiness. He loved Zachary with all his heart, and the joy that he felt was absolute.

"Leave that to me," the little boy offered. "I brought a friend." Rusty could see the tiny, brown bat as it flitted down the mountainside stopping a few times to rest on some boulders. Its wings beat quickly, as it dove straight for them. Moments after it landed, a hundred more bats flew out from the mountains, following the path of the first, and landing gently on Rusty. He could feel them resting all over his body. The pressure soothed the pain.

"What's happening?" he responded, the fear evident. He started to struggle but stopped when Zach offered reassurance.

"Don't worry, little bro. I brought little Uquay and his friends to help you." His shimmering body floated above Rusty, his smile calm and soothing.

Rusty could feel the tiny bats gnawing at the thorny vines near his hands and waist. They were not biting into his flesh, though, and he relaxed. Soon, as they chewed through each of the vines, his bindings fell away. Some of the thorns remained dug into his flesh. Rusty could feel some of the bats, even the ones on his face, chewing through them gingerly. It took a few minutes, but the remaining vines fell away. The bats had freed him.

"I need you to listen, little bro," Zach offered. "Rollover and crawl your way up this mountain. Ignore the pain. You have to get up, and you have to get moving. You do not want to be here when morning comes. They will kill you. Do you hear me? Do not stop crawling until you get to where you need to go."

Rusty's mind raced. He had been sure Zach's apparition had been a figment of his imagination. Somehow, Zach had glided down the side of the mountain to speak with him, to offer words of encouragement. Rusty, convinced that he was on death's door, was sure that his mind played tricks on him. Yet, here he was, lying on his belly, freed from the thorns by hundreds of tiny, brown bats. Looking up, Rusty expected to be alone. His neck ached, but Zach was still there.

"Where? Where do I go?" he asked, hopeful that all of this was real.

"Follow me, little bro?" the little boy offered. Zach smiled and glided slowly ahead. He looked back every so often, ensuring that Rusty followed.

Rusty crawled at a snail's pace. The muscles in his body ached, and the hundreds of puncture wounds on his skin burned. He never gave up, though, following Zach's spirit up the side of the mountain. He crawled over large rocks and small boulders, dragging his body upward, behind the glowing specter. The tiny bats flew with him, stopping ahead every few seconds and waiting for him to catch up. He was happy to have their company.

The motley crew worked their way up the side of the mountain. As they approached the ledge, Rusty's eyes fell onto the circling Dragons. Joshua had warned that they guarded against access to the cave. Rusty knew that at some moment, one of them would swoop down and scoop him up in its talons. Pausing to rest, he asked Zach, "What do I do about the Dragons?" He leaned his head down and rested it for a few seconds, enjoying the coolness of a flattened rock against his face. It was refreshing, and it energized him.

"You have to have Faith," Zach answered. "Don't you remember what mom always taught us?" Rusty could see the ledge, less than thirty feet above him. Zach glided upward and turned to face Rusty once more.

"I love you, little bro. Mom and dad want you to know that they are proud of you."

The finality of these words tore through Rusty. "Don't go," he cried, the tears streaking down his face. "I need you. I cannot do this without you." He looked up, but Zach had already disappeared.

Rusty did not have time to mourn. Sadness washed away from him like a wave returning to the ocean, replaced with a longing to reach the safety of the ledge. Zach told him it was there; he only needed to make an effort. He began to crawl once more but paused at the sound of flapping wings.

One of the Dragons swooped downward, dropping toward him like a stone. Before it could snatch him away from the mountainside, a cauldron of Uquays burst forth from surrounding caves. They flew straight at the Dragon, swirling around its face and eyes. They were joined by thousands of other bats as they burst out of nearby caverns, attacking the other two with a flurry. Tiny, brown flecks, looking no larger than a group of gnats, flew into the Dragons' eyes, ears, and faces.

Infuriated, the Dragons flew upward, swatting at the bats with their wings and their paws. The efforts were futile as the cauldron continued to grow. The mass of brown bats blocked out the Dragon faces, swirling around them like a massive cloud of dust. *There are hundreds of thousands, maybe even a million,* Rusty thought. He did not wait to count them but instead started crawling upward as quickly as his exhausted limbs would take him. He ignored the scraping rocks as he felt fresh lacerations on his skin.

Finally, with an effort that he did not know he had left in him, Rusty pulled himself up and over the ledge. Zach had gone. Lying in front of a wooden door, Rusty breathed heavily. He pushed himself upward when one of the Dragons flew by the ridge, swatting with its clawed hands at a brown, swirling cloud.

He looked down the mountain, amazed at the distance that he had crawled in the darkness. Rusty could see the distant flickering of fires below. There were thousands. The Amoraki had gone to sleep confident that they did not need to post any guards. Celebrating the pending invasion well into the night, the plain below held the sound of their sleeping in its silent grasp.

Rusty rolled back over, took a few deep breaths, and forced himself to sit up. Fighting against wooziness, he stood up, walked over, and leaned heavily against the door. It opened a fraction, the darkness inviting Rusty to safety. He looked upward at the Dragons and, without hesitation, slipped into the blackness. The door closed behind him without a sound.

"Did they have to die?" Rusty asked the large, black-maned lion standing before him like a majestic marble statue. As soon as he yelled the words, he regretted his bluntness. Joshua and his mother would have been disappointed to hear him speak like this to the Eighth Lion.

The blue eyes bore into him with an intensity that eclipsed the fury he had seen in Natus Khan's eyes. Rusty had expected darkness, but instead, the chamber infused with light as the torches lining the walls burst into flames, each burning brightly and showering the den with brightness. He met the gaze of the Eighth Lion without flinching but noticed another wooden door, to his left, closing. Rusty wanted to ask who had just left the chamber but held his tongue.

He waited patiently for an answer, though his skin, embedded with hundreds of thorns, throbbed with pain, the tiny puncture wounds burning sharply. If this had been another place and another time, Rusty would have fled in fear. The Eighth Lion was larger than he was tall. Its ebony hair shone brightly in the torchlight. Rusty was sure that he could see his reflection in the sleek, black hair if he looked close enough.

"Why didn't you save him?" Rusty demanded, referring to Joshua. "You have the power to do so? You could save all of us if you want?" His words spewed out of him without restraint, without anger, in exasperation. "You do not have to allow pain and suffering. You could have saved her?"

Rusty's reproach of The Eighth Lion did not offer him comfort. His mother had suffered. He had not been with her at the time of her death. He had doubted the veracity of Joshua's faith. He had questioned the existence of The Eighth Lion and all that it meant. Yet here he was, hobbled and suffering, standing before divineness. His mother would have demanded he be more humble. She would have insisted that he revere the opportunity of the moment. She had known of Joshua's plans and had agreed to them without hesitation. *Why?* Was it because she had faith in him that he did not have for himself? Was it because of the trust she had in The Eighth Lion? His mother had given her life so that he might cross into the Lands of the Khans. She had done so without proof that this world even existed.

What had she said to him? "You are needed." Her words reverberated, rolling into his head like thunder across a grassy plain.

Slowly, as the weight of his words sank in, Rusty lowered himself to his knees and bowed his head in supplication.

"Should I play a role in death and destruction?" The Eighth Lion's voice boomed. "Is it better than my offer of life and eternity?" He added the second question without hesitation. "Is it not better that I offer choice?" The blue eyes offered kindness and warmth, though his questions were a challenge to Rusty's own.

"A choice? About what?" Rusty asked, confused. He wanted to believe, but doubts clouded his mind. They refused to let him do so, completely.

"Faith!" the words boomed throughout the chamber, echoing against the walls. The Lion's impassive face loomed over him. Rusty looked to the large paws, retracted and offering no violence. *But I know they are there.*

"How do I know if you are real?" Rusty asked, the words tumbling out of his mouth without restraint.

"Would you have me deny my existence?" the Eighth Lion demanded, his eyes widening to the point that the bright blue pupils shined in the torchlight.

"I have doubts," Rusty admitted. "I am afraid, but I would not demand that you deny your existence."

"Well spoken, but your actions betray your true emotions," the commanding voice responded. "You doubt your senses, and thus you doubt your purpose. These doubts cause you to question your existence and mine. What do doubters do best?"

The lion shook his black mane vigorously, waiting for Rusty's response. When no answer came, he continued, "They doubt. How is it that a blind man may see while others with vision are blind?"

Rusty stammered, uncomfortable with the turn in the conversation. "What do you mean? A blind man cannot see. It is not possible." He could hear the frustration in his voice building slowly.

The Eighth Lion's eyes hardened for a few seconds, "Thus spoken, you have proven my point."

Moving closer, the large paws slapping the ground as he walked, the Lion brought his face close to Rusty. Changing the direction of the conversation, the Lion said, "I do not provide the ability to choose lightly. If I take away choice, then what is the purpose of existence. Humans can see even though they may be blind. They can hear even though they may be deaf. They can speak even though they may choose to be mute. I would not take that away from them, though many have made a choice not to believe. They have that choice, to turn their backs on faith."

"Those with doubts always demand that I prove my existence upon their command. Dissatisfied, they respond by demanding that those with faith deny my existence."

Rusty admitted, "It is much more difficult to have faith in this world. It is so much easier not to believe."

The Lion whispered, "Only to those who doubt."

Rusty's mind exploded with a newfound appreciation for everything his mother, father, and even Joshua had taught him. "When we question faith, it is because we fear what comes after." He remembered his father's words. "We hope that by questioning faith, we can knock others off their perch. We believe that if they falter, they will do so with us. Leading a faithless life is lonely, and the doubters hope that if they are in the company of others, it will assuage the fear of what comes after. We do so because we know that we have not held the Covenant. We fear that we will be refused the treasure waiting for us in the afterlife."

He took a deep breath, held it for a few seconds, and then exhaled. "My mother once told me that people without faith are like scornful little children. When denied something that they desire, children will turn their backs on their parents," he added, inspired by the lessons from his mother. "Faith means believing in something without reason and always without direct proof."

"Though I know that my family awaits me, I fear that I may not get to sit with them at our table. My mother's kitchen offered warmth and love. With them gone, I fear that I have lost that chance forever, though my mother felt it would be an eternal place for us to gather. Have I lost that chance?" He looked up, expecting an answer, but did not get one. "I know we all die; that is a part of life. I know that we should honor and cherish the gift that is the greatest above all others. I have always understood my mother's words, but I admit that I did not always heed them. She lived her life based on faith, not fear. She did not worry about what came after the storm. Her faith carried her into it, buoyed her during it, and lifted her spirits after, regardless of the damage."

"I entered your cave full of doubts, determined to exact a promise that if I did your bidding, I would survive. Short of this, I planned to demand the opportunity to sit with my family at the table. I realize now that my demands, and my fear, and my doubts are all the same."

He turned, walked past the Eighth Lion to look at a wooden table in the center of the room. "I know now why my questions have gone unanswered. I am human, and therefore I am more than capable of providing the answers for myself." He looked at the wooden table and a sword with a milky, white blade. The jewel encrusted hilt was magnetic. Placed next to a shield of interlocking, emerald-colored feathers, it beckoned to his soul. Rusty could almost hear the words in the beating of his heart. *Pick me up, pick me up.*

Without asking for permission, Rusty picked up the blade and the shield. He lifted the sword in front of him and smiled. He appreciated the weight and the balance; it was the perfect weapon. It felt lighter than the wooden one. The razor-sharp edges glistened in the torchlight.

"I go forth, not knowing whether I am the Hand of God or merely a token of despair," he started. "I choose faith, and I thank you deeply for the opportunity." Rusty opened the heavy, wooden door and walked out onto the ledge. The pain from his wounds dissipated, evaporating instantly the moment he walked into the fresh air.

The top of the sun appeared over the horizon, its golden rays showering the landscape. Looking down the mountain, Rusty lifted the sword above his head and yelled at the top of his voice, "Khan!" His words rolled down the mountain, bursting forth across the grassy plain. The howls of fifty thousand Amoraki, their blood-red eyes lifted upward in his direction, exploded in response.

Once again, he bellowed to the Werewolves below, "Khan!" This time, possibly because they were surprised at the strength and power in his voice, his words met silence. Rusty did not look back. He started his walk down the mountain.

WHEN WORLDS COLLIDE

AS HE BEGAN SAUNTERING DOWN THE STEEP, ROCKY SLOPE WITH A renewed sense of purpose, Rusty could see the mighty frame of Natus Khan, the half-man half-werewolf, standing statue still below. He envisioned a snarl on Kahn's curled lips, his sharpened canines exposed. It helped to know that his challenge would anger the Khan. An enraged opponent would be more likely to make a mistake.

Rusty pushed the fifty-thousand Amoraki from his mind. *I cannot let them be a distraction,* he reminded himself. *He is more capable a warrior than any of the others. I need to stay focused.*

Picking his way around and over the myriad of boulders that pocketed the ankle-high grass, Rusty grinned, amused by the interaction occurring below. He watched as Khan used a muscular forearm to brush away the approaching wizard. The darkened robe, with its purple hems fluttering in the wind as the wizard stumbled, brought a brief sense of joy. Unfortunately, Jochi did not lose his footing. The wizard righted himself and quickly approached the Khan once more. They looked to be arguing, the hobbled Jochi leaning heavily on his wooden staff and gesturing wildly toward Rusty. During the brief exchange, Natus Khan's eyes never left the mountainside. His fixed gaze made it clear that he intended to meet Rusty's challenge and that any prodding from the wizard would not change his mind.

"I can almost hear the wizard's words," Rusty sneered. It felt good to say it aloud. "He is not Amoraki. Have him captured and bound, and let me sacrifice him."

He slowed his pace, stepped around three colossal granite boulders, and smirked, "He will not agree to your plea, wizard. Natus Khan is a demon plagued by the sin of pride. Do you hear me? He is too prideful, and that shall be his undoing."

Rusty stopped and looked outward beyond the hoard of Amoraki gathered below. The world looked peaceful, a canopy of greens from the majestic trees spreading out in every direction. The blanket of leaves, gilded lightly by the sun's golden rays, seemed magical. The natural splendor offered serenity, and Rusty sighed with satisfaction. The breathtaking view had a calming effect. Enjoying the moment, he inhaled deeply, held his breath for a few seconds, and slowly exhaled. Wishing that this feeling of bliss would never end, he sat down slowly on a large boulder. Needing fresh legs for the oncoming battle, Rusty guessed there was less than a fourth of a mile remaining to the bottom.

The Werewolves, a mass of grey, white, brown, and black hair, howled in despair when he sat down. Frenetically, thousands of them began jumping up and down, pointing at him with their long, clawed hands. They growled at Natus Khan, barking their frustrations. Hundreds started swinging their swords wildly above their heads, pleading with Khan to give them permission to climb the mountain and seize the insolent human. The sight might have struck fear into his heart, but it did not do so this time.

Natus Khan refused to heed their cries of frustration. Outwardly, the Khan waited with his muscular arms folded across a massive chest. He tried to project patience to his warriors, but the dark eyes betrayed his genuine emotions. Natus Khan was seething with anger.

Rusty smiled inwardly, holding his emotions in check. Sitting at this height, with the green-feathered shield leaning against the boulder, he was close enough to see the fury as it spread across the Khan's face. The beast was a creature of action. This was a waiting game. Time would work in Rusty's favor, if he remained patient. If he could survive the initial onslaught of savagery that he knew would be forthcoming, he might just have a chance.

A movement beside him, a scurrying on the rock to his right, caught his attention. A black scorpion, no bigger than a field mouse, scuttled up the side of the boulder and breached the top, its stinger hovering just above its body. Mesmerized, Rusty could see a tiny drop of venom, the size of a drop of dew, dangling from its stinger. It crept forward slowly, hesitated, then moved a few inches closer. His presence did not startle the creature. Even when he lifted his hand and waved it above the ebony body, the pincers snapped open and shut aggressively. Rusty had never seen a live scorpion in the wild. His size should have intimidated it enough to send it scurrying back down the other side of the boulder. With only a few inches until the scorpion reached him, Rusty lifted the pommel of his sword above it and smashed it against the rock. A screech of pain from below grabbed his attention, and he turned to look at Khan and the wizard.

The wizard had cried out in pain. He held his right hand to his forehead, his hatred filled eyes looking up at Rusty. Rusty looked at him with understanding and smiled as he nodded to the wizard. He picked up the remains of the scorpion and tossed it away.

He knows that Khan can be beaten, Rusty thought emboldened by the revelation. *Otherwise, why would he send a scorpion?*

This time, when the wizard approached, Natus Khan shoved him back with a greater force, almost knocking him to the ground. It struck Rusty as humorous, and this time he did not try to hide his emotion. He laughed aloud, the sound audible to the sea of Werewolves below.

Thousands of Amoraki fell silent and all of them, their one hundred thousand, blood-red eyes, looked at him confounded. They hated all humans; their lust for human flesh drove them into a state of unbridled lunacy. The Khan, though part human, carried the same hatred for humanity. The wizard held the same hatred, though Rusty felt he sought power and dominion over the world. Jochi was not of this world of that Rusty was certain. He was a demon in the form of a man.

The cast of characters gathered below intrigued him. Their only purpose, the common thread that bound them together, was the annihilation of the human race.

Behind the Amoraki a group of Dragons, some lava-red and some emerald-green, dotted the landscape. Rusty counted twenty-three, but the smaller black ones blended in with, the larger ones, and he could not be sure. *Why hasn't he ordered one of them to fly up here and eat me?* he wondered. *It's pride, of course.*

His challenge had forced Khan, and thus the wizard, into refraining from using the Dragons.

Natus Khan believed in his superiority and could not refuse Rusty's challenge. Jochi had immediately recognized the danger Rusty posed. Rusty could almost read his lips. Only deep magic could arm a human with a sword and a shield when he had gone up the mountain weaponless.

His face hidden, Jochi's gestures betrayed the emotions he was feeling. He feared the unknown. Rusty could see the wizard, his hood pulled tightly around his face, pressuring Khan to refuse. Wary that the Khan might pummel him again, he remained at a distance. As the leader of the Amoraki, he was under no obligation to battle someone from another world. The purple sleeves slid up the pale forearms as the Wizard continued gesticulating wildly.

Well-rested, Rusty finally stood. He looked at the sunlit sky, captivated by the green blanket covering the forest below and then looked downward, his eyes locking onto the silent crowd of Werewolves. Lifting the milky-white blade above his head, Rusty gathered the green-feathered shield in his left arm and pulled it close to his body.

He roared, his voice echoing loudly, "I have challenged Natus Khan in front of the Amoraki, wizard. He cannot refuse me." He motioned with the tip of the sword, waving it from side to side. "I am only a human, and pride forces him to accept my challenge." Rusty started walking again. He forced himself to remain calm. He wanted to run the remaining distance, wishing he had the power to leap down the side of the mountain in one bound. His nerves tingled, charged up for the coming battle. "He cannot refuse me," he yelled at Jochi the moment his feet touched the flattened plain. He looked at Joshua's bone fragments, the only part of him that remained, and his anger boiled like wildfire. Rusty pointed the tip of his sword at Jochi and screamed with fury, "He cannot refuse me!"

The Amoraki fell into silence, stunned to hear a human challenge one of them so openly. Rarely had they faced a human with the courage to stand his ground, one who refused to cower in their presence. Slowly, by the thousands, they widened the distance between themselves and the Khan. In this battle, the Amoraki would play no part. Rusty had challenged Natus Khan to single combat, to the death.

Rusty inhaled with anticipation as his senses heightened to a new level. He stopped walking, choosing instead to wait for the Khan's next move.

They had more than two hundred yards between them, but Rusty knew Natus Khan still held the upper hand. The creature had it within his power to order him seized, bound, and executed.

Rusty watched Natus Khan. He was confident, though, that Khan would not do so.

A human had called out his name in front of his warriors. A human had raised his sword above his head, declaring that he would be Khan's superior in battle. The giant, still annoyed by the gestures of his minion, issued a final warning, "To refuse his challenge is to refuse the Amoraki. Would you have my power over them weakened?"

Natus Khan, the fearless leader of a Werewolf army, turned toward his challenger and howled with delight. The Khan brushed the wizard backwards once more and looked to Rusty with hatred. Turning to a silver-haired Amoraki he pointed wildly toward his tent and grunted a command. The younger Werewolf dashed to the tent, grabbed the Khan's sword, and returned it to him.

Advancing at a slow jog, Rusty was vaguely aware that the wide circle of Amoraki had moved to close off any retreat. The mass of Werewolves ringed in the two combatants, keeping their distance. The bloodthirsty creatures fell silent for a few moments but roared with unbridled jubilation the moment the Khan raised his sword and howled his battle cry.

Icy fear crept back into Rusty's heart, but he decided not to fight against it this time. Fear would keep his senses heightened. Fear would keep him wary, and fear might just keep him alive. He stopped less than twenty yards from the Khan and waited.

I will fear no evil, he thought. The complete words from the prayer, spoken often by his mother, escaped him. He found comfort in the part the phrase that he could remember. *I will fear no evil.*

The two combatants, a human from the earth and a Werewolf from the Lands of the Khans, sized each other up. The moment the Khan began to run, Rusty could feel the ground shake beneath him. It might be that his heartbeat pounded loudly enough in his chest that the world seemed to tremble. He could not be sure.

Rusty cried out, "Khan. I offer battle for my mother. I offer battle for my father, for my brother, and all of humanity." Placing his feet shoulder-width apart, Rusty turned sideways to his right, lifted the emerald-colored shield against the left side of his body, and leaned against it with his shoulder, the top of the shield just beneath his chin. He lowered the sword to his side, the tip pointing downward but at the ready. Rusty smiled, watching the confusion spread across the Khan's face though it dissipated, quickly replaced by anger and fury.

Natus Khan did not hesitate. He charged at Rusty, his muscular legs closing the gap between them. Rusty's eyes widened, startled by the Khan's speed. He lifted his shield above his head just in time to stop the downward chopping movement from caving in his skull. The force of the blow sent a sharp pain along his forearm and up through his shoulder. It felt like a sledgehammer had pounded into his shield. Rather than waiting for a second blow, Rusty sidestepped to the left, backed up a step, turned his body to the right once more, and placed the shield ahead of him. He tried to back up a few more steps but did not have enough time.

The Khan's second blow was seamless, following the first within a split second. Turning quickly to his right, the Khan swept his blade with a two-handed grip and brought it crashing against the emerald-feathered shield. The impact thudded loudly against the interlocking Dragon feathers as its force knocked Rusty backwards and onto the ground. Rusty felt as if he had collided with a truck. He crashed to the cold, hard earth. Rusty's mind swirled with indecision as he gasped for air. The collision knocked the breath from his body and the sword from his grasp. Barely able to breathe, he rolled over quickly and scrambled onto one knee. He reached for the sword, but the Khan, quick as a lion, leapt forward and pressed his attack. Natus Khan's ivory fangs glistened in the morning light as he lifted his blade once more above his head and swung it downward with a thunderous force.

Rusty barely had time to lift the shield high enough to meet Khan's blade in mid-strike. The jolt rattled his teeth. It felt as though another sledgehammer had crashed onto his forearm. The shield held, but his bones did not. Hearing the crack of a broken bone, he felt a sharp pain above his left wrist. He had lifted both forearms to the shield, hoping to absorb the blow, and they both throbbed in pain. Agony resonated up through his shoulders. His knees buckled beneath the strength of Khan's death strike. The inside of the shield struck Rusty in the forehead, opening a deep cut above his left eye. Blood ran in rivulets down his face, blinding him for a few moments.

The Khan hammered relentlessly, striking downward with another Herculean blow. He repeated the strike two more times, each in quick succession. By the fourth blow, Rusty's legs gave way, and he crumbled backwards into a heap.

Natus Khan could have bounded forward to use a finishing strike. He could have driven his blade through one of Rusty's exposed legs. The brute did not. Instead, he turned in a wide circle, lifted his hands in celebration, and howled loudly into the air. Fifty-thousand howls answered him in response. The Amoraki were ecstatic with joy.

Rusty lifted the shield slowly, rolled over, and scrambled to his feet. He stumbled forward, hurrying to grab the sword. *He is toying with me,* Rusty thought, not surprised but angered. He turned to watch the antics of the surrounding Werewolves. They maintained their distance, but thousands of them hopped up and down, pointing at him and gesturing toward their throats with a slashing movement.

A second round of fury rose in Rusty, and this time instead of waiting for the Khan to attack, he turned, lifted his sword, and charged.

Caught off-guard, Natus Khan met Rusty's downward strike with his blade. The sound of the two swords, their metal blades clashing against each other, echoed across the open field. The power behind Khan's counterstrike pushed Rusty back a few steps, but he did not wait for Khan to return another blow. He threw his shield at Khan, forcing him to step aside. The Khan's eyes locked with wonder onto the emerald-colored feathers. The distraction was minute, lasting a split second. Rusty attacked again, slashing at Natus Khan with all of his strength. Forced onto the defensive Natus Khan did not have enough time to strike back. Surprised to see Rusty give up his shield, he was startled when Rusty began forcing him backwards with a flurry of strikes.

Surprised by the turn of events, the Amoraki howled. Their despair did not distract Rusty from his purpose, though. He pressed Khan, swinging his sword quickly and with as much force as he could muster. Khan attempted to save face in front of the Werewolves by leaping backwards and pointing the tip of his blade at Rusty. He issued a challenge yelling his words loudly enough for the Amoraki to hear, "And now human, with your death, the invasion of the Known World will begin."

The Khan's legs coiled as he prepared to pounce onto Rusty. He stopped in his tracks, when the screams of thousands of Amoraki flooded the battlefield. Petrified by something streaking toward them from across the heavens, the beasts cried out to the Khan for protection, their loud whimpering drowning out all other sounds.

A snow-white Dragon, its immense body the size of a small castle, soared out of the clouds between the two tallest, snow-capped peaks. The massive, bat-like wings carried it high overhead, and past the Amoraki, many of whom began to flee in all directions. Gliding in a wide circle, more than a thousand feet above them, the massive, ivory-colored wings temporarily blocked out the sun.

Rusty looked to Natus Khan and then back to the heavens. The White Dragon flapped its wings, climbing higher into the sky until it looked no larger than a snowflake. Whimpering with fear, the Amoraki pointed feverishly to the skies, their bloodshot eyes searching for the snow-white beast. Suddenly, the Dragon pulled the wings close to its body and dove downward, straight at them, a massive, white-winged meteor.

Natus Khan ignored his howling Amoraki. He turned to his wizard, started to bark a command, but cried out in pain when Rusty drove the tip of the sword into his lower back. Hoping to stab the blade into Khan a second time, Rusty pulled the sword out quickly. Natus Khan turned and smashed Rusty with the back of his left hand and knocked him senseless. Natus Khan's blood ran down his blade. Shaking his head feverishly, Rusty rolled over, lifted his sword, and smiled.

I can kill him, Rusty thought. He could feel his excitement building.

Warily, the Khan barked his command at Jochi and pointed to the approaching Dragon. He turned to face Rusty, his fury returned.

The wizard removed his velvet robe, letting it drop behind him. He looked to the skies and shrieked, "Norduir!"

Rusty's eyes widened in fear. Jochi's snake-like features, fully exposed, glared wrathfully at the approaching Dragon. Though pressed backwards by Khan, Rusty could see the cobra hood as it expanded on the back of the wizard's head. Deep, purple veins bulged, pulsating with venom.

Jochi lifted his oaken staff, pointed it at the Dragon, and yelled, "Ende Wrathma Karlat! Norduir!"

The Amoraki hoard turned to watch the other Dragons, those controlled by the wizard, as they roared with fury. More than twenty Dragons leapt high into the air, beat their giant wings, and hurled themselves furiously at the plummeting Dragon.

Rusty did not know how the white Dragon could stave off an attack by this many Dragons, but he did not have time to watch. Natus Khan turned his attention back to Rusty and charged, swinging his sword wildly. It took all of Rusty's strength to block the blows. He held onto the hilt of his sword with both hands, gripping it tightly. Khan's power and strength surpassed Rusty's tenacity. The sword buckled beneath Khan's attack and fell from Rusty's hands. Exhausted, he dropped to the ground beside the weapon, waiting for a death blow that did not land. A heavy, crashing sound behind him tore Khan's attention away from the fight.

Startled by the sound, Rusty watched as the Dragons sent by Jochi began crashing to the earth, landing so harshly that the ground shook with the impact. A lava-red Dragon streaked downward, smashing a group of Werewolves beneath its lifeless body. Then a black Dragon and two more red ones, and then a green Dragon fell like giant meteors, flattening more unlucky Amoraki. Dozens of Dragons smashed to the earth, their dead bodies crashing into the screaming Werewolves before they could flee. Hundreds died in the carnage.

The two combatants looked up in time to watch the lone Dragon, Norduir, swoop around the interior of the Amoraki, breathing an ice-blue flame that solidified into a giant wall of ice. Frozen with the howls still on their faces, thousands of Werewolves became ice statues. The remaining Amoraki, those outside the frozen wall, howled in fear, confused about what to do.

Natus Khan, trapped inside the frozen arena, backed away warily and joined his wizard. They watched silently as Norduir, its thick, interlocking scales as white as arctic snow, landed next to Rusty. The large, ice-blue eyes remained fixated on Khan and the Wizard, but the Dragon lowered its head quickly. An older man, his black hair streaked with grey, slid down the side of the Dragon and ran to Rusty. He offered his right hand, lifting Rusty off the ground. Rusty found his dark complexion surprising.

He is not from this side of the mountains, Rusty thought. This man must have crossed over from the Known World.

"Warrior, I thank you," the man offered once Rusty was on his feet.

"Who are you?" Rusty stammered. His knees almost buckled, but the man helped him maintain his footing. He stared perplexed.

"Who am I? I am Landon," the man chuckled, the wrinkles along his eyes expressing kindness and gentle humor. He looked down to the sword and whispered, "Greetings *Wynde Ryder*? Our House has need of you once more." He smiled at Rusty's confusion and asked, "May I?"

Rusty nodded wordlessly. He watched, captivated as Landon lifted the sword to his face before bowing to Rusty in salute.

The man turned to face Natus Khan. He unclasped his emerald-colored cloak and let it drop to the ground behind him. He started to walk but stopped at Rusty's words.

"Be careful he's the Devil," Rusty warned. He gestured at Natus Khan with his head.

Landon turned. His dark eyes burning with intensity, "He is not the Devil, my friend. I have seen the Stygian castle with my own eyes. I hope never to return. I have spoken with the son of its Master." He looked over to Khan adding, "This creature, he may be a demon to be sure. A demon bent on death and destruction. Or, he may be a minion of the Devil," Landon continued, pointing *Wynde* Ryder at the Wizard. "But, do not fear him, for he is not the Devil."

Landon raised his sword and charged feverishly at Khan. Their swords clashed loudly.

Rusty's eyes darted back to the wizard, caught by his strange movements. The wizard yelled, the words unintelligible as he whirled his wooden staff in a wide circle above his head. "Anth ata et mgata wan wif illt."

Slamming the end of the staff into the ground, a purplish swirl of smoke enveloped Jochi's body, masking him from Rusty's view. Instantly, the Wizard transformed into a giant Dragon, its magenta scales glistening brightly. The Dragon Jochi increased in size, his frame towering above Norduir.

Rusty's eyes darted back to watch Landon and the heavily pressed Khan. Rusty admitted that though much older, the man was a master swordsman. Khan was on the defensive, his sword blocking Landon's heavy strokes. Rusty could see the worry lines as they grew on Khan's retreating face.

Rusty's eyes darted back to the Dragons, beating their wings loudly as they lifted up, back into the sky. Rusty shielded his eyes, half-blinded by the dust that had been kicked up by the heavy flapping. When his eyes cleared, he cried aloud, shocked to witness the Dragon Jochi sink its fangs deep into Norduir's left wing. Rusty could hear Norduir's bones snap, the crunching loud and foreboding.

Their shrieks echoing loudly, the two titans grappled hundreds of feet above the still screaming Amoraki. Razor-sharp claws sank into underbellies, opening up deep gashes. The beasts soared higher into the sky, their bodies rolling around each other until they were almost out of sight. The surrounding sky became a brilliant array of colors, radiated by yellow flames, and then purple ones, and then blue and green.

Tearing his eyes away from the Dragons, Rusty looked back in time to see Natus Khan turn the tables. Landon's swordplay had slowed, and the Khan moved to attack. Though deep gashes crisscrossed his massive chest, they did not deplete Khan's strength.

He is too old, Rusty thought, realizing that Khan's youth and strength offered a counterbalance to Landon's skill with the sword.

Natus Khan began to press Landon backwards. The older man was now defending himself, reacting in self-preservation as the Khan landed numerous blows. Natus Khan swung his blade like a hammer, knocking Landon to the ground. The man landed beside Rusty, his sword raised above him for protection. A loud screech brought all of their attention back to the skies. The two Dragons, locked in a death grip, streaked past them like a bolt of lightning. Neither seemed to be tiring as their claws continued to rip and tear into their armored scales.

Rusty felt the hopelessness of the moment and cried out in despair. "Why did He bring me here? I do not understand. He told me it was my purpose to wield this sword." Rusty, confused, felt his despair weighing heavily in his heart.

Natus Khan remained oblivious to his words, captivated by the Dragons and their battle overhead.

Startled, Landon turned to Rusty and asked, "What did you say?"

"The Eighth Lion," Rusty called out in distress. "Joshua. They brought me here, chose me to wield this sword." Rusty, too distraught to notice the change in Landon's demeanor, continued, "My mother sacrificed her life so that I could come into these Lands."

"He brought you here?" Landon asked calmly. "Have you been to the den of the Eighth Lion?"

"Yes," Rusty answered, his despondency weighing him down. "I was there last night."

"Last night?" Landon asked in surprise. "How is that possible?" he mumbled quietly, though he seemed to be asking himself, not Rusty.

Rusty ignored his last question and continued, "He gave me the sword, but for what purpose? I do not understand?"

Landon hoisted himself up and stood over Rusty, a new awareness guiding his actions.

"What is your name, young man?" Landon asked, holding out his right hand. He pulled Rusty up to one knee, placing his right hand on Rusty's shoulder.

"My name," he stammered, confused. "I am Rusty."

"What is your given name?" Landon asked, slightly amused. "Hurry," he insisted. A pang of deep sadness in his voice made Rusty look at him questioningly.

"My name is Reginald Rusty Rogers III," he said with pride. "I am named after my father." He waited for Landon's response but was surprised when Landon lifted the sword and tapped him gently on both shoulders with the tip of the blade.

Rusty looked up into Landon's darkened face.

"Reginald Rusty Rogers III, before the Lord of us all and his servant The Eighth Lion, I declare you to be my heir. Upon my death, you will inherit my kingdom. You will rule the House of Gheldari, hopefully with wisdom, of course. I name you heir to O'ndar and its kingdom." Landon tapped Rusty on his left shoulder and then again on his right. He held the sword before him, the hilt in one hand and the blade in the other, both hands facing palm up. Landon placed *Wynde Ryder* into Rusty's hands and removed a ring from his right hand; the large gemstone, an emerald, sparkled in the sunlight. "Place this on your finger." He nodded with satisfaction as Rusty complied.

Landon slipped out of his emerald-colored chain mail, let it slip from his fingers to the ground, and turned to walk away.

"Wait," Rusty yelled apprehensively. In response, Landon smiled, lifted both hands and stretched his arms out wide.

"Wait," Rusty demanded. Something had changed. The speed with which everything had unfolded unnerved him. His yell caught Natus Khan's attention, and Rusty watched in horror as the creature turned back toward the two of them. Landon approached him unarmed. The Khan's eyes widened, and he grinned wickedly, exposing his canines.

Landon did not look back. He did not waiver.

Khan's delighted face, exposed by the wide-toothed look of glee, burned deeply into Rusty's core. Natus Khan stabbed Landon in the chest, the blade sinking deeply.

Landon's hands grasp the blood-soaked edge, the pain spreading across his face. Landon closed his eyes in prayer, but did not cry out.

Natus Khan laughed in delight, proud that he had taken Landon's life so effortlessly.

Rusty jumped to his feet, started to charge, but ended up catching a falling Landon as Natus Khan kicked him backwards with a large boot. The beast yanked the blade out of Landon's chest, and the two separated, a large splatter of blood splashing to the ground. Landon collapsed into Rusty's arms.

Lowering him to the ground, Rusty asked softly, "Why?" Tears welled up in the corner of his eyes.

Landon's eyes fluttered as his life began to ebb away. He whispered, "*Wynde Ryder* is powerful, a gift to our house from the Dragon of the Forests. Younger hands, those with strength, must wield it to harness its true power. I am too old to defeat him. We cannot allow him to be loosened on the Known World."

"Why?" Rusty asked. "Why?" his question trailed off as Landon closed his eyes.

"Remember," Landon whispered, his words barely audible, "Anyone can make the sacrifice. It just takes courage."

The words hit Rusty like a ton of bricks. They had been words his mother had told him since the day of his birth. Joshua had used these very words, and now Landon, a stranger, had given his life with the same pledge. Rusty stood, enlightened by the sacrifice made on the world's behalf. He felt a new source of power coursing through his limbs, his muscles surging with strength when he touched *Wynde Ryder*.

"It is Faith," he said, hoisting the sword lightly in front of him.

"What do you say?" Natus Khan growled.

The world went silent. Rusty could not hear the wailing Amoraki, hidden from his view just beyond the wall of ice. The battle overhead muted as the shrieks of unbridled fury died away, replaced by tranquility. The power of the sword changed him. His muscled tingled as a surge of energy flowed through his veins, coursing its way into his entire body. A new awareness flooded his consciousness. Everyone he loved most in the world was gone. They had died, some of them sacrificing themselves so that he might help bring sanity back into this insane world. His hometown, Millstadt, was a universe away, but Landon's sacrifice, made on his behalf, had locked Rusty's purpose into place.

He looked at an astonished Khan and offered once more, "They all have faith," he thundered.

Rusty did not hesitate. He walked toward Khan, closing the distance between them and said, "They all have faith. That connection will save this world and the next." He attacked Khan with ferocity. The blade flitted, almost too quickly for the eye to see, back and forth, opening up long cuts in Khan's arms, legs and torso.

Natus Khan, astounded by the power in Rusty's strikes, demanded, "How is this possible? You are only a human?"

Rusty stabbed the tip of his blade towards Khan's stomach, a move that forced Natus Khan to lower his sword to block the attack. Then, with his upper body exposed, Rusty spun around, swinging *Wynde Ryder* in a wide arc and sliced off Natus Khan's head.

Rusty looked to the skies, watching the battle for supremacy play out between Norduir, the white Dragon with penetrating ice-blue eyes and the magenta-scaled Dragon, the wizard Jochi, transformed into a menacing beast. The two of them came crashing to the earth, each bearing mortal wounds.

The Dragon Jochi, with its mulberry eyes glowering, turned and looked at the headless body of Natus Khan. Shrieking loudly, it charged at Rusty.

Rusty did not cower. He did not run away. Leaping forward with the speed of a lion, Rusty slid on his back the instant the Dragon Jochi was upon him. Lifting *Wynde Ryder* above his body, holding the hilt tightly with both hands, he sliced open Jochi's underbelly as the Dragon crossed over the top of him. The milky-white blade, honed from the tooth of a Dragon of the Forests a thousand years before, sliced easily into Jochi. The Dragon shrieked in agony, took three steps past Rusty, and turned. Jochi's piercing eyes fixated on Rusty, the hatred intense. The Dragon Jochi roared in pain and breathed a purple flame a hundred feet into the air. Retreating from the intensity of the heat, Rusty turned to face the false Dragon.

He lifted his hands, defensively, seconds before the Magenta-colored Dragon breathed another burst of flames. Knowing the end had come, without the emerald-feathered shield to protect him, Rusty faced death bravely.

Norduir, the original Titan, bounded forward, landing in front of Rusty, and absorbed the heat from the flames. The White Dragon charged, collided with the Dragon Jochi, and flipped him over onto his back. Before the Dragon Jochi could right himself, Norduir sank his ivory fangs into the Dragon's neck.

Roaring in pain, the purple Dragon shook its head furiously but could not break free.

Rusty heard the crunch of bones and watched as Norduir released Jochi. The wizard died in Dragon form and lay unmoving before them. Norduir, its left wing charred, lifted its head and shrieked triumphantly into the sky.

WISDOM OF THREE

"WHY DO WE DALLY HERE, MY FRIENDS?" THE BROAD-SHOULDERED soldier asked his two companions. The ends of his thick, shoulder-length blonde hair swayed in the gentle breeze. "Do we now follow dreams as if they are real?"

Laughing, the darker-skinned man shrugged before responding. "Do you doubt, knowing all that we have seen with our friend and King?" Gezpar smiled broadly and chided Balthason once more.

The third companion ignored the exchange, keeping vigil stoically. His eyes looked to the mountains, the snow-capped peaks looming. Slim-wasted, Melkior had always been the most serious of the three. Even now, while his two friends bantered back and forth, his dark eyes waited patiently.

Gezpar, had awakened them an hour before the sunrise. He offered news that their Lord and King needed them once more. Donning their armor quickly, the three companions rode their horses at a quick gallop, across the knee-high prairie grass, and back to the mountains.

"What say you, Melkior?" Balthason asked impatiently. "You are quiet, as usual. What are your thoughts about Gezpar's dream?"

In response, Melkior dismounted, tethered his horse to a shrub and said, "We are summoned, once more." His two companions quickly dismounted, secured the other three horses, and jogged softly to catch up to him. He walked away, heading towards the mountains, his eyes looking to the peaks in anticipation.

"It will be dark soon," Gezpar offered. "We should build a fire." He turned to gather some twigs but stopped at Melkior's words.

"There is no need. The Queen has arrived," Melkior whispered; the sight of the arctic Dragon breaching the snow-covered peaks awed him to his core. His two companions followed his gaze, and soon the three could easily see the magical creature, soaring through the clouds, gliding softly on the wind currents, and heading straight for them.

"I must admit that even after all of his descriptions, seeing her in person is the most awe-inspiring thing I have ever witnessed," Balthason said. Kneeling quickly, with his eyes lowered, the soldier patted his leg with his left hand to indicate that his companions follow suit. They did.

Though their eyes remained downcast, they knew she had arrived the moment the breeze, created by the beating of her wings, died down as she landed a few feet away.

The three soldiers, Landon's companions, lifted their eyes. The Dragon, covered with cuts on her underbelly, and large chunks of the thick, ice-white scales torn away, set her penetrating gaze upon them. She ignored her blackened wing, large pieces of the tissue burnt. She had just been through the battle of a lifetime, though for a Dragon, that could seem an eternity. The unyielding ice-blue eyes hardened, masking her intentions.

"My Lady," Gezpar offered. He bowed his head in supplication before looking into her eyes. "What news?" His voice quivered, astonished to be speaking to the original Titan, the Queen of the Dragons.

Norduir spoke, her voice booming loudly into the evening night, "Your Liege has fallen. Chardon II is no more."

Balthason cried out in anguish, "Our friend. Can it true?"

Melkior closed his eyes, fighting back the tears. His shoulders sagged, and then a flood of sadness swept over him as he sobbed uncontrollably.

Gezpar, his eyes matching Norduir's penetrating stare, lowered his face and prayed.

Silently, as if she were giving the three companions time to pay homage to their friend, each in their own way, the arctic-white Dragon lowered her head, and two men, one carrying the other, slid off her back.

Rusty held Landon's lifeless body close to his chest, stepped forward and gingerly lowered Landon to the ground, placing him in front of his companions. "He saved me," Rusty started, the words difficult to express his emotions. "He saved us, all of us. His sacrifice has saved the Known World."

The three companions stood, their eyes travelling to the milky-white blade sheathed at Rusty's side. They spotted the Emerald ring on Rusty's finger and looked to Norduir, the emerald-feathered shield held gently between two razor-sharp talons.

Instantly, all three dropped to their knees and offered, "My Lord." Their heads lowered; they did not notice the embarrassment on Rusty's face.

"I guess I am going to have to get used to that," Rusty smiled, looking up into the Dragon's face.

She smiled back, her ivory fangs as bright as the scales on her back. "It will take some time, of that I am sure."

"Rise, my friends," Rusty insisted. He stepped around Landon's body and embraced the three of them, one at a time.

"Where will she take him?" Melkior asked as the four of them watched the white Dragon disappear into the western sky. The sun had started to dip below the horizon, and night would be upon them within the hour.

Rusty responded, "She told me that she was flying West across the Ardenian Ocean. I offered to return him to O'ndar so that we might have a burial that befits a King. Norduir assured me that there could be no greater honor. She will bury him with her own hands, and his bones will reside next to the bones of Dragons. She offered, with sincerity, for him to take his rightful place, honored for eternity. "

The four men mounted their horses, and three of them turned to the West, toward the direction that the Dragon had flown. "Do we head West, My Lord, back to O'ndar?" Balthason asked.

"In time," Rusty answered. He turned his horse south, intent on heading eventually toward the Eastern Steppes. "But first, it is time I met the Chieftains of the clans. If any wish to challenge me for the right to lead, they shall have that chance."

"Four companions," slim-wasted Melkior answered, smiling widely, "Riding across the Steppes, once more." He clicked his tongue, and his horse broke into a canter, riding out ahead of the others.

Balthason did the same, and soon the two began racing each other, galloping quickly across the fields of Prairie Grass.

Gezpar smiled, winked at Rusty, and encouraged his horse to race after his two friends.

Reginald Rusty Rogers III watched his three companions gallop away with admiration. The newly anointed King of O'ndar and the Emperor of the Known World turned and looked across the sea of flowing grass. He sighed and leaned in to pat his horse gently, enjoying the moment.

Off in the distance, far beyond the undulating waves of prairie grass, a bolt of lightning filled the grey sky. Rusty watched the dazzling web of brilliance as it spread across the heavens, replaced quickly by a blast of rolling thunder. He paused, listening as a loud rumbling reached his ears, sounding a lot like the roar of a lion.

A BRIEF HISTORY OF DRAGONS

<u>A Brief History of Dragons</u>

As told to Pelinnedes by Meeha, third daughter
of the elder Dragon Bosque.

MY DEAR PELINNEDES, BE ASSURED, IT IS NOT LIGHTLY THAT I PASS ON to humans the exalted History of the Dragons. I do this with a heavy heart, knowing the reign and influence of the Dragon Race has begun to wane. Soon, Dragons will be no more than stories and legends, their history never believed by the descendants of humankind. Thus, our saga will slowly erode down through the ages, added to the folklore of human history as an afterthought.

There may come a day in which our supremacy over this world is eclipsed by the race of man, though this saddens me beyond description. It benefits humans to remember that there has been and always will be a place and time for Dragons, whether that place is in the physical sense or in the tales of ancient lore. Be warned, though, even though the time of the Dragon is fading, our race might yet play a role in the rise and fall of many an empire. Even when the memory of Dragons has faded into legend, our fate and the fate of the world remains intertwined. The history of the world has been and will always be the same as that of the Dragon. It is a thread of commonality that binds us all.

The Dragon Race is the eldest of all living beings, inheriting the original knowledge of the Creation of Life. Remember my words Pelinnedes and let the Human Race know that there has always been one spark, one thread, and one similarity to which the universe's genesis owes its beginning. The original conception rests in the hands of Ea, the Mother of us all.

Since the existence of time there has always been Ea, the Creator of the universe. Ea is the earth. Ea is the sky. Ea is the moon. Ea is the stars. Ea is everything.

Ea encompasses all, yet there was a point in time when our mother felt the pangs of solitude; she bore the burden of loneliness for an eternity. Looking down from the mountain peaks at the abundance of all that she had created, Ea's heart yearned to share her happiness and her joy. Ea, in her infinite wisdom decided to create companions so that she would no longer be alone.

A little more than two-hundred millennia ago, Ea, in her wisdom, decided to impregnate herself. The expectant mother waited patiently for the nativity and with anticipation for the joy of motherhood. A thousand years later Ea gave birth to the original Titans, the three Daughters of Ea.

In celebration of the birth of the divine Titans, Ea commanded the earth's volcanoes to spew hot ash and fiery lava into the heavens. Ea showered the skies with meteors, a brilliant array of light that soared high above the earth in triumph. Ea was delighted beyond imagination with the birth of the three Titans. Ea was happy that her solitude had finally ended.

All Dragons look to the original Titans, the three daughters of Ea, with deference and admiration. The three Daughters of Ea are Norduir the Northern Ice-Dragon, Pahaida the Mountainous Lava-Dragon, and Bosque the Emerald Dragon of the Forests.

The Three Titans of Ea

Norduir

In the northern reaches of the Cargathian Mountains, hundreds of miles beyond the realm of man, resides the original Titan Norduir, the

Ice-Dragon. White as the driven snow, the Dragon of the north blends perfectly to the arctic landscape, feeding on whales and other animals found in the cold desolation of the polar caps. It is a rarity to find an Ice-Dragon south of the northern range of the Cargathian Mountains. The Daughters of Norduir prefer the snow and ice of the world, provided by the arctic conditions, though on rare occasions, one of them may cross over the mountain peaks, choosing to leave the snow-covered lands in the north.

Norduir, the eldest, may be the most powerful of the Dragons, though Pahaida and my mother Bosque oppose that assessment. As an original Titan, Norduir has mastered hundreds of orbs. With this power she is ferocious in her wrath and terrifying in her scorn.

Norduir breathes ice-blue flames that freeze all in their wake. Norduir, and a few of her daughters, have an unlimited supply of this power. Most other Ice-Dragons, though, have not mastered enough of their Dragon orbs. They breathe the icy-flames, but can only do so with limitations. Housed in ice-covered scales, Norduir's body has many chinks of armor more than a foot in thickness.

Norduir has grown in size and age, a compliment to her wisdom. The Titan's talons are longer than the size of an average person. Her power is equal to that of three thousand men, maybe more.

Norduir's daughters broke the original Covenant with Ea. They spurned the Dragon Race in their quest for glory and power, almost leading to our destruction. The daughters of Norduir were the first to steal an orb of another Dragon. They were also the first to kill other Dragons. It is to Norduir, and her daughters, that other Dragons lay blame for the rise of the Race of Man.

After the Dragon Wars, Ea summoned Norduir and her sisters to explain why her daughters were the first to steal the orbs of other Dragons. Enraged by their answers, Ea ordered the world cleansed of the wayward Dragons. Hoping for her mother's forgiveness, Norduir was more than willing to purge the Dragons of the north and begin anew. Pahaida and Bosque, the other two Titans, believe Norduir's daughters acted with Norduir's blessing and have never forgiven her for the atrocities committed against their daughters.

Pahaida

The domain of the Red-Dragon Pahaida and her daughters is the largest of all of the Dragons. It is equal to the length and breadth of the Cargathian Mountains that circle what the humans on the western side of the mountains call the Known World.

Lava-red scales that ripple like fire when in flight, Pahaida has more living daughters than the other two Titans combined. Like Norduir, she breathes flames. However, unlike her northern sister, Pahaida's flames burn with a white-hot intensity, capable of scorching all in its path. The volcanoes of the earth, which spew forth lava into the sky, are often confused with Pahaida when she is angered and breathing her fire.

Pahaida's scales are equally thick chinks of iron-like armor, resembling molten lava as it spews from volcanoes.

The daughters of Pahaida were quick to meet the challenge of the Ice-Dragons the moment they swooped out of their lands and invaded the Cargathian Mountains. During the Dragon Wars, the Lava-Dragons unified with the Forests-Dragons against the Ice-Dragons of the north.

Bosque

One of the first orbs stolen belonged to the Titan Bosque, the Emerald Dragon of the Forests. Unique of all the Dragons, the daughters of Bosque were the only Dragons who refused to steal orbs from other Dragons. Hidden in thick feathers of green, a mosaic of Emerald colors, the daughters of Bosque breathe an invisible, high-pitched, noise-deafening flame that renders its victims paralyzed. Even other Dragons, other than the original Titans, will succumb to the power of Bosque in all her fury. The Emerald Dragons of the Forests are unique in body stature. While the daughters of Norduir and Pahaida are sleek and lean, the daughters of Bosque are thick and muscular. It is believed, by the Dragons of the Forests, that the arctic Dragons started the Dragon War out of jealousy.

The Dragon Bosque has always been the favored daughter of Ea, which may be why some of Norduir's daughters left the arctic north to steal the Dragon orbs from the daughters of Bosque.

The daughters of Bosque were the least guilty of all of the sins committed by the Dragon Race. If the Race of Man ever gains dominion over the earth, humans should give thanks to Bosque, the Emerald Dragon of the Forests, because of the knowledge given to you, Pelinnedes.

⚜

In celebration of the birth of the Titans, the Mother Ea created the sun, placing it in the heavens so that it might always shine a brilliant light onto the world. The splendor of the golden rays, cascading across the landscape filled Ea with delight. She smiled, happy with all that she had created.

Following their births, the Mother gathered her three daughters close to her bosom. Ea cradled the three Titans and began singing the first Dragon Song to them. The three Daughters of Ea listened intently, showered with the love offered by the Mother of everything.

For thousands of years the Age of the Dragon reigned supreme in the world. Dragons communed with Ea nightly, singing to her the original Dragon Song as they perched atop the highest peaks of the Cargathian Mountains. Ea was happy and content, watching daily her descendants soar above the clouds. Ea was delighted and content, listening nightly to the melodious songs of the Dragon Race. There is no other sound in the universe as pleasing as Dragon Song.

Sadly, as thousands of years went by, the daughters of the three Dragons of Ea began to forget their connections to Ea and their relationships to each other.

Ea was saddened to see the daughters of Norduir leave their homes in the ice-capped lands of the north.

Ea was saddened to see the daughters of Pahaida leave their caves in the high-peaked mountains that encircle the lands.

Ea was saddened to see the daughters of Bosque leave their homes in the majestic forests of the world.

The wayward daughters ignored Ea and their mothers, spreading their domains across the entirety of the earth. Only the three elder Titans, the original Dragons of Ea, kept the original Covenant with their mother.

As the centuries passed and time continued to thin the Dragons' connections to mother Ea, many of the Dragons began to forget their relatedness to each other. This alarmed Ea, but she waited patiently, hoping that they would eventually see the error of their ways and return to the original Covenant. Her mighty tears flowed out of the Cargathian Mountain peaks, forming into the crystal-clear waters of broad rivers and smaller streams.

Eventually, because of the lost connections, these wayward Dragons began to stray. Slowly, much to the chagrin of Ea, the lost Dragons began to sin. Many of these Dragons began to covet the orbs of other Dragons. Watching silently, Ea endured the shame as only a mother can when her offspring become a burden. She watched quietly, wishing these Dragons would see the error of their ways and would again grace the world with the original Dragon Song, a song of peace and never-ending love.

Eventually, coveting the orbs of other Dragons was not enough. Some Dragons began to steal the orbs of other Dragons, then they began to steal the eggs of other Dragons, and finally, to the horror of Ea, they began to raid the hatchlings of other Dragons. Initially, these Dragons justified their behavior, saying they only stole the orbs of those Dragons that they hated the most. These wayward Dragons, consumed with jealousy, justified the theft from their cousins. They seemed to be unaware of the pain their discretions were causing the Mother.

Before long, much to the horror of Ea, Dragon began to kill Dragon.

Thus, without Dragon Song to guide their hearts, the Great Dragon War began. The fierce struggle witnessed Dragons fighting for supremacy of the lands and sovereignty of the skies. Vast swaths of the mighty forests burned to the ground, charred and decimated. At night the heavens looked aglow with brimstone and fire. The world shook and trembled.

Ea was saddened beyond description as she looked at the devastation to the world that she had created. It was only then that mother Ea became enraged. Her wrath violently shook the mountains of the Known World.

Ea summoned the three eldest Dragons, scolding them as they knelt before her afraid. The three had held to the Covenant, but they allowed the transgressions of their children to go on without reproach. They lowered their heads in supplication, begging for forgiveness.

Soon, the wayward daughters of Ea, those Dragons that had forsaken the Covenant looked to the heavens with despair. Their hearts filled with doom as many realized their actions had angered Ea beyond the point of forgiveness. Thousands of Dragons took flight, drawn to the highest peaks, hoping to gain Ea's pardon, though they trembled knowing that it was too late to erase their sins.

Looking at her kneeling daughters, Ea declared it was time to start anew. The Mother commanded the three Titans to rid the world of their daughters, demanding they expunge the Dragon race of those that had sinned.

Norduir, Pahaida, and Bosque, the three original Titans and the only Dragons who had kept the faith and kept to the original Covenant, were terrible with their wrath. Norduir destroyed all of the dragons of the north. Pahaida destroyed all of the dragons within the mountains, and Bosque destroyed all of the dragons of the forests.

Soon, only the three authentic Dragons remained.

Once again, Ea looked at the world and was pleased. Ea summoned her daughters before her once more. She spoke softly, but firmly to them. She commanded her daughters to begin anew. Ea longed for a world in which Dragons soared through the skies, singing Dragon Song, though in her wisdom, she decided changes needed to be made.

First, Ea decided to elevate one of the lower life forms on earth. Ea determined that man should have a more prominent role in the fate of the world. Ea warned the three Titans that man would replace the Dragon Race if the Dragons strayed from the Covenant once again.

The Titans shook with fear at Ea's words. The elevation of the Human Race required Ea to give to humans a gift reserved initially for the Dragon Race.

Ea, in her wisdom, gave humankind the ability to reason.

Ea had created humankind, thousands of years before, but at that time man lived a nomadic lifestyle, often with the tribes of man warring on each other, never worried about the past while not once considering the future. Humans lived in darkened caves, hiding from the other beasts of the world. Humans travelled the earth, following the large herds of migratory elk that populate the land. Humans had never before considered their place in the world, and had never before considered their relationship to nature. Humans had never before thought about who they were or how they came to be.

Man had been sheep for Dragons, a source of food, no more, no less.

Looking at her three daughters, kneeling before her, Ea issued her dire warning. If the Dragons faltered again in their dominion over the earth, humans would someday take up the helm and become the masters of the planet.

The Titans heard their mother and trembled with fright. They committed to hold the Covenant tightly to their Dragon hearts. They swore that their daughters would keep to the Covenant for eternity. As they began to lay new orbs, which then became eggs, which then became hatchlings, the Dragons demanded their daughters hold to the Faith. Time has a way of wearing down the faithful, dear Pelinnedes, remember that when man takes over dominion of the world.

Once again some Dragons have begun to forget the Covenant made with Mother Ea.

Ea is watching and Ea is waiting. Ea is a patient Mother, but the patience of a parent cannot remain limitless. The Dragon Race, with all its faults, is still the master of the planet. There are no other species and there is no other race like the Dragon Race.

The Dragon Race is unique. It is exhilarating to observe. Yet all Dragons, regardless of their lineage, have some similarities that I will now impart to you dear Pelinnedes. Much of what I impart to you has been cloaked in secret, hidden away from the humans of this world to keep them from gaining supremacy over the Dragons.

First, all Dragons are female. Dragons have a saying, "With the wisdom of Ea."

All Dragon hatchlings are born the same color and the same size. Their scales, a shade of charcoal-grey, will quickly change to an ebony color in the first few weeks. Before the Dragon Wars, the daughters of Norduir were born with ivory-colored scales, the daughters of Pahaida were born with lava-red scales, and the daughters of Bosque were born with Emerald green feathers. Ea changed this so that all Dragons were born the same; hoping that as they matured the Dragons would remember their similarities at birth, rather than focus on the differences. Based on physical differences, these superficial jealousies had led them astray from the Covenant and resulted in the Dragon Wars.

Though born the same, Dragons will always change to the color of one of the three daughters of Ea, depending on their lineage. This change will not occur until after the Dragons have matured enough to hatch a clutch of eggs.

A Dragon will reach the maturity to lay her first clutch of orbs once they are nearly a thousand years of age. The wisdom of Ea again embraces us all. A Dragon must be mature enough to hatch her eggs, otherwise Ea forbids her to do so.

The life cycle of every Dragon follows the same path, although the expanse is not set in stone and is not exact.

First, a Dragon lays an orb.

If the Dragon inside the orb survives long enough she will become an egg. Such is the wisdom of Ea.

If the Dragon inside the egg is strong she will then become a hatchling. Such is the wisdom of Ea.

Finally, if the Dragon hatchling is resilient enough, she will become a mighty Dragon, beautiful and majestic, graceful and powerful. Dragons are the most powerful beings on the planet.

Once she nears her thousandth year, a Dragon will become mature enough to lay a clutch of between twenty and forty orbs. Each orb has the potential to grow into an egg, and then into a hatchling, and then into a Dragon, with Ea's blessing. Only Ea knows which Dragons are worthy of her blessing.

It takes almost five-hundred years for a Dragon orb to become a Dragon egg. It takes another five-hundred years for the Dragon egg to become a Dragon hatchling. If blessed by Ea, a Dragon will be ready to lay another clutch of orbs once her eggs have hatched.

Once her first clutch of eggs has hatched a transformation will occur with the Mother Dragon. She will become one of the original Titans types, depending on her lineage.

The transformation process is painful and exhausting. It is a time when Dragons are most vulnerable. It is Ea's final reminder that we are all the same and thus, our pain is the same as the pain of our sisters.

Humans have always coveted Dragon orbs. This became especially true after the humans were gifted the ability to reason. Before that time, they remained ignorant of the world and ignorant of the blessings of the Dragon race.

During our history, cowardly thieves have snuck into our lairs to steal our orbs. Most Dragons do not track down stolen orbs nor will they track down stolen eggs, but they will always track down stolen hatchlings. Man has never successfully kept stolen hatchlings, most likely because a vengeful mother found them and ate the thieves. My fear is this may change, someday, far into the future. If this happens, the ramifications could throw the world and the universe into chaos as the Dragons and the humans would wage war on each other. Let us pray that never comes to fruition.

Most Dragons may not attempt to recover stolen orbs or eggs, though some will do so vigorously and with a vengeance. Stolen orbs and stolen eggs are of no use to man since his lifespan is very short. Before an egg becomes a hatchling, the thief will have perished, taking with him the original knowledge of the Dragon inside. Stolen orbs and eggs, if not recovered, merely harden into stone. Without the care of the mother Dragon the orbs and the eggs become useless. Sadly, though, the potential of the Dragon inside is lost for all eternity.

Man has unknowingly used some Dragon stones to build the walls of their castles and their forts. They have crushed the former orbs and eggs into gravel to line their cities' streets. Even with the ability to reason humans remain ignorant of the splendor and power of the Dragon race.

All Dragons are magical. The extent and power of this magic depends on the development while Dragons are in the orb stage. A Dragon will watch over her clutch of orbs carefully. She will care for them, using the warmth of her body to encourage their growth. Picking the four to five orbs with the most potential, the Dragon will use their magical properties to increase her astonishing powers. This is why a Dragon needs to identify the most formidable orbs in her clutch. All Dragons will keep at least one orb from becoming an egg. Some Dragons have more than one-hundred orbs under their control. The magic offered by a worthy Dragon orb is too powerful to completely give-up.

Using the power of their orbs, all Dragons can see the past, regardless of the age of the Dragon. A few Dragons have mastered their orbs in ways unknown to most others. These mighty Dragons have acquired the ability to see into the future. Dragons who master the ability to see into the future hide this knowledge from other Dragons and the race of Man.

Dragon orbs potentially have unlimited power. Very few Dragons ever master the power offered to them by the potential of the Dragon orb. This was one of the limitations placed on the Dragon Race by Ea, in all her wisdom.

An orb offers the power to master human speech. This is how I am able to communicate with you, Pelinnedes. Before the Dragon purge all of the Dragons could speak all of the world's languages, both human and animal alike. Ea removed this gift. It is not until after Dragons have matured and have hatched a clutch of eggs that they once again can develop the power of speech.

Dragons, who wish it so, may learn to speak the languages of many living things. The most potent Dragons know the languages of all living things. The three daughters of Ea were born with this gift. Following the Dragon Wars, their daughters must master orbs and the power of speech if they wish to use it. There are only eight Dragons left in the world who have learned to speak the language of all living things.

Some Dragons choose not to master the power of speech. Some choose to speak only the language of the Dragon Race. These Dragons were offended when Ea gave humankind the ability to reason. They tend to avoid interacting with humans, only coming down from their caves to feed on the horses and cattle often held by men.

Destiny, and Ea, will decide which Dragon orbs become eggs. If not used for their magical properties the mother eats them. Destiny, and Ea, will determine if Dragon eggs become hatchlings. The mother too eats these. Destiny, and Ea, will decide which hatchlings become Dragons. Nonetheless, when hatchlings are not destined to be Dragons the mother Dragon cares for them as if destined for greatness. Dragons will quickly remove these hatchlings from their nests, lest their sisters eat them. Placed in the rivers, the lakes, the mountains, the streams, and the world's forests, some of the hatchlings fall prey to animals, thus becoming food in the cycle of life.

In the north, the Dragon hatchlings released into the oceans will transform into sharks, whales, or any manner of fish. The carnivores of the oceans are all descended from the Dragon race. This is why the whale and the shark are masters of the seas.

Some Dragon hatchlings will become the Komodo or other predatory lizards in the mountains, and in the forests some will become crocodiles or snakes. In the woods, the hatchlings may also become birds of prey. Thus, with the wisdom and influence of Ea, the Dragon race is the reason the earth has an abundance of predators to help maintain the balance in nature.

Dragons have many more powers than just the ability to fly, though I will never divulge all of our capabilities, even to you Pelinnedes. While I am breaking the Covenant of the Dragon race, I will not willingly provide man with the knowledge that could lead to the world's destruction.

Following the Dragon Wars, Ea made it more difficult for a Dragon to master the power to breathe flames. The three eldest Titans can do so, without limits.

Contrary to a belief allowed to exist amongst humankind, a Dragon's ability to breathe flames is limited. It has been to the Dragons' advantage to let humans believe the power to breathe fire, to breathe ice, and to breathe the invisible flame remains unlimited. Only those Dragons who have truly mastered the power of the Dragon orbs will ever be able to master this gift in an endless supply.

Dragons are a proud race. There was a time, eons ago, when the Dragon alone ruled the world. We deserve the pride we hold in our Race. Yet, we also deserve the curse placed on us by Ea. The curse is the rise of the Human race.

Dragons are not animals. Humans should never try to domesticate Dragons, for it will only end in despair. We are not horses, mules, or donkeys, to be ridden for pleasure. In the history of the human race, only a handful of men and women will ever claim that privilege. You are one, my dear Pelinnedes. Be thankful of the gift I have given thee.

Dragons are ferocious. Dragons are powerful. Dragons are majestic.

A Dragon's nails are sharper than any metal known to man. A Dragon's scales, and our feathers, are impregnable and impervious to any weapon made by man.

Most Dragons have the strength of almost a hundred men in the first years of maturity. The eldest Dragons have the power of thousands of men.

Man can kill a Dragon, though the weapon used must be powerful enough to do so. During the Dragon Wars the claws and teeth of other Dragons breached the scales of many Dragons. The warrior who battles a Dragon must be courageous enough to strike where the Dragon is most vulnerable. All Dragons are vulnerable, to man's weapons, on their underbelly. If pierced, a Dragon's heart is vulnerable. During the Dragon Wars the first Dragons killed were the smaller ones. Many of which were simply flipped onto their backs by the more massive Dragons, only to have their underbellies torn asunder.

Many a Dragon has succumbed to old age, though it is not clear how many thousands of years the Dragon's lifespan encompasses. When a Dragon dies another Dragon will always come to claim its body.

Man can drown a Dragon. Dragons can hold their breaths for a long time. Submerging them for hours would be one way to kill them. Dragons are avid swimmers. This is why Dragon hatchlings became the original sharks of the oceans of the world.

A Dragon's nature is solitary, other than with its brood.

Dragons will only leave the northern lands, the mountains encircling the Known World, or the majestic Red-barked forests to feed, or if compelled by an instinct to survive, or to recover the body of another Dragon.

Use the knowledge imparted to you well, Pelinnedes. Humankind may benefit if they learn the Covenant of Ea and choose to follow it faithfully. If not, another being may someday lift themselves above the Race of Man, many eons into the future.

Printed in the United States
by Baker & Taylor Publisher Services